THE BACK OF BEYOND

THE BACK OF BEYOND

by

Barbara Bickmore

KENSINGTON BOOKS are published by

Kensington Publishing Corp.
475 Park Avenue South
New York, NY 10016

Library of Congress Card Catalog Number: 93-080436

ISBN 0-8217-4517-4

First Printing: April, 1994

Printed in the United States of America

DEDICATED TO
DR. JEFFREY BECKWITH
I have always been blessed with wonderful friends,
but Jeff is a rare friend indeed.
He has saved me, listened to me, shared himself with me—and
he advises me and researches medical material for all my books.

and to

THE REVEREND FRED McKAY
a legend in his own time,
the most extraordinary man I've ever met.
He worked beside the renowned Australian figure,
John Flynn, the founder of the Royal Flying Doctor Service,
later carrying on John's work for over twenty-two years.
He has extended loving friendship and encouragement,
and has been of inestimable help in the writing of this book.

and to

NAN YOUNG
a long-time Royal Flying Doctor Service
councillor who was an incomparable hostess
and has become a dear friend
and wonderful traveling companion.

" . . . the Flying Doctors is already legendary and is perhaps the greatest single factor in the successful . . . settling of the Outback."

Charles and Elsa Chauvel, *Walkabout*, 1959

"When John Flynn dreamed of a Flying Doctor service, he did not picture it as a romantic and glamorous enterprise, but as a workaday organization of professionals and volunteers dedicated to those in need of their skills . . . He saw the Service as a practical method of employing the noblest trait of our tangled human nature: the impulse to help others because they too are part of humanity.

"Often the Service is called miraculous, but the miracle is not compounded of radio, aviation, and medicine. These are techniques developed and used by human beings. The miracle is wrought by people working together for a common cause. On the whole, they are quite ordinary people, capable of normal human error, fatigue, crankiness, and pride, but the nobility of their purpose enables them to escape, at least momentarily, from the bondage of such failings into the freedom of selfless endeavor."

Michael Page, *The Flying Doctor Story*, 1977

Preface

Two million square miles of moonscape. Dry, cracked red earth. Dust. Waterless. Endless vistas.

The life is that of reptiles and millions of jewel-like birds, of marsupials and dingoes. Occasionally tracks cross the sand, signs of man like no other men on earth. Twenty-five-thousand-year-old stone paintings on rocks. The most consistently remote and barren land known to man. The most unwelcoming. Uninhabited and uninhabitable for millions of years.

And then slowly, in the middle of the nineteenth century, a few men came, searching their way across the gibber plains, across the vast deserts, across the horizon that never seemed to come any closer. With the men came sheep and, later, cattle. Along with these came death, desolation, and infinite loneliness.

It was a man's country, for few men had the temerity to ask a woman to share a life so removed from humanity. And yet, here and there, hundreds, sometimes thousands of miles apart, a woman did come with a man, came and made a home for him, bore his children who would be doomed, as was she, to be forever alienated from civilized society . . . from any society, civilized or not. It drove some people insane. It was referred to as the Great Loneliness, the Great Australian Loneliness.

The sun beats down on this parched earth, which for millennia seemed unfit for human habitation. It is the most isolated, empty vastness—as well as the oldest land mass—on the face of the earth. And the last to be populated by white man.

It is a land of infinite beauty, frightening, empty . . . a land of indescribable bird life, of reptiles, of mystical spiritualism. It combines blacks native to the land—unlike any other people known to man—and whites of European extraction who have met the challenges of this inhospitable continent.

It is a land where Biblical seven-year droughts are common, and the earth is littered with the bleached bones of sheep, cattle, horses . . . and the broken hearts of men. It is a land where flash floods appear with no warning, obliterating homesteads and drowning babies. Wind-driven fires rage out of control.

It is the only place on the planet where people dwell in underground caves to escape the blast-furnace heat of summer when the temperature hovers above 120 degrees for months on end, where a man can die of thirst within hours. It is two million square miles unlike any other, beyond anything most men can imagine.

That it has *ever* been populated, that *any* women were willing to settle on homesteads where the nearest neighbor might be as close as sixty-five miles away or as far as five hundred miles distant, is truly a miracle. And the fact that towns were born there, that cattle and sheep stations developed that led to wealth, as well as to bankruptcy and death, has all largely been due to the efforts of one man and to the radio and the airplane. These two inventions and this man, the Reverend John Flynn, opened the way for the Flying Doctor Service, one of the nobler experiments of mankind, and it made all the difference to the development of the interior of Australia.

It is called the Outback, The Never-Never, *The Back of Beyond.*

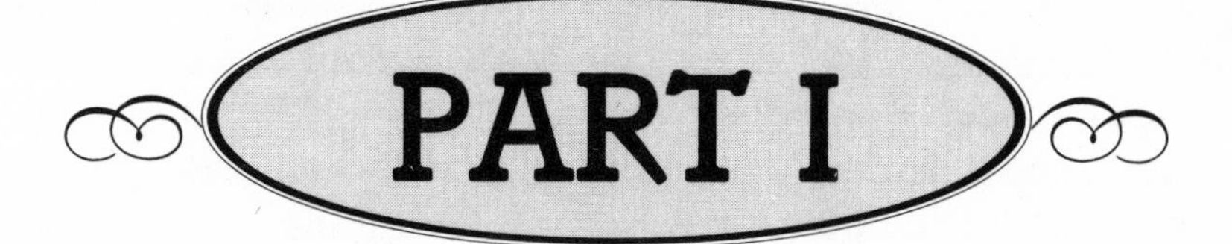

June 1938–August 1939

Chapter 1

She had never really believed love could be like this. Her whole being sang.

In her years at Georgetown—in Washington where her father was the Ambassador—she knew that if she became involved, if she were to fall in love, it would deter her from her path. She refused to let that happen. In med school she'd had to work so hard she never had time for men.

Then she'd come home, back to Melbourne, to work in the Emergency Room at the city's largest hospital, the first woman to do so. She'd been warned for years that she'd have trouble setting up a private practice, that not even women would want to come to a female doctor, so this job would give her experience and alleviate the worry of setting up a practice of her own in a country that hadn't been home to her for twenty years.

The reason, she suspected, that she was offered this job was thanks to Dr. Norman Castor, head of surgery. A friend of her father's from their days in the university together, Dr. Castor had visited them when her father was the consul in San Francisco and at the embassies in London and Washington. He'd been "Uncle Norm" to her since she was a little girl.

She knew he was proud of her. She dealt with trauma cases well, rose to emergencies, didn't hesitate to call a surgeon when she needed one or a specialist when in doubt. She had delivered babies in ambulances, sewed up knife wounds, and even performed a cesarean on the linoleum floor of a filthy third-floor apartment of a woman who'd been shot in the belly. One evening a week, on her own time, she conducted prenatal classes and dispensed birth control information at a free clinic.

In the Emergency Room one night, she met Dr. Raymond Graham when she needed a neurosurgeon for a trauma patient. She'd had to call and wake him at four-thirty. He was there in half an hour, scarcely nodding at her as he examined the patient. Then he turned and said, "You'll have to assist. Come along."

She was impressed with his skill, and when they finished sewing the patient up, he turned to her and smiled for the first time. "The least you can do is buy me breakfast after waking me up."

They sat in the hospital restaurant in their blood-stained green fatigues, drinking endless cups of coffee. She was charmed by his amusing stories and easy manner. He asked her questions about herself, interested to hear she'd grown up mainly in England and America.

He called her late the next afternoon, knowing she'd have to sleep during the day. "What nights aren't you working this week?"

"Tuesday and Wednesday."

"I don't want to wait that long. How about dinner tomorrow night?"

It was the first time she'd dined out since she'd worked at the hospital—nearly a year. The few women she'd met outside work couldn't understand why she'd rather be a doctor than a wife. The few women she knew at work were nursing sisters, unaccustomed to being friends with doctors.

Cassie suddenly realized she'd been lonely. The Emergency Room was always charged with drama, and usually she would drag home at the end of a night there, too tired to worry about making friends. But, if you didn't meet friends at work, where did you meet them?

She and Dr. Graham dined in a little Italian restaurant she'd never even noticed, though she'd walked by it a dozen times. It reminded her of Mama Leone's in Georgetown, and she felt warm and cozy even though there was a sleeting rain.

Between the salad course and the chicken cacciatore he told her he was married and had two children, but that he and his wife, after eighteen years of marriage, were separated. She'd gone back to Toowoomba to her parents and was going to file for divorce there.

They began to walk along the beach on fine fall evenings and to watch the fairy penguins. They went to movies together and discovered all the ethnic restaurants Melbourne offered. One night he reached across the table and put his hand over hers, saying, "I've fallen in love with you."

For the first time in nearly ten years, since she'd entered the university, she began to feel safe with a man, found herself enjoying his kisses and the touch of his hand on her breast. All the feelings she'd buried rose to the surface so that the night he began to unbutton her blouse she didn't stop him. She wanted to feel his kisses on her neck, on her breasts, wanted to feel the length of his naked body against her.

He'd whispered, "Don't worry. I'll see you won't become pregnant."

She gave him a key to her flat, and he'd be waiting for her when she came home at dawn after the late shift. He'd devour her with kisses and words of love, and she'd open herself to him, clutching him, drawing him into her. She could think of little else. Work became a place to put in time between hours spent with Ray. They seldom went out to dinner anymore and never to the cinema. They always ended up in bed. He taught her things she had never learned about loving. He was patient yet demanding. He would not let her lie passively, but showed her what pleased him.

"Kiss me there. Don't be afraid. Oh, God, yes, like that."

He turned her on her stomach. They made love standing up, and upside down, and she thought they must have done it sideways and maybe even inside out.

He told her she had the most beautiful breasts, the most electric body he could ever imagine. She began to be proud of herself, walked straighter, stole looks in mirrors, bought dresses that clung. She bathed herself in oils and always wore perfume behind her ears and her knees.

She had never felt so alive.

She was in love. Wildly, insanely, ecstatically in love. He told her they'd be married as soon as his divorce . . .

Yeah, well.

He called Cassie into his office early in the morning of the third Tuesday of June and said, "Cassie, Martha's come home. She wants us to try again. So, I'm afraid you and I are finished."

She sat there staring at him, into eyes that were like ice, eyes she had never seen.

"Ray?"

His lips tightened.

"Don't make this more difficult than it already is, Cassie."

"*More difficult?*" A tear slid down her cheek. Her throat burned. "Ray, I love you." It was a nightmare from which she was sure she'd awaken any second.

His fingers drummed on his desk. He looked at his watch. "I'm due in surgery in fifteen minutes."

"You're saying goodbye, just like this?"

He stared at her.

Cassie burst into tears. Ray slid a box of Kleenex across his desk and said, impatiently, "I don't find you very attractive like this."

Cassie's head jerked up and, her voice tearful, she asked, "Just like this? You really mean it's over?"

"That's exactly what I mean. And I think it would be better if you found a position in some other hospital. Of course, I'll write you a recommendation. You *are* a fine doctor. I have friends in hospitals in Perth and in Charleville that I'll contact, if you like." Two towns as remote as they could be from Melbourne, she realized. "I suspect you'll feel awkward here, under the circumstances."

"*I'll* feel awkward?" She wondered if he heard the squeak in her voice.

He lowered his eyes and sat down behind his cluttered desk. "I think you'll find it quite uncomfortable . . . " His voice trailed off as he looked her straight in the eyes. "Cassie, I don't want to fire you. That wouldn't be fair. Why don't you make your own arrangements."

She couldn't sleep. She didn't eat. She experienced spells of dizziness. She took walks and wept as she made her way through the streets. She tried a movie but wailed so loudly she left. She read the same page over and over, not comprehending a word. She sat at her window and stared into space, into emptiness as she sobbed in great, gasping moans.

She appeared at work red-eyed and humorless. She could think of nothing but Dr. Raymond Graham and, as he'd instructed her to do, she penned her resignation.

At the end of two weeks, noticeably thinner, she was summoned to Dr. Castor's office, where he sat behind his enormous teak desk and looked at her as she seated herself in the chair opposite him. He sighed heavily. "I don't want to accept it."

"I've been in the ER long enough," she murmured, not looking at him.

He sat back in his chair and studied her. "What are you thinking of doing?"

How should she answer? Putting one foot in front of the other. Hibernating. Going back to Daddy in Washington. Climbing the Himalayas. Becoming a nun.

When Cassie didn't reply, Dr. Castor said, "You want to run away."

She looked at him. Did he know? He answered her unspoken question. "Everyone knows."

Tears gathered in the corners of her eyes. Castor stood and walked around his desk, sitting on the edge of it in front of Cassie, reaching out to take her hands in his.

"I can't stay," she whispered, tears sliding down her cheeks. She wondered bitterly if she would *ever* stop crying.

Dr. Castor walked over to look out the smudged windows, his hands clasped behind his back. When Cassie stopped sniffling he asked, "What do you know about the Flying Doctors?"

She looked over at him. "The ones who fly out to patients in the Outback?'

Castor nodded. "It was started a decade ago by one of the finest men I've ever known, Reverend John Flynn. It's his theory that the great center of this continent can only be settled if women are willing to live there. He saw that there were hardly any homesteads in all this vastness. No women or children or warmth. No love.

"He was sure the only way to get women to live hundreds and even thousands of miles from their nearest neighbors was to assure them of medical care and find a way to relieve their isolation. In 1928 his dream began to come true; the first Flying Doctor base was started in Cloncurry.

"In the latest medical journal I saw an ad for another Flying Doctor. They're ready to open up a fifth base, I'm not sure where. They pay very well and John Flynn only hires the best, people who will share his dream and help develop the great interior of our continent."

He paused. "Interested?"

Nothing interested her. "It's a long way away, wherever it is, isn't it?"

Castor nodded and, without waiting, picked up his phone and gave the operator a Sydney number.

"John, glad to find you in. It's Norm. No, I'm not in Sydney. I'm calling to see if you've filled that position."

Castor listened for a minute.

"Now, wait—before you make any decisions, let me send you a candidate I bet you can't beat. Or even equal. She's . . . Yes, *she.* For the last year she's been one of our Emergency Room surgeons." He was quiet, obviously having been interrupted.

"Wait a minute, John. You're out there way ahead of everyone else in your thinking. Why not give a woman a chance? At least talk with her, will you? She's bonzer, really first class." He winked at Cassie.

Castor listened to the other end, then he said, "How do you think women feel with their legs up in the air as a man examines them?"

Silence again. "Yes, well, think about it that way. Look, John, I can get her on the night train and she can be in Sydney in the morning. How about seeing her at ten? Someday you'll thank me for this. Her name's Clarke. Dr. Cassandra Clarke."

He hung up the phone and grinned at Cassie. "Well?"

She stared at him blankly. This was happening far too quickly. Where was her life heading? Well, wherever, it would at least be heading away from Ray Graham.

"You don't have to say yes. Neither does he. He's not thrilled about the idea of a woman in his outfit. Said he'd never given it a thought. Well, go give him hell, Cassie. You'll wow them out there."

Out where?

Chapter 2

Augusta Springs was a dusty little town with a 180-degree view. As Cassie's train—it ran once a week—slowly chugged into the station, the first flicker of emotion she'd felt in two months fluttered in her chest.

Fear.

What was she doing here, nearly a thousand miles from civilization? What did she know of this town? It had a small hospital and two local doctors. It was a railhead for shipping cattle from the north to the big markets. It had a school through the sixth grade and maybe—give or take—twelve hundred inhabitants.

It didn't look like anyplace she'd ever seen, not even the American west. It was so flat you could see forever, except that gum trees proliferated in the sandy earth.

Reverend Flynn warned her she might have trouble being accepted. "But when there's no choice, they'll have to accept a woman." Not much comfort. He'd also told her *the* big aboriginal problem was venereal disease. "And they're not likely to let a woman examine them."

So, why had he chosen her?

Why had she said yes? Because it was a long way from Ray Graham. Because she didn't have the energy or interest to think of anything else to do, any other place to go.

She felt more alone than she'd imagined anyone could feel. Her life for the next year would be lived in this remote hamlet and in the air. She'd never been in an airplane. Would she be sick? I'm not afraid of dying, she told herself, but being sick?

She steeled herself, stiffening with resolve, staring out the train window into the blinding sunlight. "I've nothing more to lose," she said aloud. At the same time she was sure there wasn't much to look forward to.

The Flying Doctor Service pilot, Sam Vernon, stood on the station platform, a blade of grass in his mouth, his baseball cap pushed back on his head, looking around the station through his dark glasses. Cocky-looking. Tall and thin as a stringbean, tanned. She noticed how his gaze followed every young woman. She was sure that behind those sunglasses he was mentally undressing each one. Not that there were many girls disembarking. Not many of anything.

Cassie picked up her overnight bag and walked over to him, brushing back her short, thick chestnut hair.

"Mr. Vernon?"

He jerked his head to look at her and murmured, "Ma'am?"

Setting down her bag, she said, "I'm Cassandra Clarke." She held out her hand.

He stared at her for a moment before reaching out to grasp her hand.

"My bags are over there." She pointed to the baggage rack.

He looked at them, then back at her, and began walking toward the luggage. "Yes, ma'am."

He grabbed the bags and nodded toward his dusty blue pick-up. "The utility's over there." They walked to the truck in silence. He tossed the bags in the back and opened the door for her. As he walked around the front of the truck, got in the driver's side, and inserted the key in the ignition, she studied him.

The engine chugged into life. She looked out the window. "There are more trees than I expected. I thought it would all be desert."

"It is, further south. You'll be treating a lot of stockmen and abos . . . "

"Abos?" She turned to face him.

"Aborigines. Don't mean disrespect," he put in hastily, "just seems easier. Anyhow, none of them're gonna let a woman look at their bodies, at their private parts."

She tried to see his eyes through his dark glasses.

He looked straight ahead as he continued talking. "They're not going to accept you easily."

"They'll get used to me." *Thanks for your encouragement,* she really wanted to say as they passed houses that either had trees and tidy gardens or were littered by debris and assorted goats. "Why do you think people move out here?" she asked, more to herself than to him.

"Pioneering spirit." Apparently that didn't seem like an adequate answer. He went on. "Freedom. Individualism. Wanting to be rich. Liking to be one's own boss. To get away from people and rules." He grinned and turned to look at her. "Some men just feel more comfortable never having to dress up."

"For a woman, you mean?" Their eyes met.

"Personally, I think women are one of God's great gifts to mankind." She had a feeling he wasn't so sure about her, though.

"Why," he asked, "did you come out here?"

"I'm not sure." What she really wanted to do was get back on that train.

Sam swung his legs out of the truck. He took off his dark glasses and tossed them on the dashboard. "Most women come out here to find love." He led the way up the street to Addie's and held the swinging door for her. Addie's fronted on two streets so that a person could enter from either one. A balcony ran along the second story. "You're going to be rooming with one of the local schoolteachers. I told her we'd meet her here."

The air was thick with smoke and the smell of stale beer. Men lined the bar and gathered around the dart board at the back of the long room. Sam turned right and led the way to the dining room, where tables were covered with red and white checkered tablecloths. There was just one empty table and Sam went to it, holding out a chair for Cassie.

"I don't know many people yet," he said. "I've just been here a week. If I don't introduce you to people it's because I can't remember their names."

"We won't be working with people in town anyway, will we?"

"But we'll be living here," he said. A waitress with thin hips and an enormous bosom appeared, smiling coquettishly at Sam.

"Wanna beer, right?" she asked.

He nodded and winked, then cocked an eyebrow at Cassie. "Want one?"

"Sure, why not?"

"How d'you like your steak?" he asked.

"Medium rare."

"Yeah," said the waitress, "and I know you'd like yours so it's just stopped breathing." She brought them their beers, leaning over Sam so that Cassie wondered if her breasts would spill right out of her blouse. Sam smiled appreciatively.

A jukebox blared American music. Cassie poured her beer into a glass, while Sam picked up the bottle and drank from it. "Your age is going to work against you, too."

She straightened up. "*Too?*"

His eyes danced around the room. "I like it here, in Addie's. In Augusta Springs."

The bosomy waitress brought their steaks. Chips. Canned string beans. Tomatoes on a bed of wilted lettuce. Steak sauce.

Cassie looked at it and up at him. "This is the best food in town?"

Chewing on a thick slab of steak, Sam nodded happily. "Taste it. Feels like velvet going down."

Just then a laughing, red-haired woman about their age wove her way through the crowded room. She stopped to greet most of the diners but her goal, Cassie could tell, was their table. Sam waved to her and, when she approached, he stood up. When she spoke, her voice was husky. "This must be the doctor," she exclaimed. Not waiting for an introduction, she said, "I'm Fiona Sullivan," and held out her hand. "Has Sam told you you're going to be living at my place?"

Sam sat down again and began to attack his steak as the women surveyed each other.

Fiona reached to the table behind her, dragging its extra chair over so she could join them. "Well, well." There was amusement in her eyes. "I just dropped in to say the front door's open and there's a trail of notes leading you to your bedroom. Please make yourself completely at home. We can talk in the morning. I'm on my way to a party. Race week, you know."

"Fiona, here, is Miss Hospitality of Augusta Springs," Sam said. He ordered another beer and tipped his chair backward.

Cassie began to cut into her steak. It was tender, wonderfully so. "Do I detect an Irish brogue?"

Fiona sipped the coffee the waitress had plopped on the table. "I can't fool anyone despite having been here over five years."

"From town gossip," Sam said, "Fiona is *the* best teacher in this part of the country. Maybe in the whole country."

Fiona leaned across the table and put her hand over his. "An exaggeration, but it's nice to hear."

Just then two young stockmen whooped into the dining room and, upon seeing Fiona, headed for their table.

"Come on, Fi," pleaded one. "They sent us to look for you. Party can't start without you." Each one took an arm and urged her from her chair.

"I'm coming. Put me down." She leaned over to Cassie. "Welcome. I couldn't be more pleased."

Warmth washed over Cassie and she smiled for the first time since Ray Graham had told her he was returning to Martha.

Fiona left with the two men. Sam's eyes followed her. "Tomorrow," he said, pushing his chair back, "I'll drive you out to the base station to meet Horrie, and we can talk about what we'll be doing and how we'll get organized."

He took a cigarette out of his packet and glanced at Cassie. Then he rolled it between his fingers, scattering tobacco over his gnawed T-bone. His eyes met hers and she sensed his resentment.

"Does it bother you to be working with a woman?"

"I'm not about to quit or anything. I'm willing to give it a go." His voice had a grudging edge to it. "I was surprised when they told me it'd be a woman doc. I've never worked with a woman before."

"Is it impossible to imagine?'

His grin was shy, like a boy's. "Well, I can think of better things to do with women than work with them. By the way, what would you like me to call you?"

When Cassie looked blankly at him, Sam grinned. "How about Doc? Anybody call you Doc before?"

She shook her head. "No. Never." She hated it.

"C'mon, I'll take you over to Fiona's so's you can get settled in. It's just a couple of blocks. I'm paying. It's on me tonight, Doc."

Doc. She gritted her teeth.

Chapter 3

Fiona's house was the prettiest place in town. A colorful border of snapdragons edged the picket fence that surrounded her front yard. In typical Outback style, the verandah encircled the entire house. Fiona had sprinkled it with pots of bright marigolds, zinnias, petunias. The wicker furniture on the porch had been painted a bright yellow, and the comfortable cushions were white muslin. It was where Fiona said she really lived.

"I better warn you," Fiona said, leaning her elbows on the table. "I'm a lousy cook. My heart's not in cooking, though heaven knows, I love to eat."

Cassie grinned. "Cooking's the one household chore I'm any good at."

Fiona whooped. "We're going to get along, I can tell."

Being with Fiona made Cassie feel good.

Fiona's living room was white with splashes of primary green and blue pillows tossed around. So unlike the dark horsehair sofas Cassie was used to in the cities, the dark scratchy velour with antimacassars on the arms.

On the four-poster bed in Cassie's room was a hand-crocheted bedspread. "It's gorgeous," Cassie murmured as she fingered it. "An heirloom?"

"I did it a couple of years ago," Fiona had said, "when I was recovering from an unhappy love affair and needed something to occupy my time and mind."

The room could have been stark with so much white, but splashy pillows and a gaily-colored impressionistic painting above the bed made it light and airy, with paned glass doors opening onto the side verandah.

"I love it."

Fiona wore a light blue shirtwaist dress and sandals. Her bright red hair looked wanton, like her garden. "My bedroom's on the other side of the house, so we needn't fall over each other."

"I might not be here every night to cook, if that's to be my assignment. I don't know what our schedule's going to be."

"That's okay." Fiona waved a hand through the air. "I can always eat at Addie's. I think what you're going to be doing is awfully exciting. We can ask Sally—she's the phone operator—to cut through any other calls when Horrie rings."

Fiona looked around the room. "There's plenty of space to move a desk in here if you'd like. We could put it there by the window."

"It's awfully kind of you." Cassie felt herself unfolding like a flower.

"Not really. It's an act of pure selfishness. I can use the rent money and I want access to the ton of books you say is on the way. Also I do think we're going to hit it off. I'll introduce you around. After I get home from school this afternoon I'll take you over to meet Dr. Adams, the hospital superintendent, and hope he'll let you keep your medicines in their cooler. No one else around here has an icebox. Most of us make do with a Coolgardie safe. Of course, he's such a curmudgeon he'll probably make it difficult for you."

Difficult was an understatement.

Dr. Christopher Adams stood as erect as an army officer. Though only in his early forties, his dark hair was graying at the temples, his trim mustache salt and pepper. There was no humor or warmth in his ice-blue eyes.

He nodded to Fiona, gesturing for the two women to sit in the chairs opposite his tidy desk.

"I heard they sent a woman." He said "they" as though it were the enemy, and "woman" with scorn.

"I wonder if you'll let me keep some of my medicines in your cooler?" Cassie asked.

Adams didn't answer but tapped his fingers on his desk. "I've talked with your Reverend Flynn and with Steven Thompson, leader of the pastoralists. You understand this hospital is not your province, don't you? You have no medical privileges here. Patients you bring in will be treated either by me or by Dr. Edwards. We can send an ambulance to meet the plane should you require such. Once you enter the hospital, your patient becomes our patient."

"Yes, I understand that's regular Flying Doctor Service procedure." Cassie tried to keep her voice even.

"Just want to make sure you know the ground rules."

"As I understand it," she said, keeping her voice light, "the FDS will not be flying out to any patients you could possibly reach, but only those beyond present medical care. Is that right?"

Adams hesitated a moment and then nodded. "That's how it's supposed to work."

Cassie leaned over and put her hands on the doctor's desk. "Let me reassure you, Dr. Adams, I have no desire to steal patients from you, if that's your worry."

He didn't say anything for a minute but looked at her, his gaze never wavering. "I can have one of the sisters clear off a shelf for your vaccines, I guess. As long as we understand each other."

"I suspect it will take us a long time to understand each other, Dr. Adams." Cassie stood up, stretching out her hand. "For now, thank you for your willingness to help."

Adams did not reach out to shake her hand but took off his rimless glasses and rubbed them on his tie. Then, not looking up, he said, "Better you should have been a nurse, you know."

Fiona arose and said, "Thanks, Chris. I knew you'd help. Cassie's going to be staying with me."

The doctor did not say goodbye.

"He's a charmer," Cassie said.

"He does lack a bedside manner," Fiona admitted. "However, he's a fine doctor, a far sight better than Dr. Edwards. And his bark is worse than his bite." She opened the door of her car as Cassie got in the other side. "Let's stop and buy some food. I'm starving."

"It's all ready. I fixed a casserole—all I have to do is heat it."

Fiona keyed the engine. "Dinner waiting? How wonderful."

"Why is he such a—what was your word? Curmudgeon?"

"Who knows? I'd blame it on his current situation except that he's always been rather testy."

"What's the current situation?"

"His wife."

Fiona pulled up in front of the house. "Isabel's dying. She's been his nurse all these years, too." Opening the front door, she continued. "They've been together at work and at home all their twenty-some years of marriage."

Fiona headed to the Coolgardie cooler and took out a beer as Cassie lit the oven, shaking her head at the beer Fiona offered her.

Fiona wiped her mouth with the back of her hand. "He's the school doctor and once he's with kids, he takes off that protective mask and is a gentle—I'd almost say loving—man."

"What makes you stand up for him?"

Fiona sipped from the beer bottle. "Probably because I always tend to defend the underdog. It wouldn't take you long to discover that on your own."

Cassie nodded. "How long has she been ill?"

"Isabel's been bedridden a couple of months. God, that smells good."

Cassie was chopping greens for a salad. Fiona ran outside and clipped some flowers, artfully arranged them in a vase, and put them in the center of the table.

"I got this front verandah screened in just last month," she said. "In summer the flies are unbearable."

Cassie brought the salad to the verandah. "If you're up to cooking for more than two," Fiona said, "we could invite your handsome pilot and that engineer to dinner some night."

Cassie thought flying with Sam would give them more than enough time together. "Does Mrs. Adams stay by herself all day?"

"Dear me, no. There are two ladies who come in to feed and bathe her."

"Maybe I'll go over there when I have an hour free and offer to read to her."

Fiona looked at Cassie and grinned. "Whatever's in this casserole, it's nothing short of divine." She chewed a minute, then said, "So, you're going to attack Chris by being a diplomat?"

"I'm anything but a diplomat," Cassie said. "People accuse me of being too straightforward."

"Is that a euphemism for lacking tact?" Fiona asked, laughing.

"Exactly."

"Doesn't that turn men off?"

A veil seemed to drop over Cassie's eyes. "I'm not interested in men."

There was silence for a minute, and then Fiona leaned back in her chair. "There's no way you can keep men away here. The country's lopsided with single men. Most of them just want to have a good time though I get a half-hearted proposal every couple of months, but . . . " her voice faded away.

"But?"

"The only man I ever *really* wanted didn't want me."

Cassie didn't know what to say. Wouldn't any man want Fiona?

"I got over it," Fiona assured her, "after a while. I'd like children, but I'm just twenty-six. I have time. For now, I like my life just as it is."

"Right now," said Cassie, "I do, too. Despite Sam and Dr. Adams, I feel I'm on the brink of a great adventure."

The adventure took off early the next morning when Horrie came dashing up in his truck, shouting. "A stockman's been trampled by his horse couple hundred miles north of here."

Chapter 4

"Scared?" Sam asked as he slid into the cockpit seat next to Cassie.

Not waiting for an answer, he began turning dials, waving to someone on the ground as the engine began to rev.

Cassie clutched the arms of the seat much as she did in a dentist's chair even before the drilling began. She shoved her medical bag under the seat.

A tingling sensation feathered across her chest and she hoped she wouldn't be sick. The aircraft began to roll across the tarmac, the noise of the engine deafening. She watched as everything began to move by faster, hardly realizing the plane had taken off until the ground began to distance itself. She couldn't believe she was flying.

Augusta Springs, already half a century old in 1938, didn't look like much from up here. Trees, numerous but not yet tall, lined most of the streets, laid out in rectangles. A desert oasis. Cassie could see the rail terminal easily, the tracks leading east by southeast. The race course. A cluster of buildings in the center of the town. The two largest must be the school and the hospital. Neither looked very impressive from this height. As they gained elevation, all she saw was clumps of trees widely scattered across the endless red earth.

Gradually Sam leveled the plane out and turned his head to shout over the engines. "Most of it looks like this. Miles of what seems to be nothing. Thousands of miles of it, though this has trees and south of here doesn't. The farther north we go, the more trees."

How could those flimsy-looking wings possibly keep the plane aloft? Her knuckles were white as she clutched the arms of her seat.

"We'll probably get lost now and then," Sam said with a grin.

"There aren't even any road maps to guide us. We've got to notice landmarks—homesteads, rivers, a mound of land higher than others, a clump of trees, a dry riverbed. We'll get used to it."

It all looked the same to her. How could you tell a dry riverbed if there was no water in it?

"What happens if we *do* get lost?"

He turned his head to look at her and she was glad to see his eyes twinkling. "We'll face that when it happens. It's not going to happen today," he reassured her. "Over there," he nodded to where the stretcher was tied to the wall, "in that box is a thermos of coffee. Wil-lya pour me a cup? Do it in little bits, or it'll spill all over. Have some yourself if you want. Milk in a little can and some sugar, too, if you've a mind for it."

She managed to pour two cups without spilling any, despite the plane's dipping into what Sam explained were air currents. "Nothing much to worry about at this time of year. The Brits and Americans can't believe we never have ice on wings or don't have to fight the kind of weather they do. Most of the year the flying conditions are near perfect. Except for three months of the Wet. Then we'll have some fun. But that's not until December or January. Of course, if there's no Wet and a drought comes, then we have to fight duststorms.

"We're flying at fifty-five-hundred feet," he said, and she realized his voice had a rough edge to it. Rather nice, scratchy like sandpaper. She sipped her coffee and studied him. Too thin, really, but he had a nice face. Tanned. She guessed she would soon be, too. Firm chin. What she'd call dirty blond hair always topped by his baseball cap, which he wore even when flying, though he had pushed it back on his head. Sharp, straight nose.

Leaning forward to look out the window, she understood why he had told her never to fly without dark glasses. The sun was blinding, bleeding down on the red land below them, into big dry cracks opening into the bowels of the earth.

They were following a barely visible, narrow dirt road. The landscape was dotted with a station every so often, dozens of miles apart. She wondered what made people build homes so far from anyone and anything else.

The plane jolted and Cassie wondered if she were going to throw up.

"Where gum trees and coolibahs dot the land is where water flows in the Wet," Sam shouted at her. "In those cracks down there and under the smooth sand that looks like a dry river next to the stands of trees, well, where there's no water now can spread out miles wide when it floods."

She couldn't imagine a flood over this land.

"In a couple of months," Sam went on, "before the Wet begins, a lot of this land will be cracked wide open with dryness."

Cassie kept her eyes glued to the window, observing the monotonous vastness of the unending landscape.

Sam jotted something in a small notebook strapped to his right leg. "Pilot's log," he explained. "I'm noting idiosyncrasies in the landscape so when we fly out here next time I'll know where I am. Hey, look down there! It's a whole herd of roos." She looked out her window to see hundreds of jumping kangaroos. How and where had they found food in this desolate land?

Two hours later, by the time they circled over a cattle station, Cassie was more relaxed, though she still clung to the arm of her seat. Wilkins, the name of the station's owner, was painted in enormous letters on the tin roof of the homestead.

"I'm trying to find claypan or any smooth place to land," Sam said. Cassie saw a man running from the house, waving his arms in the air.

Sam said, "Okay, here we go. Hold on."

They plunked over stones, and the plane quivered as it touched the uneven terrain. By the time Sam was out of his seat and had the door opened, the man was waiting for them.

Sam reached out a hand to help her down the steps. She felt her legs wobble.

"Got me a Land Rover and we can get over about ten miles in it," the man said, without waiting for introductions, "but after that you're going to have to go in on horses. No way for a car to get through there."

"How far is it altogether?"

The man ignored her and continued talking to Sam. "Better leave your nurse here with my missus. That country's tough to travel through, no place for a woman."

"This here's the doctor," Sam said. "I'm the pilot."

The man turned to look at her, his lower jaw falling open. He scratched behind his ear. "Well, let's get going," he mumbled. "The stockman might be dead by now. It's been over twenty-four hours since the horse fell on him, if you can believe the runner. Of course, these natives have no sense of time, so who knows? The runner's waiting at the next station to guide you. Country out there is rocky and filled with ravines."

"Why were they droving in such country then?" Sam asked. He was tamping metal stakes into the ground and tying the plane down.

"On the other side of them canyons is some of the best grass in the world."

It took them over three-quarters of an hour driving over dry, cracked, sandy red land to travel the ten miles to the next station, which was no more than a shack. Nevertheless, it was probably the headquarters for thousands of acres of cattle. A lean, dirty drover ambled out of the shack, pointing to the black man lying under one of the trees. "He'll guide you." He went over to kick the sleeping aborigine awake, saying something unintelligible. "Got a couple of horses you can use. Had them saddled up and waiting."

Sam turned to Cassie. "You ride?"

She nodded. She'd had riding lessons three times a week ever since John Flynn told her the job was hers, but she'd never ridden outside a riding ring or the city park.

"It's close onto twenty miles, if you can believe that one." He pointed to the black, who stood waiting.

"Doesn't he have a horse?" asked Cassie.

"He's a tracker. He's better on foot."

"But twenty miles?"

"He made that much last night," answered the man, not bothering to look at her.

The first three or four miles were easy riding, through mulga scrub and sand. Thankfully there wasn't spinifex, that prickly bush whose spikes sent despair through cattlemen and lamed their animals. After that the canyons started, rocks jagged against the afternoon sky. Sam handed her a sandwich. "What about our guide?" she asked.

Nodding, he reached into the saddlebag and drew out a waxed paper bundle, calling out to the man running steadily ahead of them. The man stopped, turned, and then, seeing he was being offered food, came back to them and reached up his hand. He smiled his thanks. Several minutes later he stopped again, holding up his hands and gesturing to them to descend. He left the trail and a few yards from it knelt down, drinking from a trickle in the ground.

"We'd never have found that," Sam said, following the man. The water was refreshing. Cassie followed Sam's example, splashing it over her face and hair, slapping it on her neck.

"How ya doin'?" he asked.

"I'm fine. How much farther is it?"

"I don't know. I can never figure mileage on the ground. Couple more hours to go, I'd guess."

The black man started his rhythmic, even running. They climbed back on their horses, Sam forming his hands into a cup so Cassie could step into it and mount. He jumped onto his. She was glad Reverend Flynn had suggested she buy men's pants, even if wearing them did shock people. She'd gone to R. M. Williams, who manufactured shirts, breeches, and boots for sheepmen and cattlemen. Cassie had opted for the latter, with the more pointed high-heeled elastic boots rather than the flatter-heeled boots worn by sheepmen. Whereas the sheepmen's trousers were invariably a creamy white, Cassie had bought two pairs in the colors preferred by drovers, and today she'd left behind her blue pair and wore dark grey riding breeches. None of Williams's shirts fit her, as the shoulders were far too broad. She wore a pale green silk blouse that clung to her, accentuating the very thing she was trying to hide—her femininity. Her wide-brimmed Stetson was a pale grey, and her eyes were hidden behind dark glasses.

This was a different world from any she'd known. A thrill ran through her. She would never have dreamed, back in Georgetown, that she'd be flying two hundred miles and riding through red-rocked canyons under a technicolor sky to attend a patient.

By the time they reached their destination, Cassie guessed there would be another two hours of daylight—and that she'd have saddle sores the next day.

In the shade of a clump of tall gums lay the man they'd come so far to tend. He was surrounded by three of his mates, their horses hobbled a short distance away.

Sam jumped down from his horse, then reached up to help Cassie. The prostrate man's eyelids fluttered open, and Cassie could see his pain. Kneeling next to her patient, her voice gentle, she said. "Tell me, where's the pain?"

The man wet his cracked lips with his tongue, his head barely shaking as he mumbled something she couldn't understand.

"In your belly?" she asked.

He nodded weakly.

"I'm afraid I'm going to have to hurt you more. I have to feel to see if anything's broken." She unbuckled his belt. "Does this hurt?" She prodded his stomach.

"Jesus Christ!" he yelled, clenching his teeth as her hands expertly touched him.

She turned to Sam, aware that all the men were staring at her. "Get him out of these trousers, and let's lower his underpants."

Sam knelt down and with his left hand raised the man's buttocks from the ground, smoothly sliding his pants below his hips.

"I think he has a broken pubic bone. Try to lift him as gently as possible while I pull his pants down all the way." Cassie turned back to the patient. "Have you been able to urinate?"

"Jeez," she heard one of his mates say.

"Hurts like hell," whispered the patient, his voice broken.

"Look," she said to Sam. "Blood on his underpants." Turning again to the patient, she asked, "Does the pain come in waves? Does it well up and then seem to go away, but never quite completely?"

In response, the man just moaned. He could move only slightly and, as her fingers touched him again, he cried aloud.

She pulled her stethoscope from the bag and fastened the blood pressure cuff on his upper arm. "Pulse is fast at 150." *Mine must be, too. Am I going to have to operate out here?* "Blood pressure's normal, though, 140 over 80. Can you tell me exactly where the most pain is?" *I'm afraid I know what it is*, she thought. *What will I do out here in the wilderness?*

The patient ground his teeth and raised his left arm, pointing to his lower abdomen, which was swollen and tender. Cassie didn't touch it again. "The genitalia look normal," she said. Sam couldn't tell whether she was telling him or talking to herself. The other men stared.

"There's no swelling in the sac. I suspect he may have a fracture of the pelvis because his abdomen is so distended." She pointed to the affected area, adding, "And since the urine is bloody, he's probably ruptured his bladder." What the hell could she do about a ruptured bladder out here? Well, something had to be done or it could lead to infection and possibly fatal blood poisoning.

She'd never faced such a problem outside a sterile operating theater. "What I'm going to try first," she said to Sam, "is inserting this catheter . . . "

"Aw Gawd," said one of the men.

" . . . to relieve the bladder distension." She inserted the tube through the man's limp penis but only a small amount of urine and blood emerged.

She glanced at Sam, who was still kneeling on the other side of the patient, watching her. "The broken pelvis doesn't need any specific treatment as it'll heal by itself, but a ruptured bladder is a surgical emergency." She sat back on her heels.

"You going to operate—out here?"

"There's no choice, and it's going to be dark in a couple of hours."

The only sound was the buzzing of flies. She recognized the knot of fear as it tightened in the center of her belly.

Cassie stood up and turned toward the three men. "Gentlemen, I'd appreciate your building a fire. I'll need sterile water." She turned to Sam. "You'll have to help."

He drew back. "I'm a pilot, not a nurse."

"I have news for you," she said, pulling a packet out of her medical bag. "You are a pilot *and* an anesthetist. See this?" She held up the gauze mask.

"I can't do that." Sam's voice had a rough edge to it.

"Of course you can," she said. "I'm going to give him an intramuscular injection of ten milligrams of morphine to help sedate him. Then, when he starts to doze you hold the mask in one hand and this bottle of ether in the other and drip a drop of ether every three to five minutes onto the gauze. Make sure it's just a drop or you can kill him."

"How do I know how much is too much?"

Cassie took out a hypodermic needle and a bottle. Sliding the needle into the bottle, she drew out ten milligrams. Jiggling the needle, she spurted a bit of the clear liquid into the air and knelt back down beside her patient. With her left hand she grabbed a cotton swab from her pack, undid the bottle of alcohol, and dampened the cotton swab. Then she rubbed the swab on the upper part of the patient's arm and plunged in the needle. One of the men standing by the tree let out a moan as she heard Sam's quick intake of breath.

While the patient relaxed into a gentle sleep, Cassie looked around for a place to lay out her sterile pack. She said, "It's either this or he'll be dead by the time we could transport him back to the plane."

"What's that?" asked one of the men.

"It's a pack of sterilized instruments," she answered, sliding on rubber gloves. The pack also contained novocaine, a surgical knife, gauze, sutures, and a needle. She surrounded it with sterile towels.

"Now," she said to Sam, "every three to five minutes just a drop of ether on that cloth."

"How can I tell how many minutes?"

"If he's restless, three minutes. If he seems under, five minutes. Just a drop, mind you." She cleaned an area in the lower abdomen with an alcohol-soaked cotton swab, following that with tincture of iodine. She took a deep breath and then, picking up a sharp surgical knife, she made a two-inch vertical incision immediately above the pubic bone, holding it open with her left thumb and forefinger. The adrenaline began to flow, as it always did when she began surgery.

"I've got to go through several layers." Cassie took it for granted that Sam was interested, knowing that if she talked aloud some of her nervous tension would vaporize. "This second layer of slippery fat, there where those vessels are oozing blood, then this layer of thick gristle."

There was the sharp, tearing sound she expected. Blood seemed to be everywhere.

Sam jumped.

"It's supposed to do that," Cassie reassured him. "Then I cut down through this thick layer of muscle, there, right through the rectal muscles."

One of the men behind her made a strangled sound and ran from the tree, vomiting into the sand.

"The purpose is to provide drainage of urine from the bladder and help get rid of the blood and urine that have accumulated outside the bladder in the abdominal cavity. I need to drain the bladder itself. As soon as the incision goes through the muscle layer, there, ah . . . " A gush of urine and blood leapt forth. It smelled terrible.

"I can see the small part of the bladder but I can't see the tear exactly." Pushing a rubber catheter into the bladder, Cassie explained, "That's to facilitate the discharge of liquid." Her hands moved with dexterity as she inserted two rubber drains around the bladder to help siphon out the blood and urine that had already escaped. With one hand she used a suture to hold the rubber catheter tube in place, then went inside the bladder, using two sutures to close the muscle layer and two more to close the skin. All the tubes came out through the lower part of the two-inch incision.

Everything had gone smoothly.

"All I have to do is sew him back up." The knot in her stomach loosened.

Sam's eyes never left her fingers.

"Okay, you can stop the ether."

Aware that her whole body was relaxing, she let out a long sigh of relief. The tightness in her shoulders began to dissipate.

She smiled at Sam. "You did a good job. Thanks."

He tossed the gauze mask on the sterile towels and set the bottle of ether in the sand. He stared at her for a minute and then got up and walked away, out to the hobbled horses in the distance.

Turning around to face the patient's mates, she saw only one of them was still there. She asked, "Can you make a stretcher so we can carry him to the plane and get him to the hospital?"

She wished she had a Coke, or some of Sam's coffee.

She stood up to stretch and hugged herself as she watched jagged fingers of red bleed across the darkening sky.

Chapter 5

After a meal of beans and damper shared with the patient's mates, the quiet of the empty land was broken by the raucous cries of thousands of rose-breasted galahs, darkening the sky.

"Heading toward a water hole someplace nearby," Sam said. More birds congregated than Cassie had seen in her lifetime. Cockatoos settled on trees, making them look like ghost gums. Finches and budgerigars headed toward the upper branches, adding their cries to the galahs.

There were cattle troughs in the distance; birds darted down onto the backs of the cattle, drinking along with them. Where had all the cattle suddenly come from?

There was no possibility of talking above the cries of the thousands of birds until dusk, when the sky changed from pale lavender to violet, and then to the color of dried blood before turning a lustrous royal purple.

Cassie sat next to her patient while Sam and the three drovers stood talking and smoking.

Suddenly there was a silence, as deep as death. She saw Sam stamp out his cigarette and come walking toward her. An excitement filled the air, yet there was no sound at all.

When darkness hit only the glowing lights of the ends of three cigarettes could be seen.

As Sam reached her, it began—the lowing of what sounded like thousands of cattle. "C'mere," Sam's hand touched her shoulder, and he reached for her hand, pulling her up. "You want to see something you'll never forget?" Holding onto her hand so she wouldn't trip in the darkness, he led her out from the trees, through the gentleness of the soft night air. As her eyes grew accustomed to the dark she saw figures moving in the night, men on horses, bringing the cattle into a tight circle, encouraging them to lie down.

"They're abo stockmen," Sam said in a low voice, letting go of her hand.

Ten-gallon hats were silhouetted against the star-filled tropical sky. She could see cattle tossing their heads and milling within the circle around which rode a dozen stockmen. Sam stopped, and they watched the outlines in the night.

Softly at first, the stockmen began to sing.

"It's called 'singing the cattle,' " Sam explained. "It makes them aware that men are around them, so they know they're safe. See, if even one of the cattle panics, the whole herd could stampede within minutes and then no man can stop it. But if they 'sing the cattle,' and keep 'em calm, they won't get scared."

The voices of the stockmen were high, like no singing Cassie had ever heard. The contented lowing was the background music. Then the same rhythm was repeated, this time a tone lower, followed by an unearthly sound, a deep throbbing that carried across the miles of emptiness.

Cassie's spine tingled. Nothing she had ever experienced had prepared her for this.

As the moon rose, the singers passed, riding herd on the cattle. Wild, primitive rhythms filled the night.

She and Sam must have watched for an hour when he said, "We better turn in or we won't be any good tomorrow."

Cassie wanted to sleep next to her patient. Nearby, Sam lay on his back, his arms under his head, his baseball cap across his face, and fell asleep immediately. Cassie lay staring at the stars, thinking that this had been a real adventure. She had felt alive every minute of it. Every single second. And she had thought she might never be able to feel again. For the first time it dawned on her that this year might be fun. Perhaps leaving Melbourne was the best thing that could have happened to her. Uncle Norm knew what he was doing when he sent her out here. Maybe she could forget Ray. Maybe time did heal all things.

She dozed off and on all night, not wanting to miss a minute of this opera under the stars. Toward morning, she slept soundly.

When she awoke, they were gone. A thousand cattle, the men in their hats, their horses, the birds—all vanished. Only the flat, grassy plain, already burning under the sun, remained. Empty. Silent.

The patient's voice, stronger than it had been yesterday, said, "She saved my life, didn't she?"

Cassie turned over to look at him and saw Sam standing above them. She couldn't see his eyes behind his sunglasses as he responded. "I think that's just what she did. Saved your life."

"You helped," she said, pulling herself up, her body stiff from sleeping on the hard ground.

His lips curved in a smile. "Yeah, well. *We* saved your life."

Sam was an odd one. She had been able to see his irritation change to grudging respect while participating in the operation. He'd not hidden his annoyance at the thought of working with a woman doctor, making that clear as soon as she'd met him three days ago at the Augusta Springs train station.

Reverend John Flynn had told her, "The Outback's basically filled with two kinds of people: those searching for adventure and those running away from something." She wondered which kind Sam was.

And which kind she had become.

Back in Augusta Springs the ambulance was waiting, with Dr. Adams standing beside it. He was dressed in a long white jacket over his shirt, neatly pressed pants, and regular shoes—not high-heeled boots like Cassie and the drovers wore. Adams's black hair was trim and neat, his rimless glasses lending a professional air. He stood erect, looking competent if not friendly.

He reached out to open the back door of the ambulance as the plane taxied up to the hangar. Cutting the motor, Sam waited a minute before crawling out of the cockpit. He opened the door to the cabin and slid the steps down into place. Adams appeared in the doorway.

"You have an emergency here?" he asked, his voice cool and clipped.

"No," Cassie replied as she stood up and walked over to the door.

"I had to perform emergency surgery last night, but he needs hospitalization."

"What was it?"

"A ruptured bladder," she answered. "I need help getting this stretcher out of here."

Both Sam and Dr. Adams looked at her. "Of course," Sam said, gently elbowing her out of the way as he took hold of the end of the stretcher. "Ready, Doc?" he asked Adams.

Adams took the other end, and they moved the patient to the ambulance.

With her medical bag in hand, Cassie started to crawl into the back of the ambulance, too.

Dr. Adams put a restraining hand on her arm. "Where are you going?"

"With my patient," Cassie answered, looking up at him.

"He's no longer your patient," Adams said. "Remember?"

"But I operated on him last night."

"I have perfectly capable nurses. And, it may surprise you, but I've done a ruptured bladder or two and can follow through quite well. Once a patient is in Augusta Springs, he's no longer the province of the Flying Doctor Service. You know the rules. Or at least you told me you did." He slammed the door shut and walked around to the side of the ambulance. Opening the door, he got in and said to the driver, "Okay, Ed, let's go."

Cassie stood staring after them as the van pulled away. Sam heard her sigh.

"Well, you knew they're only your patients when they're over fifty miles away."

Cassie nodded. "Adams didn't have to be such a prick."

Sam studied her. She not only dressed like a man but talked like one as well. "I'll shout you a beer."

As they walked towards his utility, he grinned. "Well, this has been quite an adventure, hasn't it? What a way to start a new job."

Cassie got in the truck and took off her hat, putting her medical bag on the seat between them. "A grand way, I must admit." But irritation at Adams prickled her.

As they drove toward Addie's she said, "I knew before that I couldn't handle any patients within fifty miles, but somehow I guess I thought . . . "

Sam reached over and put a hand on her arm. "You'll get used to it," he said. "Adams is probably nervous. We're a threat to him. We treat patients for free. We fly to rescue them wherever they're in trouble. We're gonna make legends, Doc—I feel it in my bones, and he doesn't know how that's gonna make him look."

Cassie looked at him. Maybe he wasn't going to be an antagonist. "You bought my dinner last night. Let me shout you a beer today."

He laughed. "Well, I guess I've got some things to get used to, too. I never had a lady buy me a drink."

"We both have things to get used to." Much to her surprise, she liked the idea.

Chapter 6

The next morning Sam was driving to Addie's for breakfast. Ahead of him he saw a battered old utility racing toward the train station. He didn't recognize either the pick-up or the young driver. The young man screeched to a halt, jumping out of the truck and running toward the train, which was already blowing its warning whistle. The young man raced up the steps of one of the steel cars and before Sam had even driven past, two suitcases were hurled off the train and the young truck driver jumped down the steps of the car, holding onto the collar of another young man.

Sam grinned. A fight? Over some girl? Two brothers who had had a falling out? As he drove past, he saw the two young men leaning down to pick up the suitcases, one brushing himself off. In his rearview mirror, as the train began to pull out, he saw them make their way along the platform and walk over to the utility.

He had nearly forgotten the incident three-quarters of an hour later when he sat finishing his breakfast and sipping his third cup of coffee at the counter in Addie's. Suddenly he felt a hand on his shoulder. Someone said, "You're with the Flying Doctors?" He turned to see the dusty young man he'd seen driving the utility.

"I'm Conway Sellars," said the young man. "We need a doctor down at my dad's, at Kimundra."

Sam looked at the kid. "What's wrong?"

"My sister's about to have a baby. We need the doctor bad."

Ah. So the lad he'd pulled off the train must be running away from fatherhood.

"My dad told me to get a doctor and stop by for Padre McLeod—he's over at Dexheimers' station—on the way to Kimundra."

Sam pulled the map from his hip pocket.

"My dad's got a flat stretch of land that'd be right fine for landing a plane on right next to the house, he said to tell you. And we gotta take him, too." He nodded to the young man he'd pulled off the train.

OK. Himself, Cassie, the minister, and these two young men. Sure, the plane'd be able to handle that, as long as there was no baggage and they didn't need the oxygen tank.

"When's the baby due?" Sam asked, getting down off the high bar stool.

"Any minute."

"Okay, let's go get the doctor." Sam threw a bill on the counter and waved to the waitress behind the bar.

As he drove toward Cassie's with the young men following in their utility, Sam chuckled. What was it going to be like when they formally began operations if this was what it was like already?

Cassie came to the screen door with her robe still on, her hair dishevelled and sleep still in her grey eyes. "Oh, Sam," she murmured, pulling the robe tight around her. "What time is it? I think I've been sleeping the sleep of . . . "

"C'mon," he said. "A baby's about to be born and you're needed, and it's a couple hours flight from here."

She was ready in fifteen minutes, during which time he'd taken the liberty of brewing coffee in Fiona's kitchen. He poured it—black, strong, and steaming—into the thermos he always kept ready in his pick-up, and was behind the steering wheel when she came running out with her medical bag and sunglasses.

"No hat?" He raised his eyebrows.

She threw her bag on the seat and ran back into the house, returning quickly.

"Who are those young men in the truck behind us?"

"One drove all the way up here from some station down south. He slammed into town and dragged the other one off just as the train was ready to leave. Then they found me at the pub and the driver said his sister's about to have a baby. I suspect the other one was running away from a shotgun wedding. Or maybe just a shotgun. The girl's father wants us to stop and pick up Padre McLeod on our way."

"Reverend Flynn mentioned Padre McLeod. He marries couples . . ."

" . . . and sometimes baptizes their babies the same day."

She cast a glance at him.

"Well, he only gets to most places every year and a half or two. It's a big territory." He drew out the word *big.* "Sometimes he's the only human being people on stations see for a year at a time. He performs funerals, sometimes even when the person's been dead a year or more. He's been known to conduct a service on the porch of a homestead and then roll up his shirt-sleeves and repair a truck or help mend a broken windmill. I don't know anyplace where he's not welcome. He doesn't act like he puts God before people. He's a rare, fine human being from all I hear. Guess the girl's father wants his grandchild christened and his girl married right away."

Sam stopped at the base station before going on to the airport. He jumped out. "You stay here. I'll let Horrie know where we're going."

He was back directly. "All Horrie did was laugh. He says we're in business whether we planned to be yet or not."

The young men gazed at the plane with admiration, walking around it, staring up at it in awe.

Cassie walked over to them as Sam conferred with Pete. "Tell me about this woman who's going to have a baby."

"My sister," said Con, his pale blue eyes still gazing at the plane. He nodded at the other young man, obviously more interested in the plane than impending fatherhood. "He's about to become my brother-in-law."

"Had pains started?"

"No'm," he replied and shook his head. "Not when I left night before last."

Sam and Pete began wheeling the plane out of the hangar. Sam said, "C'mon, get in," as he pulled out the stairs. "I'll need some help. We got to bolt two more seats to the floor. This is built to hold four passengers and that's just what we'll have. C'mon, boys, give me a hand here."

It was a morning worthy of an artist's paintbrush. The sky was cobalt, and as the plane rose above the ground, Sam could see the red earth mottled with dark green trees, scattered widely apart. He sighed. It was good to be alive. He turned to call out to Cassie, "This'll be different scenery from yesterday. We're going south, into sheep country. There won't be near as many trees. Sheep can live with less vegetation than cattle," he explained, taking for granted the fact that a city slicker wouldn't know that.

He saw her jotting in a little notebook as she glanced out the window. He smiled. She was going to try to locate landmarks, too. Well, good luck, Doc.

He twisted around to look back at the two passengers. Con and his soon-to-be brother-in-law were gazing out the window. Sam felt for the young man. There, he thought, but for the grace of God, go I. Didn't seem quite fair. Having to marry a girl he might've just had an evening's fun with. Have to spend the rest of your life with someone you hardly know just because your sperm happened to meet her egg that night. What the kid should've done was be more careful. Probably no place to buy condoms a thousand miles from nowhere. And human nature isn't easily controlled. Guess I've just been lucky not to have been caught, he thought. Makes you stop and think, though. Be prepared. Be a good Boy Scout.

Ah, keep an eye on that thin line that seems to keep disappearing. It's supposed to be the road out to the Dexheimers' station. Past a grove of mulgas along a dry river bed, turning like a hairpin and then about three miles farther . . .

He could have landed anywhere, it was so flat. A pathway through the scrub and, as he coasted to a stop, a woman and a man came running out of the nearby house, enclosed behind a fence designed to keep the blowing sands out. The woman was wiping her hands on a flour-spattered apron covering a faded housedress. The man was broad shouldered and of medium height, wearing a white shirt with rolled-up sleeves and city shoes, not boots like everyone wore out here. Sam guessed he'd be the padre.

He was. Sure, he could fly down to Kimundra with them, so long as they could fly him back to get his truck. He asked them to wait til he got his hat and a few things, including his robe if he had to perform a wedding and a christening.

His brown eyes danced as he climbed into the plane. "Never expected a bird to come out of the sky just for me." He sat down next to Cassie. "A woman doctor? No fooling?" But he did not make it sound like an insult.

Sam could only hear parts of their conversation as he took off again, heading into the wind.

"Call me Don," he said. "Everyone does. No formality out here. One of the reasons I like it. Everything's down to the bone."

Yeah, thought Sam, that's for sure. He studied the terrain. The only road he saw was tracks that must've been ground into the sand by iron tires of bullock wagons. Rolling sandhills, mile after mile of them ruffled by the wind. Here and there a station, surrounded by what looked like a million sheep.

He looked ahead of him, into the atmosphere; it seemed like they were flying right into the heart of the sun. There was nothing purer, he thought. When he'd been a kid and looked up at a plane flashing silver across the sky, he thought it spelled freedom. Shake the bonds of earth and be alone above civilization, away from pretense and pressure and responsibilities. But it wasn't like that. Right now he was responsible for the lives of four other people in this plane. He was also responsible maybe to the mother and about-to-be-born baby. He looked at the prismatic compass and nodded. Shouldn't be more than another half-hour. He settled back comfortably in his seat trying, in vain, to hear the conversation in the cabin behind him.

They arrived before noon, landing on the level area next to the homestead. Con had told him his father was trying to construct a landing area so the Flying Doctor could land when necessary. They didn't have a wireless transceiver yet, but hoped next time they came to town or next time Padre McLeod came out he'd bring one. They were greeted at the gate by three young children, probably ranging from eight to twelve or thirteen, wide-eyed at the sight of an airplane in their front yard. A tall man followed them, walking up to the plane as Sam opened the door.

Peering inside, the man said to the minister, "Glad to see you, Padre." He looked at the young man whose name Sam didn't yet know—and kept on looking.

Cassie grabbed her bag. "I'm the doctor. Am I in time?"

The big man started to say something, then changed his mind. "My missus is in helping her now. The girl's hurtin' bad."

Cassie ran down the steps toward the house, not waiting for anything else.

Con and the padre walked down the steps. Sam followed them.

"C'mon, git down," said the big man to the boy who sat clutching the arms of his seat. "It's your baby bein' born."

Sam hoped the kid wasn't going to burst into tears. McLeod and Con walked in front of him towards the house. Suddenly they heard a scream, and by the time they reached the verandah the faint mewling cry of a baby made the padre smile.

"A new member of the Lord's flock," he said.

Cassie hadn't even had time to wash her hands or open her medical bag.

The big man, talking to McLeod, turned to Con and said, "See if they'd like some coffee or tea."

Sam nodded. "Coffee'd be fine. Think the doctor would appreciate some, too." He turned to the young boy, the new father. "Bet you'd like some, too, huh?"

The boy nodded appreciatively. Sam wanted to put his arm around his shoulders but refrained. He hadn't said anything yet.

A woman in her forties appeared in the doorway to the bedroom. Her tired eyes smiled. "It's a boy," she said, looking at the silent young man. "You've got a son. You can go in if you want to, in a minute."

He shook his head and looked at the floor.

"Hello, Maude," said McLeod. "Is it all right if I go in?"

"Sure, but wait til the doctor's through and we get clean sheets on the bed," said Maude. "Millie'd like that."

"How is she?" asked Mr. Sellars.

"Tired. But she's going to be fine. The doctor's taking care of her now and examining the baby."

The woman headed toward the kitchen.

The big man said, "Don, I want a wedding in ten minutes. Millie can get married from the bed. Then you can christen the baby. You hear that, boy?"

The young man nodded, his eyes miserable. "Yessir."

"You better go wash up and make a decent appearance if you're marrying my girl," the father said.

The young man reached up and tugged at Sam's shirtsleeve.

"Will you be my best man?" he asked.

"What's your name?" Sam grinned.

"Tyler. Tyler Edison."

"Why, Tyler, I'd be honored. Of course I'll be your best man. That'll be a first for me." He reached out to shake the young man's hand.

He looked up and, in the doorway, there stood Cassie, holding a baby that resembled a squirrel more than a human being. Cassie looked soft, the way a woman was supposed to look. For a second, Sam thought his heart skipped a beat. But only for a second. I'd better wash up, too, he thought, if I'm going to be a best man.

Chapter 7

At twenty-six Fiona realized she was verging on becoming an old-maid schoolteacher. Yet she also knew that she was having the time of her life.

She'd been ready to settle down five years ago, just after arriving here. She'd been so madly, crazily in love she couldn't think straight, blinded by a passion she'd never experienced . . . and knew she never would again.

Sure, she'd marry. She wanted children, wanted to be part of a family, but it would be a marriage of companionship, of sharing, not overwhelming passion that took over her whole being.

The first time, he'd torn her clothes off her. She loved the feel of his skin next to hers, shivered as she felt his hand between her legs, his tongue brushing across her nipples. His lust excited her, and she spread her legs wide as he bit the soft, tender flesh on the inside of her thigh. Her nipples stood erect as his tongue licked her belly, his fingers playing between her legs, opening her.

"My God, you're so beautiful," he'd whispered.

By the end of two months there wasn't a part of her body or her mind that he didn't know, that he couldn't manipulate to give her intense pleasure.

Then he just stopped calling. When she saw him he'd nod in a friendly, impersonal way. Pain and terrible emptiness welled up inside her.

In a frenzy, she threw herself into any and all of the town's activities, swearing that her only involvement would be with her students. With time the pain abated, even though she still spent every moment hoping he'd appear. She jumped every time she heard steps on the porch, felt her heart skip a beat whenever the phone rang. After a year or so she was no longer tied in knots waiting for his touch, for his voice, for the look in his eyes. She vowed never again to let a man own her.

So, instead of opening her heart to one man, she opened it to everyone who entered her life, and it became so crowded there was no room for just one person. In four years she'd never dined alone.

Then Steven Blake had phoned her from three hundred miles away, telling her that he and other station managers had contacted John Flynn of the Flying Doctor Service about supplying a doctor for the vast area. The doctor was going to be headquartered in Augusta Springs and Flynn had done the damnedest thing—he'd hired a female doctor. As a representative of the station managers in the area, Steven had agreed to give the lady a go, and now they had to find someplace for her to live. Though he, himself, had never met Fiona, half a dozen of the ranchers suggested that since she lived alone, she might let the new doctor room there. Certainly it would mean getting the doctor off to a good start.

Fiona didn't hesitate.

"If it doesn't work out," Steven said, "we can find a diplomatic way to get her another place." Fiona liked his voice.

"My wife and I'll be coming down there for monthly FDS meetings once we get this thing going, and I look forward to meeting you," he said. "Everything I hear has always been very affirmative."

"I've met your son a couple of times, at dances and parties."

Steven laughed. "You and every other good-looking girl within five hundred miles, I imagine."

Yes, his son did have that reputation.

And now, Fiona was glad she'd gone along with the idea. Not since her girlhood in Ireland had she had a close friend, one to whom she could unburden herself, someone to be silly with, someone on her . . . well, on the same wavelength. And this Cassie certainly had that potential.

They'd packed a picnic supper and walked in the cool of the evening out to where the creek flowed, to a sandy embankment under a grove of giant eucalyptus, whose stringy bark waved in the gentle breeze.

"Sometimes in the Wet, this is a raging torrent," Fiona told Cassie.

"I don't believe it."

"Well, you'll see," and they settled back with potato salad and deviled eggs and cold chicken breasts and bottled olives and pickles and bottles of Coke to share the stories of their lives.

It was amazing, they agreed, how many of the same ideas and beliefs they shared.

"When I arrived here what I missed the most was greenness. But I soon realized I'd rather have the sun every day. I guess it's a choice." Fiona picked a blade of grass and feathered it across her cheek, smiling. "Of green below and grey above or blue above and gold below."

"Gold?" Cassie laughed. "Brown, isn't it?"

"It depends on whether you love it or not, I suppose. I can't imagine wanting to live any other place. My family writes asking what in the world there is to do in a little town in the middle of no place and all I know is I'm busy all the time. I'm never bored. They can't figure why I wanted to come so far away."

"Why did you?"

"Oh, for the sheer daring of it. For the excitement of a new place. I don't like cities, and Ireland, oh, I don't know. It seems so inbred, though heaven knows the people are as friendly as here. But it's insular. It's closed in, like there's no future. I felt hemmed in by its grey skies and stone walls. And here," she waved her arm expansively, "I'm not bound by any traditions—it's all so new and such fun. I'm welcome at every home in town. Someday I want to be able to get out to the countryside, too, though I guess that's not what one calls it here."

"Maybe you can fly out with us some time, if we get an emergency call on a weekend."

Fiona's eyes shone. "I'd like that. I've never flown and I've wanted to ever since I was a kid. I guess I like anything that's new and different . . . "

"And a bit dangerous?" interrupted Cassie.

"You hit the nail on the head." She sat back on her heels, hugging her knees and gazing at Cassie. "What about you?"

"For twenty years," Cassie began, "all I saw of my native land was three weeks every summer when my mother and I came home to visit my grandparents."

Her father had worked his way up as a career officer in the diplomatic corps. His first posting, when she was six, had been to San Francisco, where she had entered school. The other children had made fun of her, saying, "Who says Australians speak English?" She'd worked very hard to sound American. Her parents loved San Francisco, where her father was the consul. She'd longed for Sydney and her grandparents' large Victorian house with its red roof and view of the harbor and children who talked like she talked and played games she knew. Six years later, just as she had become Americanized, just as she knew the forty-eight states better than her classmates did, just as she used American slang expressions more easily than the Aussie ones she'd nearly forgotten, her father was transferred to London.

They spoke an even different English there. Cassie was depressed by the grey weather and cold, clammy winters. Even her mother moaned about the fact that this climate with no central heating gave her "chilblains." She found the British terribly stiff and formal after Australia and America. They revered tradition while the two other countries rebelled against authority. She never felt at home in London, and hated being sent to a boarding school, where she saw her parents only on weekends.

When she complained, her mother patted her head and said, "Now, darling, education is different over here. There aren't any really good schools that you can go to each day. They rely on boarding schools. You know your father went to one, living in the Outback. There was no other way to be educated. The only good schools in England, darling, are boarding schools. Most of the children don't even come home weekends."

Cassie knew that. And she knew that when she was home her parents went out evenings. Weekend evenings were invariably social for the diplomatic corps. Some embassy or other was always having a party. Important people were always inviting her parents to dinner. But Sundays were reserved for family, unless her father had to help solve some crisis. The three of them took Sunday afternoon drives, exploring country roads near London. And they always stopped in a village pub on the way home. "Get to know the real people this way," her father had said every single time.

She hated the steak and kidney pies that he doted on, but she loved his company. He was funny and witty and charming. Her mother was beautiful and usually very quiet. Never once did Cassie hear her parents argue; never did she hear her mother disagree with her father, except to tell him he was working too hard. Often Cassie wondered how her mother managed to keep her mouth shut. Didn't she have *any* opinions of her own? Her mother laughed at her father's jokes, even if she'd heard them a hundred times before.

The high points of Cassie's life had been spent on ships and in her grandparents' home. She loved summers. She loved the trips she and her mother took, first from San Francisco to Sydney and then from London, by way of the Suez Canal and the Indian Ocean. Several times their ship stopped overnight in Bombay and Calcutta, and Cassie and her mother roamed the streets, even though they were told it was dangerous. They dined in elegant hotel restaurants and her mother bought fabric for a sari, which she then wore on formal occasions in London.

Her mother was a different person in the summer—she laughed more and seemed younger. She told Cassie she should begin to think of a career.

"Don't let the limits of your horizons be tied to a man," she had said.

"Aren't you happy?"

Her mother looked at her quickly, her eyes unreadable. "Of course I am. But you're a new generation. You can do more than live your life vicariously through a husband and children."

At fourteen, Cassie wasn't sure what her mother meant.

When Cassie turned sixteen, her mother developed cancer, and Cassie watched as she wasted away, her pain-filled eyes eating into Cassie's heart. There was nothing that could be done, not even to alleviate most of the pain. Morphine was the only help.

One day her mother took Cassie's hand and said, in a weak voice, "What I regret most is leaving you. I won't be around to see your success. I won't be around to cheer you on. I won't be around to . . . oh, Cassie, I won't be around for you," and she broke into tears.

"You know what, Mama? I'm going to be a doctor. I'm going to see that people don't have to be in pain like you are, and I'm going to help people feel better."

Her mother's eyes lit up. "A doctor? My daughter, a doctor? Oh, there's no reason you can't be. You can be whatever you want, but how wonderful! A doctor. I like that. Oh, yes, I like that very much."

From that moment on, Cassie never doubted. Certainly not after her mother died, and not even when her father tried to dissuade her.

By that time he'd become the Ambassador to the United States and together they settled into the Georgetown house that was far too large for them. "Well, we don't have to argue about that now," he said. "Women aren't doctors, Cassie. Get that through your head. But go on to college—we've always planned that. Let's see if you can get into Georgetown so you can live here with me. You wouldn't want to leave me alone, would you?"

No, she wouldn't. And she zipped through Georgetown with honors, much to her father's amazement. Her mother wouldn't have been surprised.

Summers she sailed back to her grandparents alone. She took the five-day train cross-country to San Francisco, and loved every bit of the ten days it took the ship to reach Sydney. Every summer she had a brief and mild romance—it was the only time she allowed men romantically into her life. She had long ago resolved that no man, no marriage, would deter her from her path. But she allowed herself the shipside romances, for they had a definite end when the ship sailed into Sydney Harbor.

Her grandparents' big Victorian house, with its four stories and gingerbread eaves, was the only place Cassie ever felt at home. It was the only constant in her life. It was where she found unconditional love, though not always approval. The one thing both grandparents disapproved of was her decision to become a doctor.

"Ladies don't prod into men's bodies," her grandmother whispered with a look of distaste.

"What about men peering into women's bodies?"

"That's different."

But they could not dampen her resolve. Her grandfather invited her out to his greenhouse one afternoon and told her, "What you need to do is come home and let yourself meet some nice men. You've been too long in foreign countries." He was working with tweezers, trying to cross-pollinate an orchid. Ever since he'd retired, orchids had been his passion.

"I'll come home, Grandpa, but not to get married." The sight of her mother in pain for so many months was always there.

When she was just twenty-five she graduated from Johns Hopkins Medical School. It had been a hard four years. She had felt pressure to perform better than the men to prove that women were just as capable. She had suffered practical jokes that were obscene. She had been the butt of ridicule in anatomy classes. Even most of her professors treated her as though she should not have been there. But they could do nothing to stop her. She graduated in the top five percent of the class, but it was a difficult journey. The men she'd been surrounded by were cruel and unkind and power-hungry. They made it clear she was trespassing in what they considered to be a man's world.

There was one other woman in her class, and they became friends because their goals and their problems were the same, but otherwise they weren't alike at all. The day Cassie graduated she told her father, "I'm going back to Australia." Home.

But by then both her grandparents were dead.

Her father called Norm Castor. He vouched for her, and with her impeccable records at Johns Hopkins, Cassie spent six months at the Victoria Lying-In Hospital, delivering babies, performing cesareans and D & Cs. Then Dr. Castor wangled her a transfer to the Emergency Room at the Melbourne Hospital.

Cassie found herself an alien in her own country. After twenty years abroad, she did not speak like an Australian, she was not used to driving on what she considered the wrong side of the road, and she didn't even think like an Aussie. She was more American than Australian, yet she had never qualified as an American because she was Australian. She wondered if she would ever fit in anyplace . . .

She told Fiona about Ray Graham.

Fiona's remark was, "Join the crowd, honey. It happens to all of us. You'll recover."

Which showed her how much Fiona knew.

Chapter 8

Cassie liked Horrie the minute she met him. He was a stocky, chestnut-haired man in his early thirties, laboring in a tiny, three-room, tin-roofed shack that, as he'd said, "will boil water all by itself come summer. It's the nerve center of the Augusta Springs Flying Doctor Service," he said with pride in his voice.

They were sitting in front of his radio equipment. "Only thirty-six homesteads are prepared for a plane now. Some others have radios and are working on landing strips. I don't know how many others there are who don't even know about us yet, since they have no way of communicating or knowing anything until they come to town or meet a neighbor, who might be a couple hundred miles away. It'll take time for them to get underway. Some can't afford the labor or materials for an airstrip."

All calls were to come through him. All contact with people for a 450-mile radius, a territory larger than France, would come into this little bungalow baking in the sun. There wasn't even a typical Outback verandah stretch around it, just an overhang in front. It was a mile and a half northwest of town, where there'd be little shortwave interference.

"How do people contact us?" Cassie asked.

"Used to be by Morse Code," Horrie answered, a cigarette dangling out of the corner of his mouth, "but too many couldn't learn that. So Alf Traeger—he's the genius who invented the pedal wireless—came up with a typewriter that can translate regular typed letters into Morse—brilliant man. Now, it's telephonic. An hour is set aside three times a day—at eight, at eleven, and again at four forty-five—where we check in with the bases and ask if anyone needs emergency help or advice. If you're not here, I check in anyhow. Probably mainly questions that'll be easy for you to answer, things like what to do for a cold or sore throat, or maybe a knife wound." He laughed. "Bet there'll be a bunch of them!"

"What if an emergency comes up in the middle of the night?" Cassie looked at the radio equipment and wondered if she'd ever understand it.

"Just has to wait. We both have to be tuned in at the same time to talk with each other. Besides, you're not likely to fly at night. If we think an emergency has to be monitored, we can make arrangements to talk with each other at a certain time. I can say 'call back at seven' and I'll stay here waiting for the call."

"What if we're out on a clinic run or I'm not here for some other reason?"

"The plane's equipped so we can talk to each other and I can relay messages. You can even talk to one of the AIM hospital nursing sisters or a station and give emergency directions if necessary. If you're already out on a call, I can divert you."

Sam was leaning against a wall, the front legs of his chair in the air, his baseball cap turned backwards. "I suggest we arrange for scheduled clinic runs just twice a week til we get our bearings and see what it's going to be like."

Cassie nodded. She was wearing trim tan gabardine pants, a pink cotton shirt, and high-heeled riding boots favored by stockmen. She'd tossed her new Stetson on a chair.

"How will all those people out there know when we're ready to start a regular schedule?" she asked Horrie.

Sam answered. "When will we have time for a regular schedule if we've been as busy as we have before we've even officially begun?"

Horrie laughed. "Betty's going to be arriving in ten days, just about the time we get formally started. We're going to get married right away. I don't know anyone else really so I'd appreciate you two standing up with us."

Cassie was inordinately pleased.

"Think I ought to be near the radio all the time, so maybe I can live here a while."

She looked around, already sorry for this Betty.

"Betty says she'll learn how to use the radio so she can spell me."

The front legs of Sam's chair hit the floor.

Horrie said, "I'll ask if some of the larger stations will let us have clinic runs. We'll play it by ear. Learn as we go. Everyone will be eager. Of course, you'll go to the AIM hospitals routinely."

Cassie hugged herself. Despite the dismal landscape, she felt the excitement of a new challenge surge through her body.

Horrie seemed to accept her easily. Not like Sam. Sam knew how to handle the sweet, young girls who gazed into his dark eyes and smiled at him, teasing him, daring him to kiss them, to hold them. He'd know what to do with those women, Cassie thought, but he didn't quite know what to do with her. He acted as though a thinking human being and a woman were two different things. It wasn't that he had said anything, or that he'd been anything but cooperative, but there was a tension between them. Cassie knew he didn't approve of women doctors . . . or lawyers, she assumed, or engineers, or pilots or any of those professions that were supposed to be male provinces. Though he certainly was polite. But why couldn't he be like Horrie? Open and friendly, welcoming.

Sam and Dr. Adams. Two thorns in her flesh already.

"Well, that was some bash," Cassie said, drying the dishes as Fiona washed them. They had just given a party for members of the Flying Doctor Service Council, who had gathered in Augusta Springs to meet Sam and Cassie and discuss operating procedures.

"At least it got me someplace," Fiona remarked as she wiped her damp forehead with her arm, her hands full of suds. "Honorary member of the Council!"

"Yes," said Cassie. "How come no women are on it?"

Fiona turned to look at her, raising an eyebrow. "Maybe you haven't heard."

"You mean it's a man's world?" Cassie reached up to put some cups in the cupboard.

"Speaking of men, let's."

"Let's what?"

"Talk about the men here. God, that Steven Thompson is something. He may be fifty, but oh, my!"

Cassie smiled. "You're right, and I liked his wife, too. She's gorgeous."

"So's their son. He's the heartbreaker of the whole territory. Loves 'em and leaves 'em, yet I don't know of a single girl who wouldn't risk heartbreak just to dance with him."

"No one can be *that* good!"

Fiona slushed the dishwater down the drain. "Someday you'll see. But I did like Papa. I agree Mrs. Thompson is pretty swell, too. The Thompsons are the big landowners, the powerhouses around here. I understand their place, Tookaringa, is fantastic. Something like five or ten million acres."

Cassie knew Fiona was exaggerating, but she got the idea. "Well, at least they seemed to accept me, even though they warned me I'll have trouble with the men out there."

"I have never known any worthwhile relationships between men and women that weren't complicated," Fiona said, grabbing a dishtowel to help Cassie. "I bet we went through gallons of booze tonight. Well, you're a lucky duck, I can tell you, working with guys like Horrie and Sam."

"Horrie and Sam are just people I work with. I don't think of them . . . *that* way."

"I'm twenty-six and my hormones are whirling around," Fiona giggled. "Attractive men are males to me. And Sam and Horrie are certainly attractive—not that Horrie is sexy like Sam, but he's awful nice."

"Sam, sexy?" Cassie hung the dishtowel on a hook.

"Oh, come on. No woman could miss that. Look how he walks, or rather, lopes. He seems like he's going to throw you right on a bed, and when he talks he looks you right in the eye but you get the idea he's mentally undressing you. He's different with men. Sort of no nonsense. He's what I'd call a man's man—he's himself with men, but flirts outrageously with women."

"He doesn't do that with me."

"He's probably intimidated. You're a doctor. I've an idea he'll stay ten feet away from you. But tell him I'm not always professional, will you? I could have fun with him."

"Oh, Fiona, I think you've had too much to drink."

"Well, I'm not saying you have to run out and sleep with them, but aren't there any men you've met whom you think it'd be fun, well, you know . . ."

Cassie smiled. "Don McLeod. Now, there's a man. Too bad *he's* getting married. He's heading back to Adelaide next year to marry the girl he's been engaged to for three years. They haven't even seen each other in a year and a half."

"So, give him a go."

"No," Cassie replied as she walked into the living room and collapsed onto a chair. "He's not that kind. And I don't have those particular urges. But he's one of the finest men I've met, here or anyplace. He just sort of emanates love."

"Not sex, you mean?" Fiona sprawled the length of the couch. They'd clean up the ashtrays and toss out the empty beer bottles tomorrow. It had been a real wing-ding. Nobody, Fiona thought, partied any better than Aussies.

"Well, maybe Don has a bit of that about him. But he's loyal to his girlfriend, I think. No, he just seems to love. Humanity, I mean. You're pretty much like that, too, you know."

"And I suppose you decided to be a doctor for the money?"

Cassie could hardly keep her eyes open. "I'm in there with you and Don. I was going to save humanity, too."

"Is that a past tense?"

"Okay, okay, so I still think I'm going to save this particular geographical area of humanity. But mine wasn't so simple. I've also had to prove I can do what men do."

"Why? I like being a woman. At least I do when I'm not in love. Love is hell."

Cassie got up. "Fiona, my dear, I'll agree with you on that. Love is hell. Now, I'm going to bed."

In the morning, they were awakened by the insistent ringing of the telephone. Fiona bounced out of bed first, barely able to see her way to the phone.

"It's for you," she called. Not waiting to see if Cassie even heard her, she stumbled back to bed.

It was Steven Thompson.

"Jenny and I are heading back to Tookaringa, but we're going to breakfast first and hope you'll join us. Can you be ready in half an hour?"

Cassie looked at her watch through sleep-blurred eyes. It was barely seven-thirty.

"I guess so," she said, not really ready to awaken.

She took a quick shower and ran a brush through her short hair, donned a pale blue linen dress that was one of her favorites, carefully applied lipstick, and grabbed her dark glasses. High heels, she decided, kicking off her more practical looking shoes. And maybe that wide-brimmed ecru straw hat. She'd taken to wearing hats under the Outback sun, and this one was far dressier than her Stetson.

The Thompsons pulled up in a half-ton truck. She'd expected something more luxurious, sleeker. But of course, if they were going to drive nearly four hundred miles through desert and desolation, they'd need something that could handle the terrain.

"You're not going to travel all the way back home in just one day, are you?" Cassie asked as Steven pulled away from Fiona's. Jennifer sat between them.

"No," Jennifer said, her voice clipped, high-class British. "We'll stop at friends' overnight. We know everybody between here and there. In the Outback you're always welcome. We all get company so seldom that anyone who passes through is a pleasure." She laughed. "Well, most everyone."

Steven pulled up in front of Addie's and jumped out of the car, walking quickly around to open the passenger door.

Cassie followed Jennifer into the pub. She might be nearly fifty, but she was slim and beautiful, her salt and pepper hair elegantly coifed. Wherever could she get it done like that? Cassie wondered. Jennifer wore a white silk suit with an emerald blouse, brown and white spectator shoes with very high heels, and looked as though she were weekending at an English estate. She did not look like she belonged in Addie's, but she also did not look as though she felt a shred of self-consciousness.

Steven held out Jennifer's chair first, then Cassie's. As the Thompsons studied the menu, Cassie studied Steven. Fiona was right. He was something. Broad shoulders tapering to a slim waist, and tall—taller than other men around, perhaps six-four or five. His tanned and rugged face reflected the outdoor life he had lived. He was a big man. Big hands. Big feet. An expansive smile. Clear blue eyes. He emanated power. Big and powerful. Those would be the first words that would come to mind to describe him.

He'd been elected President of the Council Friday night. No one else could hold a candle to him, at least not in this neck of the woods.

After they'd given their orders, and he'd requested coffee right away, he leaned his elbows on the table and said to Cassie. "We'd like you to have your first clinic at Tookaringa. It's the biggest station up north. Come up Friday. We have many aborigines working for us and a lot of them have families. We also employ over a hundred others. Jennifer and I think it'd be nice if you and Sam would fly up on Friday and stay the weekend. You could hold a clinic at Tookaringa Friday afternoon, and go over to the abo mission, Winnamurra, on Saturday. It doesn't have a phone, but I can send a rider over there to tell the missionary to expect you and to round up the sick and infirm. You two can work out a pattern for future months. I imagine a number of your clinic runs will be overnights. The radio will keep you in touch with Horrie for any emergencies, or even your three daily question sessions. Anyhow, we'll have a barbecue Saturday night and invite people to meet you. You can leave early Monday and fly to the AIM hospital in Yancanna and make contact with the sisters there."

"Sounds good to me." Cassie wondered if coffee would get rid of her headache. Had she had *that* much to drink last night?

"We think it'll take these people a while to get used to a woman doctor," Steven continued. "We'll do all we can to help. We need a doctor up here."

The waitress brought their coffee. Cassie drank it black.

"You'll find, really, that the friendliest people in the world live here," Jennifer said. "I couldn't believe it when I first came."

"Where did you come from?" Cassie turned to look at the beautiful woman.

"Cambridge," she replied, her voice clear and musical. "England, that is. That's where I met Steven." She looked at him, her eyes dancing, and Cassie could sense they were still in love.

"How did you meet in England?"

Steven gulped his coffee quickly, waving to the waitress for more. "I went to university over there. My mother insisted I get a proper education, but I resented every minute of it. I wanted to be back here riding herd, mustering, watching sunrises, not cooped up in claustrophobic towns hemmed in by trees and fences. I only stayed two years, just long enough to talk Jenny into coming back here with me."

The waitress brought their steak and eggs and a mountain of toast.

Cassie asked, "So, you're not from England then?"

Steven shook his head. Eating did not stop him from talking. "I was born here. My mother came out from England in the mid-1880s, as a governess for a family a couple hundred miles to the south of here. One of the young drovers there saw her. It only took one look and he was a goner. Made him decide to stop droving and get himself a station. So they bought a few acres up north, built a tin shack, got a few cattle. I have pictures of it. You'd never have thought it'd last a year, much less over half a century."

Cassie smiled. The food helped her headache, and she was beginning to feel better.

Jennifer leaned forward. "We need a doctor here so much. If we'd had one twenty-five and thirty years ago . . . " Tears welled in her eyes but did not spill over. "We only have the one child now. Blake's twenty nine . . . " her voice faltered.

Steven put his hand over his wife's. "We lost five children, two of them miscarriages." Cassie liked his saying "we" had miscarriages. "Finally, by the time Jenny was pregnant the third time I sent her off to the city where she'd be near a doctor. And that's what we did the next two times."

"If we'd had a doctor up here, well, now that we do maybe more women won't go through what we did." Jennifer looked at Cassie. "We also had a child die of measles, another . . . well, I don't have to go into all details, but it's been pretty difficult. I wouldn't wish it on . . . "

Cassie looked at them. Never would she have guessed the tragedy behind these faces which seemed to reflect happiness and contentment.

"How have you been able to stand it?" she asked.

Steven smiled. "We've had each other. We've had our victories and our joys, too. But we didn't get you here to talk about Jenny and me. We want to do everything we can to help get the FDS off to a flying start, if you'll pardon the pun. And anything, we mean anything, we can do to help, you're to let us know. We're going to keep the radio on all the time, as I imagine most people who have them will, and we'll hear any messages and can respond to anything you want. The other members of the Council will be just as helpful. We all know the value of a doctor up here, and have been too long without one. We're here to help you."

At that moment Horrie Wallace stuck his head in the door, yelling as he walked toward their table.

"Got an emergency out in the boonies," he called. "Sam said he'd be ready in ten minutes. I'll drive you home to get your medical bag."

Cassie stood up.

"And to change your clothes," Horrie grinned. "You'd never make it in those shoes."

Cassie turned to the Thompsons. "Thanks. For breakfast, for the meeting this weekend. For the fun at last night's party. For everything. And as far as I'm concerned, we'll be out at Tookaringa this weekend, unless you hear to the contrary. Set up a clinic and let Winnamurra know we'll be over there on Saturday."

"We'll slaughter a calf for the barbecue," Steven said, standing. He reached out his hand to shake hers.

Horrie grabbed her other hand.

"Let's go," he shouted, though he was standing right next to her.

They began to run.

Chapter 9

On this, her third flight, Cassie was able to look around and give more attention to the plane itself than she had on either of the earlier flights, when the landscape below held her initial fascination. The noise of the engine was considerable. One had to shout to be heard, which cut down considerably on idle conversation.

She leaned over to ask Sam, "Is this the kind of plane you've always flown?"

"This plane," he said, turning to look at her, "is a pile of junk, Doc. A hand-me-down from I don't know how many years in the past. Listen to that vibration. It's paper-thin and leaks all around the edges, which rules out high altitude flying . . . "

"How high have we been flying?"

"Anywhere from 2500 to 6000 feet," he said. "It makes for slow flying. But don't get me wrong, it's got some advantages. I think it's the first aircraft to be able to lift its own weight, and it has a real short take-off and landing run, which is great for the kind of work we're doing. But it's held together with band-aids. I have very little faith in it."

"That makes me feel great," Cassie said.

Sam grinned. "But then I have complete confidence in me. We'll get a better plane soon's we can afford one. Being a charitable organization and dependent on donations, the FDS doesn't have much money for modern planes. It's a marginal organization and can't afford to pay us," he added, meaning QANTAS, "for the kind of aircraft we *really* need.

"Pour me coffee?" Sam said. "It's only another twenty minutes if I'm on course."

They were met, upon landing, by a burly man waving his arms to guide them onto the landing strip.

As soon as Sam opened the door, he said, "Where's the patient?"

The big man grinned. "That's me. I feel fine now."

Cassie and Sam exchanged a look. She grabbed her medical bag and walked down the steps. "I better examine you anyway."

"Must've been heartburn," the man said, reaching out a big paw and introducing himself. "I'm Leonard Neville. My wife drove over to the next station, 'bout sixty miles away, to phone you and she's not even back yet. I feel fine now."

It turned out that Leonard Neville was a better diagnostician than Horrie.

"Better talk to Horrie," am advised as they flew back. "This isn't an aerial ambulance service, you know. It costs a lot of money every time we take off."

"Yes, I'll tell him to let me talk to any prospective patients before we do this again," Cassie said.

A wasted trip. Wasted time and money. Both were of importance to them.

"Our first scheduled clinic's going to be Friday," she told him. "Up at the Thompsons. Steven suggested we stay the weekend and go on to Yancanna Monday. They're going to have a barbecue Saturday night and introduce us to people."

Sam nodded, looking straight ahead. "Tookaringa is noted for its hospitality. I've heard of that place for years."

Cassie leaned back in her seat and closed her eyes. She was feeling better than she had all day. I came to get away, to withdraw from life, she thought, and I've never known anyplace as vital. It was the most action-packed two weeks she'd ever lived, so different from her sedentary, studious life in England and America.

Here, strangers started conversations with you. As soon as the bush people learned you were the new doctor, they seemed to open not only their doors but their arms. She had to admit, though, sometimes she had difficulty understanding some of the fast talkers who used odd expressions. But no one made fun of her American accent. She'd spent so many years acquiring it; now, she'd like to shed it.

There was no greyness like London and San Francisco, no humidity like Washington. Her urbane father would be lost out here, she thought, and then remembered he'd been brought up in a small bush town in western New South Wales.

It wasn't possible, and she knew it, that she had always felt like an alien wherever she'd lived only to find herself with a sense of belonging after just two weeks in this isolated part of the world. Whatever she was feeling was nice, though.

Her reverie was interrupted by Sam's asking, "You play tennis?"

"No." Her eyes stayed closed.

"Interested in learning?"

She opened one eye. "Not really. Sorry." She didn't consider herself athletic. Learning to ride a horse had been a great achievement. She gazed out the window at the land that stretched to the horizon. It was nice of him to make the offer. Showed he was reaching out. She didn't want him to think she was rejecting him. "Want to pick up Horrie and come to supper? Just leftovers from the party last night."

Sam raised an eyebrow and turned to look at her. "Sounds good to me."

Fiona would like that, too, Cassie knew.

And, as it turned out, Fiona knew how to play tennis. Soon she and Sam began spending late afternoons at the town's lone tennis court.

Cassie, instead, spent her late afternoons reading aloud.

At forty-two Isabel Adams was so thin she was emaciated. She was lying on a sofa, covered with a quilt, her chestnut hair cascading onto the pillow. She greeted Cassie with a wan smile.

"How lovely of you," she said, her thin voice warm with welcome. "Somehow I didn't expect you to come calling. Chris told me about you. But I don't expect newcomers to come visiting." Isabel turned to the portly woman who had answered the door. "Grace, how about tea for us all? Dr. Clarke, this is Grace Newcomb." She reached out to touch Grace's arm. "I don't know what I'd do without her."

Grace smiled. "Tea coming up. Do you like cucumber sandwiches?"

Cassie hated them. "Just tea," she said. "I'm not really hungry." Isabel's arms weren't much thicker than matchsticks.

"I'm never hungry," Isabel said. "I used to work so hard to stay thin, and now look at me. But let's not talk about me. A new face, how refreshing. Word of the outside world!"

"I came to see if there's anything I can do to help. Two big boxes of books arrived, and I have records . . . "

"That's so kind of you. But somehow I don't seem to have the energy to read, to hold a book for very long . . . "

"Would you like me to read to you? I've some of the newest books."

Isabel's eyes lit up. "Oh, would you? Chris hates to read aloud. I'd love it. That would be so kind of you. By any chance, do you have *Gone with the Wind?*"

Cassie nodded. "Yes, and it's wonderful."

"You've read it? Well, then rereading it wouldn't be much fun for you . . . "

"On the contrary, I'd enjoy it very much."

"And *Rebecca?* I've heard that's wonderful, too."

"I have both," Cassie said with a smile.

She couldn't promise to read to Isabel every day for she didn't know her routine, but they did decide that Cassie would go over to the Adams house late in the afternoons, after the four-forty-five radio contact with patients, if she wasn't needed somewhere else.

She spent three days that week reading to Isabel, and what propelled her to that act she never understood. Isabel was obviously disappointed on Thursday when Cassie announced, "We're doing our first clinic flight this weekend, so I won't be around."

They didn't talk much, for as soon as Cassie arrived, Grace placed tea on the table beside her and settled herself into a chair. Both she and Isabel were scarcely able to contain their impatience, waiting for Cassie to continue with the adventures of those who lived at Tara and Twelve Oaks.

Cassie did not see Chris Adams at all. He was never there by the time she left at nearly six.

In the other part of her life, she had difficulty adjusting to diagnosing over the radio. She did find it easier than trying to prescribe over the phone, where the other end of the line could interrupt her train of thought. She could not just prescribe from the symptoms described but had to take a medical history of the patient and the illness, which often irritated those on the other end of the line. She needed to know exactly where a pain was and what kind of symptoms, and the caller was usually unable to describe just what the patient was feeling. Cassie was frustrated by every call. Sometimes the patients called in, she suspected, because they were lonely, especially the women. They were vague about their own symptoms, hysterical about their children's. They were desperate to hear another voice. Cassie found herself adopting a more formal manner of speaking than she ordinarily used, as though she were on stage.

One of the calls bothered her for days. It came from a station far to the north. The owner, Ian James, described the symptoms of one of his aboriginal trackers. "The old black fellow is going downhill fast. Didn't come to eat breakfast, and in thirty years I don't think he's missed a meal. My wife's been keeping an eye on him and says he looks awful. He seems to be gasping for breath, and I'm afraid he's dying. Can you come get him?"

"First, look in the medical chest and you'll find a thermometer. I want you to take his temperature and feel his pulse. Count the number of beats you feel in the patient's wrist for fifteen seconds, then multiply by four. Got that?"

There was silence at the other end of the line and then an irritated voice. "Doctor? Look, I've known this man since I was a child. I don't have to take his temperature and feel his pulse to know how sick he is."

"Nevertheless, I can't prescribe without the necessary information."

"You don't have to prescribe. Just come get him and take him to the hospital."

Cassie was impatient. "You may be right, but certainly it'll only take a few minutes to get the information I'm requesting."

"Look," Mr. James shouted in anger. "I want a doctor to see this poor bastard now!"

"I sympathize with you, but I really need more information before we fly several hours up there. We're not an ambulance service. This will only take a few minutes . . . "

The radio went dead. He'd hung up on her. She knew that dozens of other stations were listening in. Even though they might not have any emergencies or illnesses, these radio hours were the highlight of their day, listening to their neighbors' problems, hearing other voices that made them feel less alone.

For the next two nights, when she closed her eyes all Cassie could envision was a black man, dying while she asked for details of the symptoms. But she forgot about it when she and Sam set out for Tookaringa early Friday morning. They'd only had one short flight all week, and that was to bring a patient into the hospital for an appendectomy, which Chris Adams performed. This time he had the courtesy to report to her that the patient was doing fine, but the information reached her via Isabel, with whom he left the message.

She and Sam decided to leave for Tookaringa after the eleven o'clock patient call-in on Friday, arriving in time for an afternoon clinic. Sam said, "From all I've heard, having an invite to one of the Thompsons' barbecues makes us two of the luckiest blokes anyplace."

Cassie seemed to have neatly solved all the eight and eleven o'clock call-ins, promising they'd stop, en route to Tookaringa, at one of the stations where a woman had scratched her leg badly on barbed wire. "I can get a tetanus shot in her at least, so gangrene won't set in," Cassie commented to Horrie.

They flew north by northwest, the sun straight above them. "I'm going to stay low with this bucket of bolts," Sam said. "We're in no rush. Figure it's about an hour or so to—what's their name?"

Cassie looked at the pad on her lap. "Martin. Heather Martin. She said their airstrip's not finished but they're working on it. The terrain is pretty flat."

"Yeah, I always wonder what people mean by that. Their idea of flat and mine are usually different."

There wasn't another station for a hundred miles, so the Martin homestead was easy to pinpoint. Around a rectangular area were dozens of red ribbons flapping in the breeze. Cassie heard Sam laugh. "Who in the world would ever have that much ribbon?" he asked, not expecting an answer.

Waiting for them, waving them in, were six long-legged women, all dressed in men's pants and bush shirts, all wearing the same high-heeled elasticized drovers' boots as Cassie's. She couldn't help pointing to them as the plane taxied across the airstrip that was smoother than most any they'd landed on.

"I see, I see," mumbled Sam, unable to stop grinning.

When he opened the door and kicked the steps down onto the ground, the six women were lined up like a receiving line. Although the oldest was obviously the mother, a woman about forty-five, all of them were stunning.

"I'm Estelle Martin. These are my girls," said the mother, advancing as the plane's propellers wound down. "I'll introduce you later. Miranda's in the house—her leg looks pretty bad." All the daughters smiled at Sam as Cassie walked by them, following their mother. They must've ranged in age from about sixteen to twenty-two or three.

Miranda lay on the sofa. She looked like her sisters, golden hair haloing her head, cascading onto her shoulders. Her tanned skin enhanced the bright blue of her eyes, around which were crinkles from years spent in the sun. Her blouse was stretched tight across her voluptuous breasts, and her hands were scratched and leathery from hard work. She smiled, showing pearly, even teeth. Miranda wore shorts, and Cassie suspected Sam would have liked to whistle. The red gash on her leg was ugly, and Cassie could tell from the way it was beginning to fester and the look in her eyes that Miranda must be in pain even though her smile showed no sign of it.

"Helluva thing to let happen, isn't it?" Miranda said.

Cassie knelt down next to her, then turned to Estelle. "Boil me some water. I want to wash this out, then I'll have to cut it open to get at the bacteria. It's a good thing you called or this could have turned gangrenous."

Sam had walked into the room, surrounded by the bevy of beauties. All he could do was grin.

The room was large and cross-ventilated—the nine of them did not crowd it. Carpets covered the floors and the furniture had obviously been chosen with care. There wasn't a speck of dust . . . in a country where sand blew constantly. Cassie imagined the men were off doing whatever it was men did on ranches. She'd seen a large herd of cattle from the air.

While Cassie removed the instruments and alcohol from her bag, the Martin women divided their attention between what she was doing and gazing openly at Sam. Maybe Fiona was right. Sam had sex appeal for certain women.

"Need any help?" he asked.

Cassie shook her head. "No, thanks. This'll be easy."

One of the daughters walked forward and knelt down next to Cassie, observing every move she made.

Cassie said to Miranda, "I'm going to give you a shot so you won't feel pain when I cut. It's going to hurt."

"No," Miranda said. "I'll try to stand it. I don't want any drugs."

"It's just something to lessen the pain."

"No," reiterated the young woman, whose age Cassie guessed to be nineteen or twenty. "I'd rather not. Let me watch it. If I can't stand the pain I'll tell you."

Cassie shook her head. She heard the mother's voice behind her. "We're strong. She can take it, I imagine."

Cassie turned to look at Estelle and saw the other daughters, sitting in chairs or leaning against the wall, one seated on the carpet, watching intently. Sam had become invisible.

When one of the daughters brought the boiled water, Cassie slit open the red running sore, watching pus ooze down Miranda's leg. She felt the girl flinch but when she looked up at her, Miranda just nodded her head, her teeth clenched. Guts, thought Cassie. I might expect this out on the range, where men try to prove they can handle anything, but not here. Not with all these women.

She was through in ten minutes. "I don't want her on her feet for ten days to two weeks. And then just a bit each day."

The mother nodded, but one of the girls said, teasingly, "Okay, Andy, you just did this to get out of work. You know we're fencing in that far pasture."

"Oh, shush," Estelle laughed. "If anyone here likes working that far from the house it's Andy."

"I'm just foolin', Ma."

"I'll get cabin fever and you know it," said Miranda.

"Come on," said Estelle. "You girls, get the smoke-o ready. These people will be wanting a cuppa tea before taking off."

There was tea and fruitcake and toast and raspberry jam. "What I yearn for once in a while is scones," said Estelle.

"Or oatmeal without lumps in it," said Cassie.

They were sitting in the immense kitchen, around a table that could easily seat a dozen people with elbow space left over.

"My husband died six years ago," Estelle said. "Since then my girls haven't seen many men. That's why they're staring at you so," she apologized to Sam.

"Ma'am, you mean you ladies run this outfit?"

"You better believe it," one of the girls spoke up.

"That's Alberta," said her mother. "In fact, better make the introductions, not that you can remember all these names. Let's start at the top. The eldest one, she's over there, that's Heather."

Heather stared admiringly at Sam, her gaze not wavering. "That one's next, Wilhelmina—Billy. After her comes Andy, lying on the couch. That there is Alberta, Bertie. Over there," she pointed, "is Louisa—Lou. And last, our little girl Paulie." Cassie realized that except for Heather, their nicknames were all boys' names. "Sure, we run it. Two hundred and fifty thousand acres. Over six hundred head of cattle."

"Don't you need men to do the hard work, the physical labor?" Sam asked.

Estelle shook her head. "Not for a minute. Even when Earl was alive, he and the girls and I did it all. They've grown up doing what you call men's work. They're bored with inside work."

"We get stores delivered twice a year from Teakle and Robbins," said Heather. "I'm the only one's ever been to town. No one else, exceptin' Ma of course, has even been off the station."

"What about clothes and shoes and . . . " Sam began.

"Oh, Mr. Teakle keeps our sizes and sends us clothes when we ask. We don't need dresses, and men's work clothes last a long time."

Cassie leaned back in her chair and laughed. "Well, you do take the cake. I never heard of six women running a station and never going to town."

"I taught them to read and do their figures," Estelle said. "I grew up in Sydney and went through school. That's where I met Mr. Martin. Earl. I was the secretary in the tool shop where he worked and all he wanted in the world was his own cattle station. We saved enough money for a down payment and bought an old Dodge truck and got married and drove up here and never left the place. Never regretted a minute of it."

"We regret it, Ma. We regret you never learned to cook," said Lou.

"You girls aren't so great in the kitchen either. We all take to the outdoor life here." Yet the house was clean and neat, and full of women's touches.

Sam's eyes met Cassie's and she could tell he was trying not to laugh aloud. "Don't you want to go into town?" he asked of no one in particular. "See a movie? Have a choice of clothes, pretty dresses maybe?"

One of the girls hooted. "What we want dresses for?"

"Well," Sam said, "don't you want to see how other people live, talk with them . . . "

"They know how others live," said Estelle. "Each year we send to Penguin in London and order fifty-two books. One for each week of the year. Bet mine's the best-read family in Australia."

The girls were silent. Then Billy—at least that's who Cassie thought it was—said, "We're not prisoners. If any of us wants to go, we could. But there's nothing out there that we haven't got here."

"A man?" Sam asked.

"Well, now," Estelle said, "we've talked about that. If you can ever find a cook, I mean a really *good* cook, send him out." She slowly looked around the table and grinned at her daughters, "It'd be nice to have a man around, for the sake of variety. But we'd be mighty particular. He'd have to be a man who could really cook. And he'd have to like reading nights. There's nothin' else to do."

As they took off for Tookaringa, Sam said, "I'd think any man could find something to do nights other than read with all those good-looking women around."

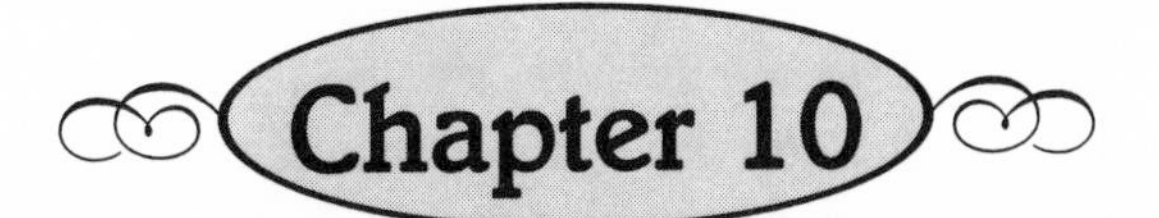

Chapter 10

Even from the air Tookaringa looked like no place else. Hundreds, thousands of trees . . . not a forest, too widely spaced for that. Mile after mile of eucalyptus, herds of cattle wandering through the trees, others grazing on open land.

A narrow ribbon of blue river widened as they flew further north, with thick growths of towering gums along its banks.

"D'you think that ever dries up?" Sam asked. "Look there. That must be the homestead up ahead. Wow!"

At least a dozen buildings were scattered among a clump of trees on the west side of a billabong. As the thicket of gums thinned out a clearly-marked rectangle, surrounded by flapping white flags, marked a landing field.

The plane shuddered, the only indication they'd touched ground. It came to a halt in front of an enormous barn-like structure, whose west side was exposed. They could see that it really was a garage. Unlike the other homesteads they'd seen, Tookaringa was neat. Tools hung on one wall of the immense garage. Tractors gleamed instead of gathering dust as in most Outback stations; two pick-ups were in mint condition.

About a dozen men, two of them black, approached as the dust created from the landing churned behind the plane like a cyclone. Sam cut the engine. Cassie saw him wave in response to the oncoming men, who all waved simultaneously.

Sam slid from his seat and walked back through the cabin, pulling the door open and bending down to toss the steps into place. Turning to Cassie, he stretched out an arm, his hand beckoning.

"I can make it without help," she said, reaching for her medicine bag.

Sam shrugged and walked down the stairs ahead of her. The men were walking around the plane, pointing, their faces filled with interest, if not awe.

From behind the garage, at a fast trot, came Jennifer, whose salt and pepper hair was pulled back in a smooth chignon. She wore jodhpurs and a pale turquoise blouse. Her waist and her walk were those of an eighteen-year-old. As she neared the plane she held both arms out.

"Welcome to Tookaringa." She smiled dazzlingly at Sam as she put her arm through Cassie's and began to pull her along. "We've set up our version of what we think you'll need for a clinic on the verandah."

They walked along a well-worn path, passing bungalows. Jennifer pulled Cassie toward the third one. "This is the men's bunkhouse. One of our stockmen fell from his horse yesterday and we don't know whether he's got a broken leg. He's in some pain, so look at him first." She walked through the open door into a large communal room, with mismatched comfortable old chairs and a sofa. A radio and magazines were scattered around the room. A bookcase held dozens of books, most of them well-thumbed from the looks of their covers.

"Walt's down this hall," Jennifer offered, leading the way to another large room, filled with a dozen bunk beds. Lying on one of them was a man, asleep. "I imagine his mates gave him something to help him sleep so he wouldn't feel the pain." Jennifer smiled and went over to him and shook his shoulder. He moaned but didn't awaken.

Cassie leaned over and looked at his swollen foot. He didn't wake even when she pressed his ankle. "A sprain, but a bad one. Not broken, fortunately, but it looks like one of his toes is. The nail is purple here and the toe is swollen. Of course, there's nothing to do about a broken toe. The only thing that will take care of that is time. I'll come back later when he's awake." Sober would be more accurate. He'll be off his feet for a week or so, I'd imagine."

"Well, thank goodness it's just that," Jennifer said. She walked back through the rooms and out onto the verandah, again linking her arm through Cassie's and leading her to the homestead itself. As they went along she pointed out the various buildings. "This is where we keep our stores. Deliveries come out just twice a year. We send orders to Teakle and Robbins and they deliver what we want, but we have to store it someplace. We have what amounts to our own grocery store. I have to make up lists of things we think we'll need over a six-month period. And that is where the girls bunk, much cozier than the men's. That over there, the one before the main house, is Steven's office—the accountant and overseer have rooms behind it. And this . . . this, my dear, is Tookaringa."

They'd stopped in front of the other buildings and now came to a slope. Overlooking a wide expanse of closely mowed lawn and a dozen regularly spaced royal palms was a three-story yellow and white Victorian house—gingerbread, curlicues, and all. A wide porch surrounded it.

It rose majestically, looking out of place in this land of few houses—and those always close to the ground. At the bottom of the gently graded lawn, perhaps two thousand feet away, were towering gums and a pond. Black swans and ducks floated on it.

"Even after thirty years I'm not tired of it," Jennifer said, squeezing Cassie's arm.

"No wonder. It's lovely." A long-beaked dark and white bird rose from the trees by the water's edge, silhouetted against the cobalt sky.

"A jabiru," Jennifer followed Cassie's gaze. "We used to have picnic suppers down by the billabong and Steven would row us around in our little boat." It was obvious that Jennifer missed those days. "But, come, we've set up on the verandah and you must tell us what else you'll need. But let's have you wash up first and have a cold drink. How about a sandwich?"

Cassie observed over a dozen black women and children seated on the lawn at the foot of the steps.

"These are some of the families of our stockmen. They live in lean-tos over there, way beyond the trees. You can't see them from here. We supply food and now that we have you, we want to see about their medical needs also. When Blake had a governess I welcomed any of their children who wanted schooling. Regrettably only a few took advantage of the offer. We're two different cultures and much as we want them to adopt ours, they don't do it willingly." She shook her head. "They probably can't understand why we don't adopt theirs, why we insist on living in houses and working as hard as we do."

The two women were at the top of the wide stairway. A long table, covered with white linen, had been set up on the right side of the verandah. On the left half, which was screened in, there was comfortable porch furniture, including a wooden swing, which hung from the ceiling. Cassie had never seen such a large house.

"Look and see if there's anything else you need."

Cassie wouldn't know until she discovered what ailments her patients had. "How about some sterile water. I think I have everything else. I hope Sam's bringing the box from the plane." She set her medical bag down on the table.

"Iced tea?"

"Sounds good. You must have your own generator."

Jennifer smiled. "Steven told me if I'd leave England he'd see I'd never lack for anything I could have there. He's been true to his word. He's recently built a swimming pool out behind the house. All under glass, with cages of parrots and budgerigars and cockatoos. Next time, bring your swimming suit."

"I thought this was the arid Outback."

"The springs here have never run dry, but three times in the thirty years I've been here the droughts have been so bad across the land we've lost ninety percent of our stock."

Cassie stared at her.

Jennifer patted her arm. "Oh, it hasn't all been easy. But then, how boring *that* would have been. It's been an exciting life. There, you can wash up in there and I'll see to the iced tea."

Half an hour later, when Cassie went out onto the verandah to her first clinic, the box with medical supplies was there, sitting on the table, but she saw no sign of Sam.

That evening, as they dined with Jennifer and Steven, Sam said, "I don't think I've ever had a better meal."

"Ruby's been with us for over twenty years," Jennifer said. "When they tell you that the aborigines aren't hard workers or go take walkabouts they don't know our help."

"Well," Steven said, "our house help and the stockmen maybe don't take walkabouts regularly, but lots of the others do."

Jennifer smiled. "I'm not going to say none of them do, but certainly we've had faithful and hard-working help around here for years."

"What's a walkabout?" asked Cassie.

Sam answered. "Depends on who you're talking to. Most of the station managers, most anybody I know, actually, will tell you it's just a black man's way of taking off when he's not in the mood to work. He never announces that he's going to leave, he just disappears one day and someone tells you eventually that he's gone 'walkabout.' But I think to them it has a spiritual meaning. A journey, searching for something, contacting their ancestor spirits, perhaps."

"I agree," Jennifer interrupted. "We're upset when they won't adopt our culture. We . . . "

"She means whites," Steven said.

"The people who have come to occupy the black man's land," Jennifer went on.

"Well, let's not go that far." Steven's voice took on an argumentative tone.

"But we do want them to wear our clothes, believe in our God . . . "

Sam interrupted again. "That is, the Christian white man's God . . . "

Jennifer nodded. " . . . And live in houses as we do."

"They'll never do that," said Steven.

"They get claustrophobia in our houses," explained Jennifer. "They much prefer making shelters out of tree boughs, temporary housing that's outdoors, keeping them in touch with nature, that they can move out of when they get dirty or they want to collectively go 'walkabout.' "

Steven said, "When they live in houses they trash them. They don't have our values . . . "

"But then, we don't have theirs," Sam interjected. "They're more—well, I think they're more spiritual than we are. They're more attuned to nature, they respect their ancestors."

Smiling at the kindred spirit she was finding in Sam, Jennifer chimed in. "They're a gentle, non-warlike people."

"Jenny's in love with abos," said Steven. "The noble savage bit. She never sees them as dirty or slothful. All her pictures are of them and their land."

"All her pictures?" asked Cassie, who felt as though she were in a foreign country. This was so unlike the Australia she knew as a child on summer vacations. She'd seen several aborigines in Melbourne, but their culture was alien to her.

"She paints," Steven explained. "She's terrific."

"He's prejudiced," smiled his wife.

"May I see your pictures?" asked Cassie.

"Of course. I don't have many right now. I always find people to give them to. Wedding presents. Birthdays. People who drop in and like one. I discovered painting years ago when Steven would be out mustering for weeks on end, home maybe only once in a six-week period. Now, Blake does that for him. He stays closer to home nowadays, thank goodness. But painting kept me sane when I first came out here and thought being alone meant loneliness."

A dark-skinned lubra brought in dessert, a large, flaky, round pastry covered with whipped cream and red and green fruits. Her dress was neat over her ample body, and what amused Cassie was that the maid wore no shoes, her bare feet slapping across the hardwood floor.

Sam started to light a cigarette, looking at Cassie, then returned the pack to his left shirt pocket.

The lubra brought coffee.

"We have several pregnant women scattered around the land," Jennifer said. "Next time, we might see if you can talk them into examinations. Getting them to submit to such may take time. Steven has ideas of ways to bribe them."

"How come you have so many aborigines?"

"They're great trackers," Steven answered. "Drovers. Handle stock like no one else. They belong on horses. And they take pride in it. Never saw a lazy drover. Natural instinct, I think. And when you hire one, he automatically moves his family onto your land. We don't pay them much or we could never afford to employ as many as we do, but we feed their families, offer them schooling if they want . . .

" . . . Which they usually don't," Jennifer said.

"True. Sad but true."

"Why sad?" asked Jennifer. "What can we teach them about the way they want to live?"

"We can teach them about a way of life they have to fit into," Steven answered, though Cassie had the idea they'd covered this issue many times before. He turned to her. "Tomorrow will be your first experience at an aborigine mission, won't it?"

"Yancanna?"

"No, that's an AIM hospital. That'll be Monday. Tomorrow will be at Narrabinga. It's run by a Catholic nun."

The missionary wore shorts. Cassie thought that was a good beginning. Something she'd like to do up here in the tropics, where it was too hot for long pants. The men she'd seen all wore shorts and knee-length stockings. She thought the latter a bit pretentious. Maybe if this woman could wear shorts, Cassie might have the nerve to try it. After people got used to her in men's pants, that is. Change would have to come slowly.

The missionary's shorts were baggy and long. Certainly they didn't add to her femininity. She had no allure whatever. Her mousy graying hair looked as though she'd put a bowl over her head and trimmed along the edge. She wore tortoiseshell glasses perched on the end of her nose.

"Thank God," said the woman. "I'm Sister Ina." She stretched out a hand and gave Cassie a firm handshake. "We hope soon to get a pedal wireless but right now we have none and we do have a medical emergency."

With no more introduction, she turned on her heel and half-trotted toward the low corrugated iron building, which was shaded by towering palms.

Medical bag in hand, Cassie followed. Stretched out on the dirt floor, facedown, was a black man. His face was turned away from the doorway, but his hands were spread out on either side of him as though he'd fallen in place. Between his shoulder blades, halfway down his back, a spear protruded. It was nearly five feet long.

"Oh, my heavens!" cried Cassie.

"He arrived less than an hour ago, and we don't know how to get the thing out."

Cassie knelt down next to him. "How long has he been unconscious?" she asked.

The missionary's tone was grim. "He's not unconscious." She said something Cassie did not understand, and the man opened an eye. He grunted, and closed his eye again. She could tell the spear had barely, but just barely, missed the spinal cord. It had obviously not shattered the vertebra or death would have been immediate. She guessed, from the angle of the spear, that it was close to the heart, but if it had punctured the aorta he would not be alive. Nothing in med school had prepared her for this.

Just then Sam marched through the doorway.

"My God," he said.

"Mine, too," said Sister Ina. "We're trying to figure how to get it out. Sticky wicket, what?"

"That's an understatement! We need tools other than those I have." Cassie stood up. "Do you have pliers, or wrenches?"

"Sure, in the workshop," said the missionary. "Follow me."

Cassie looked over at Sam. "I've a feeling you're going to be needed. You obviously have more muscle power than I do."

"Well, thank goodness for that," he grinned.

She didn't smile back.

In the workshop they found Stillson wrenches and pliers. "Let's hope these will do it."

When everything was ready, Cassie said to the nursing sister, "You'll have to administer the anesthetic." She took the gauze mask and bottle of ether from her bag.

"Not me this time?" Sam asked, relieved.

"No, I need you to pull this damn thing out."

Sam looked at her.

"You have to be careful," she went on, "not to break the vertebra." She noted the blank look in his eyes. "The vertebra—one of the bony segments composing the spinal column. What you'll have to do, in order not to chance breaking it, is to pull straight. Don't use any force other than just a straight pulling." She turned to Ina. "While you're administering the ether and Sam is pulling we'll need some more people to hold the patient down, so Sam can exert pressure. Can you call a couple of strong men in to help?"

Ina disappeared.

"What happens if I do break the vertebra?" Sam asked.

Cassie shot him a glance. She'd thought of that, too. "Don't."

Ina returned with two large aborigines and explained that they had to keep the patient pinned to the ground so that Sam could pull the spear out.

"Don't let him move," Cassie ordered. She nodded at Ina. "Okay, now a drop of ether at a time," she said, and explained how to administer it. Kneeling next to the patient, her hands pressing down on the skin by the spear, she suggested to Sam, "Put a foot on the man's buttocks for leverage. He can't feel it. Now, pull, gently but firmly."

The spear didn't budge.

Sam began to sweat. It was hot in the hut.

"Okay," Cassie said. "Just a little bit at a time, try to turn it with that wrench."

It twisted a little, but just a little. "Now, pull gently," she said. "Try twisting, then pulling." As he did so, skin stuck to the spear. "Wait!" she cried. "Look. When you twist it out the skin sticks. You'll have to pull it out a tiny bit, then let it ease back and I'll push on the skin to loosen it from the spear."

"Oh, the poor man," Ina moaned as she poured a speck of ether onto the gauze.

"Guide it out, now," Cassie ordered, pressing down on the back, so that skin would not twist itself onto the spear. "But push it down every few turns. Don't let the skin tear." She realized all her perspiration wasn't from the humidity.

Sweat glowed on Sam's face, too. He stopped to rest a minute and Cassie glanced up at him. Then he rotated the spear with the wrench and pulled deftly.

"Wait, the skin's coming up with it. Turn it slowly and don't pull up. Ah, there. Okay, go on, twist."

It took about fifteen minutes for Sam to get a rhythm. Then he rotated the wrench a little, twisting and pulling, while Cassie made sure the skin did not stick to the spear. It began to ease out.

It was more than an hour before the spear came out with a sucking sound; blood gushed like a geyser. Cassie quickly pressed the wound together with her finger and thumb, reaching for the collodion pad which she placed firmly over the hole. Then she grabbed a hypodermic needle and injected a shot of adrenaline.

"How did this happen?" Cassie asked, standing up.

Ina handed her the bottle of ether and the mask. "Probably some tribal law was broken. We'll never know exactly. Whoever was assigned to carry out the death sentence didn't succeed. Is he going to be all right?"

Cassie had no way of knowing. "Sam did a good job." She noticed he'd disappeared. "I've no idea. I've never dealt with anything like this before. He'd have been dead if we hadn't arrived just now."

"God works in mysterious ways . . . " Ina smiled. "Would you like a cup of tea?"

"Not really," Cassie said. "I need something cold."

Ina shook her head. "Sorry. Not here."

Sam was standing under one of the palms, smoking.

What Cassie saw in the clinic were sores and scars of leprosy, which had been pretty much eradicated by now, and yaws. Old injuries long neglected. All women. Or children.

One young girl, who couldn't have been twelve yet, had lines across her belly. "If I didn't know better I'd think they were stretch marks," Cassie observed.

"They are," said Ina, who had stood at her elbow all morning. "They have babies while they're still babies themselves. You have to understand, men use women and girl children whenever they want them. They can be walking down a path and see a woman or girl they want and they take her right there. It means nothing to them."

"Nothing to the women either?"

Ina shrugged her shoulders. "Who knows? It doesn't distress them as it does us. I figure if I let their ways dismay me, I shouldn't be here. I'm in their country, after all. I do try to see that the women and children aren't beaten so much. Actually, the aborigines are a gentle people. They just don't think like we do. They live in the moment, with no thought of the future. Whatever they want at the moment, they take.

The tribal laws don't apply to women, or, if they do, the women don't know it. Women aren't allowed to witness tribal ceremonies or even know the laws."

Cassie stared at Ina. "How do you stand to live among them? Doesn't it drive you batty?"

Ina smiled, though there was a melancholy to it. "I'm not sure why. I thought it was God. That's why I came. Now, I like it here. I couldn't go back to England. At least here I can blame their problems on ignorance, or innocence, whichever you want to call it. What can I blame the problems of modern civilization on? Men know better in our world than to do the things they do, but they do them anyhow."

Actually, the most prevalent problem was toothache. Cassie pulled eleven teeth. The only dental forceps she had were for upper and lower teeth and for broken stumps.

"The women, you'll notice," Sister Ina said, "are invariably more stoic about having their teeth pulled."

Half-crazed with pain, scared of both doctor and instruments, once the tooth was pulled the relief evident in each patient was transforming. Pulling the tooth caused less pain than the patient had already endured. The patient was usually amazed after losing the tooth and realizing the terrible pain was gone.

It was three o'clock before she was ready to go. Perspiration poured down her face, dripping into her eyes which stung with the salt. She kept wiping the sweat away with a handkerchief that was soon soaked.

"Only the hard cases have come today," Ina told her. "But word of the end of toothache, of your saving that man's life, will get around. I hope by your next visit to talk some of the pregnant women into letting you examine them, but I can't promise anything. Perhaps they'll let their children be vaccinated. It will take time. They've never been offered medical care before."

"How long have you been out here?" Cassie asked, so enervated she didn't know if she had the energy to walk to the plane. She knew it would be scorching inside, after being out in all the heat and humidity for over six hours.

"Seven years," the woman replied as she wiped perspiration from her temples.

* * *

Sam was standing in the shade of a palm tree, not far from the plane. He stamped out his cigarette when he saw Cassie coming and reached out to help her with her medical bag.

"I can manage," she said.

"See ya next month," he said to the nun, jumping up into the plane ahead of Cassie. He stood by as she entered and pulled the steps up into place, slamming the door shut.

"Thanks a million," Ina called.

Cassie sank into the seat and closed her eyes. God, it was hot.

Chapter 11

Jennifer took one look at Cassie and insisted she nap before the barbecue that evening. Cassie might not have awakened for hours had not Jennifer tapped lightly on her door at seven.

There were no other ranchers within more than a hundred miles, but the Thompsons had invited everyone who was within several hours of them. Their overseer and his wife, Steven's accountant, all the help on the station, the drovers and ranch hands who weren't far out in the bush, the gardener and his wife, the two mechanics, the veterinarian—everyone who worked for them had been invited to meet the new doctor. That included more than two dozen children.

"I love it," Jennifer said, as she sat on the edge of Cassie's bed. "Australia is the most egalitarian country in the world. In England you'd never invite help to a party. Then, of course, there are all the hands who are miles and miles out on muster. I wish Blake were here. He'll like you."

"I don't know that I bought anything that's right to wear," Cassie said, looking at Jennifer in a peach-colored silkish dress that clung to her splendid figure.

"Oh, half the women coming don't even own anything partyish. But, don't tell me you're going to wear jodhpurs."

"No, I do have a dress with me."

Jennifer told her she thought it was lovely. As they walked down the stairs together, all eyes turned to look at them. Cassie's short chestnut-brown hair haloed her head. Her red and white polka dotted dress of fine lawn created interest among the women—they hadn't seen anything like it. They were used to Jennifer's elegance and took it for granted, but seeing the new woman doctor in such a pretty dress made her seem, well, less professional. Less awesome.

"Every man here will want to dance with you," Jennifer whispered.

"I'd just as soon spend my time talking with the women," Cassie murmured. "After all, they're the ones who'll need me the most."

"Not necessarily." Jennifer let go of her arm. "And, besides, you can talk with women anytime. Dances are for spending time with the opposite sex."

Cassie looked around. She didn't see any potential Ray Grahams. Didn't see anyone dangerous. Maybe she could allow herself to have fun tonight. Dance with the station hands, the horse lovers, the mechanics, the roustabouts and jackaroos. Let herself go a little.

The smell of barbecued beef permeated the air. All day it had been roasting over open coals. There were huge bowls of salad and beans along ten-foot tables that had been set up on the front lawn that sloped down towards the billabong. Biscuits and pumpkin bread, enormous red tomatoes, slabs of cheeses, pitchers of milk and iced tea were repeated down the long trestled tables.

Steven appeared. "Good evening, ladies. My, you two look lovely. Come on over here—there are two Tom Collins I mixed with my own hands, just waiting for you."

"As long as it's tall and cool," said Cassie.

"Your man over there," Steven nodded towards Sam, who was talking with several of the station hands, "seems to go for beer. D'you know that we Aussies drink more beer per capita than any other country?"

Cassie wondered if that was something to be proud of.

"These gangling station hands are going to be looking you over tonight," Steven grinned. "They're about as shy with women as any group of men can be, but they're all going to want to dance with you, even if you are a doctor. Don't get nervous when you see them staring at you. We don't get many women who look like you up here."

"We don't get many women at all up here," Jennifer said. "In fact, hardly anyone but the girls who work here. The men liked it when we'd have a governess when Blake was young. But that's been a long time."

"You are far from any schools, aren't you?"

"It's a shame," Jennifer said. "We could always afford governesses, but of course after a year or so they always got married. One woman among so many men, after all. But there are hundreds of families out in the bush who can't afford a governess and who aren't educated enough to teach their children anything. Sometimes the children are lucky to learn the alphabet and how to add. It's one of the big drawbacks to having families here. When a child does reach twelve or so we have to send them off to the cities to boarding schools. That's a horrendous cost, too, and most people can't afford it. Those of us who have the money, pay for it in another way. We lose our children early. It's a high price to pay for pioneering."

"We're luckier than most," Steven said. "We could afford governesses and good schools. Blake graduated with a degree in business, not that it does him a bit of good or that he wants to do anything other than ranch. But he got a good background."

"Well, well, Doc," Sam's voice came from behind Cassie. "I wouldn't have known you."

She turned to find him looking at her. Self-consciously, she held up her drink and pirouetted. "Do I look unprofessional?"

"You look all woman," he said. Turning to Steven, he asked, "Mind if I help myself to another beer?"

"So, you're the one killed my black boy?"

Steven put an arm around the speaker, a stocky, grey-haired man. "Ian, you don't know who this is. This is the new doctor . . . "

"She wouldn't come see one of my boys when I asked her to and he died."

The hair on the back of Cassie's neck stood up. She noticed Sam turn around and come stand beside her.

"All I asked for was his temperature and . . . "

"He died."

Steven spoke. "Probably no one could have saved him."

Ian James looked at Cassie. Then, turning on his heel, he walked away. Cassie wanted to sink out of sight.

"Don't let it bother you," Steven said. "We all make mistakes."

"It *will* bother her," Sam said. "And it wasn't a mistake. He hung up on her. I heard it. He didn't cooperate. There's a difference between the FDS and an aerial ambulance service, you know. Cassie has to be sure it's a medical emergency before I'll even let the plane leave the hangar. The expense is enormous and it would also be a waste of time."

Oh, thank you, Sam, Cassie wanted to say.

"To make any kind of evaluation I need a patient's medical history and symptoms. Mr. James refused to give me either."

Steven patted Cassie on the shoulder. "Take it in stride," he advised.

Within a minute several other men sauntered up, allowing Steven to introduce them to Cassie. Sam ambled over to talk to several of the young women who were gathered together. Cassie lost sight of him after a while.

After recovering from Ian James's attack, she realized it was fun to be surrounded by men she didn't care about, to have them look at her appreciatively and say outrageous things. She found that by putting on a party dress she left her brisk manner—her doctor's persona—behind.

As the sun sank slowly in a vermilion sky, the evening began to cool off and the party took on a convivial atmosphere. Jennifer and Steven made sure Cassie was introduced to everyone. She decided she had never met such friendly people.

At dinner, she found herself seated between two of the stockmen and across from three others. Only one of them was a real conversationalist, and Cassie had to search for things to talk about, but it was most pleasant anyway.

After dinner, when stars began to shimmer into the sky, she heard a violin tuning up from the verandah. Pretty soon the wail of a trumpet, smooth as Harry James, wafted through the night air. Then several other instruments joined in and the dancing began. The French doors to the living room had been thrown open so that the spacious verandah and the immense living room became a ballroom. Rugs were thrown back and the floors shone from fresh waxing. Chinese lanterns were strung across the verandah, and the band played zippy American songs interspersed with slow foxtrots.

Cassie found herself handed from one man to another all evening long, with never a chance to rest. She was dying of thirst when Sam cut in. After a few minutes, she said, "You dance very well." He was quiet as they moved slowly across the floor. "I think you're a fine medical assistant, too," she added.

He laughed. "I was pretty impressive yesterday, wasn't I? With that spear."

Cassie's eyes twinkled. "Shall I tell all those young girls over there how great you are?"

He shook his head, spinning her around. "You needn't bother, thanks anyway. They'll find out for themselves."

The band broke into a fast American jitterbug melody, "Elmer's Tune." Most of the couples backed off the dance floor.

"Wanna give this a go?" Sam raised his eyebrows.

"Do you think I can't?" she asked, teasingly.

"Okay, Doc, let's wow 'em," and he began to swing her out, twirling her around, catching her hand as she spun back to him. "My, my. I'm impressed," and off they went, Cassie following his lead.

The dance floor had cleared and everyone watched them, clapping along with the music. Cassie's skirt swung wide as she circled around Sam. His hold on her hand was light but firm and his face was alight with pleasure. He was good, and he made it easy to follow his lead. She could tell he was adding extra steps, challenging her to keep up with him.

When the music ended applause broke out. They grinned at each other and Sam bowed low. He was obviously a show-off. Cassie curtsied. She was letting a part of herself out of a box, she could feel it. Not with Sam so much, but with the Outback. With life. Everything was novel to her and she found herself loving it.

* * *

When Cassie and Sam left for Yancanna Monday morning, they agreed they'd had an extraordinary weekend. They were both impressed with the quality of Jennifer's paintings, which were of aboriginal faces and of the open red land, its trees, its cliffs, its vastness.

They had learned much, they had relaxed, they had played bridge last night and laughed a lot. Cassie felt she had found two new friends in the Thompsons.

She and Sam had shared so much. They had worked together and played together. He had held her in his arms when they danced, yet she did not feel she knew him better at all.

Maybe that was just as well.

Yancanna was directly below them, but from the air one could hardly see it. It didn't look as though there were as many buildings as at Tookaringa. There was a post office, the AIM hospital, and a store. There were only five houses, unless you counted the police station, which served as the one policeman's home as well. Cassie wondered why they had a post office, but learned it served an area of seven thousand square miles.

The two nursing sisters, Marianne and Brigid, were in their early twenties, and had been in Yancanna nine months. Brigid was out in the bush delivering a baby, but Marianne and the six-foot-five policeman, Walt Davis, whom everyone called "Chief," met the plane when it landed on a cleared field behind the hospital.

Marianne was wearing the traditional white nursing uniform. She was a good-looking young woman, her dark eyebrows accentuating her nearly black eyes, and she constantly pushed back her unruly hair which seemed to match her eyes.

"You can't possibly know how happy we are to have a doctor here," she said, reaching out to shake Cassie's hand.

The Chief relieved Cassie of her medical bag. He was the biggest man she'd ever seen. Broad shouldered, suntanned, he had a craggy face that was already seamed from years spent in the sun, even though he still had to be in his twenties. He reached over to shake Sam's hand.

Explaining that Brigid was sorry to miss the doctor's first visit, Marianne began leading them to the hospital. Like other Outback hospitals, it had two stories and was built of concrete, to ward off termites. Wide stairs led up to the verandah, whose wide double doors opened onto a good-sized lobby. The floors were of burnished jarrah wood, and the large ward and dispensary were sparkling. The dispensary, which was also used for minor operations and out-patient treatment, was excellently equipped. To the left of the lobby was a three-bed ward, presently unoccupied. On the other side of the lobby, to the right, was a large sitting room, and beyond that the kitchen. These two rooms were the social center for thousands of square miles.

"Everyone for miles around comes in for Christmas," Marianne said. She smiled up at Chief. "He read Dickens's 'Christmas Carol' to us and it was wonderful."

Cassie could tell Marianne was smitten with the Chief. Marianne continued leading them through the hospital. There were two bathrooms with porcelain baths and sinks. Upstairs were the sisters' bedrooms, commodious rooms with doors opening onto an upper verandah. From there they could see for miles, see the coolibahs along the riverbed and perhaps a river when there was water in it. They could see the dust rising in apricot puffs, and herds of brumbies racing across the desert. They could see strangers approaching from miles away.

"We let people know you'd be here by eleven," Marianne said, "but we don't have any emergencies right now. Actually, we serve as doctors half the time. We pull teeth . . . " Yes, that seemed to be the single greatest complaint out here, so far from civilization, Cassie mused. " . . . And if the women can't afford to go over to Brisbane or down to Adelaide or even up to Augusta Springs to await the birth of their babies, Brigid and I deliver babies, too. We're always nervous that someone's going to need a cesarean, of course, and we're not really qualified to do that. We've delivered breeches and had some chancy ones, though. We try to get them into the hospital, but usually we end up going out to their stations."

"I'm impressed," Cassie said. She was awed, too, thinking she'd volunteered to spend two years in what she'd thought was a remote place—but Yancanna was really in the middle of nowhere.

The Chief was talking with Sam. "We've had a recent tragedy. Three weeks ago that scrub out there," he pointed at the endless miles of mulga, "swallowed two victims again. Two little boys, three and four years old, just disappeared. Mrs. Benbow left them on the porch while she went to get tucker and when she returned they were gone. Not a sign of them. No tracks. Out about seven miles east of here. Everybody within thirty miles came to help search. They even searched nights, but no sign of them even with the best aborigine trackers helping. No luck. The mother's wild with despair."

"I would be, too," Cassie said, shivering at the thought.

Marianne nodded in agreement. "I hear she goes out nightly, calling to them. She fixes dinner every night and when she sits down at the table she tells her husband they must wait for the children to come in from playing."

"Let me fix tea," Marianne said. "I don't think there will be many people today. What we mainly need you for is advice when we find we can't solve a problem or if we have an emergency. We could have saved at least half a dozen lives if we'd had a doctor available, I'm sure. You just don't know how thrilled we are to know you're here. Excuse me a sec."

Cassie looked out the window. She heard the Chief telling Sam, "Yeah, I administer an area larger than any other in the country. I didn't know what I was getting into when I came out from England five years ago. I'm the only lawman in a territory larger than most European countries!" He laughed, and there was pride in his voice. "I wear many hats. I'm protector of the aborigines—people I've grown fond of. They invite me to their corroborees and initiation ceremonies, the first white man. Of course, women aren't allowed. Women are nothing to them. But I feel privileged to have their trust. I like them. Seems to me they have integrity and skills. They can track like a white man never could. They have tribal laws and traditions I respect. They know what they should and shouldn't do. It's a simple society that knows right from wrong, but they get confused when we insist they operate by our laws and traditions."

Sam said something Cassie couldn't hear and then Chief continued. "I'm the clerk of the courts. When it seems like some problem should legally be solved right here I call the court into session and I'm both the judge and the jury. People would rather have that than wait around for whatever justice might come this way."

Cassie walked out onto the verandah and looked at the landscape; it overwhelmed her. "Doesn't that stagger you?"

"Nope." He grinned, his broad shoulders looking like they could carry the weight of the world. "I like being head man. I like it here. The hotter it gets the better I work. There's not a person out in these parts I don't know, not a homestead where I'm not welcome. And now that the sisters have a wireless, we can sit around evenings and find out what's going on all over the world. When someone out in my district talks over the pedal wireless to you, over in Augusta Springs, I can listen in and if I think it's something I can help with, I ride out."

"Do you always use a horse?"

Chief shook his head so that his blond hair fell over his forehead. Absent-mindedly, he reached into his shirt pocket and pulled out a toothbrush and began brushing his teeth. "Where there are roads I use a truck, but most places don't have roads that're usable. If there is a road it's not always in repair. In the Wet it may be washed out. In drought, sand blows over it, though with all the trees up here that's not as much a problem as further south."

"Doesn't it get lonely?" It was all Cassie could do not to laugh out loud at the toothbrush bit.

The Chief plopped his toothbrush back in his pocket. "All my relatives in England keep asking that. I haven't had a lonely minute in the five years I've been here. I never get through everything I plan, not in any day."

"Neither do we," said Marianne, bringing in a tea tray with four cups.

Just then they heard someone coming up the stairs, and through the open doors came a woman of indeterminate age, her face lined and leathery from years spent in the open.

"This is Hermione," said Marianne. "She's the postmistress—her husband runs the store and pub."

Cassie couldn't imagine that either of them would be overworked.

Hermione wore a shapeless dress, one white sock and one yellow one and dirty sneakers, one of which had the toe cut out. On her head was an old battered wide-brimmed straw hat. She held out a packet of letters. "Thought you could take these with you, instead of their sitting around here waiting for Mr. Miner, who prob'ly won't show up for another ten days."

Sam took them.

Marianne went to fetch another cup.

Cassie wondered aloud where the mail came from, where patients came from, where people came from. There couldn't be more than a dozen in the whole town.

"Some of the mail's to and from the education department," said Hermione, her voice sounding as though she'd smoked all her life. "That's how children get educated around here. By mail."

"This is along the stock route," added Chief. "The hospital is a gathering place. Every man within a hundred miles finds some reason to come to town just to look at Brigid and Marianne." He laughed as Marianne blushed. "They always have a meal for whoever drops in."

"We also serve as the library," Marianne said. "Anyone who's finished reading a book brings it here. We've gotten a pretty good collection. When a bunch of drovers come through, though, and each one of them takes out a book, then we get sort of low. But people are always giving us books. Keep that in mind if you find extra ones. We can always use books. I bet the Outback people are about the best-read people in the world."

"If you don't read, you can go nuts," said Hermione.

Since there were no patients, they did not stay long at Yancanna. Before leaving they tuned in to the eleven o'clock Flying Doctor radio session, checking in with Horrie about any emergencies, and Cassie gave advice to two stations that had called in with minor problems.

"Do me a favor, will you?" Horrie asked. "Get back here as soon as you can. Betty's here and we want to get married tonight. You can do the four-forty-five session and then we thought we'd get married and we can all have dinner together."

As Cassie relaxed in the plane, closing her eyes, she reflected that as much as she liked Horrie she was glad she wasn't Betty. Imagine having to live in that little tin shack. Imagine loving a man enough to put up with that. Imagine that being the outer limits of your life. And, much as she liked Horrie, she couldn't imagine him being the inner limits, either.

She wondered what her life would have been like had Ray not decided to return to his wife.

Well, now there were no limits on her life. Were there limits—inner and outer ones—only when men were in your life? She sighed; she had no answer to that. Maybe she'd even gotten to the point where she was glad Ray Graham had made the choice he had. Maybe being here, so far from any city, was where adventure was. Where else would she have taken a spear out of an aborigine? Where would she be flying hundreds of miles a week, thousands maybe? How else would she know people like Steven and Jennifer? Like Fiona? Like Don McLeod? Like these people in Yancanna and Sister Ina in Narrabinga.

Nowhere else, she knew that. A smile drifted over her face as she fell asleep in the seat next to Sam.

Horrie and Betty were waiting at the airfield. Betty was a perky, curly-haired blonde with a baby-doll face who barely came up to Horrie's shoulder. She wore a white shantung suit and her little straw hat had a veil and flowers cascading down the side, over her ears.

She had clung to Horrie's arm all the way to the church and all during the ceremony and as they exited down the aisle.

"She's cute," Sam said as he and Cassie followed them down the aisle. Horrie hadn't even let them take the time to change their clothes.

"Betty Wallace," Betty was saying. "Isn't that a pretty name? I wonder if I'll ever get used to it."

They headed towards Addie's where Sam ordered champagne to toast the newlyweds.

Betty giggled. "Isn't this the greatest thing? Just think if I'd married someone back in Kerrybree, I'd just be a housewife. Here, I'm going to be a real helpmate."

"That you are," Horrie grinned, holding her hand tightly. "But I think I'll wait till tomorrow to teach you Morse code."

She smiled at him. "Isn't he the mostest?" she asked no one in particular.

Sam said, "This is on me," as the waitress brought the bottle of champagne. "And so are the steaks." He held his glass up. "To a lifetime of happiness."

Horrie gave him a look of appreciation.

Just then Cassie felt a hand on her shoulder. She turned to look up at Chris Adams.

"Sorry to interrupt," he said, with no hint of apology in his voice. "I've been trying to trace you down for over an hour."

Cassie looked up at him, raising her champagne glass to her lips. Chris's hand came down and touched the glass. "No," he said. "No champagne. I need you."

He needs me?

"I have to amputate a hand," he said. "Some crazy guy tried to use dynamite and didn't get away quickly enough and he's blown off his hand. All but the bones. I need to amputate and quickly."

Cassie set her glass on the table. "Why me? Certainly Dr. Edwards . . . "

"Dr. Edwards," said Chris, his voice as rigid as a straight line, "is incapacitated."

No one said anything.

"He's dead drunk, and I need an anesthetist right now."

Cassie stood up. "Of course."

She turned to Horrie and Betty. "I'm sorry. Maybe you'll still be here when I'm finished. I'll check and see. If not, tomorrow . . . "

Chris turned on his heel and walked ahead of her, not even holding the swinging door for her or opening the car door. He waited, turning the key in the engine, while she opened the passenger's door and climbed in.

He didn't say a word all the way to the hospital.

Chapter 12

"What's the problem, Mrs. Anderson?" Cassie wasn't yet used to diagnosing long distance, without seeing a patient.

"He's got pressure in his chest. Says it feels like somebody's standing on it."

Cassie flicked a switch. The big advantage, she thought, was that neither could interrupt the other. The switches had to be synchronized. "Does the pain travel?"

"Just a minute." Cassie could hear the woman shouting.

In a moment, a man's voice came on the phone. "Yeah, it travels. I feel it going up into my neck and into my shoulders and down my left arm."

Angina.

His voice continued. "I can feel it in my elbow but there's nothing wrong with my elbow. I haven't hit it on anything."

"When does this pain come on?"

"Well," the voice crackled through the air, "I especially get it in the early morning when I'm up doing chores. Hurts so bad sometimes I have to stop what I'm doing and just sit down till the pain goes away."

How much to tell him? "That's pretty typical signs of heart pain or angina. You better quit exerting yourself until we get a handle as to what's going on."

"What can I do?"

"Take it easy. Don't strain yourself. Get someone else to do your chores. We'll come out tomorrow and do an EKG and bring some nitroglycerin tablets."

"I can't get anyone to do my chores."

"You better. Is your wife listening?"

A woman's voice chimed in. "I'm right here."

"Okay, you heard all I said. Don't let him exert himself too much right now. But the symptoms aren't dangerous. If he gets worse or there are new symptoms, let me know. We'll come out tomorrow."

"I'll do what I can. Should I put him to bed?"

"That's not necessary. Just keep him from doing too much and make him rest when he feels the pain."

That ended the radio calls for the day. It was five-thirty. Cassie turned to Horrie. "You heard me tell the mother of that little girl you'd check in at seven to see if her fever had gone down? I'll be home all evening, as far as I know. If I'm someplace else I'll let you know."

"I thought you were going over to the Adams place."

Cassie grinned. "Small town. How did you know that?" She didn't really expect an answer. Yes, she was going to stop off and read to Isabel on her way home. She and Fiona were having leftovers—chicken salad made from the stewed chicken they'd had last night. No hurry to get home.

She'd hardly read to Isabel since she'd been out at Tookaringa, and she hadn't heard from Chris since the amputation two nights ago. He'd barely thanked her.

She looked around. In only two days the tin shack had taken on a different look—especially the room next to the radio room, the room that was the kitchen and sitting room for Horrie and Betty.

"Horrie promises we can build a verandah around the house," said Betty, "especially off the back, so we can sit out nights." She didn't seem dismayed at all by the housing arrangement.

"She already knows five letters," said Horrie, meaning Morse Code. "She's a quick learner."

"Either you're a good teacher or you're prejudiced," Sam said. He had to drive Cassie out to the medical session at eight, eleven and four-forty-five until Flynn was able to provide her with a car of her own.

"Drop me off at Dr. Adams," Cassie said, as she got into Sam's utility.

"Maybe you're going to get to be buddies."

"I doubt that. He acted as though he resented every second I assisted him the other night."

"Did he even thank you?" Sam shifted the visor of his baseball cap around to the back.

"Barely. But I've got to give him this . . . he's a damned good surgeon. I was impressed."

Sam didn't say anything, so Cassie looked out the window. "What's it like in winter here?"

Sam looked over at her. "Trying to change the conversation?"

"Not really," she said, still staring out at the town of Augusta Springs. "As far as I'm concerned I exhausted it. I've nothing more to say about Chris Adams."

"It's cold. Nights in winter can be frosty. As for the rest of the year, as you can already see, it's dusty." The entire area had a constant pink glow to it, the effect of perpetually swirling dust. "When there are dust storms you batten down the hatches and still can get a couple pounds of dust over everything. Same with flying. Most of the time a plane can fly itself, but in dust storms, wow! Or when it's really hot, you'll see in a couple of months, then there's lotsa turbulence. There where the Orilla River barely is, in March we can go swimming in it. Look at the way that sand winds its way through the eastern edge of town. We'll take picnics beside it next March and April. Maybe earlier."

"Why are all those aborigines always camped in the middle of it?"

Sam shrugged. "Why not? They don't like living in town, in buildings. You and I got here right after the high point of the year, the river races."

"Boating, you mean? Where? Certainly not on the Orilla?"

Sam laughed. "I should wait and let you see for yourself next year. They copied it from the Henley-on-Todd in Alice. They have bottomless boats, and I understand the decorations are outrageous. It's *the* big event of the year."

As they drove into the center of town, Cassie looked around. In a long, low wooden building was the general store, Teakle and Robbins, Ltd.; the barber was next door. Next to that was one of the town's two butchers, and then a hairdresser and a shoe store. Combined with the pharmacy, there was a milk bar, famous for serving excellent sodas.

Outside of it was the town's single gas pump. On the opposite side of the street was the electrician, and then the fruit and vegetable store, an airline office, a pool hall, and a hostel—mainly occupied by government workers who hoped they wouldn't be in Augusta Springs long enough to buy a home. On the next corner was Addie's, and next to it the picture show and the veterinary office and lab. Beyond that was the office of Doctors Adams and Edwards. Further down was the saddlery, combined with stockmen's clothing and boots. The last building housed a building materials center, the other butcher, the one dress shop, and a Chinese restaurant. Over in the next street was the school, through the sixth grade. It, like the AIM hospitals, was two stories high, and the gymnasium dominated the ground floor. Near it was the court house, which contained a single jail cell, occupied mainly by several drunken aborigines, incarcerated for a night. Next to it was the hotel, an attractive building on the outside, but rundown inside, with peeling wallpaper. Transients who could find no room at Addie's turned to this as a last resort. Its single claim to fame was the stand of towering trees from which it had taken its name, "The Royal Palms."

"Royal, indeed," Sam muttered as they drove past it.

"A bit pretentious," Cassie agreed.

"Do you need a defender?" Sam asked as he stopped in front of the Adams'.

Cassie shook her head, thinking it was a nice gesture on Sam's part. Nicer than she would have expected. "No, he's never there. I'll read to Isabel for an hour, and she'll probably tell me that Dr. Adams appreciated my help Monday. He never talks to me directly."

"I'm going to stop and see if Fiona will shout me a beer," Sam said. "Want me to tell her you'll be late?"

"Just let her know where I am. Dinner's in the fridge if she gets too hungry to wait. It's all cold. I should be home before six-thirty." So, Sam was stopping in to see Fiona?

Isabel and Grace were waiting. Grace had watercress sandwiches and pound cake on the table next to the chair where Cassie sat. She ran to get tea as soon as Cassie arrived. What Cassie noticed, however, were Isabel's eyes, filled with pain. Wasn't she taking the morphine? There was no reason to suffer so.

"Oh, we're so glad you're back." Isabel reached out her thin arms in welcome. "We can hardly wait to go on. We refused to peek to see if Ashley is going to renounce Melanie once he hears Scarlet loves him."

In half an hour the little alarm clock next to Isabel rang. She shook her head, so unaware was she of anything but the story Cassie was reading. "Time to take my medicine," she said.

Grace arose and went to the kitchen. She returned in a minute with a hypodermic syringe. Isabel would be asleep soon. Grace sat back down.

Cassie had continued to read barely five more minutes when the front door opened and in walked Dr. Adams, carrying his black medical bag. He looked as fresh and neat as though he had just dressed. Cassie could tell from the paper in which it was wrapped that one of his bundles was from the butcher's. He disappeared into the kitchen but returned before she finished her reading, standing in the archway between the living room and the foyer, a glass of something tall and cold in his hand, listening to her read, watching her.

Cassie could see Isabel's eyes glazing, thanks to the morphine. She closed the book.

"Tomorrow," she said, "barring emergencies."

Grace's eyes sparkled. "This is the highlight of our day." She stood up, nodding at Chris. "Evenin', Dr. Adams. Guess it's time for me to get going." She leaned over and patted Isabel's hand. "Tomorrow morning." She picked up her purse from the mantelpiece and left.

Isabel sighed. "A nap," she said, hardly able to hold her eyes open. "Just a little one before dinner." She and Chris had not exchanged a word.

Chris put down his glass and went over and picked her up, carrying her from the sofa to the bedroom, where he laid her on the bed and covered her with a light blanket.

"Don't close the door," she said.

"Of course not," he said. "I never do."

When he turned to Cassie, he asked, "Join me in a cold drink?"

She shook her head. "I really must be going, too. I have to fix dinner for Fiona."

"I make the best Tom Collins around," he said. "You're not on duty at night, are you?"

Cassie smiled. He was trying to be pleasant. It was his way of telling her he appreciated her help. "Well, maybe, but then . . . "

"I just bought the two best steaks in town. Isabel is never hungry enough to eat. I'd hoped you'd join me. Not that I'm much of a cook," he said, "but I do know how to broil a mean steak and I'm pretty fantastic at chips."

"How can I say no to such an offer?" She really wanted to go home to Fiona—but he was making such a heroic effort. "Let me phone Fiona."

Fiona said, "Your airman's here. I'll offer him your dinner."

"Horrie's going to check on someone at seven. If he wants me, you know where I am. I won't be very late."

"My, my. So Chris is making amends, huh? He knows he's got a better ally in you than with that sot Edwards. Don't give an inch. Make the bastard work for every smile."

Cassie laughed.

She walked out to the kitchen where Chris was broiling steaks. Lettuce, tomatoes, and onions were sitting on the porcelain table in the center of the room.

"Want me to make the salad?" Cassie offered.

Hunched over the broiler, Chris nodded. "Fine."

He was not a man of many words, Cassie decided. She wished there were some green peppers. Maybe she'd start a kitchen garden, grow some herbs, too. They certainly never seemed to have much in the local store. She'd order some seeds: spinach, radishes, peppers, onions. She'd start a garden out behind the kitchen window, where it got shade in the late afternoon.

Chris flipped the steaks over. "How do you like yours? Just don't tell me well done."

"No, medium to rare. Not bloody, though."

He took some silver out of a drawer and walked over to the kitchen table. "I suppose if I were to thank you adequately for your help the other night I should fly you to Sydney's best restaurant."

"I'm glad I was able to help. It was a grisly operation. I had never seen an amputation before."

"God, I hate them. Most of the time patients can't accept it psychologically. They think their missing legs pain them, they refuse to look where a hand used to be. They never feel quite whole again. But that guy, he's amazing. He's already joking about it. Says it was his own damn fault and next time he'll be more careful."

Cassie placed the salad on the table.

Chris leaned down to the broiler and slapped the two steaks on a platter. She noticed he'd cut out the tenderloin from the one on his plate; he was saving it for Isabel.

She fished around for something to say. He didn't make it easy.

"How long have you been out here?" she asked, as she sat down.

He shrugged. "About eighteen, nineteen years, give or take a couple. We came right after I graduated."

"What in the world made you come?"

He glanced at her. "What makes any of us come out here, or to places like it? Into the Back of Beyond. It sounds surreal, doesn't it? I imagine everyone out here and in every town and on every station of the Outback is a bit off-center. Some of them are way out. You'll see. You'll run into a lot of them out beyond even this pale of civilization. Izzie and I thought we'd come out here for a couple of years, no more than three." He laughed, but it was a mirthless sound. "We thought it would be an adventure."

"Has it been?"

"I don't know that that's the word for it. I haven't done much adventuring. After about a decade I advertised for a partner and Jon Edwards showed up. Together we raised enough money for the hospital, got us some nursing sisters. We've grown along with the town. There weren't more than a couple of hundred people when we arrived."

"These potatoes are great. So's your Tom Collins."

He nodded, without looking at her.

"Why did you stay?"

Now he looked up. "Inertia."

She smiled. "Certainly not. You don't seem lazy."

He shook his head. "I'm known here. I've put energy into this town and I don't have that kind of energy left anymore."

Cassie looked at him. He mustn't be past his early forties. Where had his vigor gone?

"So, you're off-center, too, I gather?"

He reached up and took off his glasses, rubbed them on his tie, put them back on, and said, "Square peg in a round hole is more like it."

The phone rang. It was Horrie. "Sam's on his way to pick you up. Think you better talk to Mrs. Dennis. Kid's running a high fever, over 105."

Cassie turned to Chris. "I have to leave. But thanks, thanks a lot."

They heard Sam's steps on the verandah stairs. He stood in the doorway, baseball cap pushed back on his head. "Ready?" He barely glanced at Adams.

Just then Isabel's thin voice called out, "Chris?"

Chris headed to the bedroom and Sam turned and walked quickly down the steps.

"Horrie's worried," said Cassie.

"Yeah, well, he was worried about a heart attack that never was, too." Sam started the utility.

They reached the radio station in less than fifteen minutes.

Horrie was waiting. "Told Mrs. Dennis we'd call back at seven thirty-five. Wait three more minutes."

Cassie could tell from the woman's voice that she was near hysteria. "Rosie won't wake up." There were tears in her voice. "She's burning with fever."

"Do you have any ice?"

"No."

"Dampen washcloths and towels and lay them on her. Keep her as cool as you can." She turned to Sam. "Can we fly out at night?"

He cocked his head to the side. "Unlikely. Here, let me ask about landing possibilities, though I don't know where the hell the place even is."

No, they didn't have a cleared landing site. Yes, they were surrounded by trees. They only had one car so they couldn't use their headlights to light a landing field, though there was a level field about three-quarters of a mile away.

Sam handed the microphone back to Cassie. "No way," he said. "We could leave here before dawn, but it'd have to be light by the time we got there. I think it's about an hour by air."

Cassie repeated this to Mrs. Dennis and said they'd make contact at five a.m. to see if they were needed.

At five, when it was still dark, Mr. Dennis told them they were still worried sick. The girl's temperature had gone up to 106 and she had completely lost consciousness.

"Let's leave," Sam said.

Cassie had barely slept, worrying. She had wanted to leave at four-thirty, when Sam picked her up to drive out to the airport, but he wanted to perform a thorough engine check, followed by a cockpit check, paying attention to the gyro-operated instruments, and said they needed to wait until it would be light enough to land. "At least we have a lighted runway for takeoff," he said.

"Airspeed and rate of climb will take care of themselves if the plane's climb attitude is right." Sam seemed to be talking to himself.

Cassie thought it seemed immeasurably lonely, flying into blackness. They climbed to eight thousand feet and then droned on into the northeast. Cassie wondered how Sam knew whether they were flying right side up or upside down. She felt weightless, disoriented except for the thin line of dawn to the east.

They arrived at six sharp to learn the girl had died fifteen minutes before.

"If we'd gotten here half an hour ago," Sam asked, "could you have saved her?"

"Who knows?" Cassie answered, wondering if one ever got used to death.

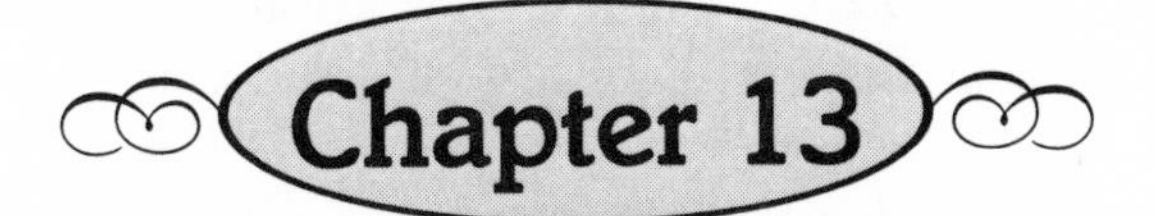

Chapter 13

"But everyone goes to the Saturday Night Dance."

"Not everyone does," Cassie said. She wanted to stay away from men in a social way. "I'm tired. I've had a rough week. I want to shampoo my hair and not talk to anyone and read a book."

Fiona, standing in the doorway, looked over at Cassie, who was slumped against the pillows on her bed. "You got problems?"

"What is that supposed to mean? Can't I do what I feel like doing?"

"Of course, sure. But people are going to be disappointed. This place is so lopsided with men. They ride in from miles around just to get a peek at a woman. It takes all their courage for some of them to ask for a dance."

Cassie said, "I'm sure they can get along without me. I need time to myself."

Fiona shrugged. "I've got a feeling it's more than that. But, so be it."

"Well, I can suggest something that should please you. I asked Sam if we could fly out to Burnham Hill next weekend. We were going to go Wednesday, but I thought if we flew out on Saturday you could come. He was agreeable. How about you?"

"Oh, Cassie!" Fiona came into the room and bounced onto the bed. "That's super. I'd love to!"

"Okay, then don't nag me about the dance tonight. Or any Saturday, okay?"

"You dance, I know you do. Sam told me you were terrific."

"He probably just wanted to brag about himself."

"Don't you two get along? I mean . . . "

"As far as I know, we get along fine. He's an easy person to work with, although he resents working with a woman."

"I think he's over that. He respects you."

"And that's just where I want it to stay. I respect him, too."

Fiona stood up. "Okay, I'll go have fun and you'll stay here and waste away."

"Do you realize what I've done this past week? Aside from having no free time because of Tookaringa and Narrabinga last weekend, I spent Monday at Yancanna, got Horrie and Betty married, assisted in an amputation, and on Wednesday flew out on an emergency only to find the girl dead when we arrived. Then I had a clinic on Thursday and I think I must have pulled about two dozen teeth this week alone . . . "

"Okay. Okay."

But, after Fiona left, Cassie wandered around the house restlessly. She shampooed her hair, but she couldn't make herself sit still long enough to read. Around eleven she wandered, in her old terry cloth robe, onto the verandah, and sat staring out into the dark until she could see the leaves on the trees down the street. Music, coming from Addie's three blocks away, filtered through the night air. The cry of a saxophone engulfed her with a feeling of terrible loneliness. Maybe she should have gone with Fiona.

Yet she knew that simply being with others would not alleviate the feeling of isolation she seemed to carry within her. She'd thought—for far too brief a time—that maybe at last she'd belonged with someone, felt that she was the most important person in the world to someone, that maybe she fit with someone. But Ray Graham had shown her it wasn't true. She was alone, after all.

Despite the friendliness of everyone up here, Cassie knew this was but a waystation. She'd go away after a year or two and, shortly thereafter, no one would remember her name. "Oh, yeah, that woman doctor." No one would mourn her leaving their lives . . .

Someone was walking down the street, quick definite steps. Cassie peered out into the night from the vantage point of her chair. It was Chris Adams, striding along, looking neither to the left or right.

As he passed in front of her house, she called out, "Good evening, Chris."

He stopped abruptly, peering in her direction. "Fi? Is that you, Fiona?"

"No." She didn't get up from the chair. "It's I, Cassie."

"Oh, good evening," he said, and she swore if he had a hat on he'd have doffed it, so formal was his manner. "What are you doing at home on a Saturday night?"

"Are you taking your evening constitutional?"

"I guess that's what you'd call it." He stood there for a moment, but in the dark she could not see his face. "Well, good evening." He started his swift march again, heading down the street toward the end of town.

Strange man. Awkward in social conversation. Never giving an inch about anything. He was even abrupt with his patients, a bit condescending. M.D. as God. A common syndrome. She wondered if ice water flowed through his veins.

Falling asleep as she held the book she'd tried to read all evening, she awoke in the morning with it sprawled on the floor and her covers in bunches, as though an army had marched across her bed. Tears had dampened her pillow, and she remembered why. She had dreamed of Ray Graham, felt his lips on hers, remembered how it felt with his arms around her.

Never again, she told herself. Never, ever again.

They only flew out once that week and that was to a clinic at one of the stations, where the owner's wife was seven months pregnant. Their other three children, all under five, had never been vaccinated. None had even seen a doctor as they were over two hundred miles from town. Cassie also inspected the cook's ingrown toenail and the sprain of one of the jackaroo's ankles. From there they flew to a neighboring station, where Cassie found herself setting a dog's broken leg as well as vaccinating the children there, including three aborigines. The nanny had had diarrhea for three days, so Cassie insisted she return to Augusta Springs with them. The poor young woman could barely stand. Sam helped her to the stretcher in the plane. Most of the time, when they were on the ground, he just stood around, talking to everyone. Wherever he was, Cassie heard laughter.

On Saturday, when Fiona was free from her teaching duties, the three of them breakfasted in Addie's before flying south to Burnham Hill, a sheep station of over two million acres. Sitting at a table near them were Heather Martin and one of her sisters.

Sam leaned across the table, his voice low. "Damnedest thing last night. The Martin girls knocked at my door and said they were in town and didn't know where to stay. Could they stay with me?"

Cassie raised her eyebrows.

"No, no," Sam grinned. "I got them a room here, at Addie's. They drove their old utility all the way to town to see me. I told them we're flying out today."

Cassie laughed. "You can't help it if they find you irresistible."

"Well, they are good-looking, but I *am* the only man they've even seen, except their father and the delivery men."

"They're gorgeous." Fiona had been studying the young women.

"I told them to go meet Cully," Sam said. "He's a great cook and they want a cook."

"He's not likely to leave here to go live in the country," Fiona ventured.

"Yeah, well, there are five more like that at home," Sam said.

Cassie waved at Heather and her sister, and the girls rushed over to the table.

After introductions, Fiona suggested, "You should attend the Saturday night dance tonight—there'll be an abundance of young men."

Heather hadn't stopped looking at Sam. "You going to be there?"

He nodded. "I suspect so."

"Okay, we'll go," said Bertie. Or was it Billie?

As they flew, Cassie watched Fiona, who had scrunched up on the floor of the plane, as near as she could get to Sam, listening to him in rapt attention.

"Okay, you'll have to kneel to look out the window," Sam told Fiona. "See, these are cumulus clouds. Whenever you see white ones, those that look like castles, that are bunched in big puffs looking like cotton candy, they're always high . . . those are cumulus. Well, they're safe while they stay up high, far above land, and continue to roll and swell, but they become hazardous when they build to a huge towering solitary rounded mass that lowers itself close to earth."

Cassie looked out the window, watching a falcon swooping, climbing, diving, flying along beside the plane. Sam began his descent. This must be a larger place than she'd expected—there were dozens of cars and trucks, more than she'd seen anyplace except Augusta Springs.

Sam turned his head and called back to her, "Well, look at this turnout! Everyone for a hundred miles must be sick!"

Fiona pushed herself up from the floor and crawled back to the seat behind Cassie, strapping herself in.

"I never suspected flying was this exciting."

"It's not always, when you're just sitting here for a couple of hours."

A car was chasing a herd of horses across the landing ground. They circled and pivoted, galloping in an ever-wider circle as the truck chased them. Sam proceeded toward the landing strip anyhow, heading right into the oncoming herd, which swung past the plane, on either side of it, in a cloud of dust. God, he had nerve.

The plane came to a smooth stop, and Cassie could see that rocks had been cleared from the ground, for they were gathered along either side of the airstrip. I wouldn't make a very good pilot, she thought. I'd be too careful. Sam took chances she'd never dare. "I think you get your kicks out of courting danger," she called to him as the plane halted.

Grinning, he jumped out of his seat. "Well, ladies, here we are. Burnham Hill, biggest sheep station you're likely to see."

"Looks like a town to me."

"Nope." He opened the door and kicked the steps into place. He jumped down and held a hand up to help Fiona. Cassie stood in the doorway a minute, surveying the crowd of people. It was a beehive of activity.

A tall, lean man, wearing the creamy white riding breeches favored by sheepmen, shook Sam's hand. Cassie walked down the steps.

"This here's Dan Mason," Sam said as he introduced them. "He owns Burnham Hill."

"Where did these people come from?" Cassie asked.

Mason waved his hand. "Some of them have come from the opal fields, near three hundred miles away, and camped here overnight. Others are from every neighboring station around here, from as far as seventy-eighty miles. The blacks have come from the hills mainly, and the railroad people who live along the tracks, they all joined together and came in that truck that looks like a bus. We have a full day here for you, Doc."

Doc again.

Cassie said to Sam, "We haven't seen this many people all together in our first month."

"Need help?" he asked.

She shrugged her shoulders. "Why? Do you want to flirt with the pretty girls? Go on. I'll call if I need you."

Sam gave her a funny look and leaned over to say something to Fiona before walking away.

Dan Mason said, "When we began to realize, early this morning, how many people were comin' in, we set up this tent, which we usually keep for parties, to ward the sun off. Knew you couldn't stand in the sun all day. M'wife, Nancy, she'll be down from the house pretty soon. She's trying to fix a meal for all these people. Says if you need something, let her know. Like water, or anything at all. We got this table set up here, too. What else do you need?"

"This is fine," Cassie said.

"Can I do anything?" Fiona asked.

"Sure. I need medical records on each patient. Want to keep them for me?"

"I'd love to." Her eyes were shining as Cassie handed her a notebook.

Cassie gave inoculations and pulled more teeth. She had had no idea that so many people suffered from toothache—it seemed to be the overriding ailment of the Outback. Someday, maybe, they should think of bringing a dentist on trips. She lanced a boil, and wondered why all the aboriginal children had sore eyes and running noses. Flies gathered around their eyes, infecting the already-contaminated areas further.

There was a strep throat, a broken ankle, torn ligaments, upset stomachs, bruises, burns, a broken arm that hadn't been set properly, and three pregnant women, whom Cassie said she would examine in one of the bedrooms, if that was all right.

At one o'clock Nancy Mason came down from the house, wiping her flour-dusted hands on an apron that covered her ample body. "Dinner's on," she cried. "It'll have to be buffet style. I don't have enough tables and chairs for all of you." But she did have enough food.

There was an enormous ham at one end of the long table that had been moved from the dining room to the verandah. "Form a line over here," Nancy instructed them, "and it should go pretty smooth." She turned to Fiona. "I hope to heavens there's enough. Who'd have expected forty-four people to show up?"

There were scalloped potatoes and large loaves of homemade bread. There were trays of relishes and a mountain of cabbage, carrot, and apple salad. There was a parsnip and carrot bake and sliced tomatoes, green beans with slivered almonds. On another smaller table were five cakes. Nancy answered Cassie's unspoken question with, "These cakes were brought. I didn't do any of them. In fact, all I did was the ham and the potatoes."

"This is real neighborliness," said Sam. "You're not used to this, huh?"

Not in Washington, D.C. or London or even San Francisco. Cassie listened to women exchanging recipes, and talking of spending enforced weeks in the city—Adelaide or Brisbane, once in awhile Augusta Springs—awaiting the births of their babies. Men, gathered in clusters at the opposite end of the porch, talked sheep and horse racing. She looked down on the narrow strip of lawn that surrounded the freshly painted white house and saw Sam, his ubiquitous baseball cap jammed into the pocket of his pants, with his arms around two girls, grinning while they laughed, looking up at him.

It would take until after dark to fly back to Augusta Springs. "We can make it," Sam said. "They have lights at the airfield. It's not like landing at a station, where they're not prepared for night landings. They have a beacon, too."

But Nancy and Dan Mason talked them into staying overnight. Sam checked in with Horrie, and there were no emergencies. No calls of any urgency at all.

"We can leave early in the morning, if that's what you'd like," he said to Fiona and Cassie.

"What about the Martin girls? They'll be disappointed." She'd meant to sound teasing, but it didn't come out that way.

Sam squinted his eyes and looked at her. "I don't want a woman to choose me. I prefer to do the choosing."

"So, a man always has to do the leading?" Her voice had a hard edge to it.

Sam leaned over and picked up a blade of grass, sticking it in his mouth. "Sure."

"Isn't this fun?" Fiona asked as she joined them. "Thanks so much for inviting me. I'm having the time of my life. I didn't know flying could be so—oh, I don't even know how to say it. So exhilarating." Fiona wasn't even tired. "I had no idea your life was so filled with . . . well, I imagine you never feel lonely, do you? All these people just ready to love you for helping them so. You're part of their lives the minute they meet you. That's how I feel about walking into a classroom. I'm going to be part of those children's lives forever, whether they remember my name or what I teach them or what my face looks like."

You must never feel lonely . . . Cassie mused.

At six a.m. a cowbell clanged noisily. Cassie had been lying in bed, trying not to move so as not to awaken Fiona. Now, she punched her arm.

"Hey, time to get up."

"Mpf," murmured her friend.

Cassie swung her legs out of bed and looked out the window. Was every dawn in the Outback glorious? She donned the clothes she'd laid over the back of a chair and ran her tongue across her teeth. She hated not having a toothbrush with her. She would put one in her medical bag so she needn't have a mouth that felt like a bird's nest when they stayed overnight unexpectedly someplace. Pulling her boots on, she looked in the mirror above the dresser and reached for a comb, brushing it hastily through her hair. She didn't even bother to put lipstick on before walking out to greet the dawn.

Dan Mason was already outside, talking to his foreman. Dust rose around the hooves of the horses being rounded up and saddled by three of the jackaroos. Cassie took off across the spikey grass to a ridge about a quarter-mile to the east. She saw Sam already giving the plane a once-over.

Although it was light enough to see clearly, the sun had not yet broken over the horizon. As Cassie crested the hillock, hoping to see the sunrise, she was surprised to observe a creek winding its way between banks of tall gums. Behind the line of trees the sun rose. Not as dramatic as it would be if there had been clouds, or even a large amount of dust, it was nevertheless startling in this landscape. Cassie could see to the horizon in every direction. It was flat, flat, flat. When the immense orange ball rose, sending blinding rays, like tentacles, across the land, the whole landscape was covered with the golden glow that presaged another day with no escape from the heat.

Cassie wondered what summer here must be like, if three minutes after sunrise she could feel so hot in early October.

"Makes you feel holy, doesn't it?" Sam's voice came from behind her.

The cowbell clanged again.

"Guess breakfast is ready. Then I'd like to take off. It *is* our day off and I've got things planned." He watched her walk down the ridge and then followed, shaking his head.

Chapter 14

"Sam's going to teach me to fly," Fiona said excitedly. "Isn't that marvelous?"

Cassie glanced up from cutting vegetables. "What brought that on?"

Fiona poured herself a cup of tea. She'd just come in from playing tennis with Sam and looked a picture of shining health. "I told him flying seemed to me like a romance and how I'd fallen in love with it that time we went to Burnham Hill. You know, at night I lie in bed and close my eyes and see myself up there, floating in the air, like an eagle. He said, 'If you feel that way, I'll teach you how to fly.' My first lesson's going to be Saturday. I'm so excited."

Cassie placed the carrots in a pan and, not looking at Fiona, asked, "Is there something between you and Sam?"

"Yes." Fiona's eyes shone. "And it's brand new to me—friendship with a man. I don't know that I've ever had a male friend before. I mean a *real* friend. We like each other, but there's no chemistry, if that's what you mean. But I have a wonderful time with him. We talk about everything."

Cassie turned to face her. "Can you really be close friends with a man? I doubt it."

"Oh, Cassie, stop taking it out on yourself and all men because you've been rejected. I had a miserable love affair, too. Who hasn't? It's taken me years to get over it. But I think we're all richer for it. What abominable beings we'd be if we never experienced that. How could we empathize with others? I'd wish a bit of unhappiness and at least one rejection for everyone. Keeps us humble, too."

"Oh, screw that. I'd be a much better person had I never been treated the way Ray treated me."

"You might be happier right now, but I bet you're growing from the experience," Fiona argued. "The way you feel is not Ray's fault," she argued. "So, he was a bastard. But rejection doesn't end our lives. It's how you've reacted that's made you bitter. Now you don't let yourself trust *any* men. You deny yourself so that you won't get hurt again. Cassie, you're a lovely, beautiful person most of the time. You let your hair down with me and you're at ease with other women. You're wonderful with children. From all I hear, you've got a great bedside manner. Patients love you. But, you hide from attractive men who might tempt you."

Fiona reached out and put a hand on Cassie's arm. "The wall you build around yourself, between you and men, is almost visible."

"Hey, I'm pretty happy with my life right now."

Fiona sat in the straight back chair, the only one in the kitchen. "You're nicer to Horrie than to Sam. And you're nice to Steven Thompson because he's old enough to be your father. But wait til you meet his son. Blake's going to threaten you, and how, and you'll be even more aloof with him than you are with Sam. Do you realize you act like a man when you're with men who might be attractive to you?"

"You're off base. I have reasons to be aloof with men and not all of it has to do with Ray Graham. I had to fight my way through med school. Do you know that every anatomical class I ever had they made snide jokes about women, and they'd look at me to see if I could take it." The memories of that time tensed her. "Do you know how much men are threatened by a woman in what they think is their province?"

Fiona tapped on the table. "You know what? I'm not even sure the sexes like each other. I think we feel threatened by the opposite sex. They make us unsure of ourselves. But we *are* attracted to them. Maybe it's as elementary as sex. Maybe it's the desire to feel we're the most important person in the world to someone else, and it's likely a man we're going to spend our eternities with. Maybe it's because we're two parts of a whole. Yin and yang. And we may not *like* each other but we can love each other, we want to see ourselves as beautiful in a man's eyes. We play games with the opposite sex, but not with our good friends. Yet for thousands of years men and women have not felt complete unless they've a member of the opposite sex in tow."

Fiona was right. Much as she knew she built walls around herself whenever an attractive man entered even the periphery of her life, some part of Cassie was all too aware that at those same moments she wondered how she looked, if her hair was combed, if she still had lipstick on, if the man was looking at her.

"I don't understand it, Cassie. I *like* women better. I can become closer with my women friends, though certainly I don't talk like this with most of them. Only with you and Ally . . . " Ally was Fiona's younger sister. " . . . Can I talk about these things, Fiona went on. Only with you and Ally can I say, yes, I've slept with a man and not been married to him, and Jesus H. Christ, I liked it. I loved it. And part of me still loves the guy, though I don't like him very much now."

Cassie sighed. "Fiona, you're about the nicest person I've ever known. Even when my mother was alive I couldn't talk with her this way."

"Oh, Cassie, we never tell our mothers what we're *really* like because we care about their approval too much. My mother would have a shitfit to hear me say shit. But with a good friend, we unclose ourselves and that helps to solidify the friendship. We can be honest and true and then we look for that in a man, hoping he'll be our best friend as well as our lover, and it just doesn't happen. We have to please him. We don't have to please our friends. Don't get me wrong. We have to nurture friendship, and give time to it, and we have to cherish it. It's the one area of life where we can be our true selves."

"I think you're the first real friend I've ever had," Cassie said.

"I've had good friends all my life, but never one like you. I'd never told anyone else the things I've told you."

Cassie walked over to Fiona, reaching down to put a hand on her shoulder. She leaned down and kissed Fiona's cheek.

"I came to the Outback, running away, to escape. And instead, I may be finding myself, thanks partly to you."

Just then the phone rang and Fiona jumped from her chair. She was back in a moment. "It's for you. An emergency from Tookaringa."

"Not the radio at the station?"

"A direct call. Horrie told them where you were."

Since the few telephone lines in the Outback were simply strung along fences and trees, the system did not always function.

Jennifer's tone was urgent. "Cassie, thank God. We've a problem here. Steven's not here, but talk to my son, quick."

An unfamiliar male voice started talking. "We were playing tennis when our guest, Eva Paul, threw down her racquet and began clutching her throat, stamping on the ground, spitting. A hornet had flown in her mouth and stung her. This happened not fifteen minutes ago. It stung her on the back of her tongue. Her tongue's swollen and she's having trouble breathing. She's in a state of panic. We're giving her cold drinks and ice to try to stave off the swelling."

In the background, Cassie could hear Eva's labored breathing.

"She's turning blue, her face and lips are a pasty color, and she's sweatin' like a stuck pig."

Oh, dear God in heaven, Cassie thought.

"How soon can you get here?" Blake Thompson asked.

"By the time I can get there she'll be dead. You'll have to perform a tracheostomy."

"What?"

"You'll have to perform . . . "

"I'll have to do what?"

"Now, listen carefully. Swelling in the epiglottis blocks off the entrance to the trachea and can result in death by suffocation or choking. You're going to have to cut an opening into the trachea just below the Adam's apple."

There was silence at the other end.

Cassie continued. "While we're talking get someone to sterilize a small, sharp knife, quickly, and find a short piece of rubber tubing, maybe in the barn. Maybe you have one for siphoning gas. Hurry!

"Listen to this carefully so you understand. At the base of the tongue is the pharynx, below which the throat is divided into two tubes. One is for swallowing food and fluid, and the other is for air. That's the trachea. It has a flap valve which closes when food's being swallowed. Swelling obstructs the passage to the trachea; she'll suffocate or choke to death unless something is done quickly. If we were in a hospital a tube could be passed into the trachea, but you're four hundred miles from a hospital."

"The only operations I've performed are castrating young animals."

"Either you do this or she'll die, and I mean within minutes. She'll soon be comatose from lack of oxygen. Put your mother on the phone and while I'm talking to her, drag the sofa close to the phone. Get some of your men in there immediately. You'll need strong men to help hold her down."

Jennifer's voice came over the line. "All right, Cassie, he's pulling the sofa over, but I think Eva is passing out. Oh, my Lord! Thank goodness we do have two other strong men here. What can I do?"

"You can stand there and hold the phone to Blake's ear or relay every word I say to him. Now, if the sofa's close to the phone where he can operate and hear me, too, get her head and neck jutting out over the arm and get the strongest man in the room . . . "

"That's Blake."

"The next strongest, then." For heaven's sake, don't quibble, Cassie wanted to shout. "Get the strong man to hold her head between his hands, so tightly that no matter how much she may jerk she can't possibly move. Tell him not to look at what's going on, so he can concentrate on just holding her head and nothing else. This is absolutely critical. Now, have Blake run, I mean *run*, and wash his hands and get back here to the phone with a sterile knife."

Jennifer's voice came back on the wire. "Cassie, he'll be back in a minute. Oh, my dear . . . "

"Don't say it, Jenny." She turned to Fiona, who had come to stand next to her. "Get me a chair, will you? I'm going to be on the phone awhile."

Blake's voice was back on the line. "I'm here."

"Give your mother the phone and she'll repeat to you every word I say. Don't hesitate or the girl will be lost."

"Okay," said Jennifer.

"Have Blake feel for the Adam's apple and start a vertical cut half an inch below it. The cut should be about one and a half inches long.

"As soon as he starts to cut and is positive he's right in the center of the neck, exactly in the middle, have him keep cutting until air flows out. Don't worry about the bleeding. As soon as you get air gushing in or out the bleeding will slow down."

In the background Cassie could hear the girl's labored breathing.

"She's gone blue and her eyes have rolled back like she's dead. She's unconscious." Jennifer's voice was filled with fear.

Blake said to his mother, "I think she's gone."

"Tell him to keep going. Make sure, really sure, that he's in the very middle. And stay there. If he's sure of that he'll have to cut through the windpipe whether she's dead or alive."

"She's breathing again," said Jennifer.

"Then something's terribly wrong," Cassie realized she was shouting. "Either he's gone to one side or he's not deep enough. Make sure he's right in the middle."

"He's opened the windpipe and air's gushing in and out. Oh, God, there's blood all over!"

"Good. Place the tubing into the hole. Cover the area with clean cloths, handkerchiefs, or napkins. Put a large safety pin at a ninety-degree angle through the part of the tubing that protrudes so it doesn't slip down her windpipe. Is she conscious?"

"Yes, and having the tube inserted is painful."

"Tell him to put his fingers on either side of the cut to plug the bleeding, and keep the hole dry. It doesn't matter where the blood is going or how much is lost as long as none of it goes back into that hole!"

There was a moment's silence before Jennifer said, "The blood is just oozing now."

"That's fine. Someone will have to take turns sitting up with her all night to make sure the tube is all right. It's nearly dark so we can't possibly fly out. But we'll leave here by dawn and be there a bit after nine. She should be all right. Give me the doctor again," she said, a smile in her voice.

Blake's voice responded. "Here," was all he said.

"Good job."

"Yeah. Well."

* * *

At nine twenty-two the next morning they landed at Tookaringa. Blake Thompson met them at the landing field in the utility. He stood leaning against it, his big Stetson shadowing his face as Sam pulled the door of the plane open. Blake walked toward them with slow, big steps, his high-heeled boots scuffed. He walked as a man used to days in the saddle, yet there was a grace about him, almost leonine. He reached out to shake Sam's hand.

"Blake Thompson."

Sam nodded, and Cassie imagined he was introducing himself to Blake, though, with his back to her, she couldn't hear what he said.

She reached out her hand before she was off the steps. "Dr. Thompson?"

Blake laughed. "You sure knew what you were doing, leading me through that."

They started walking to the truck.

"How's the patient?"

"Seems okay. She slept a lot. Doesn't seem to be in pain this morning."

God, he was good-looking, even more so than his father. Well, what had she expected with parents as handsome as his? He was large-boned and towered over her. He must've been a good five inches taller than Sam. Maybe six-four. Broad shoulders.

"With a bit of squeezing, three of us can fit in the front seat," he said. He held the door open for Cassie. She slid to the middle of the seat, while Sam placed her medical bag in the back.

"I'm glad I was at a phone," Cassie said. "Another few minutes and she'd have been dead."

Blake stepped on the brakes in front of the house and turned to look at her. His eyes were a cobalt blue.

Sam said, "You go ahead. I'll bring the bag."

Cassie ran up the steps and into the living room where Jennifer sat next to the patient, who was sitting up. After an examination Cassie announced, "I couldn't have done better myself. The swelling's already gone down, and when we get her back to the hospital we'll remove the tube. Tomorrow we can close this opening. You'll hardly see it," she assured the young woman.

"Have you had breakfast?" asked Jennifer.

"We can't stay," Cassie said. "We have another call to make and I want to get this young lady to the hospital."

"She's visiting from Brisbane," Jennifer said. "I better get her clothes and bag and she can take the train or a plane from Augusta Springs when she's out of the hospital. She was going to do that anyway."

"I better gas up," Sam said to Blake, both of them standing in the doorway.

"Follow me," Blake said. "Can you taxi the plane to the pump?"

"If not, we can fill drums and load it that way."

Jennifer said, "I'll get Eva's belongings and drive her and Cassie out to the garage, so we won't hold you up."

Sam nodded as he and Blake took off.

After Eva was strapped into her seat in the plane, Cassie took the seat next to her. Blake jumped in and hugged Eva. "Sorry for the rotten luck."

She smiled weakly. "Thanks for saving my life."

He looked over at Cassie before he ran down the steps. Sam slammed the door and went to the cockpit.

As they taxied down the field Cassie observed Blake and his mother, standing watching the plane, he with hat in hand, both of them waiting there until they looked like small specks.

As they flew out of sight, she thought, *So that's Blake Thompson.* Eyes of sky blue.

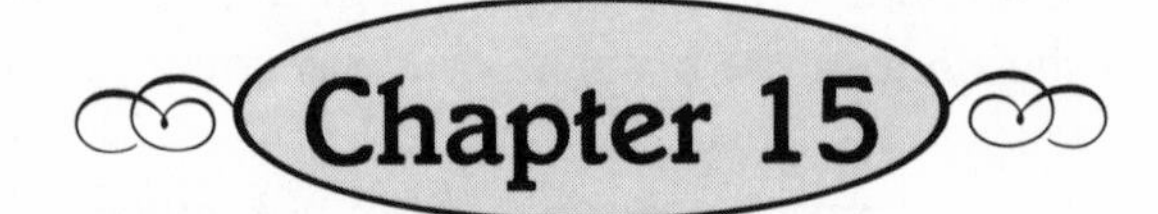

Chapter 15

They'd arranged for their regular Tookaringa clinic to be held the day of New Year's Eve. Cassie had heard that people came from as far away as Sydney and Melbourne to Tookaringa's famous New Year's Eve parties.

She had urged Fiona to come along, since the Thompsons had invited her, too, but Fiona begged off. She didn't give a very good reason, considering how fond she was of parties.

"It'll be the gala event of the year," Cassie had said.

Fiona waved a hand in the air, as though dismissing such a thought. "All the more reason to stay here and help light up Addie's."

"You've never even seen Tookaringa."

Fiona nodded. "It's not high on my list of priorities. I can see Jennifer and Steven whenever they come to town. No one will miss me. Don't nag me about this, Cassie. I don't want to go."

"But why not?"

Fiona stood up and walked towards the kitchen. "I have my reasons."

Fiona had helped Cassie make a new dress for the party. Certainly she couldn't find anything glamorous in Augusta Springs. Now she wondered if she'd be overdressed.

"If you don't want men in your life, why wear a dress like the one we've just made?" Fiona asked.

"You're keeping yourself from enjoying life," Fiona continued. "After it happened to me, I knew I couldn't go on living that way, cut off from the world. The only ones I was letting into my life, into my heart, were my students. But that wasn't enough. I finally decided I'd let everyone in. My heart's big enough for everyone. And once I started doing that, it became much easier."

"You let *everyone* in? But you'll get hurt again."

Fiona shrugged. "Maybe. But not as much. Not as much as when one man owned my heart, my mind, my every breath. My heart's so crowded now that no one person can control it. And, Cassie, I swear it's healthier than the way you go about it, not letting any man at all in. You must be the only single woman for a thousand miles that men aren't clamoring to date. And if you'll look in the mirror, certainly the men who judge by looks alone should be lined up outside our porch. But you say no man's even made an overture in the months you've been here. You intimidate, Cassie, that's what you do."

"I don't mind." She slid the new pink chiffon dress over her head and pirouetted in front of the full-length mirror on the back of the closet door.

"Look at you!" Fiona's voice was filled with admiration. "You don't even have to get involved. Just treat 'em like ordinary human beings. Don't make them feel inferior. Be a little nicer to men, Cassie. I don't intend to get involved, at least not for now, but it sure is fun to flirt."

"I've never known how to do that."

"You're always so serious. Now, don't get me wrong. That's also one of your virtues. A doctor should be serious, I guess, so people'll have faith in him. Her. But you don't always have to act like you're a doctor. Now, go on up to Tookaringa and let loose on New Year's Eve."

Maybe she would. She hadn't yet seen a man she should protect herself from out here. They were mostly like Sam, preferring silly, giggling girls who looked up at them worshipfully. Who kissed them out behind barns while she held clinics. Sam was okay to work with. No, he was better than that. He'd become fine to work with. He flew the plane and didn't talk to her too much, not unless he wanted to point something out that he thought might interest her. He helped uncomplainingly when she needed it. He was pleasant to the people they came into contact with, more than pleasant. He seemed to get to know them on a first-name basis. He remembered who had how many kids and where they'd come from before arriving here. He knew how long they'd lived on their stations. If they were drovers he remembered who they worked for. He knew how big each of the stations was, and he recognized landmarks in a personal way. *Down there's the road Dick Highland built with his own hands.*

Or, *See that cairn? It's been there for over seventy years. A stock route runs through there, and long ago some drovers piled stones and created that mound on it to signal to others that water's there.*

Or, *Matt Warden's shipping out six thousand cattle this year.*

But he didn't talk much about himself, and he didn't ask her much about what it was like growing up outside Australia, about her past. Aside from knowing that he played tennis with Fiona and gave her flying lessons on weekends, Cassie had no idea what Sam did in the time they weren't together, though she heard people speak of him. The men liked him. He sat around Addie's evenings, shooting darts and drinking beer, listening to the yarns that the drovers told, participating in the life of the town.

She could also tell that the girls were crazy about him. But he didn't favor any in particular. "He's with a different one every Saturday night," Fiona told Cassie after she'd come home from the dances. "He's not leading anyone on. And, wow, is he a dancer! He makes me feel as light as air when I dance with him."

"If you're not careful, you'll fall in love with him, even if you think it's platonic. It happens when you least expect it."

Fiona thought a minute. "Not likely. I really do treasure Sam as a friend, period. But if I do fall in love, I do. If I never open myself to the possibility of being hurt again, I suppose I never open myself to the possibility of ecstasy, either."

"You're not consistent, you know."

"I'll quote one of my favorites, Ralph Waldo Emerson. He said '. . . consistency is the hobgoblin of little minds.' " She laughed. "Never let it be said that I have a little mind."

"Or a little heart." Cassie wished she were more like Fiona.

After the clinic, at four, Jennifer said, "It's going to be a late night, in case you want to take a nap after working all day. You look like you could use one."

Cassie nodded gratefully.

"Do you want a snack to hold you over? We won't be eating until late. How about a cold lamb sandwich?"

As soon as they'd landed, Sam had bounded off. "He's out in the kitchen," Jennifer said, pointing toward the low building visible through the glass that surrounded the swimming pool. "I think it's the new cook. She's cute as a button."

"I thought your cook was a man."

"Steven fired him. If someone can't learn to broil a steak rare after a year, Steven said there was no hope. This new girl has all the boys coming up to the kitchen as often as they can. She not only cooks wondrously well, but has a smile that would light up a dungeon."

Well, that's where Sam would head for sure.

"Come tell me if my dress is a bit much for this party."

"Nothing's out of place at one of our parties. Mary Ellen Fonteyn will put us all to shame. And the rest of the people from around here wouldn't know style if they saw it. You can wear anything. I'll love you no matter how you look, as though you could look anything but stunning."

Cassie didn't see herself that way.

"Blake's in from the bush for a couple of weeks for the holidays. I think you two will hit it off."

"I hope not too much, Jenny. I don't have room in my life for a man right now."

"You don't have to marry him," Jennifer said.

There were over a hundred people at the party. A dozen of them were staying in the big house, and Cassie had already met several of them. An orchestra was out on the lawn so that all the space on the verandah and in the living room could accommodate the dancers. Lanterns were strung, and even the palm trees had Christmas lights wound around them. All the members of the Augusta Springs Flying Doctors Council were present, with their wives. Even Don McLeod had arranged his itinerary so he could attend. Cassie was delighted to see him. She decided she better not follow Fiona's advice and cut loose. She had a reputation to preserve.

The Tookaringa parties, the two she'd attended, were the first ones she'd really enjoyed. Aussies were the nicest, most hospitable, open people she'd known. Americans had a reputation for friendliness, but they were pale in comparison to these bush people who treated you like they'd known you forever, pulling you right into their lives. It was a good feeling.

"How about a dance?" Steven's voice came from behind her. "Someone's got to get it going."

He took her hand and led her across the lawn, up the verandah steps, and into the screened portion that opened into the living room.

"Sad song," he said, "but danceable."

Cassie recognized it immediately . . . "I'll Never Smile Again."

He held her lightly, humming along to the music, as he moved smoothly across the floor. "You're a big asset to this region, you know."

"I hope so," Cassie said, easily following his lead. "I like it here."

"Even those of us who wondered about the viability of a woman doctor have been won over."

"Oh? You weren't enthusiastic about the idea?"

Several other couples moved onto the dance floor.

"Did you think anyone would be? There are still many—only those who haven't had to deal with you yet—who are skeptical about a woman's ability to diagnose or operate properly. But you'll win them all over eventually."

"I hope you're right. They don't have any other choice, do they?"

The orchestra segued into a fast tune. "How do you dance to this?" Steven asked. "Do you jitterbug or do the Big Apple?"

Cassie started to answer when Sam appeared. "Sorry, Steven, this has to be mine." He grabbed Cassie's hand and began swinging her out. Last time there'd been a party here they were the star attraction on the dance floor. This time, they captivated an audience, too, but several other young couples joined them. Sam made it seem effortless, and she could follow wherever his footwork led without even thinking about it.

When the music finished, Sam said, "Come on. Let's find a cold drink."

But Cassie's eyes were riveted on Blake Thompson, leaning against the door frame. He stood straight as a gun barrel and was staring at her, a look of amusement on his face.

Sam followed her gaze. "Uh, oh," he said.

Cassie, in thinking about it afterward, didn't remember if Sam had disappeared, if he had turned to someone else, what happened to him. He ceased to exist. So did everyone else.

No, she thought. No. Just no.

Blake threaded his way through the dancers and reached for her hand, putting his other one around her waist. He didn't say anything, but drew her close and began to dance, looking down into her eyes. She could feel his body against hers, feel the next step before he took it.

For a moment all she wanted to do was run, wanted to find Sam and say, *Let's leave. Let's fly out tonight.* But she felt Blake's leg against hers, felt his firm hand pressing the middle of her back.

"Shall I tell you what I know about you?" he asked, his voice like smooth stones in a pool. "Your competent veneer covers a soft heart. You're an idealist. You fought every inch of the way in a man's world and now you're afraid to show your femininity. But you can't hide it. You have a woman's body that moves like a woman, and you have been hurt by some man. You're not going to let any man take advantage of you again."

She missed a step and nearly fell over his foot.

"And I imagine when you kiss you put all of yourself into it." He pulled her closer, so that their bodies moved as one.

Cut this out, she told herself. Shape up. Don't dare let him do this to you.

"And what do I know about you?" She tried to sound flip. "With a line like yours, you must leave a string of broken hearts all over the countryside."

Her body came alive in Blake's arms.

As the music stopped, he took his arm from around her, but he did not let go of her hand. He started walking from the verandah, leading her through the screen door. "Come tell me why you have an American accent, and why a pretty lady like you is a doctor instead of being married and a mother."

"What about you?"

"All you really need to know about me right now is that I'm the next man who's going to kiss you."

They had reached the long table that served as a bar. "What do you want to drink? A lemonade?"

She laughed. "How about a beer?"

He grabbed two bottles from the table. "I imagine you don't even require a glass, do you?"

"What makes you think I'll kiss you?"

His face was serious. "I doubt that either of us has a choice about what happens in the next twenty-four hours. Maybe after that we will, though I'm not sure. I knew it the minute I saw you. You knew, too. I could tell when you saw me tonight you felt the same way."

She wished the feeling would go away. But it didn't. Her blood flowed more quickly through her veins, and a pulse in her neck began to throb. She reached her hand to still it.

Brushing the spot with his fingers, Blake said, "Later, I'll kiss it."

Chapter 16

Wherever she was, in whoever's arms she was in as she danced the night away, he watched her. At midnight, he came back to her, taking her in his arms as though she belonged there, not saying anything, holding her so close she could feel his heart beating. The length of their legs moved together, and she looked at the hand that held hers, his left one. It was scarred.

He saw her looking and said, "Burns. A long time ago." He watched her mouth. He was going to kiss her, he'd said, before the evening was over. A kiss wouldn't hurt, would it? One kiss.

He stopped dancing in the middle of the song and took her hand. "Come on. Let's walk down to the billabong."

The music followed them down the slope of lawn, into the darkness. Blake did not stop, but held Cassie's hand, surefooted as he walked in the night. He must've come down here many times at this hour, perhaps as a boy for a midnight swim.

A crescent of moon outlined the towering gums along the water's edge. He stopped beside them and turned to look at her. She could dimly see his features. "My Reverie" floated across the night air, the orchestra mellow.

He pulled her to him, his arms encircling her. Looking down at her, he said, "I may possibly have been waiting for you all my life," and his lips were upon hers, tender, soft until his tongue ran across her lips, opening them, urging her. Cassie didn't even want to resist. Her mind ceased to function except that she realized she had never been kissed so thoroughly.

He kissed her ear and the pulse in her neck, his kisses feathering across her cheek until his lips met hers again, and she heard herself sigh.

Unexpectedly, he laughed, and broke away from the embrace, taking her hand again and pulling her to the water's edge.

"Okay, tell me," he said.

"Tell you what?"

"Everything. I want to know everything about you."

She could still taste his mouth upon hers. "You'd find me really uninteresting."

"Don't start this relationship on such a ridiculous premise. I know better and you know better. I want to know why the American accent. What made you come to the Outback, why you're not married, who you are, what you feel and think. Why a doctor. I want to know what men you've loved and if you have brothers and sisters, and what your relationship is with that pilot. I want to know if you can ride a horse and how you feel living over a thousand miles from a city. What you feel about aborigines and a new moon. If you like dogs, and let's see, have I covered everything of importance? I think so."

"How about whether or not I believe in God?"

He laughed. "Look up at those stars."

The tropical sky was studded with diamond points. "I keep telling myself that some night I'm going to sleep out under them," she said.

"Some night we will. I spend a good part of my life doing just that. They are God. Look at that moon. It is, too. I don't have to ask you a question like that."

Her body was alive. She wanted him to kiss her again.

"I grew up in England and San Francisco. My father's in the diplomatic corps, our Ambassador in Washington now. My mother had just died and I didn't want him to be alone, so I went to Georgetown University and then on to Johns Hopkins Medical School. I hadn't lived in Australia since I was six years old. I've only been back a little over a year and a half."

"Why aren't you married?"

"Why aren't you?"

"Fair question," he nodded, holding her hand more tightly. "I don't have an answer. Until tonight I hadn't met anyone I'd consider spending my life with, or even sleeping under the stars with. Now, your turn."

"The one man I thought I loved went back to his wife."

Blake was silent.

"What else? I forget all your questions. Oh, yes, I've never met a dog I didn't like, and I do ride."

"Aborigines?"

"I guess I can't give you an answer to that. Ask me if I like your mother or Mr. Highland or someone in particular and I can tell you. But a whole bunch of people? A whole race? I have to judge them individually."

He was quiet a moment, staring at her as a cloud, sailing across the sky, hit the moon, darkening their faces. "Well, Cassandra, I think we're in for the long haul." He leaned forward, his mouth meeting hers. She felt his tongue and wanted it on her breast. She wanted to feel his lips surrounding her nipples, feel him bite her gently, feel his tongue against her body.

She pulled back. "Hey, slow down," she said, aware that she was trembling.

"Okay. We have a lifetime."

Stop it!

He reached for her hand.

"How did you know so much about me?" she asked, as they began to walk up the gentle rise toward the brilliantly lit house.

He laughed. "You mean about being hurt? It's that look you wear. An angry young woman. At the same time you keep your eyes veiled, as though that'll ward off danger. Yet you're as vulnerable looking as—a wounded deer." His hand tightened around hers.

The strains of "Frenesi" drew them into the party's gaiety.

"It's a good orchestra," Cassie said.

"We import them annually from Adelaide," Blake said. He stopped and turned her to him. "I was right, wasn't I?"

"I don't even know you well enough to tell you anything, really."

"Don't give me that bullshit," he said, his eyes piercing her. "We already know each other better than we've known most people in our lives. It's only the details we don't know about. They'll be fun to discover, but are really irrelevant."

From across the lawn, Jennifer waved at them. Sam and the cook were nowhere to be seen.

Hadn't Fiona warned her? Hadn't she said, *Tonight you'll meet the son and heir, Blake. Be careful. He's left a string of broken hearts all over the countryside, maybe all over the continent.*"

Arriving at the table, still laden with food, Cassie reached for a plate, helping herself to slices of ham. She looked around desperately, wanting to get away from Blake Thompson—yet at the same moment, all she wanted to do was feast her eyes on him. See if he was real. She turned to speak to him, but he wasn't there. She saw him down the table, talking to some man she didn't know, but staring at her.

"Want to know what I found out about him?" Don McLeod's voice came from behind her. Plate in hand, he wandered over to her. "I can't find anyone who doesn't like him."

"What are you talking about?"

Don grinned at her and ate for a minute before continuing. He looked more like a roustabout than a Presbyterian minister. "Even the men who work for him think he's close to walking on water. He can outshoot any of them; see a buffalo in the high grass at two hundred feet and get it with one shot. He can outwrestle any man he meets and make the bloke like it. He can outdance anyone here. He doesn't ask any of his men to do anything he won't do, and he'll do it with more bravado and daring than any of them will, and they don't even resent it. He doesn't seem to be afraid of anything. He's also got a sense of humor . . . "

"Whoa," Cassie said and couldn't help laughing. "What makes you think I'm interested in all this?"

"Listen," Don said as he placed his empty plate on the table. "I haven't spent this last half-hour playing spy to let all this information go to waste. Are you going to listen or not?"

"Okay," she said, grinning at him, "but I don't know what for."

"He can outrun, outshoot, outyarn anyone else. He works as hard as his hired hands do, he graduated with honors from the University in Sydney. What he cares mainly about is Tookaringa. He loves his mama and daddy, but is hardly ever here. He thinks big. He likes living outdoors and goes on six-month cattle drives for the sheer joy of it. He's as famous for his way with the ladies as with men and cattle. He is to be trusted with everything he touches except women. And from what I hear he touches a lot of them."

Cassie's eyes narrowed. "Are you trying to warn me?"

Don's eyes were serious and he put a hand on her arm. "All I'm telling you, my dear, is that the bloke's pretty great, like his parents. But I'm also telling you to be careful."

"Don," Cassie began, pleased he cared so much, "I appreciate your warning; in fact, I'm even touched you'd go to all this trouble, but I'm quite capable of taking care of my own life."

He nodded. "I knew it was none of my business. I can tell I was right by the look in your eyes."

"Don, I've just met him!"

"And I've known it would just take the right man, and you'll . . . oh, forget it, Cassie. Dance with me? I may be the only man here who hasn't had that pleasure tonight. You know, if it weren't for Margaret . . . "

Cassie leaned over to kiss his cheek. "Yes, Don, I do know. If it weren't for Margaret . . . " She moved into his arms. She had been letting her defenses down far too quickly. "I appreciate your caring."

She hadn't slept until eight-thirty in years. When she came downstairs, Blake was standing on the porch, waiting for her. His ten-gallon hat set firmly on his head, he moved slowly towards her, his legs hard and muscular in their tight pants and concertina leggings. He took off his hat, tossing it on a table.

"Has everyone eaten?" she asked.

"I waited." His eyes were riveted on her.

"I'm starved, ready for some of those famous Tookaringa cinammon rolls," she said, as she headed to the dining room, trying to still the hammering of her heart. The rolls were gone so she settled for scrambled eggs and bacon and strong chicory-tasting coffee.

A cat appeared and jumped on Blake's lap. Absentmindedly he stroked it. "It's fate, you know."

She looked at him for a long time. "Blake Thompson, you don't even know me. But let me tell you something. You were right about me. I got hurt. I had a real unhappy experience. It happened last year and maybe I'm still recuperating. You're going too fast for me. I'm not ready for this, this coming on so strong. I don't trust it, and that makes me not trust you."

He reached across the table and put his hand over hers. "Your having been hurt makes this all the more important, doesn't it? Okay, Cassandra, we'll play it your way, but you must already know this is no ordinary thing."

She remembered his kisses.

Just then, Sam came bursting in. "I've just been talking with Horrie. You'd better speak with him, too. He thinks we have an emergency down at Bagley Waters."

"What's wrong?"

"You better speak with him. No one seems to know what it is."

Cassie, Blake, and Sam ran out to the plane, and Sam got Horrie on the radio.

"Don't know," said Horrie. "The daughter out at Bagley Waters is mighty sick. They thought it was flu or appendicitis. I told them you'd call in exactly fifteen minutes. Okay? I'll put you through. You wait right there."

Cassie grasped the microphone. "Where's Bagley Waters?"

Sam reached into an oilcloth-lined bag and drew out his map.

"It's about five hundred fifty miles southwest," Blake said. He'd followed them to the plane and was standing in the doorway. "Bill Miller runs it. Helluva fine man. One of the best stations I know of."

Sam received Horrie's signal.

"Okay," Horrie said, tension in his voice, "I got you connected with the Millers."

A man's voice crackled over the air waves. "Dr. Clarke?"

"Mr. Miller? What's the problem?"

"We don't know. For two days my daughter, Sara, she's had a little bit of nausea, a little bit of diarrhea. We thought at first she'd come down with the flu, then maybe it was her appendix. Wait a minute, my missus wants to say a word."

"Dr. Clarke? Maybe it's her period at a weird time? She's been bleeding a bit." She paused for Cassie's comment.

Cassie was puzzled. She turned to Sam. "We better go find out what's wrong. We might have to take her into the hospital."

He nodded. Too bad. He and the cook had planned on a picnic after she'd prepared lunch for everyone else.

"We'll be there," Cassie said. "Here, the pilot will find out about landing from you and tell you when we'll arrive."

She handed the mike to Sam and stood while he talked, hearing him say, "It'll be six hours, anyway."

"Does this happen often?" Blake asked.

"No, this is the first time."

"You're not coming back today?"

Sam had hung up and was studying the map. "No way."

"Bagley Waters will have gas," Blake assured them. "You need any from here?"

Sam shook his head. "Just finished filling up before I talked with Horrie. The plane can only carry enough for four hundred miles. I'll load up some drums just to be safe." He turned to Cassie. "You ready?"

"Of course not," she answered. "I've got to get my bag and say goodbye to Jennifer and Steven."

"They're out riding with some of the guests," Blake said. "I'll tell them." He reached out to help Cassie down the steps.

"I'll be right back," she said to Sam as she began to trot toward the house while Blake strode along at her side.

As soon as they arrived at the house he reached out a hand, stopping her, turning her to face him. He pulled her close, looking into her eyes, and said, "I want you to remember this." He kissed her, and Cassie felt herself swirling, engulfed by the passion he ignited in her.

"Remember that," he murmured.

Then he walked ahead of her to her room, waiting while she threw her clothes into a suitcase. He reached for it and took her hand, striding so quickly that Cassie had to run to keep up with him all the way to the plane.

As Sam slid the stairs up, Blake reached up to shake his hand. "See you again."

Sam nodded his head. "Sure." He slammed the door and slid into the cockpit seat.

Cassie watched out the window as this man who'd plummeted into her life became but a dot on the earth, and then finally invisible. She closed her eyes and Blake's face danced before her, his electric blue eyes smiling at her.

We already know each other better than we've known most people, he'd said. She sighed as she remembered the touch of his lips on hers.

Chapter 17

Bagley Waters, though not quite as large as Tookaringa, was big enough to have five outstations. Cattle roamed in the north and west, and in the southeast there were ten thousand sheep. Unlike Tookaringa, where trees and scrub country were predominant, Bagley Waters was filled wide, with undulating downs covered with thick grass. Along its numerous dry watercourses, which intersected each other, were mulga, gums, and Mitchell grass. It was part of the Channel country whose rivers gathered water far to the north during the spring rains and raced south, eventually flowing into the usually dry Lake Frome. Well watered by Artesian bores, it produced some of the finest grassland in the world. Even with most of the riverbeds dry, it was still watered by one river that never dried up. Only in years of extreme, prolonged drought was Bagley Waters in trouble. It produced some of the finest merino wool in the country and, therefore, in the world.

A fence of red and pink bougainvillea surrounded an orchard of peach and lemon trees. Cassie also observed grapevines and date palms and, nearer the house, gardens lush with flowers.

Several cars and trucks raced around a rectangle, outlining the landing field they'd prepared. Cassie couldn't even tell at which point the plane touched the ground.

A man about fifty, wearing a red and white bandana around his neck and a bush hat, greeted them. The first words he said, when he saw Cassie standing in the plane's doorway, was "Sara's sicker'n shit."

He grabbed her bag and began racing toward his utility, swinging the passenger door open, waiting for Cassie to catch up. Sam jumped in the back. The house was a quarter-mile away.

"She's got a pain in her belly and has been sick at her stomach, throwing up just a little and then being okay for a couple hours. We can't figure out what it is."

From the symptoms they'd described on the phone, Cassie couldn't either. "How old is the girl?"

"She'll be seventeen come March," he said. "She's our youngest."

The southern horizon stretched into infinity, a blending of earth and sky, while red sandhills rose to the east and north. The homestead, a monstrosity rising three stories high, looked out of place, standing like a sore thumb, a lonely sentinel in this flat land.

Bill Miller stepped on the brakes so hard Cassie nearly hit the windshield. "Sorry," he apologized, grabbing her bag. "Sara's upstairs."

"You want me?" Sam asked as he swung his long legs down from the truck.

"Come along," Cassie answered, following Bill up the steps. They rushed through the immense foyer with its high ceilings and ran up the winding staircase. In one of the bedrooms Bill's wife, Marian, sat beside her unconscious daughter. She jumped up as soon as they entered the room.

Cassie went immediately to the girl on the bed.

"She's been complaining of very severe stomach pain," Marian said. "And she started bleeding a lot about an hour ago."

Cassie looked at the sleeping girl, pale and sweating, in shock. She turned to the girl's parents and Sam and said, "Wait in the hall, please, while I examine her."

Within minutes Cassie could tell it was an ectopic pregnancy.

"Is it appendicitis?" asked the mother, when Cassie appeared in the hallway.

"Looks that way," Cassie answered. "If I don't operate immediately peritonitis will set in."

"Operate?" Marian's hand flew to her mouth. "Here?"

"There's no time to get her to the hospital. Sam, come in here. Mrs. Miller, boil me water. I need clean sheets and an area in which to operate. What about the kitchen? Do you have a long table there, or can you move one in? I'll give you half an hour to get it as clean as humanly possible, and to have water boiling." These emergency operations under non-sterile conditions always made her nervous.

Marian stood and stared at Cassie, until Cassie went over and took her by the arm. "Do you understand?"

Marian shook her head and ran out the door.

"Sam. I need you."

When he walked in the room, she closed the door behind him.

"The girl's pregnant," Cassie said, "and I'm sure her parents don't know. Maybe *she* doesn't."

He glanced at the girl on the bed.

"She's probably barely a couple of weeks or so, but it's an ectopic pregnancy."

"Huh?" He scratched his head, looking at Cassie.

"It's where gestation is someplace other than the uterus . . . a Fallopian tube, perhaps, or in the peritoneal cavity."

"What's a peritoneal cavity?" He was always interested enough to ask questions.

"It's the smooth, transparent, thin, watery membrane that lines the cavity of the abdomen and is . . . oh, never mind. It's just not a natural condition and requires immediate surgery. She's in shock now and will be dead if I don't do something quickly. I've told her parents it's appendicitis. I'm not going to have them punish this girl any more than she's being punished right now."

"What if she has appendicitis years later?"

"I'll take her appendix out now," Cassie said. "I'm going to need you as anesthetist."

"I suspected as much. Better wash up, I guess."

"And help them get the kitchen in shape. Quickly. Time is of the essence."

An hour later she cut the girl's belly open, splitting the skin and then the muscle layers. When she entered the peritoneum there was a gush of blood. "I'd like to suction this out but I don't have anything. I'll have to mop it up. Hand me those gauze sponges." As Sam did so, she swept the blood away. "Ah, look. There's the bleeding lesion—you can see it in one of the tubes of the ovary."

Sam leaned over to look.

"It's the one that looks like an angry purple veil, the one with a bleeding gash where the blood's clotting at the opening." As she explained, her hands worked deftly. She placed clamps on either side of the tube to stop the bleeding. She removed the lesion, tying up the end of the tube closest to the uterus.

Sam looked up at her when he heard her sigh with relief.

"Safe?" he asked, trickling another drop of ether onto the mask.

"More of those gauze sponges," she said, soaking up the remaining blood. Then she examined the other side of the uterus and the ovaries.

"What are you doing now?" Sam asked as she probed further.

"I'm reaching up to feel the intestines and the liver and the spleen to make sure there's no other lesion or any problems in the belly. But the minute I identified and clamped off the ectopic I was sure there'd be no further blood loss. Essentially she's out of danger, except for shock. We'll have to load her up with lots of fluids. But, first, I better remove this appendix."

With retractors she pulled apart two large muscle bands. "I hate doing two surgical procedures in one operation." She grasped the colon with Alice forceps and pulled it back and forth until she could see the healthy appendix right at the end of the secum. Cutting away the fatty tissue and blood vessels, tying them so they wouldn't bleed, she passed a blade between the clamps so the appendix came out.

She reached for silver nitrate to sterilize the area, then stitched a ring around the base of the secum. She pushed the stump of the appendix down into the secum while tightening the loop of sutures, closing the hole.

"As soon as I finish sewing her up, get some water and we'll drizzle it into her mouth on a cloth."

Sam watched every movement as Cassie slowly sewed back the layers of the peritoneum, the thick, woody fascia, the muscle layers, the fat layers, the skin.

As always, after an operation, her shoulders ached with the release of tension.

"How can you be pregnant someplace other than . . . "

Cassie shrugged her shoulders, her usual reaction when she had no answer. "One of nature's freaks." She pulled off her bloody rubber gloves. "The egg gets fertilized in the tube and ordinarily floats down to the uterus. This one just didn't make it all the way down."

She closed her eyes.

Sam reached over and put his hand around her wrist.

"You've got a lot of faults, Cassie Clarke, but you're one helluva nice person."

She looked at him. "What brought that on?"

"Not telling her parents."

"I hope so," she sighed, pulling her gloves off. "Now, I'll go tell them she's okay, and to give her liquids. We better stay overnight. If not, we'll take her to the hospital with us."

"Of course," he said. "Just so's they can feed us."

Fiona was waiting for her when they arrived back in Augusta Springs in mid-morning.

"Why aren't you in school?" Cassie could hardly wait to tell her about Blake Thompson. She'd thought of little else on the trip back from Bagley Waters.

But Fiona had other news. "I received a telegram from my mother," she said. "My father's been given four to six months to live."

"Oh, Fi," Cassie grabbed her hands.

"I'm going home. I can get the noon train tomorrow, be in Sydney in three or four days, then catch a ship."

"But your job?"

Fiona broke into tears. "I can't think about that. I just can't. They'll have to find someone else."

Cassie put her arms around Fiona.

"I've already started to pack. You'll take care of the house, won't you?" She didn't wait for an answer. "Oh, God, it'll be awful in Ireland right now, in winter. I swore I'd never spend another winter in the northern grey latitudes."

They sat drinking coffee together as Fiona reminisced about her father. Finally she asked, "How was the party? You must have had a great weekend. I expected you back last night."

"We had to fly down to Bagley Waters for an operation."

"You mean you spent the day working? Here I thought you were having fun. You finally met Blake Thompson, didn't you? Did he sweep you off your feet?"

Cassie didn't think this was the time to go into details. "He is a rather commanding presence, isn't he?"

Fiona laughed. "I guess that's one way of putting it. Tell me, was the party terrific?"

Cassie nodded. "It was wonderful. I don't know when I've had a better time." Or been more perplexed, she thought.

"The people here *are* super."

"Well, they're certainly the friendliest people I've ever met."

"What about Blake? I had a feeling the minute he saw you he'd come on strong. Did he?"

"He has that reputation, you mean?" Cassie's heart sank.

"Oh, honey, new girl in town—especially a good-looking one—everyone takes for granted she's Blake's before anyone else has a chance."

"And then?"

Fiona shrugged. "Then other blokes can have their turns, but not until Blake's through. Usually it doesn't take too long."

That's what she'd been afraid of. It wasn't her. It was just anyone new, anyone he hadn't tried before. *I can't say I haven't been warned.*

"You're telling me he's not to be trusted?"

Fiona got up and rinsed out her cup. "I think he's one of the most respected men in the territory. Certainly he's the most popular, not only with women. He's got a way with people, all people. I'd trust him with money, but not with my heart."

Cassie asked, "Are you speaking from personal experience?"

Fiona's back was to her. "I'm smarter than that."

Lying in bed, later, Cassie thought how much she'd miss Fiona. Four to six months. That's a long time, she thought.

She closed her eyes and remembered Blake's lips upon hers. Felt his arms around her. She was disgusted with the alacrity with which she'd responded to him, yet even now, twenty-four hours later, when she thought of him her heart beat faster. If she saw him again she'd be more careful.

When she remembered Sam had told her she was a nice person, she hugged herself. Sometimes it didn't seem that he thought so, that he thought she was a good doctor but didn't know much about being a woman. She smiled again until she remembered he'd also said, "You've got a lot of faults, Cassie Clarke . . . "

She sat up in bed. What had he meant, *a lot of faults?*

Chapter 18

The room smelled like death.

Isabel's hands were balled into fists, appendages at the end of her matchstick-thin arms.

Cassie closed *Rebecca.* It had become a chore to come and read in the afternoons.

"I'm so glad Maxim loved her," said Grace. "Wasn't Rebecca an awful woman, though?"

"Isabel, let Grace get you the morphine," Cassie suggested. "There's no reason for you to suffer so."

Isabel opened her eyes and shook her head.

"No," Grace said. "She told me she's going to die beholden to no one and nothing."

Cassie didn't know whether to admire her or think her foolish. She looked at the woman, hardly making a dent in the pillow on which her head rested. Her skin seemed to hang on her arms.

Cassie stood up. "Tomorrow we'll be out on a clinic run, so I won't be over unless we get back very early, which is doubtful. At least it's not an overnight." Actually, she enjoyed the overnights. Everyone was so hospitable. "But next time I come, how about an Agatha Christie?"

Grace nodded. "I love mysteries. And Izzie likes anything. Takes her mind off herself, you know."

Isabel hadn't said anything all afternoon; she just lay on the sofa, her eyes closed or staring at the ceiling.

Cassie tucked the book under her arm and ran down the three steps. The heat of the day hadn't abated much, and she perspired as she walked home, down the main street past the shops and Addie's, on to the other side of town. She was angry at herself.

One night, a couple of kisses, some sweet talk, and she was hooked. She decided she had no character, no backbone. Fiona and Don told her Blake played the field and left them crying. She didn't want a man like that. She didn't even want a man. What in the world made her react to him so strongly? Why couldn't she get him out of her mind? It had been ten days and all she did was think about Blake.

She was sure she'd see him again, and whether that was something she wanted or not she didn't know. His face floated before her when she closed her eyes at night or was reflected in the plane's window as she flew over the red heart of the continent.

She missed Fiona. There was no one to share the day's events with. No one to laugh with. No one to cook for. The house was empty. She hadn't realized how much Fiona's friendship had come to mean. Cassie found herself angry at Fiona for having left her alone. It was not only the house that seemed vacant; her whole life was emptier.

Doctoring had settled into a routine. Tuesdays and Thursdays they flew out on clinic runs. One or the other of these was usually an overnight, so that Wednesday or Friday became a clinic day also. The other days they generally didn't have to fly out because most medical problems could be treated over the radio. Once or twice a week some emergency usually required their flying, perhaps to bring a patient in to the hospital for something like appendicitis, and then, of course, Chris operated. He'd become more gracious, and now invariably asked Cassie if she'd like to assist, be the anesthetist, if it was a patient of hers. He also asked for her help when Dr. Edwards was increasingly "incapacitated," particularly in the middle of the night when an emergency operation was required.

Cassie wouldn't say he'd become friendly, for there was always a tension between them which she couldn't define. They argued all the time. Not about medicine. That was the one thing they agreed about, the one thing they had in common.

Even in that area, Cassie found much in his attitude to be repugnant. Always sympathetic with patients, he was, however, seldom gentle, not seeming to invite confidences.

He couldn't stand anyone who wasn't like him, who wasn't Protestant, white, of British background. He disliked aborigines. "They smell to high heavens. They have no work ethic, no morality, no sense of responsibility. They're pagans."

He wasn't mad for people like the Thompsons, either. "Think they own the world because they own millions of acres, because they can buy anything they want."

One of the things he liked about living so far from cities was there weren't any Jews. Cassie asked what he had against them. "They crucified Christ, didn't they?" She didn't think that made much sense. He did think Hitler was going too far, sending Jews to concentration camps and isolating them in ghettos; he didn't believe in that, but he thought Jews were too smart. Jews in med school always aced courses. They were Shylocks, always entering professions that made lots of money.

He approved of Australia's whites-only immigration policy.

But he didn't believe you had to suffer or die if you couldn't afford medical help. He treated people who couldn't afford to pay for treatment, but not without grumbling.

He was invariably kind to his wife, though Cassie never noticed any warmth between them. Maybe when you see someone dying, someone you've loved so long, you try to protect yourself, she rationalized. Certainly he waited on her all the time, taking care of her himself Saturday afternoons and Sundays when Grace cared for her own family.

Cassie couldn't say she really liked him, but they'd made a truce. He couldn't fault her ability as a doctor, woman or no. He'd even admitted that. Well, not so much admitted. He wasn't the kind ever to admit he'd been wrong about something. But he let her know he thought she had medical sense. He'd observed the results of surgery she performed in the bush when she'd brought patients in to recuperate in the hospital.

She wondered where Blake was. Everything, no matter what she was thinking about, came around to Blake Thompson. She'd been thinking of Chris and then there was Blake. She walked by the saddlery and thought of Blake mustering cattle, riding twelve hundred miles with thousands of cattle over deserts and through mountains, far away from civilization, sleeping under the stars, perhaps singing the cattle to sleep.

She sat on the verandah after she'd finished her supper and sipped iced tea and remembered the feel of his kisses. She lay in bed at night and wondered how it would be to have his hands caress her body.

Stripping off her nightgown, she stood in the dark, looking out the window. Chris was striding down the street, walking in a steady gait as though he were angry, looking neither to the left nor right. Her hands cupped her breasts, for she was filled with longing. In the distance a train's whistle sounded like a moan.

At the eleven o'clock radio session Friday morning a woman's voice said, "My son is in pain."

Cassie leaned forward, close to the microphone. "Explain his symptoms."

"He's bleeding from the rectum."

Her voice was even, no sign of panic.

"How old is he?"

"Six."

A woman of few words.

"Are there other symptoms?"

"He has a bad pain in his tummy."

"Is he vomiting?"

"No."

"Does he have diarrhea?"

"No."

"Does he have a rash?"

"No."

"Does he have a fever?"

"We don't have a thermometer, but he doesn't feel hot."

"How long has this been going on?"

"Since last night."

Cassie shook her head. She had no idea what it could be. She turned to Sam. "Better get directions. Think the kid should be seen."

Sam got on the mike.

Cassie said, "Tell her to prepare a suitcase. The boy may have to be brought in to the hospital. She may want to come along with him."

Sam hung up. "We better get going if we want to get there and back before dark. You be ready in half an hour?"

"I can be ready in three minutes," she said.

An hour and a half later, they arrived at the small shack where the little boy lay in a mussed-up bed. A short, thin man in dirty jeans and an old shirt met them on the claypan near their house. The fence needed mending, and it looked like the house did, too. It was only two rooms, with the inevitable verandah swinging around three sides of it. Cassie saw no animals nearby, no garden, just flatness. Not even a garage.

"I don't think it's that bad," said the man, his voice whining. "What's a little bleeding? But my wife thinks the boy's dying."

"Maybe he is," Cassie said. She didn't like him. Maybe it was that his nose was pointed or that his eyes were little and beady. She wondered what would make any woman come out to the middle of noplace to share life with this man.

In the bedroom the young boy lay listlessly. He stared vacantly at Cassie, but as soon as Sam entered the room, panic lit his eyes and he grabbed the sheet. With her back toward them, the mother stood up, not turning to face them, her hand rising to her right cheek. Cassie could see only her left side as she approached the bed and sat down next to the boy. It was then she looked up to see the mother. The right side of her face was muddled purple, the flesh around her eye black, the eye itself bloodshot, her nose swollen.

She said nothing, but asked the boy to turn over. He began to cry. And she knew, even though she had not seen such a case before, what was wrong.

"It's going to be all right," she said to him, then turned to the mother. "He needs to go to the hospital. Do you have a bag packed? You'd better come, too, or he'll be too afraid." She wanted to get this woman out of here.

The beak-nosed man said from the doorway, "She don't need to go. You can fly the boy back when he's better."

"No," Cassie turned to face him. "The boy may need an operation and he'll be less scared if his mother is there."

"An operation? What kind of operation? How much is it going to cost?"

"I don't know. But this is very serious. Here, Sam, help Mrs. Higgins with the suitcase, and I'll carry the boy." She turned to the lad and said, "I'm not going to hurt you. You're going to be all right. Just put your arms around my neck and do you know what you're going to do? You're going to fly in a plane. High in the sky. I bet you never thought you'd fly, did you? You'll be up in the sky with the birds . . . " As she talked to him she walked, sweeping past the father, going down the one step and walking through the dust ahead of Sam and the mother. The boy laid his head on her shoulder.

"Does it hurt bad?" she asked.

"Not so much," he answered. "Not like last night."

Once she got in the plane Cassie sat holding him on her lap. "Does he do that to you often?"

The boy was silent, tears welling in his eyes. Then he began to cry.

Sam helped the woman up the steps. She held her hand over the right side of her face.

"You come back soon, Millie, you hear?"

She didn't look at the man. "He almost didn't let me call," she said to Cassie.

Sam pulled the door shut. The young boy left Cassie and crawled onto his mother's lap. Sam strapped them in.

"Jesus Christ," he whispered to Cassie as he slid into his seat, revving up the engine. "How could a man do that to a woman? Did you see her face?"

"He must have been doing it to her for ages. I'll bet her body is a mass of bruises, too."

Sam concentrated on take-off. When he leveled the plane out he turned to say, in a low voice, "The kid looks okay. Do you think she just used him as a ruse to get us here?"

Cassie hesitated a minute. "I suspect he sodomized the boy, and has been doing so for a long time. The kid is scared of men. He was afraid to turn over. I imagine his father's been saying that to him for a long time." She could hear it. *Turn over, son.*

When Cassie discharged her patients to Chris, she said, "Mrs. Higgins can't go back to her husband. We've got to find an alternative for her."

Chris raised an eyebrow. "Isn't that up to her?"

"She won't want to go back. The boy's anus has been ripped open by his father. And look at her. She's been beaten for ages. She won't go back."

"The boy'll be in trauma for years. He probably will never be able to have a decent relationship. Sex will scare the hell out of him." Chris took his glasses off, rubbing them against his tie; Cassie was beginning to realize he did that quite often, particularly when he didn't know what to do. "Is this the first case of wife or child abuse you've seen?"

"What do you mean? Of course."

"They always go back."

"Always? You mean this . . . oh, don't tell me that."

"What choices do they have? How will they support themselves and their children? You watch. He'll be in here before too long, no matter what it costs him or how far away he is. And he'll tell her he's sorry. He'll tell her he loves her and that he won't ever do it again. Wait."

Cassie didn't want to wait. Chris was wrong. He had to be.

"Can't we arrest the bloke?"

"If she'll prefer charges. But she won't."

"How do you know?" Was he so damn smart?

Chris sighed. "I'd like you to be right. These situations don't make me very proud to be male. I've seen far more of it than I've wanted to. You'll see lots more of it, Doctor. Out here so far from others. Alcoholism almost always enters into it. The wife-beating, anyhow. Not so much incest. That's sadism. These are sick people who do these things to others . . . aspects of life we're not taught in med school. These and accounting." Cassie realized he was trying to make a joke.

"You'll see," Cassie said again. "She won't go back. She called us so she could get away. You'll see."

"Find her a job. Help her. No matter what you do, she'll go back.

Or, I'll tell you what. If she doesn't, she'll find another man to beat her. Maybe the next man won't sodomize her child, but he'll beat her. It's a circle."

"Oh, Chris, you're so damn cynical. Don't you have any faith in human nature?"

He smiled one of his rare smiles, but there was a touch of melancholy to it. "I wish I were as young as you are and had my idealism intact. It's one of the pleasures of youth."

Cassie didn't think twenty-seven was so young. She was glad she wasn't in her forties like Chris if age was what made you a pessimist.

She'd told Sam not to wait for her—she'd walk home from the hospital. She stopped in the pharmacy and had a soda. Well, unless there was an emergency she was free all weekend. Thank goodness.

As she turned the corner she saw a beat-up dirty pick-up in front of Fiona's. A red one. Sticking out of the window was a pair of equally dusty boots. As she approached it, she saw a man slumped behind the wheel, his Stetson covering his face.

She leaned in the open window and removed his hat. He opened his eyes.

"Blake Thompson. I must say I didn't expect to see you."

He smiled, a slow, lazy smile. "Here I thought you might ask what took me so long." He reached out to take her hand in his. "Took me twelve hours of driving but I thought I'd get here in plenty of time to make sure you're not going to the Saturday night Dance with anyone else."

She laughed. "I've never been to one."

He sat up straight and opened the door, his long legs snaking out in front of him as he uncurled from the cab. "I've a feeling you don't lie, but I can hardly believe that."

"It's true," she said, looking up at him, feeling incredibly happy.

"Well, you are in for a treat," he said. "Come on, let's go to Addie's for dinner."

Cassie nodded. "Let me change my clothes. I've been out all day."

"Fiona home?" he asked, following her up the walk.

"She's in Ireland, or at least on her way there," Cassie explained as she unlocked the door. "You want a beer or iced tea?"

Blake cocked his head to one side and reached out to put an arm around her, pulling her to him. "I want a kiss," he said, leaning over to brush her lips lightly. "Now, beer."

"May I take time for a shower?"

"Cassandra, as long as we are here together, there is no hurry for anything in the world. I don't care if we ever get to Addie's, or anyplace else."

"Why do you call me that?"

"Cassandra? Does anyone else call you that?"

"No. Never."

He grinned. "That must be why. Look, you know already we're going to love like we've never loved anyone. You know that, don't you?"

Cassie turned away and started to walk toward the kitchen to get him a beer.

As she pulled one out of the cooler, Blake was behind her. She could feel the warmth of his body. "You know that, don't you?"

She handed him the beer over her shoulder, not turning to face him.

"Cassandra Clarke, turn around and look at me."

She did.

"You know it, don't you? Tell me you know it."

She sighed. "I do know it."

"Does that scare you?"

She nodded. "I'm petrified."

He grinned in that lop-sided, irresistible way. "Tell yourself you're just beginning to live."

"I'm twenty-eight next month and just beginning to live?" She tried to make it sound funny, but it strangled in her throat.

"We are going to live so hard and so furiously together you'll think you've been dead up til now."

Oh, God. "Is that a promise?" It didn't come out flip, the way she wanted.

"Well, part of that's up to you. Now, go take your shower and I promise not to come watch you. When I get to that stage, we'll shower together. Have you ever showered with anyone?"

No. But she didn't say it.

"We'll build up slowly, Cassandra. Take our time. Don't be nervous. Anything worthwhile, anything that's this big, has risks and should be frightening. Be scared, if you must, but I won't let that stop you."

Chapter 19

"I want you to come up to Tookaringa for a week. We'll go mustering. I'll take you out and let you see how cowboys live."

Cassie smiled. He was probably using the term *cowboys* because he knew she could understand that, having been brought up in America. She still couldn't keep straight who was a drover or a jackeroo or a roustabout. *Cowboy* covered them all. "Sounds like fun. But I can't take a week off. I'm not scheduled for a vacation til I've been here a year. That's not til September."

"If you can't make it a week, see about three or four days anyway, will you?"

"I don't know how."

"Figure it out. We've got to spend some time together, and I want you to see the life I love." He stood up and reached out for her hand. "Come on, let's go to the dance. It's the only public way I can think of to hold you in my arms. You mean you've actually never been to the Saturday Night Dances?"

It was fun except that she saw Blake only half the evening. Between them they danced with everyone there. Sam's eyes widened in surprise when he saw her enter with Blake. He danced with her, when a fast number came along, swinging her onto the floor. "So Mohammed has come to the mountain?"

"What's that supposed to mean?"

He swirled Cassie around him, catching her, their steps in perfect accord. "If you measure interest in how far you're willing to go to see a girl, he must be mighty interested. And he got you to come to the dance, too."

They concentrated on dancing, as usual creating a sensation with their jitterbugging. At the end of the number Blake was waiting on the sidelines, taking Cassie's hand, stretching his right hand out to shake Sam's. "Nice to see you again."

Sam grinned. "You've got guts."

Blake glanced at Cassie and reached out to squeeze her hand.

Just then one of the men threw a bottle that shattered against the wall. Nobody seemed to mind. Instead, others began to follow suit. Cassie looked at Blake.

"Here," he handed her a glass. "Play their game." He threw his bottle of beer, joining the others.

Cassie hesitated a moment. "You've got to be joking."

He grinned. "It's fun. Give it a go." She looked at him a minute and then laughed, throwing her glass as hard as she could, thinking this was really a male society.

"Let's get out of here," Blake said. "Let's go somewhere where I can kiss you."

As they drove along, above them in the velvet blackness glittered thousands, millions of stars.

He reached out and pulled her to him, his arm around her as he drove. She loved the feel of him next to her.

"I've wanted to do this for two weeks," he murmured, abruptly stopping the truck. His lips were upon hers, and every fibre of her being came alive. Her arms wound around his neck, and she felt the heat from his body against hers, felt his strength and his tongue and his breath.

"You've bewitched me," he whispered, breathing into her ear. "I don't think of anything else. You're not like other women I've known."

"You hardly know anything about me." She reached up to kiss his neck.

"What do I need to know that I don't know? At dinner we covered your growing up, your parents, your grandparents, San Francisco, boarding school in England."

They were silent in each other's arms. Then he asked, "How long you going to do this doctoring business?"

"I've signed up for two years here."

His lips met hers again. His hand touched the blouse over her breast.

"You know what I'm going to do? I'm going to take you home."

"It's just midnight," she said.

"It doesn't matter what time it is. It's time to take you home. I swore I wasn't going to rush this and I'm not. And if we stay kissing, well . . . I'm going to take you home."

She couldn't ask him to stay overnight, even to sleep in Fiona's room. The whole town would talk. She hoped he wasn't even thinking of staying, not even on the couch. Part of her was afraid. How far should she let him go? Certainly not as far as she wanted.

As they drove back to Fiona's house, he said, "I've a room at Addie's for the night. But I'll pick you up at seven for breakfast."

"Let me fix it," she said. "I'll get your breakfast."

He walked her to the door and kissed her good night. She watched him walk back down the path, wishing he'd come in.

At ten minutes after seven, while Blake drank coffee as Cassie prepared pancakes, Horrie phoned.

"Cassie, I think we got an emergency. Ian James, you remember him? The one who's mad at you 'cause you wouldn't go running out to see his abo and the guy died? Well, his wife's in trouble. I told him we'd call out to him at seven-thirty. I'll call Sam to pick you up."

"No," Cassie said, "I can get a ride. I'll be there in ten minutes."

Blake looked at her. "Does that mean what I fear it does?"

He wasted no time driving out to the radio station. Horrie and he greeted each other as they waited for seven-thirty. Then Horrie put through the call.

"Dr. Clarke, this is Ian James." A second's pause. "Are you there?"

"Yes, Mr. James. This is Dr. Clarke."

"Sorry to bother you on a Sunday, but my wife's rather ill. I'm worried about her."

"Go ahead."

"She's, well, it's a rather delicate matter."

Cassie wondered what was so delicate he couldn't tell a doctor. "Yes, Mr. James?"

"She's pregnant, three, four months. Late last night she started getting pains and she still has them and now she's . . . ah . . . she's beginning to bleed."

Let's hope he won't act like last time, she thought. "Take her pulse. Do you know how to do that?"

"In her wrist, right?"

"Yes, find the pulse beat. Do you have a second hand on your watch?"

"Righto."

"Count the beat for fifteen seconds, multiply by four. I'll hold on while you do that."

Horrie grinned. "He's not arguing this time, heh?"

"One hundred," said Ian James.

"Take her temperature."

"I've already done that. It's quite normal."

"Now we have to figure out how much blood she's lost."

"She's . . . she's soaked through several . . . sanitary napkins." It sounded as though it hurt the man to say the words. "It's bloodied the mattress and is spotting the floor now. Seems serious to me."

"Mr. James, this *is* serious. We'll fly out to you as soon as we possibly can."

Blake had ridden twelve hours to be with her and she was going to have to leave him. She turned to Horrie. "Get Sam on the phone and tell him to get down here now." She accented the last syllable and looked up to see Blake standing in the doorway.

"Is this what I think it is?" he asked, storm clouds in his eyes.

Cassie nodded. "We've got to take off."

Blake didn't say anything for a minute. "How long you going to be gone?"

Cassie shrugged. "I've no idea. We may bring Mrs. James right back to the hospital or I may be able to do something there." She wanted to stamp her foot or cry or do something other than fly out to Ian James's homestead. "To go there and back, they're not too far from you, are they? About five or six hours. If I have to do something there, longer."

Blake walked out of the shack and over to his truck, little dust balls kicking up behind him.

Horrie said, "Sam's on his way. Says the weather's crook up north."

Cassie walked over to Blake. She put a hand on his arm. "I'm sorry. You know that, don't you?"

He nodded, and turned to her. "Yeah, I do. I do know that. This isn't going to be easy, is it? Our getting to be with each other."

Even though Horrie was looking out the door, Blake put his arms around her. "I'm leaving Tuesday for a month or six weeks in the bush. Got to go to all seven outstations and check on them."

Five or six weeks? Two weeks had seemed like forever.

"Know that every night, every goddamn night, you'll be in my swag with me. And that means there's no way you can kick me outta your bed. I'm going to haunt your dreams."

She looked up at him. Christ, he was beautiful. She loved looking at him. He'd warned her they were going to live fast and furiously. She'd never known anything to happen so quickly. When she was with him she didn't even try to fight it.

"I'll be up at Tookaringa in two weeks on a clinic. Tell your parents that we'll probably stay overnight."

"And I," he said, "will be a two weeks' ride from the house. Well, this isn't going to be an easy relationship, is it, Cassandra?" He leaned down to kiss her. "I knew that night at the party when I saw you sashaying around the dance floor with flyboy that nothing about us was going to be uncomplicated."

Like a whirling dervish of dust, Sam's pick-up bolted down the road. He dashed from the truck, nodding to Blake and Cassie, as he ran into the radio hut.

"You live surrounded by men, don't you?"

"Don't start that," Cassie said. "I don't like leaving, you know. I've had a wonderful weekend. I'm flattered you'd drive all this way for me."

Blake glanced at his watch. "Get used to it. It's not the last time I'll drive to Augusta Springs to be with you. Get used to seeing me, even if it won't be as often as I'd like."

Sam came out of the radio shack, map flapping in the still air. "Cloud base is nearly hitting the ground along the hills north of Magic Creek. We'll have to sidetrack south of the rail line until we get to Innawarra. We've never even been there. But if we head northeast from there," he was talking to himself, "we should be able to find the James's homestead. Christ, they've had over six inches of rain in the last couple of weeks. James says he can't get his utility into high gear and it's already sunk into the dirt once. He doesn't dare bog down if he wants to get us to the house. Damn!" He looked over at her. "I don't think we should attempt anything like this unless it's a matter of life and death. What's your opinion?"

"We've got to chance it," she said. "I'm not sure, losing as much blood as she has, that she'll last the day."

"Well, what's a Sunday without some challenge?"

Blake looked at her. "Florence Nightingale on her mission of mercy."

"Florence Nightingale was a nurse," Cassie said. "And missions of mercy are what the Flying Doctors are all about."

"Sounds noble until it robs me of what I want."

"I just remembered. Run me into town, will you?" Cassie ran up to the hut and called to Horrie. "Call the hospital and tell them I'm coming in to get five units of dried plasma. I want to be in and out of there within five minutes." She ran back to Blake. "Come on, drive like hell!"

When they'd accomplished her mission and were back at the airfield, Blake said, "I may jolly well wait right here."

"I've no idea when we'll be back."

"I'll take my chances. If you're not back by dawn, I'll leave." He leaned down to kiss her lightly.

She ran to the plane; the open door beckoned her.

They hadn't been in the air half an hour when the railroad line, the

"Iron Compass," disappeared below the clouds. "We've got to skirt this," Sam said, heading west instead of north. "I have to fly low so I can identify anything possible."

They flew close to the ground, and when Cassie asked how low they were, Sam answered, "Three hundred feet. It's razor clear here under the clouds, but the cloud base makes visibility lousy. Can't gain any height or we'll be flying blind."

They flew along for another forty minutes before Sam said, "There's Magic Creek. We can head up that until we see a cluster of houses, and with luck we'll turn east there and supposedly fifty miles beyond that will be the James's place."

Rain began to pummel the windows. "The damn plane will leak like a sieve in an hour," he predicted.

Three quarters of an hour later, Sam said, "There it is. Now, to decide where it's safe to land. He's got a field clearly marked, but Jesus, it all looks like bog. Thank God the wind is westerly."

"What difference does that make?" Cassie was seldom nervous with Sam in control. He didn't answer—he was concentrating. Much as he hated this plane, when it came to a safe approach it was without equal. He was flying just several knots above stalling, and only his skill kept them in the air. He zoomed over the end of the runway and kept going for two miles, turning slowly into the wind, his eyes and mind concentrating. He decelerated the plane even more until it was only inches above the ground, studying to see where the plane might bog. In a second they were rolling over tussocky grass, but then Cassie could feel the plane sinking as Sam lifted the tail before it came to a stop. The plane sank into the quagmire.

"Well, we're safe," Sam said. "But we're likely to be here awhile."

And Blake was waiting for her.

Ian James was knocking on the door. Sam pushed it open. "You're truly bogged," said James. "We'll worry about it later. Jump in."

Sam and Cassie got into Ian's pick-up.

"She's bad," he said as he sped to the house. "Of course, she knew better'n to become pregnant again. Nearly bled to death with our other two. And they're in their teens. She knew better."

What about you? Cassie wanted to ask. It takes two.

"She's forty-one years old."

The house was gracious and expansive, painted white with black trim. The usual verandah wrapped itself around the house, surrounded by flowers and bushes of all types and a patch of grass in front. Cassie liked it. The outbuildings were as neat looking as the house itself and bespoke care and affection for the land.

The woman who lay in bed was ashen. Cassie reached out to touch her forehead, which was cold yet sweaty. Her anxious gaze met Cassie's. The room smelled coppery, of blood.

"I've a feeling that there are some residuals of conception stuck in her uterus. The bleeding will continue if these aren't removed." She didn't say aloud, *then she'll bleed to death by morning.* "What I'd really like to do is fly her back to the hospital in Augusta Springs." She looked at Sam. "How long to free the plane from that bog?"

Sam looked at Ian James, who said, "My God, not today, that's for sure. Not and get you back to Augusta Springs before dark."

Cassie sighed. "Okay, Sam, we operate."

"That's what I figured."

"He's going to help?" Ian frowned.

"He's my anesthetist," Cassie said, opening her bag. "I need boiling water and . . . "

"He's going to see my wife naked?"

Sam's eyebrows raised and he looked questioningly at Cassie.

"I assure you, Mr. James, were we in town a male doctor would look at your wife. I think you can feel quite safe with Sam. Besides, she's not going to have all her clothes off. Now, go get me boiling water and clean towels."

Sam said, "And make some coffee."

Ian James nodded.

"I'll go wash up," Sam said.

When she operated, Cassie discovered a mass of tissue in the uterine opening. "Just as I suspected," she said to Sam, who was administering ether.

"Well, whatever needs doing, I know you can do it."

She looked over at him. "No one's ever given me that kind of vote of confidence."

He grinned. "No one works with you every day."

"I can twist it off and then perform curettage."

"Does that mean she'll lose the baby?"

"You're learning, I see. Yes. And it's probably just as well. Her life's at risk, especially at this age."

Cassie widened the cervical opening and scraped the lining of the uterus with a curette. "She'll bleed a little for a couple of days and she'll have some pelvic and back pain.

"Okay, you can stop the anesthetic and go tell Mr. James his wife is going to be all right. He can come see her if he wants, though she's not conscious yet."

She wiped the blood away and gathered her tools together. Sam returned in a couple of minutes. "He says he'll come in when she wakes up. Right now he and I are going to get some of his men and try to move the plane to higher ground. He's got a tractor and landrover and we'll round up all the help that's available. We'll probably have to stay overnight."

"I knew it," Cassie said aloud. To herself, she said, *Shit.*

Chapter 20

During the next five weeks, Cassie received a scrap of paper weekly. Once a lone horseman brought one to her. Another time it was the regular postman, Mr. Broome. Again, a single-engined plane landed, not even turning its motor off. The pilot dashed from the cockpit to throw the piece of crumpled paper at the traffic control manager, who then brought it round to the radio station.

One week the few words were, "*Goddammit. All I can do is think of you.*" It was signed with a sprawling "B."

The next week the message told her that he lay under the stars and thought of her, that for the first time mustering seemed like a chore instead of a joy, because it kept him from her. He told her he wasn't going to let her live a safe life, so "be prepared."

The third week he wrote, "*Have you felt me next to you in bed at night? Have you felt my kisses as you've awakened? You've been in my swag with me all week. I want to smell you, hold you, breathe you. I want to lie beneath the stars with you, I want you to see the land I love. As I ride around I want to share it with you so, by God, figure some way to come to Tookaringa for at least the last weekend of this month. Don't tell me you can't do it. Figure out a way.*"

"I want to spend a weekend at Tookaringa," she told Sam.

His head jerked up and he grinned. "Ah-hah. Do I dare believe love comes to the good doctor?"

"I wouldn't go that far." But if it wasn't that, she didn't know what it was.

At times Cassie thought she and Sam were becoming friends, but then he'd do or say something to make her think he didn't much like her. Once he'd referred to her as "boss woman." Another time she'd heard him say to one of the station managers, "Women who think they're men." She refused to let it bother her.

Blake still hadn't returned home when Cassie and Sam arrived at Tookaringa. She conducted the clinic, and then she and Jennifer had tea on the verandah. It was late Friday afternoon and the lubras who worked in the big house lined up for their pay.

"I pay them," Jennifer told Cassie, "a small wage and keep them in dresses. I insist that each morning they come here washed and in clean clothes. I never allow them to handle the food, no one except Ruby—very few white women do, they just don't have our sense of sanitation—but they make the beds and sweep the floors and do the washing, all with a healthy sense of humor. They laugh and gossip a lot."

"Funny, but I never think of you as 'working,' " Cassie said. "You always look so elegant and at ease."

Jennifer said, "If I didn't like you so much I'd be angry. I feel I have as much responsibility as Steven and Blake. I have to order household supplies and keep track of them, and go to the storeroom daily to get whatever's needed and make sure what supplies, that includes medical ones, are on hand. Ruby and I plan the menus. At eleven every morning I have sort of a dispensary. All the aborigines who need treatment come and I dispense aspirin by the dozens each day. I have to decide whether I can treat them for stomachache or we should call you or whether it can wait for clinic.

"The festering sores I've treated, the babies I've helped deliver, the patience I've acquired. I've learned to laugh with them and cry with them about their children, I've learned what broken bones and sprains to report over the radio, but I shall never understand them. You know, I can't come near to sharing all that tranquility and closeness to nature. I can't share their spirituality or their sense of oneness with each other and the land. They live and think as they did twenty-five thousand years ago. So many of the whites think of them as slothful and dirty. They're dirty because water is such a scarcity they can't imagine using it to wash with. They don't need clean hands to prepare food, for they can live on witchetty grubs and whatever they find on the ground. We're asking them to think like we do, and they can't do that any more than we can think like they do."

"Is that why you paint pictures of them, because you love them?"

"I doubt it," Jennifer said, her look melancholy. "I am fascinated with them. I don't think I love them. I've even given up trying to understand them."

"Can't you love them without understanding them?"

"Maybe some people can love without understanding. I can't. I think love is a sharing. Shared experiences. Shared hopes. Shared dreams. Shared . . . kisses. Shared sunsets. For me, love must be something mutual."

"I'll buy that." Blake's voice preceded him as he rounded the corner of the house, his clothes dusty, his Stetson pushed back on his head. When he saw Cassie a grin spread over his face. "Well, I'll be damned. You did it."

Cassie felt suddenly shy, like she had at junior high dances.

Jennifer rose and walked over to him as he mounted the stairs. She put her hands on his shoulders and stretched up for a kiss.

"Don't get near me," he said, brushing his lips against her forehead. "I need a bath."

He hadn't taken his eyes from Cassie. "How long you got? How many days?"

"Just until Sunday afternoon."

He disappeared into the house and Jennifer turned back to Cassie. "I'm delighted with this turn of events—I hope you know that. The minute I met you I hoped for this." She gazed out at the horizon, the land covered with low-lying trees. Then she said, "Out here isolation can become a disease."

"Have you felt that lonely?"

"Oh, when I first came I thought I wouldn't last. Steven would be out mustering for weeks on end, and I'd have no one to talk to. I was scared silly of all the black people, sure they'd rape me or murder me in my bed or something awful. And I thought the silence unbearable. The solitude was so gigantic, so profound I could hear the beating of my own heart. And then I began to appreciate all the sounds. There are the wonderful birds, and the wind in the trees, the lowing of cattle, the buzz of mosquitoes, the dingoes that howl in the night. I do know that for many women Outback life becomes a nightmare. Aside from the emptiness and the loneliness there are accidents and no way to get to a doctor and, until you, no way for a doctor to get to us. There are women who deliver their own babies, there are fevers that mean death. There are some people who never adjust. They think everything looks the same."

"You obviously don't."

Jennifer tossed her head back and ran a hand through her hair. "I'm an Aussie now. I think like one, act like one. I've spent nearly thirty years here, on this one patch of land. I'm fifty. I'd be pale and bored stiff had I remained in England. I've never wanted the easy path."

Cassie looked at the older woman with admiration. "Do some of these people cave in? I'd think adversity creates two responses. One is to give up, crumple. The other is to become stronger."

"Of course, not everyone reacts positively. There are heart-breaking things up here. Seven years of drought can wipe almost anyone out, break the spirit. All one's sweat and labor and dreams and everything, gone. Children dead. Love tested and found wanting. There's loneliness and violence in the Outback. You won't like everything you see."

"Do you close your eyes to it?"

Jennifer shook her head. "No, it's part of life. It's the women, of course, who have the hardest times. They're left alone while their men go out on six months muster and they don't see anyone else—sometimes for years on end." She laughed. "It's a land of rugged individualism, that's for sure."

Steven and Blake entered the verandah together.

"It's long over the yardarm," Steven said. "What'll you drink, Cassie?" He leaned over to kiss Jennifer's cheek and stood, a hand resting on her shoulder.

In the doorway, Blake said, "We're taking off at dawn."

"Just the two of you?"

"Just the two of us. I'm taking her out to see the mustering camp, let her see what life in the bush is like. We'll be back for dinner."

It was a magical, if hot, morning. Flocks of kangaroos bounded over fences with ease.

Blake pointed to the west, where Cassie observed dozens of emus running across the land. "They run faster than horses," he said, "and emu fathers are strange in the bird world. They sit on the eggs and hatch the chicks, but emus are skittish. They're afraid of everything."

Cassie didn't say anything; she was too busy looking around.

"Did you know we're not only the oldest land mass on earth, but the flattest continent in the world?"

"I believe it," Cassie said.

As they rode on, Blake remained quiet so she could take in her surroundings. "I've never seen so many birds."

"You've never been farther north? Up to Darwin and Kakadu? *That's* where there are birds. I'll take you up there sometime. It's not like anyplace else. We'll hunt crocodiles, too."

Cassie smiled. "But don't you realize, *this* is like no place else?"

"Makes you proud to be an Aussie, doesn't it?"

"I've always felt slightly embarrassed to be an Aussie, as though I came from a country that didn't have much to it—a few small cities along the coast and nothing but desert inside. And now I find out I've been wrong all along. It's one of the most splendid countries I've ever seen."

Blake grinned as he looked over at her. "And you haven't even begun to see it. I'd like to be the one to show it to you. Up north, as I said, in the real tropics. Have you been to Alice?"

"Alice Springs? No, and that's not even very far."

"If you don't get to it before, we'll pass through it when we go to Darwin. Darwin's a nothing place, really, and about the only people who live there are government employees. It's got godawful weather most of the year. The humidity would sink a ship, but you've got to go through there to go to Arnhem Land and to Kakadu."

"I've never even heard of those places."

"They're aboriginal preserves. Twenty-five-thousand-year-old paintings on rocks, thought to be the oldest vestiges of civilization on the planet. The aborigines may be the oldest undisturbed race on earth."

"You've inherited your mother's affection for them."

He shook his head. "I don't know what it is. I have friends among the stockmen, but we don't understand each other, no matter how much time we spend together. I can go droving for fifteen hundred miles over many months and eat with the stockmen and ride with them, but they escape me. I don't even know if I like them as a group. I like lots of them individually. I suppose the same can be said for my own kind. But I sure am fascinated by them. Especially by the ones who still hold onto their traditions, like those up in Kakadu, in Arnhem Land. The only time to go up there, though, is July or August. Too damn hot this time of year. The humidity would knock you out."

There were hundreds and thousands of birds.

"Those lime green ones with the bright red on their wings are red-winged parrots," he pointed out. "Those small, bright-green ones with yellow faces and edging on their wings, they're budgerigars."

"They look like parakeets to me."

"That's what they're called in the United States. Of course those grey ones, with pale yellow faces and crests, they're cockatiels, but I suppose you know that since they're everywhere, all over the country."

Cassie nodded.

"Now that blue one—see, it's peacock blue and green on its upper part and buff down below, that's a sacred kingfisher. It's also all over the country, that and the red-backed kingfisher."

"What are those beautiful grey and pink ones that make such a noise?"

"Galahs."

Ah, so that's what the women's gossip session on the radio was named after, Cassie realized.

A lizard, about six feet long, slithered just yards ahead of them.

"How ugly!"

"It's a goanna. Heading for those trees in the distance, probably. It'll leap right up into them. They're not too dangerous. The *only* animals one has to fear in this part of the world are snakes, dingos, and some spiders."

There were few trees visible.

"Are you ever afraid you'll get lost?" Cassie asked, looking around.

Blake reined in his horse and Cassie halted, too. He reached out to put a hand on her arm, leaning over to kiss her.

"Out here, no. I've never thought of getting lost. But I'm losing my heart." He kissed her again.

He laughed when she sighed. "You're the damnedest, most beautiful woman. I want you. Godalmighty, Cassandra Clarke, how I want you." He started trotting again, and Cassie caught up with him as they entered an area of hundreds of dagger-shaped mounds.

"Be careful of the ant hills," Blake said.

"Ant hills?"

"There are millions of ant hills all over the country. Each hill contains about two million ants."

Cassie's mouth flew open.

"Millions upon millions of ant hills. Around here they're only two to four feet tall but as you go further north and get more into the tropics they can reach seven feet or more." He reined in his horse to keep pace with Cassie. "Each of these earth mounds has passed through the intestinal tracts of millions and millions of termites who built them from the soil combined with their own bodily secretions, until these rough edifices can survive any tropical monsoon or cyclone. They're as rugged as concrete. Don't run into them."

Suddenly they heard the pounding of hooves. Blake put up his hand, signaling that they should halt. In front of them, perhaps only by fifty feet, a herd of horses ran, their manes sweeping behind them.

"Brumbies," Blake explained. "Wild horses. Long ago they were domesticated but some got away, ran wild, bred. Now they can outrun most horses with riders and aren't easily captured."

"Why does anyone want to capture them?"

"They've become a menace. They eat more pasturage, animal-for-animal, than cattle."

They rode along, through the ant hills, for a couple of miles, and then, Cassie saw a large tank. "What's that?" she asked.

"It's where we store water from the bore."

"Bore?"

"Cattle can only go about five miles from a water tank to get their feed," Blake explained as they jogged along. "So we drill bores, sometimes thousands of feet deep, to get water from the artesian wells and store it in tanks for the cattle. All around each tank the ground becomes pulverized by hooves as the cattle gang up near them for water. After eating all the forage in an ever-widening circle around the tanks, the cattle have to be moved to new pastures so the land can rejuvenate itself. We couldn't raise a thing up here if it weren't for the wells. All this part of Australia's floating over infinite water resources, but it's so deep it costs a fortune to drill for it. And often it's so saline that cattle will drink it but humans can't."

He urged his horse into a canter. "Come on. We're nearly there." He rode ahead of her all the way to the camp.

Cassie saw smoke trailing up in the air. When they got close to it, Blake halted and waited for her to catch up. "Do you know anything about branding?"

"Not a thing," Cassie said. "I've seen westerns where they lasso the cattle and throw them down on the ground and put a branding stake on their forehead. It's awful."

"It's necessary," Blake said. "In this great unfenced land cattle could disappear without your brand on them. They do, anyhow, but this helps. It's not painful for long."

"How do you know?" Cassie asked. They were close enough to hear the shouts of men and the lowing of the cattle, pent-up in paddocks.

"It takes five or six weeks at each of our branding stations to complete the whole lot," Blake said as they rode up to the busy group of stockmen.

"See that man wrestling with that calf? It's the beast's first encounter with a human being. It's scared. It doesn't know what to expect."

They sat on their horses, watching. "First, the unbranded cattle are cut out from the mob. Lassoed, generally, just like you've seen in the movies. Then they're put in the paddocks, those fenced yards all around. One group of men, well, come on, we'll follow a calf through the process." He jumped down from his horse and went over to Cassie, reaching up to help her down.

He led her over to where the cattle were being branded. Two men had thrown the calf down and one held its leg and the other had a knee on its neck. With a tool that looked like a large staple gun, one of the men clipped an ear mark on it. The minute he finished, a fourth man sliced the calf's testicles off. The animal bellowed. He had scarcely finished when a fifth man began to saw off the animal's horns, two men holding the calf in place as it jerked and tried to rear back its head. Another man reached into a fire for the branding iron, glowing red even in the bright sunlight. He aimed carefully for the calf's rear flank, and Cassie could smell the sizzle as she heard the calf yell in pain and rage. The men holding it let go, and the animal reared up, snorting, bucking, kicking its heels in the air.

Blake left her and walked over to speak to one of the men. It was noisy here, spurs jingling, men shouting at each other, cattle bawling. There was the smell of sweat and of burning hides. Over it all, there was the hot red ball of sun. Cassie guessed this was what was meant when people talked of the Outback being a man's world. There was no place for a woman out here.

They watched for over an hour, until Blake said, "Come on, let's grab some lunch. I see the cook's set it up."

The cook and the head ringer were the only white men. The rest were aborigines, who went about their business with agility and seriousness.

For lunch there was beef that had been cooking slowly over logs. There was hot bread from the camp oven; not damper, but real loaves.

And tea. There were also ants and flies and dust, which covered everything.

Cassie watched as Blake participated in the branding. The cook said to her, "There's not a one of them can hold a candle to Blake."

At three, Blake said, "We better be getting back or we'll miss dinner."

"You'd just as soon stay out here with the men, wouldn't you?"

He helped her up on her horse and then jumped on his. "Not at all. I just came in from nearly six weeks of this. I enjoy it, I'll admit, but I'm ready for some of the social amenities."

Cassie, unused to so much exercise and sun, was tired.

"As soon as we get home, we'll take a swim. That'll revive you," said Blake.

"Aren't you even tired?" she asked.

"Hey, I do this all day long for weeks on end. I'm used to the outdoor life."

Jennifer and Steven were just emerging from the pool. Cassie's first inclination was to fall on her bed, but instead she went to the pool, and Blake was right. A swim did revive and invigorate her. She dove deep into the water, hoping the dust would slide right out of her hair. Blake glided up to her, reaching for her hand. His chestnut hair curled when damp and his eyes were an especially bright blue. "Do you know, Cassandra Clarke," and he gave her a wet kiss, pulling her so close that she could feel his hardness through their wet suits, "that when we make love it's going to be like nothing either of us has known before?"

"Blake, don't . . . "

"And when the time comes you're not going to be afraid. Not of me, not of sex, not of love."

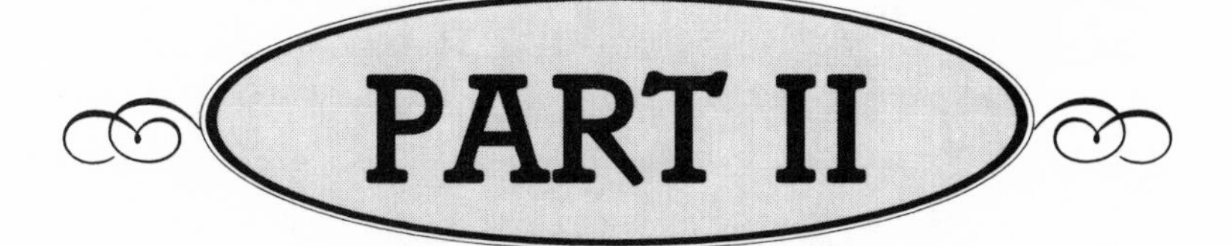

September 1939–February 1942

Chapter 21

Cassie now understood what was meant by "the Wet." When it rained, it rained.

At the afternoon radio session, the police chief in Marriott, a town two hundred fifty miles east, called in.

"Got an emergency about forty miles north of here," he said. "Man shot in the chest. Bleeding to hell and gone, so they tell me. Can't move him. Last I knew he's still alive."

Cassie handed the mike to Sam. "Find out how we get there and we'll leave immediately."

Sam looked at his watch. "We can probably get there before dark. Does it matter if we don't get back tonight?"

When Cassie shook her head, he asked for directions.

"You'll have to fly to the landing field outside of town," said the policeman. "We'll drive you from there. No way you can land back in that scrub."

"Be there in two to three hours," Sam said. He turned to Cassie. "Ready?"

She nodded, already heading toward the plane. She knew he'd given it an inspection early in the afternoon after they'd returned from a clinic at noon.

Though the clouds created a pewter sky, they were high enough that flying under them created no problems. Sam could follow the road to Marriott the whole way. Cassie slept. Rain pelted the plane as they descended to the small airfield.

"Airfield's in prime condition," Sam said.

They'd been to Marriott twice before, and had met Chief Lewis. He was a big, burly man who seldom smiled yet had a gentle voice. He was waiting for them. "I got word of it about an hour and a half before talking to you. It'll be dark before we get there."

They climbed into his car, Cassie in the back seat, and he started the motor immediately. "Packed some sandwiches," he said. "I was afraid it'd start raining again before you could get here. Damn weather. Can fry eggs on rocks in the summer and float away in the spring."

"What happened?" asked Sam.

"Who knows? We always have more killings and wife beatings and rapes this time of year. Especially when it's time for a full moon, even if the moon don't come out of the clouds."

The road was full of potholes and slippery with the slickness of the rain.

"This is out at one of the stations where there's a manager but no family, no women. We always get lotsa calls out here. Just stockmen who get bored or antsy or on each other's nerves."

It took them an hour and three-quarters to drive the forty-two miles through the rain that pounded on the roof of the car. It was dark by the time they arrived. A solitary light indicated where the house stood.

Chief Lewis preceded them up the one-step verandah and through the open door into a small room, lit only by a kerosene lantern. Two young men stood near the patient, who lay on the floor in a pool of blood.

Cassie knelt down. The wound was bad, the young man pale and in shock, breathing rapidly. She took his pulse. "One-forty," she said aloud.

"Is that bad?" asked the policeman.

"And getting worse from the looks of things," Cassie said. "He's in a coma." She looked up at the two young men in attendance. "How long since he's been unconscious?"

They looked at each other, and one of them shrugged. "I dunno. We shouted at him and pinched him but he didn't respond."

Cassie placed a knuckle on a chest bone on the sternum and pushed down hard.

"What's that supposed to do?" asked Chief Lewis.

"That'll elicit pain if he feels anything, but he's not responding in any way. He's gone if we can't do something."

"What do you mean by that?" asked one of the young men.

Cassie said, "I've got to operate."

"Here?" asked the policeman.

"Here," Cassie said.

"Come on, guys," said Sam. "Help me clean this place up."

"We don't even have time for that," Cassie said. "I've got to do it now. Can you boil water? I need some. And is there another lantern?" She turned to Sam. "I'll have to do it down here on the floor. I don't think he should be lifted."

Sam nodded. "Water," he reiterated to the young men, neither of whom had moved.

"I've got to wash my hands before I begin," she said, even though her rubber gloves were sterile. She despaired of operating under such conditions yet she could feel her adrenaline begin to flow, felt energy pumping through her.

"I don't know where there's another lamp," said the remaining young man.

"I've got a flashlight in the car," said Chief Lewis.

It was better than nothing.

Sam knelt down next to her, and whispered, "You're nervous, aren't you?"

She nodded.

"You can do it, Doc. I know you can."

"He's already lost so much blood."

"If anybody can save him, you can."

Cassie opened her medical kit and began preparing.

Within fifteen minutes she was operating. Both of the young men left the room, but Cassie told Chief Lewis, "I'll need your help. Wash your hands."

Handing Sam ether and a gauze mask, she said, "You don't need an anesthetic unless he seems to be gaining consciousness. I'll need your help with the operation itself."

She made a long cut from the breastbone out into the middle of the armpit area. "Now," she said to the men, "you've got to pull back the bones, I mean really pull hard on either side of the ribs so I can see what's going on."

The men looked at her and at each other, kneeling beside her on the floor with only the dim light to guide her. "Come on, pull!"

They pulled. "I've got to try and see in there," she said, as they held back the skin. "Pull back those bones."

Finally she saw that one of the big blood vessels, the aorta, had been cut by the bullet. "Oh, God," she said. "There's a huge amount of blood I have to suck out. Keep holding those bones back!" She didn't think she'd ever seen so much blood.

When she was satisfied that she'd mopped up all she could, she sewed up the aorta. "Okay," she said to Sam and Chief Lewis. "You can let go. I think he's lost too much blood. Sam, take his blood pressure."

Sam reached for the blood pressure cuff and the stethoscope, placing the cuff on the patient's left arm, pumping the regulator. "It's dropping fast," he said.

Cassie nodded. "His pulse is speeding up so fast it's become irregular."

The three of them still knelt on the floor, staring at the patient. Finally, the Chief stood. "My knees are giving out on this hard floor."

As Cassie gazed at him, she realized the patient's heart had stopped. "Oh, Jesus," she whispered. "I've got to squeeze the heart."

"Squeeze it?" asked the policeman, his voice sounding as though he might be sick momentarily.

Cassie placed her hand on the heart, pumping it, squeezing it like she might a tennis ball. "I've got to go eighty pumps a minute." Her own breath was short with the exertion needed. "Sam, in my bag is another rubber glove. Put it on and spell me. I can't keep it up."

He reached for the glove and put it on, watching her hand pumping. "Okay," he said, "move over."

"Maybe it'll kick back," she said.

They took turns for twenty minutes, and then she said, "Sam, stop."

There was silence in the room.

"If we had blood, *and* if we were in a hospital he might have had a chance but he's lost too much blood."

"You mean . . . ?" Chief Lewis didn't finish the sentence.

"Yeah," Sam said, "he's a goner."

Chief Lewis volunteered to put them up at his house for the night. "You'll have to sleep on the sofa," he said to Sam.

"Won't be the first time."

They were silent driving back through the drizzle to Marriott. Cassie closed her eyes but could not sleep. None of them ate the sandwiches the Chief had brought.

In the morning, before take-off, Sam contacted Horrie on the radio. "Uh-oh," he said to Cassie. "You better listen to this."

"I got a distress call," Horrie said, and they could hardly understand him for the static. "You're not going to like this."

Sam and Cassie looked at each other. "It's from Milton Crossing, about two-fifty to three hundred miles northwest of where you are. A child's in serious condition. Here are the symptoms." Cassie could tell he was reading them off. "Baby was well yesterday afternoon then bang, all of a sudden nausea, vomiting, diarrhea, and fever. By midnight it was sick, weak, cranky. It wanted to be held and kept crying. By three in the morning it lost strength and was apathetic, whether the mother was holding him or not. His mouth is yellowish this morning and wrinkled. His eyes are sunken and the skin sorta hangs on him."

"God," said Cassie. "Two days of that is enough to kill a child if there's no fluid replacement. Luckily, we always have IV equipment with us."

"They can't get the kid to keep any liquid down," said Horrie. "And I have even worse news. Storms have downed electric lines. The whole area up there is flooded. I don't know if you can even land anywhere near it. Sam, you know where Milton Crossing is, don't you?"

"Yeah," Sam said. "We flew up there to bring a pregnant woman to the hospital a couple months ago."

"Can you get enough gas in Marriott to get that far?"

"I'm sure," said Sam. He glanced at Cassie and at his watch. "We'll take off right away. I'll contact you in exactly four hours. Tell the homestead to be on the frequency then, too."

"Any other emergencies?" asked Cassie.

Horrie laughed. "How would you handle them if there were?"

Sam replaced the receiver and turned to look at Cassie. "Let's get those sandwiches we didn't eat last night and a thermos of coffee."

A fine drizzle kept them flying low all three hours, but from six hundred feet up Sam had no trouble locating their route. Finally the rain stopped, but they could see the area below them was flooded.

"Don't know where the hell we'll land," he said.

Milton Crossing was on the banks of a river, and even from six hundred feet they could see that the river was churning and fields were flooded with brown water.

"There's no place to land," Sam said, as he turned the radio on, tuning to the frequency of the base station, where Horrie was waiting for their call.

"No way can I land near here," Sam said. "Nearest open land that's not flooded must be ten miles away."

Horrie said he'd connect them with the homestead, and they and Sam could decide what to do.

"There's a hill twelve miles northwest," said Clive Young, owner of Milton Crossing. "It's flat on the top and you should be able to land there. I've already sent some of my aboriginal trackers there to await you. You'll have to walk but everything else is flooded."

"Twelve miles!" said Cassie.

Sam turned to look at her, raising an eyebrow. "I can do it. I don't know about you."

Cassie didn't say anything.

"There's the hill," Sam said, pointing, "on the wrong side of the river."

"We have to carry IV equipment to the house."

"No way," Sam said.

Cassie knew he was right. She couldn't imagine carrying that and having it arrive in usable condition, not after slogging through twelve miles of mud and brush.

The butte looked as though it had been created just to be a landing surface. "Well, it's shorter than I like. Hold on. I'll have to stop abruptly." Sam flew in on it as though he'd landed there a dozen times before.

Before he opened the door, the plane was surrounded with a dozen black men, all barefoot and soaked.

"Might as well leave our shoes here," Sam muttered as he kicked his off and grabbed Cassie's medical bag. She reached down and undid her sandals, glad she never wore stockings in this climate. They took off, sloshing behind the aborigines through mud and brush, until Cassie was not only soaked but her arms were covered with scratches. Her hair lay limp, plastered flat against her head. The aborigines never stopped. At the end of an hour Cassie was so tired she wondered if she could go a step further, but she didn't ask them to stop or slow down. Sam, bringing up the rear, asked, "You okay?"

She nodded, too exhausted to answer. Her feet were covered with cuts from twigs and roots. Her blouse and skirt clung to her.

At the end of the second hour she said, "Sam, I've just got to stop. Just for a minute or two. I can't go a step further."

"Okay," he said, calling out to the trackers. "Hold on a minute."

But they could hear the river from here, so she knew it was nearly over. Sam said, "I'll take a look. Wait here a couple minutes."

He returned in ten minutes. "The river's running about eighty yards wide. Probably not six feet wide normally. Guess the water's about four feet deep. You swim?"

"In a pool with no current, I'm pretty good."

He laughed. "I gave the medical bag to one of the men and told him he better carry it so there wasn't a Chinaman's chance of dropping it into the river. Come on," he yelled, stretching out a hand and pulling her from her perch on a log.

"Any crocodiles?" Cassie asked.

"I asked one of the men. He said, 'Oh, no, boss, not many.' Doc, we gotta take off our clothes and carry them across. Now, don't have a fit. Clothes can impede us if we get swept away. Your skirt will just be a hindrance. No one's going to look."

"How do you know? If they don't look, how will they know I'm safe?"

"Well, no one's going to be thinking lustful thoughts, how's that? We're all intent on making it across, not looking at you."

How come she could look at so many patients, male and female, and never even think of them as naked human beings, yet when it came to taking off her own clothes in front of people shyness overcame her?

"You can keep your underwear on," Sam grinned. "That won't impede you."

Cassie looked at the water, flowing so swiftly she wondered how people could keep their balance. Half the aborigines had already waded across the river and had reached the other side. Six of them stood on the bank, reaching out.

"They're going to form a line and we'll cross holding onto each other. Look, Doc, I'm right here. I won't let anything happen to you."

"What makes you think I'm scared?"

"You'd be nuts not to be."

"Are you?"

Sam was stripping his shirt off. "I'm not nuts. I've a healthy respect for nature. Looks like fun, doesn't it? Don't you like challenges?"

She began to unbutton her blouse. "Maybe I do." She did feel a certain heightening of her senses, even a thrill. Maybe living on the edge had its good points.

Sam slipped out of his pants, placing them inside his shirt and tying them into a bundle. "Pretend it's a bathing suit," he told her. "Here, I can fit your skirt and blouse into my bundle. I'll carry it. The current's swift. Hold onto my hand and the hand of that black fellow in front of you. He won't let go and I won't."

Cassie knew that despite his promise, Sam was studying her. Well, she wouldn't dwell on it—she'd think about the baby who might die if she didn't get to it. Think of the parents, frantic with worry, waiting for her. As for Sam, he looked like she knew he would: too darn thin.

But she felt comforted when his firm hand grabbed hers, holding it tight, and she reached out her other hand to the black man in front of her. He clasped it tightly, too. They began to wind through the swiftly flowing water. The bottom was smooth and sandy, and she fought to hold her balance, pushing against the current. She shuddered as a piece of deadwood floated past her. It looked like a snake or a crocodile.

Waiting on the bank, standing in the rain with an umbrella and towels, was Clive Young. As soon as Cassie emerged from the river he tossed a towel around her, throwing another at Sam.

"Sorry 'bout all this weather," he said.

"How's your child?" Cassie asked, hugging the towel that barely covered her.

"Alive," was all he said, taking the medical bag from one of his boys and leading them to the house.

Mrs. Young sat in a rocking chair holding her baby close. She took one look at Sam and Cassie and said, "Clive, find them some clothes."

The sweater and slacks he brought to Cassie were far too large, but she quickly got into them, hoping her shivering would stop.

She turned to her patient. The baby's eyes appeared sunken and the skin looked dehydrated.

"He won't keep any fluids down," said Mrs. Young.

"It's gastroenteritis," said Cassie, after examining the child. "We *have* to force liquids down him. We've got to get him to the intravenous equipment in the plane. Until we can we'll have to give it very slowly orally, a teaspoon at a time. If he doesn't vomit that up, then two teaspoons. But he really needs IV."

She looked over at Sam. His gaze met hers. They both knew that meant sloshing back across the river, *with* the baby, and going back the twelve miles through mud and brush to the plane.

"He should go to the hospital."

The Youngs looked at each other.

"One of you should come with him," Cassie said.

"I'll get my bag," Mrs. Young said, laying the child on the sofa.

"I'll carry him across the river," said his father.

"You'll need something to eat." Mrs. Young stuck her head out of the bedroom doorway.

Cassie wondered if she could possibly make it back to the plane without rest.

She felt Sam's hand on her shoulder, and in a low voice he said, "You can do it. I know you can."

She turned to look at him and smiled, brushing wet hair out of her eyes. Clive Young's flannel shirt was three times too large for Sam, who stood with it flapping around him, his long legs bare.

"No fair. I didn't laugh at you."

"That's because you promised not to look," she said.

"Well, if truth be told," he said, "I broke that promise. But don't worry. I won't tell anyone you're more woman than you pretend to be."

She turned away from him, embarrassed.

Clive reappeared, wearing a rain slicker.

"That won't help you cross the river," Sam said.

"I don't know where my mind is," Clive said, and took off the rainwear.

In ten minutes, Myrna Young said, "Sandwiches are ready. Sorry I can't offer you more."

"Aren't you going to eat?" asked her husband.

"I'm too worried to eat."

Sam said to Cassie, "We better get going. It may take some time getting the plane off that hill."

"Do you think there are easier ways to earn a living?" Cassie asked.

Sam replied, "Now, tell me, can you think of anything you'd rather be doing right now? Tell me your life isn't more interesting than at least ninety per cent of the world's."

When she didn't answer, he asked, "Is that baby going to live?"

"If we can get liquid into him quickly enough, he is."

"Well, look at it this way. If you weren't standing here now, half-naked and exhausted, looking forward to another twelve miles of rain and mud and bushes, if you weren't . . . well, I mean you're going to save a life today. If you weren't doing what you're doing this minute, a baby'd die. Think of it that way."

She reached up to touch the hand that pressed her shoulder. "Well,

I'll tell you, Sam. There's no one I'd rather have as a partner, that's for sure. You're a brick."

He was silent for a minute. "Yeah. Well."

Clive Young strapped the child in a sling across his back. "If I have to swim, at least he'll be safe," he said.

They set out, the four adults in their underwear, carrying their shoes above their heads. Sam still had Cassie's clothes in the knapsack he'd made of his shirt. It was raining so hard they could hardly see two feet in front of them and had to keep blinking to keep the water out of their eyes.

"You go first," Sam instructed Cassie, "holding onto that black's hand. Then we'll have Clive follow, Mrs. Young, and I'll bring up the rear. You're going to have to fight that torrent, but you've done it before."

Cassie could hardly see. Clive Young kept a tight hold of her hand and the aborigine in front of her seemed like a rock, so steadily and slowly did he move against the raging river. When she reached the side, before she could let go of Clive's hand, the black had grabbed it, pulling him and the child safely ashore.

Mrs. Young had lost her footing and Cassie turned to see Sam pulling her arm, trying to get her back on course, reaching out to put his arms around her, holding her close against him as he lunged through the water to safety.

Mrs. Young began to cry. "Oh, my," she said, fighting for breath. "I was afraid there for a minute . . . "

"You're okay now. Let's get going," Sam said.

"I'm scared to death with the rain beating down on that child," Cassie murmured to Sam.

He nodded. "Three hours to go."

How they made it, none of them was ever quite sure. Cassie thought the only reason the baby didn't develop pneumonia was that it was a warm rain, and by the time they reached the rocky butte and the plane, the rain had slowed to a drizzle. She dried the baby off with towels and immediately began IV.

Sam opened the knapsack—the clothes were as wet as if they'd been dunked in the river. He found two blankets to wrap around Cassie and Mrs. Young, but he landed in Augusta Springs in just his skivvies. No one at the airport understood when he emerged from the aircraft in his underwear with two women wrapped in blankets.

They talked about it at the hospital, too.

But the baby, they knew now, was going to live.

Chapter 22

Padre McLeod told Cassie, "Jennifer Thompson's stopped painting."

"What do you mean *stopped?* She can't paint *all* the time."

"I don't mean she's between paintings. She's stopped. She won't even enter her studio."

Cassie looked across the table at him. They were sitting in her kitchen drinking coffee. There wasn't anyone Cassie liked more, except maybe Fiona.

"Any idea why?"

"Nothing certain. But I've drawn my own conclusions."

Cassie waited. Don stirred more sugar into his coffee. He smiled apologetically. "I so seldom get sugar that when I do I really load up on it."

She didn't say anything.

"You know about the art dealer discovering her, don't you?"

She shook her head. "No. I don't know anything."

He smiled. "I guess I take for granted everyone knows everything. I seem to."

"People tell you everything."

"Some art dealer down in Sydney went all the way to Tookaringa to see her paintings. He'd seen a couple, paintings she'd given friends. Now, I got this story secondhand, maybe third, so all my facts may not be accurate." He sipped his coffee.

"Go on."

"Offered her a pile of money for the couple of paintings she had. Said he could make her famous."

"How wonderful, after so many years of painting. Why, that's marvelous!"

"So, why'd she stop painting?" McLeod shook his head. "The fragile male ego."

Cassie looked at him, waiting.

He pulled a pipe out of his pocket. "I don't know for sure. But from what I heard, Steven started ridiculing her. Started telling her an art dealer would take advantage of her. Then he would try to tell her what to paint, start to control her. He said she was out of her league, and that if she was going to sell her work, he ought to do it for her. I don't know what he said to her, actually. But she stopped painting."

"I can't believe that. He's been so proud of her."

"Sure. As long as she's been second fiddle. As long as she's been Mrs. Steven Thompson first. As long as her talent has just been something to keep her busy while he's attending to the real work of life."

Cassie studied her friend. "Don, I don't believe it. He'd never do that to her. He's a big enough man. He's the biggest land owner around here. He's never going to be overshadowed by Jennifer."

"What you think and how he feels are two different things."

"Are you telling me he's scared of her fame?"

"Oh, I don't think he's conscious of that. But men are funny creatures, Cassie. Not nearly as nice as women. Women are far stronger than men too, you know. Do you think men could handle pregnancy?" McLeod went on. "There are always unexpected pregnancies. Now, this is strictly off the record, Cassie, but you'll run into it if you stay around long enough. Even some of the nursing sisters in the AIM hospitals. Some of them have their babies, and can't ever practice nursing again—they're ostracized. Their families are ashamed of them. They're left to bring up illegitimate children by themselves, hardly able to provide for them. Scarlet women. Their lives ruined. Other people won't let their children associate with bastards! Yet some of these women choose to keep their children and raise them. How do you think men would react if they had to live a life like that after half an hour of fun? I imagine for many that's all it is, half an hour. Maybe less.

"And then there are those who choose to have an illegal abortion so their lives won't be ruined, so they have a chance of contributing to the world, so the world won't treat them with scorn, so their children wouldn't grow up disadvantaged, so they will not be doomed to poverty, living on the fringe financially and socially.

"They go to unqualified quacks, putting not only their bodies but their lives in the hands of charlatans, who make money off frightened and desperate women. Or they try to abort themselves with coat hangers."

Don nodded. "Psychologically, emotionally, these women have to face something men never have to. I don't think men can even understand. If I hadn't seen so much of it, I wouldn't either. And perhaps I still don't. These women all suffer and some of them cope, Cassie. Women are so much stronger than men. Maybe not physically, but in the ways that count, in moral strength and fibre."

"Moral strength? So you don't consider illicit sex immoral?"

"Oh, Cassie, my dear, you cannot ignore human nature. If we ourselves did not have these weaknesses, how could we empathize with others? Where would we learn compassion?"

She wasn't sure what this had to do with Jennifer's painting, but no wonder people confided in Don McLeod. How many he must have helped. What a source of comfort he must be as he traveled the thousands of miles back and forth, up and down his vast territory.

Cassie glanced at her watch. "Don, I'm going to have to leave you. It's time for the eleven o'clock call-in at the radio base."

His eyes twinkled. "I hear Blake Thompson may be tamed at last."

"My God," she said standing, but smiling, "is nothing private?"

"Not really," he said with a grin. "Make sure you find me and call me in for the ceremony."

"Aren't you rushing things?"

"Just letting you know I'd like to be the one to tie the knot."

"Don, I haven't seen him half a dozen times."

"Quantity has nothing to do with quality. I knew the minute I saw the back of her head, the shining black hair two pews ahead of me. I knew before she even turned around and smiled at me that Margaret was the one I was going to marry."

"And that was how long ago?"

"Five years," he said. "And we're getting married next fall, after she graduates from nursing school. Then she'll join her wandering padre."

"You mean she's going to spend her life sleeping in swags and cooking over open fires?"

"She likes the idea."

Cassie stood. "I have twelve minutes to get to the station. Want to come?"

"Sure," he said. "I'd like to see how it's done from this end."

Cassie handled most of the calls easily, but one was an emergency call from a sheep station over two hundred miles to the south, so remote that the nearest station was seventy miles away. "Gregory Carlton here," said a very clipped British voice. "My sister is very ill. She's been in pain for about twelve hours."

Why hadn't he called in at the eight o'clock session? Cassie wondered.

"She's nauseous and has a fever. She doesn't want to move because it hurts too much. The pain's diffused through her whole belly, but now she says it's focused in the lower right. Sounds like appendicitis to me."

"To me, too," said Cassie. "We better come and get her to the hospital as soon as possible. My pilot will get directions from you," she said. To Sam, she commented, "This is top priority. Let's get going."

"I'm ready," he said, grinning. "So, I'm *your* pilot?"

They left the radio room and started walking to his pick-up. "Want to come, Don?" Cassie asked, ignoring Sam's teasing.

"Oh, my," he said, trotting along, "you mean you leave just like this?"

"Just like this," Sam replied.

"My medical gear is always in the plane. I replenish it after every trip. Unless we arrive home so late it's dark, we make sure the plane is ready to take off with just a minute's notice. Come on," Cassie said. "Sam usually doesn't talk to me while he's flying. I nap or read. Come along, so I can have interesting conversation."

"I haven't even been to the Carltons', it's so far from every place else," McLeod conceded. "It'll give me a chance to meet them. I've heard of them—brother and sister who came out from England about five years ago and bought a successful sheep station from a woman whose husband had just died. No one knows much about them."

"What would make anyone live seventy miles from their nearest neighbors?" asked Cassie, not for the first time.

"I believe the name of their station is Mattaburra," McLeod said. "It's been famous as a successful station for years. I imagine they paid a pretty penny for it, despite the location."

"I think it's that kind of a day," Sam said to himself, but loud enough for his passengers to hear.

"What kind of day?" Cassie asked.

"A mirage day." He pointed straight ahead of him. Cassie unbuckled herself and stood up, walking to look over his shoulder. Shimmering ahead of them was an immense lake, in whose center were green islands, a Mohammedan mosque, and palm trees.

"You're kidding," she said. "That's no mirage."

"Watch," he said. "It'll stay ahead of us wherever we go. We won't ever be able to fly over it, and not until we get to trees again will it disappear. Atmospheric conditions have to be just right. And what *just right* is no one knows. I've never seen it before, but I've heard about it. Every pilot in this part of the country has."

McLeod crowded into the space next to Cassie, peering down ahead of them. "I'll be darned," he said. "I've heard of it, too. 'Course, I've seen dozens of mirages from down on the ground, but never one like that, with islands and a mosque."

The land surrounding the mirage was covered with red stones and great cracks in the earth. There was no sign of life anywhere. After an hour the mirage disappeared when stunted mulga trees came into sight, their pale blue spreading like a sea below. There were signs of abandoned homesteads.

A great flock of emus ran below them, through the salt bush.

"Used to be," said Don, "that people thought salt bush spelled failure, that it meant no water and land that couldn't grow grass. But now, they've found it's great feed." Trees became more abundant, interspersed with stark red plains. Great flocks of sheep roamed, seeming to thrive on land that looked as if it couldn't support life.

"There's a road," Sam said. "And a river." It was more like a series of water holes with gigantic eucalyptus trees—silver gums—along the banks, rising forty or fifty feet above what water there was. "Ah, there, in that grove of trees, there's the homestead."

Behind the long, low house and garden surrounded by a tall corrugated fence was a long, cleared stretch of land. "Bet they didn't even have to flatten it," Sam said as he turned and began to descend.

Cassie noted Don clutching the arms of his seat.

"Don't worry," she assured him. "Sam will make it so smooth you won't even know he's touched down."

"This is only my second flight," Don said.

One of the handsomest men Cassie had ever seen waved to them as he ran from the house. As Sam opened the door, Gregory Carlton reached out a hand and introduced himself. He was a bit over six feet with a muscular, lean body and dark hair to match his coal-black eyes and thin mustache.

"Alison's worse," he said after introductions were over. "I'm worried sick."

Cassie grabbed her bag and they all followed him through the gate. The garden was a wonderland of flowers, in straight even rows, but in a riot of colors. There was an herb garden, the kind Cassie had thought of starting at Fiona's.

The sick woman lay pale and sweating. Cassie imagined that she was as beautiful as her brother was handsome, but right now her black hair lay damp and limp on the pillow and her dark blue eyes were filled with pain. She and her brother looked so much alike they could be twins.

Cassie, upon examining her patient, found the muscles tense and almost board-like in the right lower quadrant of the belly. When she applied pressure, Alison winced. Cassie employed force in the left lower area and found it soft.

"It *is* appendicitis. We must get her to the hospital immediately."

Sam said, "I'll gas up. Don, you want to give me a hand? I've got forty-four gallon drums. We can't make it back without the gas."

Cassie said to Gregory, "You'll have to carry her."

"I'm going with you."

His sister stretched out a hand, which he grabbed. She said, her voice faint, "Greg, I'll be all right. You can't leave this place alone. Please, dear, don't even think of driving in to town. That's what you're thinking, aren't you? Well, don't I'll be all right."

"I'm sure she will," Cassie said, "and we'll fly her back out in about two weeks. We have a clinic at Burnham Hill about then and we'll detour through here." Like going to Melbourne by way of Perth; well, Adelaide, anyhow.

They strapped Alison Carlton onto the stretcher and Cassie said, "I'm going to give you a shot so you'll relax. Have you ever flown before?"

Alison shook her head.

"Well, we have the best pilot there is, and it's nothing to worry about. But this shot will help you sleep and relieve the pain, too."

Alison closed her eyes.

Cassie was surprised there was no ambulance waiting. When she called the hospital she was told that Dr. Edwards was out of town and Dr. Adams was at home. She ordered an ambulance immediately, then called Chris Adams. It was nearly five, and maybe he was keeping Isabel company; perhaps Grace had had to leave early.

When he answered the phone, Cassie said urgently, "Chris, it's Cassie. I've just landed. I have an emergency appendectomy here. Can you meet me at the hospital?"

There was a moment's hesitation. "Did you try Edwards?"

"I did, reluctantly. Fortunately, he's not available. Can you meet me at the hospital as soon as possible? I'll prep the patient, if you want me to, and have everything ready." She hung up.

Something's wrong. That's not like Chris. Ungracious, but . . . should she have asked if he'd prefer that she operate? Sam could be the anesthetist. She called him back.

"Chris, I can operate, you know. You don't have to come in."

"I'm on my way, Doctor."

Didn't he trust her? Or was he still so jealous that he didn't want her to operate in his hospital? She shook her head. What a strange man.

Horrie and Sam carried the stretcher off the plane. Alison had regained consciousness but was still drugged. High fever made her sweat.

The ambulance arrived in ten minutes.

"You don't have to come," Cassie told Sam. "Chris'll be at the hospital." Climbing into the ambulance, she said to Don, "I'll treat you to dinner at Addie's. I was going to cook for you but that's a bit too much for today. Why don't you wait for me at the house?"

"Why don't I take him to Addie's and we'll meet you there?" Sam said.

"Okay." Cassie looked out the window, watching Sam light a cigarette, say something to Horrie, then stare at the ambulance as it pulled away.

Chapter 23

Chris was already waiting in the operating room, dressed in his green fatigues. He was his usual curt self, taciturn and unsmiling.

Cassie ordered a nurse to prepare the patient and donned her operating uniform, scrubbing in the utility room.

When she entered the operating room Chris asked, "What stage is the patient in?"

"Could burst momentarily, I think, though not for another day probably."

Alison was wheeled in.

"You ready?" asked Chris, and Cassie began to administer the anesthetic as he examined the patient. "You're right," he said, "but then you always are."

He made a two-inch incision deep in the right lower belly horizontal to the pubic bone. Cassie watched as he reached the first muscle layer, two large bands that were split. Chris pulled them apart with retractors, long metal devices with blades on the end so they resembled right angles. She watched as the next layer came into view, and he divided the muscles, pulling them apart until he was down to the peritoneum, which he opened with a blade and then with scissors. Grasping the colon with Alice forceps, he maneuvered it by pulling it back and forth until they could both see the appendix, a four-inch, pus-filled, red structure at the end of the secum. He pulled it forward and drew the colon out a bit so the appendix was up on the belly wall where he could clearly see it. He freed the appendix by cutting away fatty tissue and blood vessels, tying them off. The angry structure stood alone like a stalk with an Alice clamp at the tip of it.

Then Chris double-clamped the base of the appendix near the secum and passed a blade in between the clamps and removed the appendix. While the clamps were still in place he sterilized the area with silver nitrate. He loosely sewed continuous running stitches that left a loop. Tying a free tie at the base under the clamp, he closed the appendix opening and then pushed down the stump of the appendix into the secum by a hemostat while tightening up the loop of sutures, closing the hole over the stump. Cassie could see he was looking around at other parts of the colon, using the Alice clamps to move it back and forth to be sure there wasn't anything else wrong. Then he closed the layers of the peritoneum and stitched the patient up.

They hadn't spoken. When he was finished, he whipped off his gloves and said, "Another few hours and it would have been too late."

Cassie nodded. "Are you all right?" She followed him out of the operating room.

He started washing his hands. "Isabel died at three this afternoon."

"Oh, Chris! I'm so sorry." She went over and touched his arm. "You should have told me. I could have done it on my own, you know."

"Good for me to take my mind off it."

"Is there anything I can do?"

He shook his head and walked out of the room, leaving her staring after him. He must feel relief as well as grief, she thought. It must have been difficult to stand by and watch someone you love in such pain, wanting to die. The strain was over, even if not the heartache. She remembered how she felt, losing her mother. Even when you expected it, losing someone you loved was never easy.

Waiting for her at Addie's, sitting with Sam and Don, were Heather Martin and her sister, Bertie. Bertie stared wide-eyed at everyone and everything. Both girls were tall, lean, tanned, and their blond hair was streaked from years in the sun. Despite their men's clothes, their breasts strained against their cotton shirts, and their tight pants accentuated their buttocks. Unaware that they created a sensation in Addie's, they were big, beautiful women who would stop traffic in the middle of Sydney, much less in Augusta Springs.

"Him," Heather nodded at Sam. "We like the looks of him."

Cassie tried not to let her smile show as she watched Sam turn red.

"We come to see if there are any more like him," chimed in Bertie, her eyes resting briefly on Don, who sat with a wide grin on his ruddy face. "My golly, the town's filled with them."

"Where are you staying? I've an extra room if you'd like," Cassie offered.

"Their swags are outside," Sam said. "They rode into town."

"That must be a couple of hundred miles," Don said, lighting his pipe, obviously enjoying himself.

Bertie's fork poised in mid-air. "This here is the best food I ever tasted." She finished the last of her steak and stood up. "Where's the kitchen?"

These girls took the cake, Cassie thought as she pointed to the swinging door.

Heather turned to Cassie. "That's mighty nice of you. We'll take you up on staying til Sunday anyhow. Last time he," she nodded at Sam, "didn't show up for the dance. You goin' this time?"

"Sure." Sam reached out and put an arm around Don's shoulder. "He'll come, too."

"Are you thinking of moving to town?" Don asked, his eyes dancing with delight.

Heather slapped her knee and leaned forward. Every male in the room was looking at her. "Never! Just thought we'd come look over the men."

"Maybe hire us a cook, too." Bertie returned with Addie's cook, Cully. She towered a full head above him, but she was grinning as she introduced him to Heather. "Tell him how good a cook he is."

Heather studied him, her eyes running up and down. "Real good. This lemon pie is heaven."

Cully, his thin face expressionless, nodded, wiping his hands on his white apron. "Ma'am," was all he said before he turned and left.

Bertie's glance followed him. "Isn't he cute as a button?"

Heather said, "You could swallow him up in one hug."

"Yeah, but he sure can cook."

"I'm tired," Cassie said an hour later. "It's been a long day. I want to stop in at the hospital a minute to see if my patient's conscious. She may be frightened waking up in a strange place, all alone."

"We'll show the ladies where your house is," Sam volunteered, unable to wipe the grin from his face.

"Bring them by in about an hour," Cassie said. "I can't stay awake much longer. Oh, by the way, Isabel Adams died."

The two girls kept Cassie awake, asking if she thought Sam could ever be happy not flying, and could ever settle into a station.

Cassie said she'd dine with them the next night, but she was too tired to talk, and no, she didn't think living on a station would satisfy Sam, but then she couldn't speak for him.

In the morning she stopped by again and found Alison Carlton to be as nice as she was beautiful. Cassie sat with her again late in the afternoon, learning that Alison and her brother lived out there alone with no help. They had close to ten thousand sheep and the only time they saw other people was when shearers came each June and during their twice-yearly drive to Augusta Springs for supplies.

When Cassie asked if Alison didn't find it unbearably lonely, Alison replied, "Not as much as when I was growing up in Southampton. I'm never bored with my own company, or Greg's, and I've never fit in anyplace anyhow."

Cassie looked at the beautiful woman before her and could hardly believe that. "What about your brother?"

Alison smiled. "We've always been misfits. We're both happier than when we lived in a city and were never part of it."

Just then her brother burst through the door, carrying a fading bouquet of flowers. "Thank God you're alive!"

Alison reached out for the flowers but frowned at him. "You shouldn't have driven all this way and left the place alone," but Cassie could tell she was pleased. He was, after all, the only person she knew on the whole continent.

"You're more important than livestock," he said, leaning down to kiss her on the forehead before turning and stretching out a hand to Cassie. His handshake was strong.

He stayed in Augusta Springs until it was time for Alison to return to Mattaburra, ten days later. Cassie dined with him every night and twice Sam joined them, but other nights he dined with Heather and Bertie, who were always surrounded by men—their laughter filled Addie's nightly. Cassie thought if Blake Thompson had not entered her life, she would certainly find Gregory Carlton most appealing.

Sam said, "He's not my cup of tea, spouting poetry and something from books all the time. But his sister, wow!"

"She quotes poetry, too."

"That's different. Women are allowed to."

"But men write it."

Sam scratched his head. "I hadn't thought of that. Well, perhaps he writes it, too."

He's jealous, because Greg is so handsome and so cultivated and so erudite yet single-handedly takes care of ten thousand sheep. Well, perhaps not single-handedly. Alison did the same work he did.

"She doesn't look it," said Sam. "She's fragile-looking. Like she should make jam and work needlepoint."

"She does that, too," said Greg. "While I read aloud evenings."

Sam raised an eyebrow.

Obviously, Cassie found the Carltons more intriguing than Sam did. She'd have missed them when they left if it hadn't been for a sudden turn of events.

The phone rang. Oh, God, she thought, don't let it be another emergency.

"Hi, there, Princess."

"Blake!"

"I just got home," he said. "I've a proposition for you."

"I've been warned about men like you."

"You've never even known a man like me," he said. "Look, I can take three or four weeks off, if you can. But I'm sick of being stranded while you take off to rescue someone or you're out on a clinic run. You told me you get a vacation after a year. You've only been there eleven months, I know, but get a couple of weeks off, Cassandra. Do it somehow. I want to take you north, to Kakadu."

"I don't know how I can . . . "

"Just do it. I'll give you five days to make arrangements and then you and I are taking off. I want to show you some things you've never seen and you'll never forget."

"I'm not sure . . . "

"Cassandra, don't give me that. In seven months we've never had more than a day together and those have been few and far between. Relationships take some knowing each other, girl. Come on, let's see what we've got going for us. I'll be there sometime Sunday. Make arrangements so we can take off Tuesday, you hear?"

He didn't even say goodbye. Cassie sat holding the phone in her hand, grinning. How could she possibly take a vacation, much as she knew she had one coming to her?

Her toes curled. Oh, just the sound of his voice. She clutched the phone to her bosom before setting it back in its cradle.

Fortunately, the next day was only a clinic run to the AIM hospital in Winnamurra. Nothing exceptional. On the way back, she asked Sam, "What do we do about vacations?"

He shrugged. "QUANTAS sends a relief pilot out for me. I don't know about you."

"Most of the time when we go out on calls it's just a matter of bringing the patient back in. I thought maybe Chris would spare Sister Claire to go out with you to bring back a patient. She's as competent as most doctors."

"You thinking of taking off, I gather?"

"If I can."

"How long?"

"Three weeks."

"What you going to do? Fly to see your father?"

She shook her head. "No. I'm going north, to the aboriginal reservations up in Kakadu."

He gave her a funny look before turning around so that all she saw was his profile.

"Sister Claire might be willing to go out on emergencies. Maybe she could even do clinics. We never seem to have crises there."

"What about the time I pulled that sword out of that black fellow?"

"That was an exception. I wonder if Chris would spare her."

"You going to Isabel's funeral tonight?"

"Of course," she said. "And maybe Chris would welcome something to get his mind off his loss. Maybe he'd take any emergencies. I imagine he's never even been up in a plane."

"And leave that sot Edwards in charge of the hospital? Fat chance."

"I'll ask him," she said, mainly to herself. "Maybe that'll give him a chance to see what the Flying Doctors are like. Give him some insight. Just extreme emergencies, the ones Sister Claire couldn't handle."

"You're optimistic. Doc Adams with insight?"

"His bark is worse than his bite, Sam. He's been an unhappy man."

"From what I hear, he's always been that way. Cold fish."

"I'm going to ask him anyhow." She had thought of little else since Blake's phone call. Sleeping under the stars with Blake. Seeing land that few people in the world had seen. An adventure. Blake kissing her every night. Listening to Blake tell her stories of the land, hearing his voice every day, watching him awaken, seeing the firelight dance across his face. She'd never camped, but she imagined how it would be.

"You know, Sister Grace is far prettier than Sister Claire. Why don't you ask for her? I've heard you say she's a good nurse."

"But Sister Claire's far likelier to make decisions on her own, and if she has to perform minor operations, she can't be beat. I'd trust her with an appendectomy and certainly if someone gives birth . . . " No one she knew was expecting in the next month, she was relieved to recall.

"Sister Grace is cuter."

It seemed like everyone in town attended Isabel Adams's funeral. Chris stood like a statue, stretching his arm out to shake hands with each mourner.

Cassie sat in the back row. These other people were all his patients. She knew them only as friends and acquaintances. Friends. She guessed maybe she didn't have any in town. It wasn't here that she got to know people.

Who were her friends?

Horrie? She guessed Horrie was a friend, though they never talked anything but business. She and Sam had dined with him and Betty at the radio shack a couple of times; they were always energetic and friendly, but they were more acquaintances than friends. But Cassie did feel a kinship with Horrie, a closeness she couldn't define—maybe because her life circled around him.

Don, certainly.

Sam. Was Sam a friend? If they didn't work together, would they be friendly? Certainly he was the most reliable person in the world to work with—most of the time. There was never anything she'd asked him to do, including anesthesia and even sword-pulling, that he'd refused. The few clashes they'd had were due to weather and the advisability of flying someplace. He alternated between trying to protect her and resenting her authority. She probably didn't know how she felt about Sam because she didn't know how he felt about her. Maybe he didn't know, either.

Certainly she couldn't turn to Chris Adams. She didn't think she even liked him, though she had come to trust his surgical ability. He didn't treat her condescendingly anymore, though he'd have liked it better if she were a man. Or if she weren't a Flying Doctor. By no means could she call Chris a friend. They had an undeclared truce, and she imagined he was grateful for her acts of kindness towards Isabel.

She looked around at all the pews in the crowded Presbyterian Church. She knew almost everyone. They nodded to her, came over and shook her hand, leaned over to kiss her cheek. At least she had a lot of acquaintances.

When the ceremony was over and the people had filed past the casket, shaking hands with Chris, Sam whispered in her ear, "If I die while we still know each other, don't let 'em have an open casket for me, willya?"

When Cassie approached Chris, he grasped her hand and held it tightly. "I've never adequately thanked you . . . "

"It was my pleasure," she said.

"A few friends are coming over to the house for coffee. Will you come, please? I'd like my sister, Romla, to meet you."

Cassie tried not to let her mouth fall open. "Of course."

When the last of the guests left, at eleven, Chris said, "Don't go yet. I don't want to be alone."

Romla, whom Cassie liked immediately, had gone to bed.

Chris was partly drunk, Cassie realized. He must have been drinking all evening. His speech was slurring as he walked into the kitchen and sat down at the table, yanking his shirt loose at the neck, untying his tie.

"Do you know," he said, looking at her, "here, sit down, please. Do you know I've been alone all my life?"

"You're not alone," she said, pouring herself a cup of coffee. "You're important in this town. And, you've been a good husband, too, I'm sure. You must know that."

He laughed harshly. It was not a happy laugh. "Good husband? That's a joke. I haven't been a husband in so long I don't know what it would be like. Do you know what, Cassie? No, how would you? I've never been so alone as I . . . oh, forget it. Why is it important now? It's over with."

Cassie leaned over and put a hand on his shoulder. "Chris, I think I better go. You're saying things you'll be sorry you've said to me. You're lost and lonely now. Your life has been disrupted. You probably feel at sea. I'm not the one to share this time with you."

"Who the hell is, Cassie? I've lived in this town for eighteen years and I don't have a single close friend." He put his head in his hands, his elbows on the table.

"You're feeling sorry for yourself, which is okay. You've just lost the most important person in your world."

Chris picked up the whiskey bottle and poured the last of it into his glass, then threw it against the wall; shards of glass splintered around the kitchen. Cassie got up and found a dustpan and broom, then swept it up.

"Good night, Chris. If there's anything at all I can do . . . would you like me to see patients tomorrow?"

He stared at her. He stared at her for so long that she finally left. The savage look in his bloodshot eyes followed her all the way home.

She woke up seeing that look before remembering that she was going to ask him to cover for her while she spent two glorious weeks in the tropics with Blake Thompson. She tingled at the thought, though she could not forget the look in Chris Adams's eyes.

Chapter 24

They'd seen no other white people for two days, ever since leaving Darwin, staying there only long enough to buy food. Tonight they were camping along the Mary River; tomorrow they'd be at that part of the ocean called the Timor Sea.

The tropics overwhelmed Cassie emotionally. The soft air relaxed her. Blake said, "We can't swim in the river, it's filled with crocs." But he took her out in a boat, staying out until long after dark, watching the most glorious sunset imaginable. Red, fiery rays lit up the sky, taking over half an hour to fade into a golden glow.

"Now," Blake said, "we'll look for crocs."

"Can't they kill?"

He laughed. "Yes, they're deadly. These rivers up here are swollen with them, but you said you've never seen one."

"I don't have to," she said.

"But you do have to."

They paddled quietly through the turgidly flowing river, heading back south, toward their camp. Blake paddled near the banks of the narrow river, using his flashlight to search for the prehistoric water beasts.

"Okay," he whispered. "Don't paddle. We'll just float along." Cassie wondered how he could see in the dark. The moon had not yet risen and the millions of stars gave little light.

She had never felt such contentment, yet such excitement. She didn't even know what name to put to her feelings, deciding it was more than love. What she felt for Ray Graham couldn't compare with the depth of her feeling for Blake. His touch electrified her. His kisses set her afire. Looking into his eyes gave her a feeling of belonging.

She found herself telling him things she had only told Fiona. He asked questions, and he listened. He leaned over to kiss her unexpectedly.

It was something more than love that she was experiencing—perhaps it was discovering another kind of love at the same time. A love of the land. Of this wonderful country that had been hers all along, this land she had never known. Every mile of the journey had been filled with discovery. She was so used to flying over it that driving through it awakened new reactions in her constantly.

In Alice Springs they had stayed overnight with an old friend of Blake's, the minister of the Congregational Church, someone from his university days. Further along, in Katherine, he knew someone else with whom they spent the night. Salt of the earth people, with whom she immediately felt comfortable. She met no one with whom she felt ill at ease—Blake's friends welcomed her as though they'd known her forever.

But it was up here, up in the far tropical north that they were at last alone. Blake pointed out landmarks, telling her the history and geography of the land, tales that fascinated her. He had a wonderful sense of humor, laughing as he told her humorous stories. As they sped north along the highway he would reach out for her hand, holding it unless he had to shift gears or point out something of interest. They drove mile after mile, hands entwined.

He asked her so many questions about herself that by the end of the third day, when they'd left Darwin heading east to the Mary River, she thought there was nothing else to tell him. She'd never had a man concentrate so on her, urging her to share herself. She'd never known such an open man, one who didn't seem embarrassed by anything. Who hugged her in front of his friends with a total lack of self-consciousness.

Once he put on the brakes so sharply she nearly hit the windshield. There wasn't another car in sight, nothing to slow them down. Just an endless straight road. He didn't turn the motor off, but reached over and pulled her to him. "I need to kiss you," he said, doing so thoroughly. And, having done so, sped on.

Remembering this as she sat in the fore of the boat, she sighed contentedly, thinking of the wonderful four days they'd had so far.

Suddenly, Blake said, "Shh" and slid into the water.

"Ohmigod," she exclaimed.

"Shh," he repeated, his flashlight aimed at reeds on the river's bank.

He handed her the flashlight. "Keep it exactly on that spot. Don't move it." He glided through the water, barely making a ripple. Cassie was suddenly aware of two red eyes reflected in the beam, not moving, staring, unblinking. Blake reached out to grab it, lifting the small crocodile into the air, holding it by the neck, saying, "Keep the light on its eyes. Light hypnotizes them.

"Weighs about sixty pounds," he said.

"Could it bite you?"

He nodded. "Could take a big bite out of me. Out of you, too." He held it out to her. She didn't let herself shrink away. "Now you can never say you haven't seen one," he said, starting back toward her.

Then, grinning, he tossed it back into the river as he leaped into the boat, and Cassie was surprised they didn't capsize.

How he knew where they were heading she couldn't tell. She couldn't even see the banks of the river, but unerringly he took her down narrow, winding channels until they arrived at their camp.

He'd set up a tent, though they had slept outside last night. "We'll keep the food in the tent," he'd said. "There are no dangerous animals to assault us if we sleep outside. I imagine it's the only continent in the world where it's always safe to sleep outside." He had placed their swags beside each other, a foot apart, and they had fallen asleep holding hands.

"Tomorrow night," he said, "we'll go to a corroboree. We'll move camp tomorrow, go to the sea. You'll like that. I do."

The moon was opaque.

Blake said, "We can't sit together. You'll have to go over with the lubras and I'll join the men."

Cassie nodded and headed toward the black women, in front of their own small fire, not nearly as large as the men's. She and Blake had arrived just after dark, when the tribe was still chanting its prayers . . . to the rain spirit and to the Great Mother of fertility. Their voices rose and fell together, rising to a high falsetto, filling the night air.

Through the darkness came the hollow, lonesome, deep moan of the didgeridoo, an oboe-like instrument. Chiming in were the gil-gil sticks, their high treble sounding like thousands of crickets. Then, softly, voices broke in, rising gradually to an extraordinary crescendo. In unison, torsos undulated rhythmically to the music. The same words were repeated, again and again, the cadence never breaking. Cupped hands beat a tattoo upon glistening thighs, and in the distance tom-toms could be heard as yam-sticks beat the dry earth. Boomerangs—crimson with blood—rattled as they were clicked together. An old man on the edge of the circle beat two tins, breaking into a wild, excited cry, sounding like a dingo wailing at the moon.

The throbbing rhythm rose to a frenzy.

Then, suddenly, unexpectedly, stillness. Not a sound.

Silent echoes pulsated in Cassie's ears. She could hear her own breath.

One voice began to sing, a high tenor coursing through the night, and the music began to pound again, quickening, the throbbing of the didgeridoo insistent.

Eyes now accustomed to the dark, Cassie saw dancers emerge from the trees, wending their way to the circle in the center of the group of men. Blake had told her that they timed the dancing to the rising of a particular star.

The faces of the dancers were reflected from the firelight. Painted grotesquely, their frightening visages were topped with silver-white cockatoo feathers, iridescent in the firelight. To these elaborate crowns were added a bizarre medley of ochred sticks and quivers. The white paint on their bodies made them look like skeletons floating in limbo. They stamped upon the ground in unison, making noises, Cassie thought, like chalk scraping over a blackboard.

Forming a line, the dancers twisted like snakes between the fires lit beyond the circle, their feet pounding, the leaves—fastened at their knees and elbows—rustling like whispers in the night.

Shivers ran up Cassie's back as the throaty, thick rasping sounds of the savage music wound into her. Lifting their feet in unison, the dancers pounded the earth with such force and momentum that it shook under them. The lubras around Cassie hit their thighs, and the men joined together in singing. The dancers wound around the large circle of men, returning to the center, imitating daily events. An iguana frantic to escape dogs that yelped after it, the ecstatic jubilation of a man finding water in the desert, the slithering of a snake, the willowy movement of a brolga in its minuet.

Then a frenzied dance, the feral vaulting of the pursued, the chase, the capture, the culmination with the kill. Sounds alien to Cassie rent the air.

The dance continued, repetitively. The staccato sound of the music, the eternal duplication of action and sound, pummeled into Cassie's nerves until she felt caught, as in a straitjacket, emotionally unable to escape. She wanted to scream, to flee, thinking she could not bear it another moment, when a high-pitched "ai-ee" came from the crowd as the dancers pounded one last time, the stomping of their feet seeming to flatten the very land under them.

Silence. The dancers, moving in a column, snaked out of the circle and sprinted back into the woods, disappearing in the night.

Cassie wasn't aware that she'd been holding her breath until she heard Blake say, "Come on." He reached a hand down to help her up.

Holding her hand tightly, he walked ahead of her in the darkness. "Careful not to trip over tree roots," he said.

Cassie's body was alive, electrified by the music and the dancing, by the lubras slapping their thighs, by their bare breasts glowing in the firelight, by the men's dancing, naked except for their headdresses, beckoning her, luring her soul.

As the sounds faded behind them, their walk through the palm trees slowed, Blake beside her now instead of ahead of her.

"We're nearly at the beach," he said, his hand around her shoulder, holding her close.

The trees ended. Only sand stretched ahead of them, into infinity. There were no forcefully crashing waves, just the pat-pat-pat of barely-lapping water.

Blake stopped, bending down to take off his shoes. Cassie followed suit. The warm sand squished between her toes.

They strolled for over a mile before arriving at their tent under the palms, at the edge of the beach.

"Let's swim," Blake said, peeling off his shirt, turning, gathering her in his arms. She kissed his chest. His hands fiddled with the buttons of her blouse, until he slipped it off. She put her arms around his chest. He unfastened her bra, and she felt her breasts against him, their skin touching for the first time. Oh, God, she thought, closing her eyes. It feels so good.

He let go of her, unzipping his trousers, letting them fall onto the sand, kicking them away. "I want to see you," he said. "I want to see you for the first time this way, by the light of the heavens, see you . . . " His voice thickened.

She slid out of her pants, thinking, his body is beautiful. All of him was.

He walked to her, not touching her, bending over to kiss her breasts. "You're as beautiful as I knew you would be."

He stood looking down at her, then turned from her and ran into the water, diving so she could not see him. She walked to the edge of the water, so alive that she wanted to shout.

She submerged herself slowly into the ocean. It was as warm as bathwater. Blake's head bobbed to the surface, far out. He swam toward her, long, slow strokes, his legs slicing smoothly through the water. A cloud covered the moon and she lost sight of him.

"You're not afraid, are you?" His voice came from beside her.

No. She shook her head. No.

He reached for her hand and pulled her down in the water with him, kissing her wetly, his tongue thrusting into her mouth as though searching for answers there. She felt his hand between her legs, touching her, opening her.

She lay back in the warm wetness, her legs spread apart, feeling his kisses on her, his touches. His lips feathered across her belly, and he pulled her legs around his waist, his mouth devouring her, kissing her neck, his tongue finding her ear, his breath coming hard.

He picked her up and carried her to the sand, kneeling down, cradling her in his arms. He kissed her, and she wound her arms around his neck as water lapped their feet.

"I want you," she said.

"I know. And I've wanted you since that night at the dance."

He lay, his body on hers, his weight on his elbows. He leaned down to kiss her again, and his body melded into hers. He rolled over, pulling her on top of him, his mouth finding her breasts, kissing them as she pressed against him, their bodies undulating in a rhythm that picked up the frenzy of the corroboree. They rocked back and forth, against each other, his hands surrounding her buttocks as she whispered, "I'm going to . . . "

He rolled her over again. As she arched her back, he thrust into her, pressing her so tightly against him she thought they were one.

"Oh, don't leave me," she cried.

The stars above her blazed like fireworks; she felt the ocean rushing into her, over her, and she whispered, "Don't stop!"

"Oh, dear God," she whispered. "I think I'm falling in love with you."

He arched his back. "Think? You *think?*" His voice cracked.

"Goddammit," he muttered, holding himself still. "Tell me! Tell me you love me."

"I love you."

He gave one final lunge, and the water washed over them. Opening her eyes, Cassie saw a star shooting across the sky.

Chapter 25

A spiny anteater in reds and ochres stared down at them from the huge rock. In yellow ochre and white there was a fish, reminding Cassie of the ones painted in her long-ago first grade class. There were primitive line drawings of crocodiles; dark handprints against white backgrounds.

"This land has been continuously inhabited for over twenty-three thousand years," Blake said. "This," he pointed to the paintings on the immense rock, "is the world's earliest known art. It's the world of the Dreamtime."

"Dreamtime?" Cassie asked, basking in the warmth of Blake's hand around hers.

"The Dreamtime," said Blake, leading Cassie closer to the rocks on which were painted such prehistoric images, "is the aboriginal way of recounting how the land was given to them at the beginning of Time, of Creation."

"Like Genesis?" asked Cassie.

Blake smiled and squeezed her hand. "Pretty much so, except they don't tell of so much begatting. They tell of how their ancestors rose from the earth in animal and human forms and created earth as it is now. The word Dreamtime has nothing to do with dreams as we know them. These drawings tell the story. You want to hear about it?"

"Of course." Cassie couldn't believe she was looking at pictures nearly twenty-five thousand years old. She reached out her hand and feathered it along the gigantic rock.

"Once upon a time," Blake said with a smile. "Well, actually before time began, the world was unformed and malleable. Then the Warramurrungundji arose from the sea. She was a woman with a human body, and She created the land and gave birth to human beings. Here," he pointed, "She's represented as a white rock. Along came other creators: Marrawuti, the sea eagle—see, there—who captures a person's spirit when he dies. He also brought water lilies from the sea, dropping them from his claws so they were planted over the floodplain. This crocodile represents Ginga, who became so misshapen because he was blistered in a fire. Ginga made this country, the rock country. The bower-bird here is Djuway, who is caretaker of the sacred initiation rites.

"All living things," Blake said, and Cassie thought his voice took on a reverent tone, "are as One. Tree, eagle, grass, earth, water, people. We are all One. When Creation was finished, the people were told by the ancestral beings that they had made everything necessary, now it was up to the people to keep them safe for all time. They were admonished not to change anything, but to revere and treasure the land and each other."

"So," Cassie said, fascinated with all she was hearing and seeing, "they were made custodians of the land."

Blake leaned down to kiss her cheek. "Exactly. But not only the land. Of each other as well. Of all animals, too. The Dreamtime is the glue that's supposed to hold the environment and man together in harmony. It has succeeded here for two thousand generations. Because aboriginals are part of the land, part of nature, they can't understand us. Why, they wonder, do we want to change it, destroy it."

Cassie looked up at him. "You have the soul of a poet, you know that?"

Blake grinned. "I don't mind your overestimating me. But it's not true. Look what I do. I graze tens of thousands of cattle on the land. Each day I help to change the landscape forever."

"You can't avoid progress, no matter how charming the Dreamtime sounds," offered Cassie.

"Progress? I'm not sure we're progressing. Look what Hitler's doing in Europe. Is annihilating people progress? Is genocide progress? Is jailing and killing those who don't agree with us progress? Is going to war over land progress? I think the longer civilization goes on the less pure it becomes. For centuries we've fought wars to force others to believe in our God. I know, I know . . . I can't move the calendar back thousands of years, but I'm not sure progress is the right word, but whatever it is, I'm as guilty as the next person. I overgraze and destroy the land. I am more dedicated to acquiring land and money than spiritual growth . . . "

Cassie stared at him. She had never heard anyone talk like this.

"Come on," he said, pulling her hand, leading her up higher on the rock formations. "Be careful of your step, but I want you to see the view from way up there," he pointed to the top of the escarpment. "I want to make love to you up there, where we can see into forever, where you'll never forget the view and what we do there as long as you live."

He was tender and gentle and insistent and passionate. He touched every part of her that was touchable. "I am going to drink your wine," he laughed as he rained kisses all over her body.

"I'm going to devour you," he muttered as he bit her.

"I'm going to inhale you," he whispered as he licked her.

They made love all afternoon on a flat rocky promontory overlooking green plains that stretched to the horizon. The sun beat down on their naked bodies as they joined together.

"We are one," he said.

Later, after they'd made love for hours, he added, "We are one with the universe."

Cassie knew there had never been a love like theirs. She was in love with his words and his ideas as well as his love-making. She was in love with his looks, particularly his hands—even the left one, which had been burned in a fire many years ago. She loved his knowledge of the history of the land and its peoples. She loved his having friends wherever they went. She loved his opening her up, breaking down her reserve. She loved trusting again, and she loved his hand wrapped around hers as they drove the thousands of miles across the red continent. She loved the taste of him, and what his hands and tongue did to her body. She loved the feel of him coming inside her, and she loved seeing him stand up and stretch. She loved his laugh and his easy smile. She loved the feline grace with which he walked, and she loved the power he emanated.

"Some day," he told her, "when I wear my father down, we're going to muster all our cattle with helicopters. We're going to use trucks instead of droving our cattle twelve hundred miles over a six-month period. We're going to bring ranching into the twentieth century."

"Your father doesn't like the idea?"

"My father thinks it would then be business. He is dedicated to carrying on as it's been done for the last hundred years. He says if I want to run a business I should take myself to Sydney."

"But you love droving. You love mustering. You love the life you lead."

He nodded. "But I'm not going to do the same thing forever." He turned to grin at her. "Learn this about me. I'm restless. I want to try new things. I want to be ahead of others. Someday I'm going to own more land and more cattle than anyone else in Australia."

Cassie, naked, sat up on the hot rock. "What were you just telling me about man and nature in harmony?"

"I know. And I do believe it. Yet I don't live in that kind of society. I live in one where you either have to go forward or get lost. My going forward may make the lives of my grandchildren less livable, but I must go forward or sink. And I'm going far forward. I'm going to blaze trails."

Cassie reached for her bra and began to put it on. Blake reached down and pulled her up, leaning down to kiss her right breast. "Why is that so important?" she asked.

"How else will I know I've succeeded? Look, look out there." He waved his arm in an arc. "I don't want to own this particular stretch of land, but I'm going to own land like it. I'm going to own so much land over so much of this country that when there's a drought I won't lose any cattle. I'm going to be able to move them across the country to markets, all on land that I own. It may be a narrow trail, but I'm going to own land from here to Brisbane or to Adelaide. My cattle will be able to be moved at the first sign of prolonged drought; they won't be trapped on overgrazed land and bottlenecked in. There will be a path from Tookaringa to the cities that will not have been grazed, but will be waiting until it's needed, waiting for my cattle."

"God, Blake, you're saying you want to own land for a thousand or more consecutive miles?" Cassie pulled her clothes on and buttoned up her shirt.

"Yup. That's it. You'll see."

It was an outrageous idea, but she thought Blake could do anything he put his mind to. She walked over to him and put her arms around his waist, leaning her head against his chest. "I don't doubt it for a minute."

His arm reached around her shoulder and he turned so that they looked from the escarpment over the miles of emptiness. "This, my dear, is the world's last frontier. This is where dreams can still come true. Within the next decade there'll come another prolonged drought that will kill hundreds of thousands of animals, that'll break families and hearts, that'll skyrocket prices of meat. The land will dry up and cattle and sheep will be too far from bores and waterholes that'll be dry anyhow, and their carcasses will be littered across the continent. The dreams and hopes and lives of scores of people will be ended. But not us, not Tookaringa. By then, Cassie, I'll have water bores all along my land running all the way to the coast, and my cattle will move along, not even losing weight. What will destroy many will mean profit for us. Not that I yearn for that. But it's inevitable. History and weather do repeat themselves, in patterns. And I'll be ready. Maybe not yet, but I'll wear Dad down. Or I'll do it on my own."

Cassie gazed up at him. He was looking far into the distance, seeing—she knew—into the future, which belonged to him.

Waiting for them back at their camp along the Alligator River, sitting cross-legged in front of their tent, was a man of medium height, sandy-colored hair, bleached blue eyes, and three or four days growth of beard. He was dressed in khaki shorts and short-sleeved shirt, and wore no socks with his boots.

He arose when they pulled into the camp, doffing his hat and saying, "Hope I've got the right blokes. Hear tell you're a lady doctor." He stretched out his hand. "George Bill. Called Buffalo," he grinned, showing a gap in his front teeth.

Cassie met his handshake. "I'm the doctor."

Buffalo nodded. "Got a problem nearby. One of the blacks has been wounded by a boomerang. He's in a bit of a bad shape."

"Never a vacation?" asked Blake, reaching into the river and pulling out a couple of beers and a Coke. He handed a beer to Buffalo and a Coke to Cassie.

"His chest is pretty badly bruised," Buffalo said, using his teeth to uncap the bottle. "I touched the bruised area and it felt like bones clicking under me fingers. The old bloke was in a lotta pain, had trouble breathing. I mean, every time he took a deep breath it was painful, you could see. But he won't let a woman look at him."

"What do you want me to do then?"

"Well, I thought you could tell me," he said, taking a swig from the bottle, gulping as it went down.

Cassie sat down, cross-legged, and Buffalo scrunched next to her, knees bent, his weight on the balls of his feet, his bush hat pushed far back on his head. "I don't suppose you have any tape," she said.

Buffalo didn't even answer. Cassie thought for a minute. "I think I have an Ace bandage in my kit." Blake had laughed when she insisted on bringing her medical bag. I'd feel naked without it, she'd said. "I'll get it in a minute. It's stretchy," she explained. "Wind it around the entire chest under the arms, just kind of a compressive splint bandage to immobilize the chest so it doesn't hurt so much to tilt or bend. Make him lie still for a few days."

"What're you doing up here?" Blake asked. "You live around here?"

"I'm a buffalo hunter," said Buffalo, "or maybe you could gather that. Damn Asians brought water buffalo over last century and they got loose and multiplied and now roam around eatin' up crops and drivin' people batty. There's a bounty on 'em. And they make good meat. I got a camp about two miles down the river. Not far from one of the blacks' camps. I give 'em the animals I kill, 'cause for sure I can't eat that much by myself. Come to dinner tonight, if you've never had buffalo meat. You bring the beer and I'll supply the rest."

Cassie looked over at Blake. His eyes met hers. "Sure," he nodded. "Right hospitable."

They dined on fried buffalo steaks, fried potatoes, fried eggs, damper, and beer.

"I'm really a water hunter," Buffalo told them, obviously enjoying the company. "For last six years, government's been sending me all over Arnhem Land locating water. You can tell I don't talk much, can't you, the way I run on when I see anyone. I only get outta here once a year, for a month at a time."

"First time I've had buffalo steaks," Blake said. "Not bad at all."

"What do you do up here without anyone to talk with?" Cassie asked. She thought buffalo steaks left much to be desired.

"Well, you can't put it that way. I got friends among the tribes. And when I'm over in Darwin, I buy enough books so I have one a week to read." Reminded Cassie of Heather Martin and her sisters.

"You read fifty-two books a year?" asked Cassie. Buffalo didn't look like he'd ever read one.

"Hey," he grinned, "I'm one of the best-educated men in the territory, I bet. I read philosophy and history and travel books as well as novels. I've been more places than most people, I bet, even if I have never left this spot of the world. I spend a lotta my time thinkin'."

He scratched at the mosquito bites that covered his legs. "The aborigines let me see their rites, initiations, things like that. First white man, I bet. 'Course, they don't let women see any of it, and I'm sworn to secrecy." His voice swelled with pride.

He turned to Cassie. "Reason no black man'll let you take care of him is that they don't think women really are people or have souls."

Cassie felt herself straighten up. "Not have souls? What are we, then?"

"The aborigines think women are vessels . . . "

"Vessels?"

Blake reached out a hand to cover Cassie's. "Hey, it's not you he means. He's telling you of tribal traditions and beliefs. You don't have to argue with him."

Buffalo nodded. "Yeah. They don't even know babies are a result of intercourse, begging your pardon, ma'am. They think pregnancy is the result of the supernatural. A woman is a vessel to carry the seed of the Great Spirit that will produce other men spirits that live in the flesh in their tribe. Being born of woman profanes the Dreamtime. A woman is unclean and it's a sin to be born to an unclean woman, so a man must be cleansed by initiation rites. Males live apart from women. They can only approach women at specified times. It used to be death, not so much so anymore, to a man or even a boy who disregarded the sexual taboos. There's still death to any male who reveals tribal magic secrets or secrets of initiation to a woman."

"My God," said Cassie.

Buffalo got up and went over to the fire, leaning down to lift up the iron coffee pot. He walked back and poured coffee into three metal mugs. "Women're happy, though."

Yeah, I bet.

"They don't have to do the major work of hunting. Men have to supply food for the whole tribe, and fight the evil spirits and outwit kangaroos and crocodiles. Sometimes hunting for food takes days. And evil spirits always lie in wait. Women never have to participate in that, in the tough life."

"What do they do?" asked Cassie, thinking that in our civilization women don't usually have to go out and supply what's necessary for living, either. They stay home and wash dishes and diapers and take care of runny noses and cook and clean the house every day. Maybe it wasn't so different.

Buffalo sat down again, holding his coffee mug. "Women collect the food—witchetty grubs, little reptiles, bugs. Firewood. You see them bent over like mules. And every white Aussie I've ever seen looks at them and feels pity, for all they see is the dirt and the hard work and the primitive thinking. You know what they don't see?"

"Yes," said Blake.

Buffalo looked at him.

"They don't see the magic, the religion, the wholeness with Nature, the unbroken chain of humanity going back to the start of time."

Cassie thought, Blake, I love you. Blake and Buffalo's eyes were locked. Buffalo nodded. "You're right. They don't see the freedom of life, either. Or the security of knowing exactly what is expected of you, of knowing just what your role is."

"Oh, I don't know," Cassie interjected. "In civilized society we pretty much know what our roles are."

Blake laughed. "Well, maybe most people do, but you've broken the pattern. You're not settling for a woman's traditional role."

"Well, all the tribes aren't alike here, either. In some of the tribes the men and women do associate, do form family groups."

"What happens," asked Blake, "if you want a black woman?"

Buffalo grimaced. "Not me."

"Well, if any white man wants a black woman?"

"He takes her. They're used to that. Whenever a man wants a woman, he just takes her. She has nothing to say about it. White man, black man. She thinks that's what she's here for. To be used. But it's not that the woman's black that turns me off. It's syphilis. I don't know of any tribe that isn't riddled by venereal disease. Me, I go spend a month each year down in some city where there's white women." He said to Cassie, "Hope I'm not offending you, ma'am."

She wanted to say, *Not at all.* But couldn't.

Chapter 26

"It's been a wonderful vacation," Cassie said, not yet opening the utility door. "I've loved every minute of it."

"Look," Blake said, putting his hand around her wrist, "you talk about all this being based on just a couple of weeks together and some great sex. That's a bunch of bullshit. You know damn well this has been no ordinary couple of weeks. Lots of people don't get this much in two years, or ever. How many people do you know who've had this kind of a time together? Nobody, right? And if you think I'm coming on strong, that's my style. If it bothers you, you better run like hell, because when I want something, I reach out and grab hold. I try to be sensitive but I'll be damned if I'll pussyfoot around. Yes, I want you. That should be pretty obvious by now." He leaned over and kissed her even though people were walking down the street in front of Cassie's house.

"How am I going to come back down to earth?"

He grinned. "Your life's not down to earth—you have to take off into the wild blue yonder. I don't know how I'll do it, either. We're carried away by all this, and that's good. But now let's focus on possibilities. If we do that, the rest will take care of itself."

Cassie had never felt such exquisite joy. He'd made it clear, or so it had seemed to her, that he wouldn't expect her to continue her professional life; he wanted a wife who would be content to be Mrs. Blake Thompson.

For years she'd concentrated on nothing but being a doctor, but now she would gladly give it all up to live at Tookaringa, to be Blake's wife, to bear his children. Nothing mattered except this man beside her.

She had another year's obligation to the Flying Doctors. They could be engaged for that long.

"Look," he said, tracing his finger across her throat. "We have all the time in the world. Let's take it slow. We'll be apart, you up in the sky and me out on the land, and we'll think of making love to each other. We'll remember each other's touch and yearn for each other. We'll see new country together, geographically and emotionally."

"You can even seduce me with words," Cassie said with a smile.

He laughed. "Look who's talking of seduction. I probably won't think of anything but your body all twelve hours back to Tookaringa. Thank goodness there won't be much traffic. Wish I had a helicopter now. I'd fly to you every night."

"I don't know if I'll even be able to sleep tonight."

"Between now and the next time I see you, figure out how I can come into your house and sleep in your bed without the whole damn town knowing about it."

"I love you," she said. "I'm crazy mad in love with you."

He leaned over to kiss her again. "I probably knew that before you did." He opened the door and stretched his legs out of the truck. Walking around to her side, he opened the door and then grabbed her suitcases from the back. She followed him up the verandah steps.

"I'll be back as soon as I can, but it might be a couple weeks," he said, pushing his Stetson to the back of his head.

It turned out to be much longer. By far.

Horrie phoned. "Thank God you're back."

"Problems?"

"When aren't there? Your friend, Doc Adams, flew out on emergencies twice. He's not as bad as I'd thought he'd be. And Sister Claire's been a brick. But thank God you're back. They've got polio out at Yancanna and Sister Brigid wants you out there like yesterday."

"Polio?" Cassie's voice cracked. "Is she sure?"

"Pretty much so. It started in the aboriginal hill village and now she's afraid it's spreading all around. Get down here for the five o'clock and you can talk to her."

But it was Sister Marianne who told Cassie, "We have an eleven-year-old boy with residual paralysis. There are six black people up in the hill village who won't come in to town." Despite her worry, Cassie had to smile at the thought of Yancanna considering itself a town. "Last night a young man in his twenties, manager of a station nearly a hundred miles away, was brought in. He's a strong, strapping-looking man but his breathing is seriously impaired."

Breathing was one of the main problems of polio, that and the inability to swallow. Cassie wondered where the nearest iron lung was. Certainly they couldn't get it to Yancanna, but they could fly Yancanna patients into Augusta Springs.

"Can he sleep?"

"No. And on the radio we just received word that another patient, a drover who's been out on muster, is being driven in. We don't even have room for anyone else. What'll we do?"

"Well, I can't get out there tonight, but we'll fly out first thing in the morning. I just got back from holiday and haven't seen Sam. Moist hot packs. Bed rest. I suppose you know all that."

She could practically envision Marianne nodding.

"I'll see if I can locate an iron lung and get it set up in the hospital here in case we need it."

"Righto." The nurse signed off.

Cassie turned to Horrie. "Where's Sam?"

"He and Sister Claire are out on a clinic run. Should be home before dark."

"I'll go see Dr. Adams and find out if he knows where we could get an iron lung."

Cassie called the hospital. Yes, Dr. Adams was still there. She ran all the way.

By the time she arrived she was out of breath and sweat was pouring down her face. The matron grinned at her. "He's in his office," she said, not waiting for Cassie to ask. "Have a good vacation?"

"Wonderful." Cassie whisked down the hall to Chris's office and, without knocking, barged in. He was seated at his desk, writing. He looked up.

"Chris, have you any idea where we can get an iron lung?"

"I've ordered one from Adelaide," he said. "They're being made there."

She stopped, raising her eyebrows. "You have?"

"I know about Yancanna," he said. "I couldn't leave here, Cassie. If it's an epidemic, whoever goes out there will have to stay for days. I can't leave the hospital."

"I wouldn't expect you to. That's why there are Flying Doctors."

"Horrie asked me to fly out, but I can't. I knew they had at least three cases so I phoned around and Adelaide sent the lung out last night. Should be here via air cargo tonight or tomorrow."

Cassie sat down. "Well, thanks."

"You'll have to air-evac respiratory cases here. I'm calling around to find out where we can get another if we need it. We may need several. We're both going to be busy, you out there and me waiting for whoever you send in. I've already designated three rooms as a quarantine area. There are two nursing sisters who married and moved to the bush whom I've contacted and, if this turns into an epidemic, they'll come back to work."

Cassie's mouth was open.

Then Chris smiled. Cassie realized that it was the first time she had ever seen him really smile.

"I enjoyed the two times I flew out. I'd never flown before. It was quite an experience. In all my years of practice I'd never performed an appendectomy on a kitchen table."

Was this the same man she'd known for a year? "I can't thank you enough."

"Well, I'm glad your holiday didn't last any longer. I'd be hard put to handle things here and a polio epidemic."

"Have you ever had polio cases?" she asked, knowing she never had.

"Now and then, remote, isolated ones. Couple of young people paralyzed, couple of kids died, several people recovered with no aftermath. But not all at once like this Yancanna thing."

"I'm flying out in the morning."

Chris nodded. "I took that for granted."

"I'm sure from the sound of it that one of the patients will have to be returned here to the hospital tomorrow evening."

"I cleared my schedule if you'd like me to fly out with you. I can bring the patient, or patients, back. I can't spare more than a day."

Cassie nodded, still dazed at all that he was saying. She'd never heard him so loquacious or so helpful. He'd taken charge, anticipating her needs, reaching out as she'd never known him to do.

"Chris, I don't know how to thank you. For being on call for those emergencies and now, all this . . . "

"How do I ever thank you for what you did for Isabel?"

"It was so little."

"My sentiments about this exactly. After all, Cassie, these are my people, too. When they arrive here they become my patients. Well," and Cassie swore his face softened, "at least, ours."

Cassie jumped up from her chair and went around his desk, leaning over to hug him. "Chris, there's a side of you I've never seen before. I have to admit I never dreamed we could work together so well."

As he turned to say something, her lips brushed his cheek. She hoped she hadn't crossed a line that would make him withdraw again. It would be so wonderful to work *with* another doctor instead of feeling defensive about everything she did.

He sat rubbing his glasses on his tie. "I've never been to Yancanna," he said. "I've lived out here nearly eighteen years and I've never known what the real Outback was like. I thought Augusta Springs was it." His voice trailed off as though he were speaking to himself. "It certainly looks different from the air, doesn't it? And that Sam, my God, he doubled as a nurse. I didn't even have to tell him how to anesthetize the patient. I had no idea all this went on. I appreciated the opportunity to see how you operate. Sister Claire enjoyed it, too. I think she and your pilot have enjoyed each other's company. I wouldn't be surprised . . . "

So, Sam hadn't minded Sister Claire after all. Cassie smiled to herself. That'll show him that looks weren't everything. There was certainly nothing wrong with Sister Claire's looks; she just wasn't as cute as the other nurses, but she was incredibly competent. Maybe Sam was growing up.

Sam drove by after dark. "Have a good time?" he asked, walking up the verandah steps, a blade of grass between his teeth.

Cassie nodded. "I hear you did, too."

"There's no chance of privacy, is there, in this town?" But he was grinning.

"We have to fly out to Yancanna tomorrow. After the eight-o'clock, okay?"

"Yeah," he said, sitting in a chair at the round table. "Got any coffee?"

"Sure." Cassie went into the kitchen to heat the leftover coffee, then came back. "I may have to stay there a few days. Dr. Adams volunteered to go with us—sounds like a patient will have to be brought back to the hospital here. You impressed him, by the way."

"We gonna cancel more clinics?"

Cassie nodded. "We'll have to. Maybe Sister Claire," she said, her eyes teasing Sam, "will fly out for any emergencies. If Chris—Dr. Adams—isn't in the middle of an emergency himself, maybe he'll fly out if it's something that sounds urgent. But I'm needed at Yancanna. Could be the start of an epidemic."

"I don't even know that much about polio."

Cassie left for a minute, turned the gas off under the coffee, poured it, and brought it out to Sam in a mug.

"Does it always kill or paralyze?"

Cassie raised her eyebrows and puckered her mouth. "No, but it does it often enough that it's as scary as the plague. Trouble is, there's no specific treatment at this point. There are cases without any paralysis, and I suppose a lot of the mild ones aren't even diagnosed. But during an epidemic anyone, especially children, who has a sore throat or stiffness of the neck and back—and the hamstring muscles—may have it. There are three kinds, if I remember correctly, the mild, non-paralytic case; then, there's the paralytic case; and finally, there's the life-threatening case. It's impossible within the first few days to tell which it's going to be. All patients are considered infectious and should be quarantined. Chris has cordoned off three rooms and has two nurses on standby if needed. He's being wonderfully cooperative."

"I didn't have a bad time with him. Not like I expected," Sam volunteered. "He doesn't have a great bedside manner, but he's not the sonofabitch I'd expected from all I'd heard."

"I remember Fiona told me his bark was worse than his bite.

Maybe it just takes getting to know him a bit. I suspect it's all taken his mind off Isabel's death, too. He'll meet us at the airport a bit after eight forty-five."

"Want me to pick you up at seven, so we can have breakfast at Addie's and I'll fill you in on what's happened while you were out romancing?"

Cassie smiled at him. "That sounds fine. And it was wonderful. I saw a part of Australia I didn't even know existed."

"The top end? Yeah, I've always wanted to get there. Well, someday." Sam stood up, put his baseball cap back on, and opened the screen door. "See ya in the mornin'."

Yancanna was a beehive of activity. "Thank heavens," said Brigid, who had run from the hospital when she heard the plane's engines. "We don't have enough beds for everyone. The man who was brought in two days ago—I don't think he has a chance. The paralysis has spread so that his breathing's severely affected. But he's as sweet and uncomplaining as can be."

Cassie nodded toward Chris. "This is Dr. Adams, the superintendent of the Augusta Springs Hospital. He's come to help and to ferry back any patients needing iron lungs or more care than you can give them here."

Brigid held out her hand to Chris. "Nice of you. Appreciate it."

"How many patients do you have?" Chris asked as they walked toward the hospital.

"The one I just mentioned. A young boy whom I fear is going to be partially paralyzed, but then I can't tell for sure. I've never even seen polio before. Another man was brought in last night, and he's dreadful bad. Two babies came in this morning early. And over in the low hills . . . "

Chris looked but the landscape was flat as far as could be seen.

" . . . They're about fifteen miles away and even then they're not much higher than ant hills. Well, the blacks out there, they've got six or seven sick. A runner came in, but we haven't had time to get out there for taking care of the people already here in the hospital. Marianne went out before dawn when a rider came to get her to deliver a baby out at the Cotters', 'bout seven miles down south."

They walked up the hospital steps, Sam bringing up the rear. As he always did, he walked back to the kitchen and helped himself to coffee, bringing it back to the verandah, where he sat and stared out at the scene. Sparse green trees sprinkled throughout the red earth, azure skies, birds circling. The sound of a horse neighing. Flies buzzing. A baby crying.

After Cassie and Chris examined the patients, they agreed that the two men should be flown back to Augusta Springs. Chris hoped an iron lung would have arrived. "I better call and get more. Looks like we're going to need them," he said.

Cassie turned to Sam. "Tell Horrie to be on the frequency at seven. I'll call in then and see how you people are managing and tell you if you need to fly back tomorrow. If not, you can be free for other emergencies. Simply cancel all the clinics until we know what's going on here."

When she spoke with Sam that night, he told her an iron lung had already arrived. "It looks like a coffin. It's a big, airtight box and we put one of the patients in it. His head sticks out through a sponge rubber seal. That's all that's out, his head. The rest is in the box. An electric motor drives a couple of kangaroo-hide bellows so that the pressure in the box is controlled to be like the rhythm of a chest and it helps the patient to breathe."

Yes, Cassie knew. When paralysis affected the motor nerves of the respiratory system the only way the patient could breathe was by being in an iron lung. Otherwise they'd die quickly.

"Doc Adams called Adelaide and they're rushing two more iron lungs up to us. They assure us they'll arrive by air cargo special delivery tomorrow."

"We got another patient today, and I'm hoping to get out to the black village tomorrow and see what's up there. Anything else I should know?"

There was a second's hesitation. "Yeah," he said. "England declared war on Germany today."

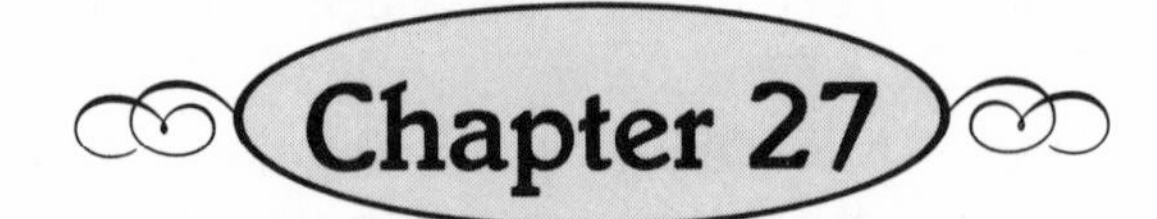

Chapter 27

Eight days later, Cassie boarded the plane with a pregnant patient. She was exhausted, as were Marianne and Brigid. She doubted they'd have kept going if Chief hadn't buoyed them all up. He cooked their meals, told them to go take sponge baths, relieved them in the middle of the night when they were sitting up with patients. And did all his other work, too.

Sam had flown out three times to pick up more patients; only one required a respirator. One of the original two patients flown back to Augusta Springs had died, as had a baby in Yancanna. Cassie felt in her bones that two others would be crippled. Five rooms in the Augusta Springs Hospital had been turned over to the polio patients. So far it was not spreading to other regions.

The day before a young man in a beat-up utility had drawn up to the AIM hospital, a cloud of dust surrounding him. Rushing into the hospital, he'd shouted, "My wife's sick. I'm afraid she's dying."

Marianne had run out, quickly gathering that this was another case of polio and that the young woman was pregnant. "Seven and a half months," her husband said.

Cassie took one look at her and knew they had to get her to an iron lung. When she spoke to Horrie that night, she said, "Let Chris know I'm coming in with her tomorrow. He's just got to have a respirator ready."

But there wasn't one. Every one of the four they'd received was in use.

"Tell Sam to do something," Cassie said. "It's too hot for her to even breathe here. We should get to Adelaide where it's cooler. And she needs to be in an iron lung."

In the morning Sam flew to Yancanna and he and the Chief lifted the young woman, Rosie Peters, into the plane. "Had trouble with the health department, but I told them you'd take full responsibility, and you'd fly with her to Adelaide."

Cassie looked at him. "Thanks a million," she said with sarcasm. She wasn't sure she was up to a long flight. "Why the health department?"

"Well, you've gotta fly by commercial cargo plane. Trans Australia Airlines is sending a freighter, which should be in Augusta Springs by noon. Then they'll fly you down to Adelaide. Since it's a contagious disease the health department is squeamish. Doc Adams contacted the hospital in Adelaide and they'll be waiting for you, ready with an iron lung. But in order to move across boundaries, the health department insists that you accompany her. You can be back by tomorrow night, or the next morning at the latest."

"I'm beginning to forget what home looks like," Cassie said. Except for one night in between her holiday and the epidemic, she'd been gone five and a half weeks.

They arrived in Augusta Springs shortly before noon, and to their surprise the Trans Australia Airlines freighter was already there. The pilot and Sam transferred the patient on the stretcher.

"Sam, I don't even have any money. I'll have to stay in a hotel overnight, and eat. And my God, look at what I'm wearing."

"Come on, Doc, who you going to know? You look okay. Just don't go to any fancy restaurants," he grinned. "You don't have time to go change. Here. Here's fifty. That ought to do it. Pay me back later."

Cassie sat on the floor of the cargo plane, next to her patient whose breathing was becoming more labored. Panic filled Rosie's eyes. "Am I going to die? Will my baby die?"

"Not if I can help it," Cassie said, putting a hand over her patient's. "I'm going to give you something to relax you." She turned to the pilot. "You can't fly over five hundred feet. Not with a patient in this condition."

He nodded. "I know. That means it'll take us longer to get there."

There was no choice in an unpressurized cabin.

"What's with the war?" Cassie asked after they'd taken off.

The pilot turned to look at her. "This is my last flight before I leave."

"Leave?" she asked. "For where?"

He looked at her as though she were slightly retarded. "For England, of course. They need pilots. They need everything, I guess."

"We do here, too."

"Not like there. Everyone's enlisting."

"Who's everyone?" she asked. "I'm not."

"Guess it's good there are women doctors, after all. Imagine all the male doctors'll be going over there."

Over there? That was the Great War. The World War.

The pilot continued. "Every man under forty's enlisting, I bet. We're all going, but we'll probably be back by Christmas. No one wants to miss it."

No one wants to miss a war? Cassie asked herself. She closed her eyes. She didn't even know what day it was. The month, yes. September. The year, 1939. She'd arrived in Augusta Springs exactly a year ago.

It was twilight when they crossed the Cooper River, a mere ribbon of green trees in the cracked landscape that looked like the moon must look. The pilot pointed to the vast sandy emptiness. "That's Lake Eyre," he said, grinning.

"Lake?"

"Only got water in it a couple times a century, they say. The Cooper and Diamantina empty into it in the spring runoff when they flood, but it doesn't stay long. It's really more a dry salt bed."

In a little while he said, "See those lights down there? That's Maree. Coming up on the left will be the Leigh Creek coal fields. Then, maybe it's getting too dark to see, some of the best farmland in the whole country."

Waiting for them at the airport in Adelaide were a doctor, nurse, and a flat-bed truck. "We have a respirator on top of it. Thought we'd get her in one right away," said the nurse. They worked quickly and efficiently, backing the big truck up to the cargo door of the plane.

"We have an obstetrician on call," said the doctor, "in case we need him tonight. Come on, climb up here. We'll ride along beside the patient."

* * *

Cassie didn't need to spend Sam's fifty dollars on a hotel. She slept in the intern's room at the hospital, not waking until summoned at five-thirty, when a plane was leaving for Alice Springs. From there she caught another on to Augusta Springs. It took all day to get home.

She wished Blake would be there. She'd had little time even to think of him since leaving Yancanna. She'd phone him when she got back to Augusta Springs. He'd probably tried to get hold of her and wondered where she was, unless he radioed and asked Horrie about her.

But when she got home she found a note pinned to her door. "*I came to say goodbye and you weren't here. Horrie told me you're out at Yancanna on a polio epidemic. I can't stay. I'm enlisting in the RAAF, and hope to blow some Nazis out of the air. From the sublime (our holiday) to war, not that this war is ridiculous. I am taking you with me (in my left shirt pocket). Remembering your kisses will help.*" Then, in a big black scrawl, "B."

Blake already gone to war?

No "Love." No real goodbye. No more of Blake's kisses. No more Blake talks. Not just two weeks, but months before she would be in his arms again, look into the blueness of his eyes, feel his lips against hers. Months? Maybe years. Years before she would feel Blake's nakedness against hers.

He couldn't have left the country already. After all, war was only declared a little more than two weeks ago. He must still be in Sydney. In Melbourne. Someplace in the country.

She'd fly to him. No troop ships could be ready to carry him away already. He couldn't be gone. He couldn't have left already. He wouldn't want to leave without seeing her again. Oh, why hadn't Horrie told her? Why hadn't Blake asked to speak to her on the radio? She'd have flown back so they could have spent one last night together.

She tried to phone Tookaringa, but all she got was static.

Hanging up, she stared into space. After a minute she began to cry. "Blake," she whispered aloud. "Come back to me."

They hadn't even said goodbye. Why that mattered so much, she didn't understand.

* * *

At six-thirty, red-eyed from crying, she answered the phone that awoke her.

"Cassie. It's Chris. That drunken sot, Edwards, has enlisted. He left last night. I've got two operations this morning. Can you assist?"

"Let me attend to the morning radio calls and see if there are any emergencies."

"Any chance you could get one in before that? Like within half an hour?"

"I'm not even dressed. You woke me."

She could almost see him nodding. "That's why I called so early. To get you before anyone else did. This is an appendectomy that won't wait. The other's just tonsils and that can wait until whenever you're available."

After all he'd been doing for her, there was no way she could refuse him.

"Sure. I'll be ready in half an hour."

"Make it fifteen minutes. I'll send someone over to pick you up."

Oh, God, she thought as she walked to the bathroom. No time even to grieve. She picked up her toothbrush but instead of brushing her teeth found herself throwing up in the toilet.

"I'm probably too old," Chris said, as they were washing up after the operation, "but then I don't suppose it makes any difference what age doctors are."

"Too old for what?" Cassie threw her rubber gloves into a hamper.

"The war, of course."

"Don't you think people here need doctors? What'll we do if every doctor leaves the country to go to war?"

He nodded. "I know. I've been asking myself that question all week. Where will I do the most good?"

"Don't you think you ought to allow yourself time to recover from Isabel's death before making any major decisions?" She took off her green cap and threw it in the hamper, too.

Chris gave her a sharp look. "Maybe a whole change of scenery would be good for me."

"Hey, it's taken me over a year to be able to work comfortably with you. Do I have to start all over with someone new?"

He stared at her. "Maybe someone new will be easier to work with."

"Maybe someone new would have a better bedside manner but none could be a better surgeon."

He finished washing. "I think that was meant as a compliment, but I can't be sure. If so, it was tempered with some sort of criticism, I think."

"I hoped you'd hear that and at least have to think about how you talk to your patients. I suppose what I think doesn't make any difference—it has to come from inside you. But I think you're needed here, Chris. Personally, I'd hate to see you go." She walked out of the room, stopping to phone Sam, telling him she'd be waiting in front of the hospital where he could pick her up on his way out to the base.

While she took calls on the radio, Sam and Horrie talked in low tones. There were no emergencies, Yancanna had no new polio cases; she solved everyone's problems on the phone. She turned to Horrie. "I think we can resume regular clinic calls in two days," she said. "Give me a day or two to recuperate."

Both Horrie and Sam gave her strange looks. Sam took her arm and steered her out of the shed. "Doc, got somethin' I need to tell you."

She looked up at him.

"I've enlisted," he said.

Chapter 28

"You can't do it," Cassie exclaimed, anger rising in her chest.

"Hey, Doc, if we don't go fight Hitler we may end up with nothing worthwhile here."

Cassie just stared at Sam.

"What are people here supposed to do? Everyone's abandoning us." Blake. Now Sam. And Chris thinking of it. It was all she could do not to cry.

"No one's abandoning the people here. QANTAS is going to send out another pilot, a family man who's too old to go to war."

"Too old? Then what good will he be to me?"

"For Chrissakes, Cassie," and it dawned on her he hadn't called her *Doc,* "you're going to keep on doing what you've done, what's necessary. Think what a good thing it is there are women doctors to keep the home fires . . . "

"Don't you dare say anything so trite!" She balled her hand into a fist and hit his shoulder.

Amazement swept over his face. "Hey, Doc . . . "

"Don't you *hey, Doc* me! I hate being called Doc. I hate it! You men all think running to a war is so glamorous, so heroic. Maybe it's just as heroic to stay here and do the humdrum everyday things that ordinary people need, but no, that's not heroic enough, is it?"

Sam grabbed hold of her shoulders, shaking her. "You're getting hysterical," he said. "Look, Doc . . . Cassie. This shit in Europe has to be stopped. We're at war with Germany. We have to go fight. There's not a man around who could hold up his head if he didn't try . . . "

"What are you going to do, leave the country to women?"

"If they're like you they can handle it. Doc . . . Cassie, you can handle anything. Look at what I've seen you do. I thought having a woman doc was the worst thing the Flying Doctors could do. I thought men wouldn't let you examine them, that you'd go over like a lead balloon. But you fooled me. I don't think many people out here even think of you as a woman. They treat you like a man. You've succeeded. I'm proud to have worked with you."

He patted her arm. "You'll have another pilot who'll be fine, and you'll go on just as you have. No one's deserting the people here, or you."

Cassie burst into tears. Sam put his arms around her. He made her feel good and safe even though he'd just ripped her security away from her. "Oh, Sam, whatever in the world will I do without you?"

"I just told you, another pilot's coming and QANTAS wouldn't hire him if he weren't tops . . . "

"That's not what I mean," she wailed, her head buried in his chest. "What will I do without *you?* I mean, you're my nurse and anesthetist, and whenever I feel inadequate or you sense I'm scared you always, *always,* tell me, *You can do it. I know you can.*"

"Do I say that?" Sam smiled, his arms still holding Cassie close.

"Well, you always do." Absentmindedly, he kissed her hair. "You're a real pal, Doc. I sure never dreamed you'd become one, that first day you got off the train. You're a little feisty but I can't imagine anyone I'd rather work with. Don't get too fond of this new pilot because, by God, Doc, I'm comin' back. We'll be flying together again, just you wait and see."

"Sam, if you get yourself killed I'll never forgive you."

He laughed and hugged her tighter. "Not a chance."

Sam stood back and put his hands on her shoulders. "You *are* going to be without a pilot for a couple of weeks. I'm leaving in two weeks and QANTAS can't get this man out here on a permanent basis for another week. It'll be okay, Doc."

"How the hell do you know?"

He grinned. "You know what's so nice about you? You don't pull your punches. You don't act pretty—yeah, you look pretty—but you don't act it to impress people. You say what you think, and shoot straight, like men do."

Cassie found a handkerchief in her pants pocket and wiped her eyes. She'd cried more in the past twenty hours than she had since . . . since Ray Graham. And now Ray seemed shallow compared to what she was going through. Blake. For heaven's sake, Ray couldn't even hold a candle to Sam Vernon. She figured she'd miss Sam and Blake more than she'd ever missed Ray Graham. Men weren't lousy after all, just that one neurosurgeon in Melbourne. So, just as she discovered that, the two nicest men in her life were being ripped away from her.

"Shit," she said.

"See, that's what I mean. I've never heard another woman talk that way."

"So why is it okay for men to say it and women shouldn't?"

He grinned. "Shucks, Doc, thought you knew women are supposed to be pure and sweet."

"Isn't that a bit dull?" she asked. "Why on earth do men find virgins so appealing? They don't even know what to *do.* Men have perverted ideas about women."

Sam stared at her and she could see color rising in his cheeks. She turned away, embarrassed that she had embarrassed him. What in the world had made her say such a thing? That was the sort of stuff she should save for Fiona.

Oh, Fiona, where are you? Her best friend and her lover all gone. She began to cry all over again. The emotion she felt made her queasy. She just wanted to get in bed and lie there, in the darkness, with shades drawn and an ice pack on her head, and not think. Just close her eyes and have nothing there, nothing she had to think of, nothing she had to face.

"Well," Sam said, "if we only have a week more of working together, how about getting in as many clinics as we can—barring emergencies, that is."

She sensed that from now on the quality of her life would never be the same. The whole fabric would be different. Something was irrevocably changing, nothing would ever be as it had been up until this minute. Even when Blake and Fiona and Sam came back, something would be different. She knew it. And she didn't like what she sensed. From this time forward, the world would never be the same, the whole world, not just her world. She knew it as surely as she knew she was going to throw up right here on the ground in front of Sam. With Horrie looking on from the radio shack door, with his arm around Betty, who was large with child.

Large with child? Oh, shit a brick. Could she be throwing up so much because she was pregnant?

She stared at Sam.

"I have to go home," she said. "I don't feel well."

"C'mon, Doc," he said, his voice hinting of irritation, "don't do this to yourself. It's beyond your control. Just face it. This isn't like you."

Damn you, Sam. Goddamn you. It's not that.

She put a hand on his arm. "I'll be okay. Just give me a bit of time. I think I'm tired from these last ten days." She didn't want to throw up here. She felt lightheaded, dizzy. The sun's glare hurt her eyes.

"Okay, I'll drive you home." He headed toward the truck, opening the passenger door as he passed it but not waiting for her to get in.

They drove along in silence, and Cassie closed her eyes. Blake and she hadn't even talked about the possibility of pregnancy. She guessed they'd thought they could get married even though they'd never even talked marriage. And now, how could she contact him? Tell him? Even if she knew how to get in touch with him there was no way he could get leave to come all the way back to Australia to get married. No way.

Maybe she wasn't pregnant. Maybe it was the exhaustion of the polio epidemic, of flying overnight to Adelaide, of knowing that both Blake and Sam were being torn away from her, that her whole life was turning topsy turvy. One could be queasy, one could throw up, one could want to lie down for other reasons than pregnancy, after all.

She felt Sam's hand on top of hers and turned to look at him. He smiled. "Doc, working with you certainly makes this one of the top jobs of the world. I can't think of any other reason I'd ever leave except war. If I didn't enlist, they'd come get me anyhow, you know. Trained pilots are in great demand. Blake's left, too. I know. I'm sorry, Cassie. You in love with the bloke?"

She nodded.

"You planning on marrying him?"

She nodded. "We didn't talk about it, but yes."

"Come here," he said, pulling her next to him and putting an arm around her. She laid her head on his shoulder, tears again welling up in her eyes. He tightened his hold. "It's going to be harder on women, I suspect," he said. "Waiting is always harder."

"I didn't even get to say goodbye to him." Now she did start to cry again.

Sam didn't say anything until they drew up in front of her house. "We'll go out on our regular clinic call tomorrow, okay? Right after your morning radio session."

In the morning, Cassie felt fine. So, she probably wasn't pregnant after all.

They covered two clinics that day with time to spare. "Let's stop at Yancanna on the way home," she said. "It's not much out of the way and we can see how Brigid and Marianne are holding up."

They brought one of the polio patients back to Augusta Springs with them. Cassie hardly talked to Sam all day. She felt anger toward him for leaving her. She knew she was being unfair but she couldn't control it.

"I'll tell Horrie to schedule clinics every day, while I'm still here. That okay?"

"Do whatever you want," she snapped.

He gave her a long look but she didn't notice.

Three days later she could hardly climb out of bed. She was so dizzy she fell on the floor and had to crawl on her hands and knees to the bathroom where she threw up.

Damn.

She couldn't be pregnant, just couldn't be.

By the time Sam picked her up she felt better. At least she wasn't dizzy. He said, "You don't look well."

"I'm fine." Her voice was curt.

But all the time they flew out to Kypunda that day she sat in her seat, eyes closed, fists clenched, wondering what in the world she could do.

What were the alternatives? Have the baby, lose her job, be ostracized by any community where she might live. Have to leave Augusta

Springs. How could she support a baby—would anyone come to a doctor who was also a scarlet woman? Her own life, her ability to do good for people, would be over. Her father would be mortified. It would create a scandal. And she would be tied to this baby for the next twenty years or more, tied with no one to help her, no way to earn a decent income. She knew there was no place she could practice that would not rise up in arms and dismiss her when they found out. Oh, God, what could she do?

Try to contact Blake? What good would that do? She couldn't fly to the front to marry him. And maybe he wouldn't want to marry her. Well, no, she knew that wasn't true. Of course he would.

There was no possible way to marry Blake now that he'd flown off to war. No way to marry him, or even see him, before the baby was born unless the war ended quickly. Oh, God, how unfair. For two weeks of ecstasy she would have to bear this cross forever and the man could escape scot-free, not even knowing she was carrying his seed.

She couldn't eat lunch.

She couldn't sleep. She thought of nothing else. She had never been so scared in her life. And there was no one to turn to. *Oh, Fiona, where are you?* She couldn't tell her father; he'd be ashamed of her. There was no one else.

Everything she tried to eat came back up. She took to setting the alarm for four a.m. so that her sickness could be over by the time Sam picked her up for clinic runs. He commented that she was looking peaked.

Peaked, indeed. If he were carrying a baby around, he'd look peaked, too.

She wanted someone to talk to. What about an abortion? There were ways to get one even if they were illegal. But she didn't know where. She had visions of dark alleys, a quack with dirty fingernails, and dying of peritonitis. Blood poisoning. Bleeding to death. She thought of women who had tried to abort themselves with knitting needles and ruined forever their chances of conceiving again, or who had died as a result of unsanitary conditions or someone's butchery.

How could she find a reliable doctor who might perform an abortion?

And just as she needed him, Don McLeod came to town.

"You look awful, Cassie," he said. He'd appeared at her door as she arrived home from the afternoon call-in. "Is it Blake? Is that why?"

She burst into tears.

"Come on, fix me a cup of tea and cry on my shoulders. So, you've fallen in love, huh?"

As she boiled the water, she told herself she couldn't let Don know she was pregnant. He'd lose any respect he had for her, he'd be disillusioned, he'd tell her she wasn't fit to be . . .

"I'm pregnant, Don."

Silence.

Then, "Are you sure?"

"No," she sobbed, unable to control her tears. "But I have all the symptoms."

She sat down, her head in her hands. Don got up and turned off the gas, found the tea, and steeped it.

"And there's no way to contact Blake?"

"Right." She blew her nose and wiped away the tears. "I can't have this baby, Don. I just can't. You know my life would be ruined. I couldn't continue my work here . . . "

He poured the tea and placed a cup in front of her. She looked over at him as he sat down opposite her.

"Are you disgusted with me?"

He reached out to put a hand over hers. "Rid your mind of that, my dear. Disgusted because you're human? Sorry, but not disgusted, Cassie."

"I should have been more intelligent; after all, I *am* a doctor."

They drank their tea in silence.

"I don't know who to turn to. I don't know anyone who performs abortions."

"Are you sure that's what you want?"

"Tell me," she challenged him. "What other choice do I have? That won't ruin my life, I mean."

After a minute, Don said, "I suggest you talk to Chris Adams. He must have been faced with this problem, patients not wanting children . . . "

"Chris? Talk to Chris Adams? He's the last person . . . "

Don nodded. "He's not an ogre, Cassie. I have a feeling he can help you. He must have dealt with many unwanted pregnancies in the years he's been out here. Maybe he would even perform the abortion. A nice, clean, medically safe one."

At twilight, two nights before Sam was to leave, she walked over to Chris's house. She felt what she was doing was dangerous. Of all the people in the world to go to, Chris seemed the least likely. Yet, Don had encouraged her and she didn't know where else to turn, or to whom.

Chris was sitting on his verandah, smoking a cigarette, drinking coffee. She realized she'd never seen him without the formality of a jacket, except in his operating room uniform. Now he sat with his sleeves rolled up and his collar open.

When he saw her turn down his walk, he stood. "This is a surprise."

"I hope I'm not interrupting."

"Just finishing dinner. Would you like coffee?"

Cassie shook her head. "No, thanks. But I'd like some talk."

He indicated a chair and then sat down himself.

He was silent.

"Looks like the end of the Yancanna epidemic," she said.

He nodded.

"Thanks for all your help."

He nodded again, silent.

"And for going out on emergencies while I was up north."

"I enjoyed it. I forgot the practice of medicine could be so exciting."

Silence again. He snuffed his cigarette out in the ashtray.

Cassie sighed. "Sam's enlisted."

"All the young men," Chris said.

"Someone has to take care of the people at home."

Outside the screens, mosquitoes buzzed.

"I'd like to talk to you about something confidential."

Chris raised his eyebrows and reached across the table for his cigarettes, pulling one slowly from the packet. Waiting.

"You must have women who become pregnant and don't want to be."

The only noise was the scrape of his match. He inhaled as he lit his cigarette.

Cassie looked at him, but he stared beyond the screen, into the trees. Finally, he met her gaze and asked, "Are you asking me if I perform abortions?"

After a minute, she asked, "Do you?"

He studied her. "I'd like to, Cassie. I've seen so many brokenhearted women who will be forever doomed because they have to bear illegitimate children, and I've wished I had the courage to break what I consider an immoral law, but I'm a coward. I'm not willing to jeopardize my practice—have my license revoked—to help them. The most I can do is arrange adoptions. I often send them over to Townsville, to my sister's, and she takes care of them until they have their babies. But it's the most I have the courage to do. I'm sure Romla would help your patient, too."

His chair squeaked as he rocked.

"It's not one of my patients, Chris. It's me."

She imagined what he'd do. Look at her over the rim of his glasses, give her a censuring look, tighten his lips into a thin line and stare.

But he did none of these things. When he offered no response, she said, "I don't know what to do."

"You want my advice, is that it?"

"I don't know," she said. "I don't know who else to talk to."

"Why me?"

She shrugged her shoulders. "You're a doctor. I've come to trust your medical expertise."

"I'm not an expert in moral dilemmas."

"Is that what I'm in?" she asked. "Maybe I will have a cup of coffee. Or tea, if you have some."

Chris stood up and walked into the house. Cassie sat alone for nearly ten minutes, listening to chickens nearby, roosters crowing at sunset. She heard cicadas in the trees and sounds of children playing in the street several houses away.

When Chris came back he brought two cups, setting one down in front of her.

"What shall I do?" She sipped the hot tea. It burned her tongue.

"What do you want to do?"

"I don't know," she answered. "Having a baby will ruin my life. Gossip travels around here, especially about a woman doctor. Having a baby will cause scandal . . . "

"For someone who knows better, you *have* been careless." Chris's voice was clipped and cold.

"I'm all too aware of that. But we didn't foresee a war."

"There's no chance of marriage?"

Cassie shook her head again. "Not right now."

"Does he know about it?"

"No."

"Ah," Chris said in a tone of recognition. "So, he's gone off to war. It's that Thompson fellow you went north with, isn't it?"

Cassie nodded, wondering if she'd ever felt more miserable. They sat there while she waited, she wasn't sure for what.

"I'm flattered you've come to me, Cassie. I really am. But I won't do it even though I think it's immoral that women have to have children they don't want, have to bear the brunt of illicit sex."

Illicit. "Do you disapprove of me?"

He thought a moment and smiled a tight smile. "I disapproved of you more the first day I saw you than I do now. Who am I to approve or disapprove? Let he who is without sin cast the first stone."

"I don't want to be a social outcast, Chris. I don't want my life to be ruined by bearing a child without a husband, and I'm not ready to have a baby."

"Would you feel this way if Thompson could marry you?"

Her eyes filled with tears. "I suppose not. But he's not here and I can't get married. And I'm not about to give up the Flying Doctors."

"Are you sure about this pregnancy?"

She nodded. "Pretty sure."

"Let me examine you tomorrow, take a urine sample and have a rabbit test."

"But that means we won't know for another week."

"Surely you can wait that long. It wouldn't be too late if you choose an abortion. I have a friend in Townsville. He feels so strongly about the right of a woman to have a say about her destiny that he performs abortions, legal or not. He's willing to risk his career for his beliefs. You would not be the first patient I've sent over to him. It would be safe and clean. No danger at all."

"Do you recommend an abortion?"

He looked at her, and there was a smile in his eyes. "Have I suddenly become your doctor?"

She nodded. "I guess so, if you'll take me on as a patient."

"I'll call him if you're sure that's what you want."

When Sam was leaving two days later, she was already waiting to see if the rabbit would die. Die? Maybe Sam would die in war. Maybe she would die in a dirty back room someplace . . .

"Hey, Doc . . . Cassie, don't cry like that. I'll be back. We'll work together again."

"Oh, Sam," she sobbed, unable to see through her tears. She threw her arms around him. "I don't know what in the world I'll do without you."

"You'll be just fine," he whispered. "You can always handle anything."

You don't know, she wailed silently. *You just don't know.*

"Come on, Doc. Smile for me. I don't want to remember you like this. Just a little one, for me."

But she couldn't. There were no smiles inside her. Only an unwanted baby, created in the primeval land of Kakadu.

Chapter 29

All the way across the country, for a day and a half as the bus jiggled along—adding to her already-nauseous feelings—Cassie thought of Blake. She wondered how he'd feel when he came home from war and she told him she'd aborted his child? At the moment she felt no resentment toward him. It was just as much her fault. She was not only an intelligent woman, but a doctor who should have known better. They should at least have talked about it. But that would have taken away the spontaneity, the excitement . . . the romance.

She had suspected they would make love. Why hadn't she taken along a diaphragm? She prescribed them for patients. They had never once mentioned what might be the consequences of their love-making. She knew it was because they never dreamed they would part; they knew that if pregnancy resulted, they'd marry. And now, here she was left alone to take responsibility. She wasn't ready to have a child. Certainly not one out of wedlock. She was not ready to be accused of immorality, either.

She knew she had to go through with this. And she knew when Blake came home she'd have to tell him. Would he understand? Oh, why wasn't Fiona here? She could have talked it all out with her. Maybe Fiona would have come on this trip with her, to hold her hand, to reassure her. God, she missed Fi.

Her mind flipped back to Blake. *Oh, Blake, come home.* She knew she would give up her career, her life, anything for him. And be happy being Mrs. Blake Thompson. Cassandra Thompson.

They'd have other children. Three, four, a dozen. However many he wanted.

* * *

Townsville was a slumbering tropical town whose soft, languid air washed over Cassie. The fragrance of flowers filled the air as their colors assaulted her senses. Bougainvillea, hibiscus, plumeria, and frangipani blossomed everywhere. Royal palms rose high in the air, their fronds waving from the ocean's breeze.

The town itself had a colonial look—quite delightful, Cassie thought as she stood in the bus station looking around. A woman of medium height with straight, shoulder-length brown hair waved to her, calling, "Yoohoo." A scarlet slash of lipstick paled under her vivid green eyes, which danced with life. She approached Cassie and stuck out her hand, offering a firm shake. She was more good-looking than pretty, and her joyous attitude was contagious. Cassie wasn't sure she'd have recognized her.

"Remember me? I'm Romla Peters," she said, clasping Cassie's arm. "Come, I have the car waiting out front." She led Cassie at a fast pace to where she was double-parked outside a row of cars whose horns were already blasting.

"I'm glad you remembered me." Cassie slid into the passenger's seat of the Dodge.

Romla pulled out of the lane and drove expertly but fast. Many of the wooden houses stood on stilts and Romla pointed at them. "That's so they're high enough to catch the ocean breezes and air can circulate under the houses as well."

"It's charming." Cassie had never seen a maritime tropical town before.

"*Quaint* is the word," Romla said, heading into a driveway in front of a small, square house much like the houses on either side of it. "It's a backwater."

"Do you yearn for a city?"

Romla shook her head, opening her door. "Not necessarily. But I'd like a little excitement. I'd like more to do." She tossed her head. "But that has to come from within, doesn't it? Finding what one needs?

"You look a little peaked," Romla said, just as Sam had. She lifted Cassie's suitcase out of the back. "Would you prefer supper in bed?"

"Gracious, no. I'm better in the afternoon and evening than any other time."

"You have an appointment with Dr. Hatfield tomorrow morning at nine. Is that too early?"

"No, that's fine."

"He's wonderful. I go to him for my annual checkups and he delivered Terry. Pamela was born before we moved here." Romla inserted the key in the door and they entered a small room made bright in shades of pastels and white. It was so small it could have been depressing but Romla had given it personality and gaiety.

"We'll take tea in about an hour. Roger will arrive from work, and Terry and Pam will be home from school. Terry's just six, so be prepared for noise. Pam's the quiet one, at eleven. Imagine you'll want a bath after such a long bus ride. Here, this is the bathroom, and your room is right next to it. Ours is across the hall. As you can see from all the toys, it's Terry's room, but he's all excited about sleeping on the sofa."

"I don't mean to put you out."

Romla shook her head. "Nonsense. Here," she said, tossing Cassie's bag on the narrow bed. "Take your time. When you're ready I've lemonade in the cooler." She left the room, then her head jutted back into the doorway. "My husband thinks you're here to see the doctor about a gynecological problem. Just so you won't be embarrassed."

"Well, it's true." Cassie unpacked and walked down the hall to the bathroom, soaking in the tub until she heard a man's voice, figuring this must be Romla's husband. A policeman, Chris had said, now also in charge of civil defense. Certainly no one was going to attack Townsville. How frenetic people became in wartime. Who would attack Australia? She supposed it lent drama to war at home, when the real war was being fought over ten thousand miles away.

After she dressed in a navy blue linen skirt and pale blue cotton blouse, she walked down the hall to the parlor. Seated in the one overstuffed chair was Roger Peters, drinking beer from a bottle, his feet on a hassock. He didn't get up when she entered the room, but Cassie noticed he was dazzlingly good-looking, a big man with dark hair and a trim mustache. His dark eyes smiled at her as he nodded. "Patient of Chris's, I hear. How's the old boy doing since Izzie died?"

Cassie sat down on the sofa. "Seems to be holding up. I imagine it's hit him harder than he lets on."

"One never knows what Chris thinks," Romla said from the doorway of the kitchen. "He's never been one to share what's inside him." She looked at her husband. "But then men never seem to. Chris is just more contained than most."

"He does seem to keep everything inside."

Romla laughed. "That's the nature of the male beast. Sometimes I have to wonder if there *is* anything inside. Come on, want a lemonade?"

"Sure." Cassie warmed to Chris's sister. She followed Romla into the kitchen.

"I admire someone like you," Romla said. "A woman who makes a place for herself, other than being what every woman is supposed to be, a housewife and mother. I get so damn sick and tired of my life being circumscribed by these four walls and all I hear about is Roger's day at work. I'd like to have the courage to take life by its horns and buck and jump, take the bit in my mouth and do something on my own. Be someone other than Mrs. Romla Peters. Or am I romanticizing your work?"

"I feel lucky," Cassie replied, accepting the drink. "Though someday, of course, I'll marry and have children."

"And give up your career?"

"Well, love does make us yearn to nest, don't you think?" Cassie was thinking of her recent change of feelings, of the way Blake made her feel.

"I suppose," said Romla, opening the oven door and peering inside. "But once you sit back and the bloom is off the romance part and all you do is cook and clean and have a man come home who doesn't talk much or all he talks about is his work and the horse races, you begin to wonder if this is all life's going to offer you."

Romla did not sound as though she were complaining. She seemed to be thinking as she talked, wondering aloud. "Well, this is no way to begin your visit. All I really meant to say is I admire what you're doing."

"Thanks," Cassie said. "And I thank you also for helping me."

"I've been helping Chris out this way for years. We've always done it so neither Roger nor Izzie knew about it. They wouldn't approve.

But Chris and I, though he's so much older he really wasn't around while I was growing up, we've always been on the same wavelength."

Cassie was surprised. She'd have thought the Chris Adams she knew and this sister of his had nothing in common. Romla turned to face Cassie. "When I was little, he was the gentlest, most patient person in the world. He was my god as I grew up. I was crushed when he married Izzie and moved far away. But we've written to each other every month."

Was this the Chris Cassie knew?

"I used to wonder why they lived so far out, so far from anything civilized, so far from . . . from me. But he likes being a big fish in a little pond. He built that hospital, you know. He raised the money for it single-handedly. It took him five years. Of course, Isabel always resented living out there. I've only been out there a couple of times. But maybe, now, I'll come visit again."

"You and Isabel didn't get along?" Cassie knew it was none of her business.

"No." Romla's voice was crisp. "We didn't." She opened the oven door and pulled scones out. They smelled wonderful. "Here," she said, tossing an egg beater at Cassie. "Beat the cream in that bowl, will you? We'll have strawberries, too. Doesn't that sound worth coming nearly a thousand miles for?"

"It does."

Romla moved around the small kitchen in a no-nonsense fashion. Her actions were sharp, clipped, like her voice. But they did not reflect the warmth she emanated. Cassie felt as though this woman were wrapping her within a cocoon.

"You obviously like to cook," Cassie said as she whipped the cream.

Romla laughed. "I hate it. I'd much rather be doing something exciting than working all afternoon and then having my family demolish it in fifteen minutes.

"I wish I had some form of rewarding life outside of a house." Romla looked out the small window above the sink. "Terry should be here momentarily. Pam may be a bit late. She's on the girls' soccer team. If we wait for her, then Roger gets irritated that his tea's not ready. I either have his tea ready on time or he stops at the pub and is there til it closes at six, and then by the time he gets home he doesn't care whether he eats or not. So, I work tea around him. Though he'll go out later, to play darts probably. I don't know what he does."

Cassie did not think it sounded like an ideal marriage. Blake would never be like that, she knew. Steven wasn't. Her father hadn't been.

Terry, Romla's tow-headed six-year-old, came tearing in the door, his knickers spattered with mud, a lopsided grin on his freckled face. Romla leaned down and hugged him, never mentioning his dirty clothes. She kissed his ear as his arms wound around her neck. Then she straightened up and mildly said, "Wash your hands, love."

She set the kitchen table and went to the door of the living room. "Roger. Tea's on."

There were sandwiches and a pitcher of milk, the scones and berries waiting to be topped off with the whipped cream. "Roger comes home for a big meal at noon," she explained. "So do the kids. I hope this'll be enough for you."

Cassie hadn't been able to look at a whole meal in ten days. The sight of the food made her queasy. She put her hand across her mouth. "I'm sorry," she said, heading for the bathroom.

Romla walked back a minute later. "Why don't you just get in bed? I'll bring you a cup of tea later."

When she did come, an hour later, with tea and a scone, sans berries and cream, she sat on the end of the bed and said, "Not fun, eh?" Then, as Cassie gratefully sipped the hot tea, Romla continued. "How do you feel about all this? Getting rid of a child, I mean?"

Cassie stopped to think a minute. "It's not a child to me. It's an inconvenience which could become a tragedy. It's not a human being to me until it's born. It could be a tumor. I don't feel any guilt, if that's what you're asking."

Romla curled up on the bottom of the bed. "I don't know what I'm asking. Maybe I'm also asking how you feel about the bloke who got you in this shape."

"It's my fault, too. But I guess I do feel some resentment that he's away not even knowing I'm going through this and I'm the one paying the piper. Of course, it's not his fault he's so far away."

"Would you want to marry him?"

"Lord, yes. I love him."

"Well, then, why this? Not that it's any of my business, of course. It's curiosity. He doesn't love you?"

"War. He went off to war before I even knew I was pregnant. He'd marry me. We're in love. But somehow before we could make any plans, he left. I don't even know where he is. There's no way to contact him."

"So that's what makes you so sad, more so than being pregnant?"

"Do I look sad? I'm heartsick he's gone. We never even said good-bye. But I don't have any misgivings about having an abortion." She thought of the D and C she'd performed on the Bagley Waters girl whose parents never knew their young daughter was pregnant. She'd have to talk to the girl sometime. Warn her about not doing this again, about taking precautions. She herself would be smarter next time, too. "Maybe subconsciously I didn't mind. Something to tie us together. I'd love to have his child. I want to have many of his children. But not now. Not alone. Not single. Not . . . " Her voice trailed off.

"I had an abortion last year," Romla said. "Not even Chris knows. And Roger doesn't have an inkling. I just didn't want another. I can't stand to be so tied down, much as I adore Terry and Pam. I keep thinking life has more for me than cleaning and cooking, and I just didn't want . . . I don't feel guilty. All I felt was relief not to be pregnant. I thought I'd been careful. I don't know how it happened.

"Some of the young women Chris sends to me are wracked with guilt. Their parents have pounded into them that sex without marriage is the most sinful thing a woman can do. They spend their time here crying. Roger never understands. But then he's not basically curious."

They sat in silence while Cassie munched on her scone and finished her tea.

"Are you and my brother good friends?"

Cassie looked at her. "I wouldn't say that. In fact, I'd have thought he was the least likely person I'd ever confide in. But my best friend is in Ireland. My pilot, who's a good friend, has left for war and besides, I think he'd be disillusioned if he knew. And the baby's father . . . well, I didn't know who to turn to. Your brother and I've helped each other out before, but no, we're not close friends."

"We had screwy parents," Romla said. "I don't know how we

turned out as well as we did. And then, of course, Izzie held him on such a tight rein. I'm surprised they stayed out there all these years, knowing how much she didn't like it. It's probably the only thing he ever did to purposely provoke her."

"Everyone I know seems to have loved her."

Romla cast a baleful glance at Cassie. "Here's one who didn't."

Chapter 30

Cassie decided every doctor should have the experience of being a surgical patient. However, knowing how simple a D and C was, she wasn't nervous. Dr. Hatfield had been formal but obviously compassionate. Romla had registered her as Mary Stewart. Hatfield asked no personal questions, no whys. He did ask, "Are you sure this is the path you want to take?"

She never hesitated. "I don't want a baby at this stage of my life."

He said, "We'll examine you to determine how far along you are."

"I'm between three and a half and five weeks," she said.

He raised an eyebrow. "You sure?"

"I'm positive." The rabbit had died.

"Well, let me explain what we'll be doing."

She wanted to say, *I know. I've performed a D and C for* various reasons, just not for an abortion. But she acted as though it were new to her and she listened. She liked his explaining. Perhaps she should do more explaining to patients—then perhaps their fears might be somewhat alleviated.

After he'd explained, he said, "May I prescribe a diaphragm? Abortion is not something you'll want to do again."

She had dozens of diaphragms in her dispensary back in Augusta Springs, but she said, "Yes, thank you." And, "I know it's not."

She'd never been under ether. She tried to remain conscious as long as possible, wanting to remember everything so she could empathize with patients. But as she lost consciousness all she remembered later was feeling anger at Blake. He might be away fighting a war, but she had to pay the price for what they'd shared. And she knew that throughout history, it had always been so. Aloud she said, "Damn men." The next thing she was conscious of was seeing a clock on the wall, and although she tried to focus with all her might, she could not read the numbers on it. A soft voice said, "You'll feel woozy for a few hours, so just lie still. Your friend will be in to pick you up about four o'clock."

The doctor came back shortly before four. "Romla's here. Stay in bed for two days in case there's bleeding. If any occurs, call me. If you're all right in twenty-four hours it's safe to return home."

"I can't thank you enough." At least the queasiness had disappeared.

"The worst thing in the world to me would be having something bad happen to one of my children. The next worse thing is bringing an unwanted and unloved child into the world. The third is having a woman be a lifelong prisoner to momentary passions. I'm glad to have been of help. Now, take care in the future. A diaphragm is in this box. Make use of it." He smiled kindly. "And give my regards to Dr. Adams. Fine man."

Romla was waiting for her. "Come on, I'm putting you in bed and I've a good book for you. You're going to be fine in no time. How d'you feel?"

"A little shaky. Otherwise, okay. No pain. And no more queasiness." It had really been very easy.

In the morning Cassie felt almost like her usual self. She even got up for breakfast. Roger had left for work but Romla had tea and porridge and freshly squeezed orange juice waiting for her. Pam and Terry had already left for school. Cassie hadn't even seen Pamela, but then maybe Romla hadn't wanted her to.

While Cassie ate breakfast Romla sat at the table with her, sipping coffee, jumping up every now and then to pick up a stray toy or some other clutter. "I long for a big house. One doesn't see the untidiness in larger rooms."

"Have you thought of working so you could afford a larger house?" Cassie asked. "I know a policeman's salary mustn't be very large."

"A job?" Romla looked puzzled. "What could I do? And Roger would have a fit."

"Why? Would he rather have you sitting around cleaning up clutter and being dissatisfied?"

Romla laughed. "He'd have a fit," she repeated. "And besides, I don't know how to do anything."

Cassie looked at her. "Think about it."

"It would rock the boat," Romla said. "I'd give in before I'd do that."

"I've always thought it unfair to blame the man for not earning more when a woman is perfectly capable of going out and earning some money to help buy the things she wants. He's a policeman. He wants to be a policeman. If he feels guilty not to be earning more, he'll resent you for making him feel he should find another job."

Romla looked at Cassie a long time. Then she got up and walked over to tidy up the coffee table. "Do you know how boring it is to do nothing but dust and do the wash and dishes and plan meals? I listen to my kids and I listen to my husband, and that's my life."

"Who listens to *you?*"

Romla smiled. "You are."

"You have little things with which to fill your day but you seem to me like someone who needs challenges, needs to have your mind occupied."

"My God." Romla sat down again, reaching out to put her hand on Cassie's for a minute. "We've only known each other a bit over twenty-four hours and already you're the first person who's ever looked inside me and seen what's here." She moved her hand to her chest.

There was a minute's silence. "Sometimes I ache," Romla said. "I wonder what's wrong with me that I'm not happier. I have two children I love. A husband who doesn't run around. I was brought up to believe that marriage and motherhood would give me everything necessary for happiness, but I have this terrible yearning. I don't think it's just money, but that's part of it. I want to accomplish things, I don't even know what. And I find that a man is not the answer to everything."

"Well," Cassie remarked as she finished the last draught of tea. "At least not *your* man."

Romla jerked her head up.

Cassie bit her lip. "Oh, Romla, I'm so sorry. That's not what I meant to say at all. What I mean is—oh . . . " Cassie found herself blushing with embarrassment to have said such a thing to someone she scarcely knew.

"It's okay," Romla said. "You're saying aloud things I've tried to push out of my mind. Yeah. He comes home and just sits there or goes out and plays quoits with a neighbor or . . . well, we never talk except about the kids or . . . nothing ever about any real feelings. You know what I fell in love with? His uniform. I was seventeen and he was twenty-three and I saw him standing on a street corner directing traffic and I thought he was the handsomest thing I'd ever seen, and I set out to have him notice me. I didn't know there wasn't anything behind that uniform. Jesus, I feel guilty to have said that. I haven't even allowed myself to think it."

"Well, do think about it," Cassie advised.

Just then the phone rang.

Romla came back from the living room after speaking animatedly for a few minutes. "Chris wants to speak with you."

His formal-sounding voice was accompanied by static. "Just thought I'd check and see if you're all right."

"I'm fine. I'll probably get a bus back the day after tomorrow."

"Good. I just wanted to make sure there were no complications."

"I do appreciate all you've done for me, Chris. And your sister's wonderful."

"I thought you and Romla would hit it off."

The line went dead.

When Cassie returned to the dining room, Romla said, "It

wouldn't hurt for you to spend the day in bed. The kids won't be home til mid-afternoon. I've shopping to do. You can have peace and quiet."

Cassie was grateful.

As Romla prepared to leave with her shopping bag, she said, with the toss of her head that swung her hair across her face, "I don't suppose you and Chris . . . "

Cassie put up a hand. "Don't do that, Romla. I scarcely know your brother. We're professional compadres, that's all. Besides, I'm in love with someone else."

"Wishful thinking on my part," Romla said, and closed the door loudly after her.

The thought of Chris Adams as a lover made Cassie grimace. Old Stone-face. Getting mellower, but Chris Adams was not a man she could imagine wanting to inflict on anyone she knew. Cold. Passionless. She couldn't imagine Chris Adams touching a woman with any warmth. She'd felt sorry for Isabel, wondering how she could have stood living with Chris for so many years. Yet, she realized, whenever she'd seen him at home with Isabel, he had never been anything but thoughtful, patient, devoted. He'd waited on Isabel, catering to her every wish as she lay wasting away.

Two days later Cassie boarded the bus back to Augusta Springs. She hoped a letter from Blake would be waiting when she arrived home. The scenery palled after a while. The towns they stopped at briefly for refreshments were uninteresting. They were few and far between and then for hundreds of miles, further west and dripping south a bit, were towns hardly worth the name. Like Yancanna. A cluster of buildings and nothing else. Sometimes a school. A general store, almost always Teakle and Robbins.

They're right when they call it The Back of Beyond, she thought. It's beyond anything, though when I'm home it seems like the center of the universe. For the first time since she'd arrived a little over a year ago she realized how isolated she was from the rest of the world.

During the night she dozed, sleeping only fitfully. Where was Blake? He had no idea she was on a bus in the middle of nowhere, coming back from aborting his child. When he thought of her he would imagine her flying out to her patients, or dining in Addie's, or holding a clinic at Tookaringa. He would never dream she was doing what she was.

He was probably still in training. Some flying field in Scotland or Ireland . . . Ireland, Fiona. Would Fiona be trapped in Ireland now? Would she not be coming back? Oh, God—Blake, Sam, Fiona . . . all gone? Would she have no one left? Sure, Horrie and Chris. Well, maybe she could get close to Betty. And the nursing sisters, especially Claire if she and Sam might get married some day. She didn't need men. She had Blake tucked away in her heart.

Was he thinking of her this minute? Writing her a letter perhaps, in his barracks. Or was he out drinking with his buddies, laughing before battle? No, he couldn't be flying yet. He'd only been gone a bit over a month. Why hadn't they trained him in Australia and then sent him to England, to fly out to bomb Germany from there? Maybe he wasn't in England. God, the man she loved more than anything in the world and she had no idea where he was. She didn't even know how to write to him.

What she'd do when she got home was start writing him something every night, and then when she learned how to contact him, she'd send it all together. After that, she'd write to him every night and send it every week. *Blake, I'm waiting for you. I'll wait for you for however long it takes. I love you. There isn't a thing I do that I don't carry you with me, within me. You have become part of me.* It's true. She wondered how she was even functioning without him. She thought she had never really lived before he'd entered her life.

With her eyes closed she remembered his hands upon her, his lips against hers. She imagined their bodies touching, lying next to each other naked, her hand tracing images down his arm, his lips burrowing into her neck. She remembered the words he'd whispered to her, words of love . . . she sat up straight and opened her eyes. Had he ever said "I love you"? She couldn't remember his saying that. But he must have. All the words he used, his actions, his touches . . . the way he looked at her. No one had ever looked at her that way, as though he knew her every thought, as though he delved into her soul. When he was inside her they were one. It wasn't just romance; it was real. They were united. They were what no one else in the universe could be. He felt the same way. It was magic.

She closed her eyes again.

Of course he had told her he loved her.

But, try as she might, she could not remember that he had. Well, it didn't matter. His actions showed how he felt.

But she'd have liked to carry that around. Would have liked to have been able to hold onto those words.

In the morning, when they arrived in Augusta Springs, she couldn't decide whether her depression stemmed from the physical ordeal she'd been through or whether it was because she could not remember Blake ever telling her he loved her.

Chapter 31

The new pilot and a letter from Fiona were waiting for her.

Warren Plummer was a week early. In his mid-forties, he was a nice-looking man, but in no way distinguished. He had brown eyes and brown hair and fair skin. He smiled easily and smoked too many cigarettes, never asking if the smoke bothered her. He was thin and already a bit stoop-shouldered.

He and his Mary had taken over Sam's quarters.

Mary, an attractive woman with brown hair and eyes and fair skin, said, "I don't know what we'll do for room when the kids come home for holidays." They had three teenagers, all away at school. "They live with my family in Melbourne," she said.

They made little initial impression on Cassie, and she imagined it was because she was ready to resent anyone who tried to take Sam's place.

"If there are no emergencies on the morning call-in, we'll head out on our regular clinic run to Witham Downs tomorrow. It's an AIM hospital down south in sheep country."

He nodded. "I'll study the map."

Cassie waited until she was alone to read Fiona's letter. She felt a lump in her throat as she read the first sentence.

My father died last month, Cassie. Much as we miss him, it's a relief. He was in agony the last weeks. My mother is standing up bravely. I may have started for home by the time you get this. What with the war and bombing, my mother wants me to leave. I've begged her to come with me, but this, she says, is her home. She is surrounded by the rest of the family and a legion of friends. She knows I must live my own life, and my life is out there.

Oh, yes, news. I've seen Blake Thompson. He's stationed outside Dublin at the Air Force base there. Running into each other was sheer coincidence. I was in Dublin where I go weekly to roll bandages for the Red Cross, and they have a center there for soldiers away from home, serving sandwiches and coffee and that sort of thing, and in walked a face from home. He was as surprised as I was. It gave us both a feeling of oh, I don't know what, but it was good. We ended up having dinner together that night, and a couple of nights later went to the movies with three of his buddies and then out dancing. Sort of fun to be the only woman with four men. He looks handsomer than ever in a uniform and he and his buddies act like they're the ones who are going to win the war. It was marvelous to see a familiar face, and I'm going to get together with him again before I leave.

Anyhow, dearest Cassie, I am coming home . . . and I must tell you how much I'm looking forward to it. It seems like too many eons since we've sat around talking into the early morning hours.

Cassie looked up from the letter, aware that her emotions were churning. Fiona coming home. Thank God. Blake in Ireland, laughing, going to movies and dancing? Blake carousing with buddies while she'd been going through an abortion?

How come a letter had arrived from Fiona but not from him? Why had he not written?

* * *

As the days passed there was still no letter from Blake. Then weeks passed. Cassie's life again settled into a routine, except that flying with Warren did not carry the same joy that being with Sam had.

He certainly was a competent pilot. He learned how to find homesteads and remote stations. He willingly assisted her in emergencies, but he lacked Sam's—Sam's what? Devil-may-care attitude? Sam's ability to find laughter in so many things? Sam's always giving her a look of encouragement and putting a reassuring hand on her shoulder or her arm?

Warren was a more careful pilot than Sam. No, that wasn't fair to Sam, who was a marvelous pilot. Perhaps it was that Sam was willing to take risks that Warren wasn't. Sam could land on a postage stamp. Sam would fly under clouds at five hundred feet and seem to make nothing of it. Sam would see a storm coming and loved the challenge of circumventing it, or of conquering it. Sam never took a foolish chance, but Warren didn't take any chances at all.

It was weeks before Cassie figured out what it was. Warren and Mary were so . . . dull. Mary had been a nurse and was willing to help in the hospital and even fly out with them on clinics. Cassie thought Mary enjoyed it, but she never expressed her pleasure. She and Warren were alike. There was no nonsense about them. They did their jobs, spoke in monotones, and didn't talk much. They weighed everything very carefully.

Cassie liked the fact that they didn't seem to differentiate between aborigines and whites as patients and she began more and more to invite Mary to accompany them on clinic runs, letting Mary pull teeth and give inoculations while she took care of less routine problems. It doubled the territory they could cover or cut their time in half. Mary didn't accompany them on emergencies because there wasn't enough room for patients and oxygen plus an extra passenger, but it soon became routine for her to fly out on clinic runs.

All the joy had gone from Cassie's life. Sam was not there to share her days, her worries, her accomplishments. He was not there to talk over problems with. And Blake . . . she developed insomnia. She still had not heard from him.

Out at Tookaringa they'd received only one letter, enclosing his postal address.

She felt she'd become like Mary, treating life matter-of-factly, meeting it but neither giving nor getting joy from it. Perhaps that was what wartime meant.

Instead of worrying about Blake, she began to feel anger at him. Oh, come home, Fi. I need to talk with you. And maybe Fiona would bring her a letter from Blake. She would smile and hold it behind her back, teasing, and say, "Guess what I have for you."

Cassie had barely gotten to sleep one night when the phone rang shortly after ten. So few Outback folks had phones that the ringing always startled Cassie.

It was Steven Thompson. The minute he said, "Cassie?" she could tell there was panic in his voice.

"It's Jennifer. Jesus, Cassie. She was adjusting the kerosene refrigerator and it exploded!"

Cassie came wide awake. "Oh, my God."

"She can't see. She's blind! Her head is bleeding and cut. Cassie!"

There was no way at all they could fly out until nearly dawn. If Sam had been here, he knew the way so well, but . . . God, they'd lost children because they lived so far from medical help. Now Jennifer?

"Steven, we'll start before it's light. Here's what to do until I can get there."

"Christ, Cassie, she can't die."

"No, of course not."

She could not return to sleep. All she could think of was Jennifer. Blind. Bleeding. Burned.

She phoned Warren at four-thirty. "We have to leave immediately," she told him. By the time they'd been in the air an hour dawn would be coming.

She phoned Chris from the radio station, knowing she'd be waking him. However, he answered on the first ring, not sounding sleepy at all.

"Chris, sorry to bother you so early. Jennifer Thompson's been burned badly." She told him what Steven had said. "I'm flying out there now. If she's as bad as Steven said we can't handle her here, can we? Not if they're third-degree burns?"

She could almost see him shaking his head. "Best burn center's Adelaide."

"That's what I was afraid of. If I think she's too bad off, we'll head straight for there, though God knows it'll take us eight to ten hours. Will you phone them and warn them we may be bringing someone in?"

"Of course." There was just a second's hesitation. "Want me to come along?"

"You don't have to do that. What can two doctors do that one can't?"

"Give moral support. I know you care a great deal about the woman."

My God, Chris was becoming absolutely human. Would she want him along? "We're leaving in ten minutes."

"Make it fifteen and I'll be there."

She realized it was Sunday and his day off.

Warren had flown out to Tookaringa once, a month before, so he was familiar with the landing area. Half a dozen men waved them in. Cassie practically leapt out of the open door, grabbing her medical bag and running toward the house. Chris was close behind her. He'd never been to Tookaringa.

Her face so disfigured Cassie could scarcely recognize her, Jennifer lay on the bed, her breath rattling. Steven, eyes bloodshot, sat beside her, holding her hand.

"She's not conscious," he said, his voice as unrecognizable as Jennifer's face.

Thank goodness for that, Cassie thought, bending over her friend.

Chris went around to the other side of the bed and leaned over the patient, too. "My God," he said in a whisper.

Whatever happened, Cassie thought, she'll never be beautiful again. But that was secondary. Would she ever see again? Would she even live?

Jennifer shivered; her arms were covered with gooseflesh. "Pneumonia," Chris said.

Yes, I know, thought Cassie. She looked at Chris. "Adelaide?"

"Yes."

She hadn't needed him for this. He couldn't quell the beating of her heart, the butterflies in her stomach. She turned to Steven. "We'll fly her to the burn center in Adelaide right away." God, would Jennifer even last that long? "I'll give her a shot to keep her asleep so she won't feel anything. But time is of the essence."

Steven looked at Chris, who nodded in agreement.

"I'm coming," Steven said.

"Of course," Cassie said, placing her hand on his arm.

He turned and threw his arms around her, bursting into tears. "Cassie, I can't live without her."

"Let's go," Chris said.

Oh, damn, Cassie thought. He's not good with relatives of patients. He's not good with patients who are dying. Why did I bring him?

But, Chris had picked up Jennifer and was carrying her out the door, down the verandah steps, toward the plane. Carrying her as though she weighed nothing, as though the charred and leathery skin did not smell foul, as though the deformed figure he held was not repugnant. Perhaps it was as well he'd come. Neither she nor Steven could be objective about Jennifer.

Warren was refilling the gas tank from the pump. They'd need to stop at least twice to refill it before reaching Adelaide. Oh, dear God, Cassie silently prayed, let the weather be good.

It was. As soon as they'd taken off and leveled, Cassie took bandages out of her medical kit. "Here," Chris said, reaching for them, "I'll do it." Gently he wound the bandage around Jennifer's face and arms so her skin would be protected. It was a relief not to see the ghastly burned skin, even though they could smell it.

Why, Cassie wondered, did it have to be so hot? It must be over a hundred. Jennifer lay alternately covered with gooseflesh and sweat, her breathing becoming more labored the further south they flew.

It was the longest seven hours Cassie had ever spent. Steven never said a word the whole time. He sat beside Jennifer's stretcher, his hand touching her, his lips working in silence.

As they flew over Lake Eyre, nearly four hundred miles north of Adelaide, Jennifer's breathing became tortured, her chest heaving. Loud rattles gurgled from her half-open mouth.

With panicked eyes, Steven looked over at Cassie, who—in turn—

caught Chris's glance. He shook his head. Cassie stood up and walked over to Steven, putting her arms around his shoulders, bending down as they both looked at Jennifer.

Death rattles.

She was surprised to notice Chris staring at Steven, unable to take his eyes from the grief-stricken man.

The gasping for breath, the strangled sob-like sounds stopped. Jennifer's chest stopped heaving.

Steven threw himself across the stretcher, clutching Jennifer's hands, crying, "No, no, no."

Chapter 32

There was no comforting Steven. Once he returned home, he withdrew from the world. He resigned from the Flying Doctors Council. He was curt when Don McLeod called. He absented himself when Cassie held her regular monthly clinic at Tookaringa. Cassie had planned to stay overnight, as usual, and dine with him, hoping to take his mind off his grief. But he did not appear and she, Warren, and Mary flew back to Augusta Springs that night.

The second time Cassie held the clinic there, he was waiting for her, thrusting a letter from Blake into her hands. After she finished reading it, he took it back, went into his study, and she didn't see him again. The letter was filled with mourning for the loss of his mother. It was filled with remembrances of her. It was filled with empathy for his father. But he said nothing about himself, nothing of the war, nothing of Cassie.

In three months there was not another word from Fiona, but Cassie did receive a letter from Sam.

Dear Doc,

Surprise you, huh? I bet you didn't expect to hear from me.

Every day I wonder what's going on back there, who's had a baby or an operation or who's died or what new thing is happening. I'm hoping the pilot is good (if he's with QANTAS he has to be, I know that), but not too good. I'm coming back, as I told you, to that job and that town and to the FDS.

I'm where it's cold and grey; I'm where everyone I know wants a chance to fly across the channel and kill as many Germans as they can, be they women or children or old, be they innocent or not. Well, I guess they can't be innocent if they're willing to go along with that madman's Napoleonic dreams.

I'm spending most of my time instructing. There are so few trained pilots that we spend our time training others when what we want to do is be out there participating. Yeah, I want to be a hero. I want medals all over my chest. I want to come home and have you look at me and think I'm a hero. I want a tailgunner who machine-guns Nazi Messerschmidts out of the air until there are none left.

Okay, that's the kid in me. The man thinks this war will not be over soon. Might go on for years. The sounds of air raid sirens cast a pall over England. One begins to get used to it, and there is a spirit of camaraderie in air raid shelters deep underground. Friendships grow and we get to gut-level quicker than anyplace I've ever known. You meet a pretty girl in an air raid shelter and before the evening's over you find yourself kissing her, without even knowing her name. That could never have happened in normal times.

Consider it your patriotic duty to write to a lonely airman and cheer him up, keep him in touch with home. I think about all of you and yearn to hear about everyone and everything.

~~Best wishes~~ ~~Sincerely~~
Warm regards,
SAM

By the time she received Sam's letter he had been gone seven months and Blake had been gone eight. She had a pile of notes that she'd kept, things she'd wanted to send Blake. Letters she'd written in the lonely evenings. She went through and tossed out all the references to love, jammed them into a big envelope, and sent them off to Sam.

Bertie Martin and her sister Andy rode into town. They arrived at noon on a Saturday, parking their beat-up utility in front of Cassie's, strolling across the verandah and into the parlor, calling Cassie's name. She heard them from the kitchen.

Bertie hugged Cassie and nodded to Andy. They could have been clones, so alike were they in shape and blondness. The voluptuous, tall bodies, walking like jungle cats, strength emanating from them. Yet there was about each of them a sweetness and innocence, a sense of joy that was irresistible.

"Brought Andy in to see what town life's like."

Cassie welcomed them. "I suppose you timed this for the Saturday Night Dance."

Bertie nodded. "You'll be disappointed, I'm afraid. There are so few men left."

Bertie sprawled on the couch, using her kerchief to wipe dust from her face. "Why's that?"

"They've all gone off to war."

Bertie and Andy looked at each other. "No foolin'?" asked Andy. "All the men?"

"Well, not all, but most. There's still a dance tonight, but it won't be like last time you were here."

Bertie said, "That cook still around, or did he go off, too?"

"Cully? He's still here. I think he's flat-footed or something. Some reason he couldn't join up, so I've heard."

"Probably too scrawny," said Bertie. "But he sure can cook."

They left two days later, disappointed that the town wasn't as Bertie remembered it. "I offered Cully a job," Bertie said. "But he's not interested in livin' so far from town. He don't talk much, does he?"

The next week Padre McLeod and his Margaret came to town. Margaret was a pretty girl with coal-black hair gathered in a bun and blue eyes as bright as robin's eggs.

Cassie invited Don and his Margaret to stay with her and sleep in Fiona's room while they were in town. She asked Horrie and Betty and their new baby to come to dinner, too, realizing it was the first time she'd entertained, except for the party she and Fiona threw the second week she was in town nearly two years ago. Well, maybe she should make a real party of it. Invite Warren and Mary. Maybe Chris, too. She felt she owed him a great deal. And she knew he must be lonely, with Isabel gone. She never saw him except when they assisted each other or met in the hospital.

The unspoken agreement they'd come to pleased her inordinately. It made her work far more interesting. Without Dr. Edwards, Chris was far too busy to handle the FDS patients, too, so he permitted her to perform surgery on her patients. She was able to follow through with post-surgical attendance, getting to know the Outback people in ways that had been prohibited before. Though Chris was still the prejudiced, narrow-minded man who drove her up a wall, he had become a pleasure to work with. They might not function harmoniously outside the hospital, but they had come to rely on each other for second opinions and for assistance in complicated surgery. He had trained Sister Claire in anesthesia, but now she was leaving to join the armed forces.

Cassie planned her dinner party for a Saturday evening, knowing she'd have to spend the whole day in the kitchen. It was a welcome relief.

She needed welcome relief. She spent fifteen to twenty hours a week in the air, with her eyes closed thinking of Blake. Bitterness grew large in her heart. He'd won hers, he'd battered down her carefully built-up defenses, he'd seduced her—well, that wasn't quite accurate. He'd made love to her—mad, passionate love—for two and a half weeks. He hadn't just made love to her body; he'd seduced her mind and heart. He'd shown her a wilderness she hadn't known existed and their primitive rhythms undulated to the wildness in that land. She had lost herself in him. A part of her was still gone. Was it her heart? She grieved as much for him as for Jennifer. A sense of malaise clung to her. Could those weeks in Kakadu have meant so little to him? Had he forgotten so quickly the magic they'd shared?

In her heart she could not believe he had forgotten. She still waited daily to hear from him. Look at the one letter he'd written his family—response to his father's loss. Nothing about what he was doing. Perhaps he just hated writing letters. Perhaps he *was* carrying the memory of her in his left shirt pocket, as he'd said he would.

She was so angry she cut her finger slicing tomatoes for the salad.

Just then a horn sounded and she looked out the window to see one of the town's three taxis rounding the corner, stopping in front of the house. Out of the cab stepped an elegantly dressed woman. The cab driver began to unload suitcases.

Cassie clutched her chest. Tears stung her eyes. She stood there staring until finally she was galvanized to run out of the kitchen, down the steps, her arms open, sobbing happily.

Fiona's face screwed up into tears as she held her arms out to Cassie. They clung to each other, murmuring each other's names over and over.

"You're home, oh, you're back," Cassie cried. "How I've needed you!"

Then they began to laugh, pulling back to look at each other, kissing each other's cheeks. Cassie thought her heart would burst with happiness. Oh, Fiona was home. She could unburden herself at last, tell Fiona all that had happened since she'd gone. Fiona didn't even know she'd fallen in love, much less all that followed that. So much to share. It would be so wonderful. She could tell Fiona everything.

"First thing I have to do," Fiona said, "is get word to Tookaringa."

"Why, what's wrong?" Cassie imagined Fi couldn't yet know of Jennifer's death.

Fiona laughed, her face radiant. "Nothing. I have to tell them the news."

"What news?" *Was Blake all right?*

"That they have a new daughter-in-law." She looked into Cassie's eyes, grinning. "I'm the new Mrs. Blake Thompson." She held out her hand so Cassie could see her wide gold wedding band.

Cassie pounded her pillow, already damp with tears. She tried to muffle her sobs—great, gasping moans that she could not stop. Pain zigzagged through her chest and ribs. She shook uncontrollably.

Blake and Fiona.

Another wail escaped her.

It had been the hardest thirty hours of her life. There had been no time to mourn. No time to think.

It wasn't until Don and Margaret had moved on that she and Fiona had time alone, and she hadn't known whether she could face it. Fiona wanted to tell her all about her marriage, and Cassie didn't want to hear any of it.

"Remember I told you I'd had an abortive love affair? I crocheted your bedspread while recovering? Well, I guess I never did recover. And when I saw him again in Ireland, I felt the same thing all over again. I knew I'd never gotten over him. I knew I was a fool to get involved with him again, but I couldn't help it. And when he kissed me for the first time in over four years, I dissolved. I told myself no more would come of it than the first time, yet I couldn't say no. Two days after I'd made reservations to return here his unit was ordered away. I don't know where. And he said, 'Darling, who knows if I'll come through this or if we'll ever see each other again, but I want to think of you waiting for me. I want to think of you to come home to. I want to hope that perhaps you'll be carrying my child. Let's get married.' So we did. Oh, Cassie, I never imagined, all those years I dreamed of him after he never really said goodbye, that he'd look at me again. Even though we're not together, even though I worry about him flying over Germany, even with all the awful unknowns, I'm so happy I could burst."

Blake and Fiona? *He* was the one she'd loved all along? The one who broke her heart years ago?

Oh, Cassie moaned aloud, pounding her fists into the pillow, sitting up, grabbing it to her, weeping as though the world were about to end.

Fiona had always been in love with Blake. Even while I was making love with him he was in Fiona's heart. And now that Fiona is married to him, he is still in mine.

She told herself she wasn't in love with him, not the real Blake. She had been in love with a figment of her imagination, someone she thought he was.

She remembered he never had told her he loved her. But when she'd felt his hands on her breasts, when their naked bodies melded, when he came inside her and cried her name, she'd been sure he had felt what she did: eternal love. Damn him. All he probably felt was release. Did it even matter who it was? Damn him, goddamn him.

"Never again!" she screamed, though there was no echo of her voice in the house. Never again would she let a man do to her what Blake Thompson and Ray Graham had done. Never again would she fall in love. Next time, if there was a next time, she'd be in charge. She would never, ever be the victim again. Never again the victim of love. Never!

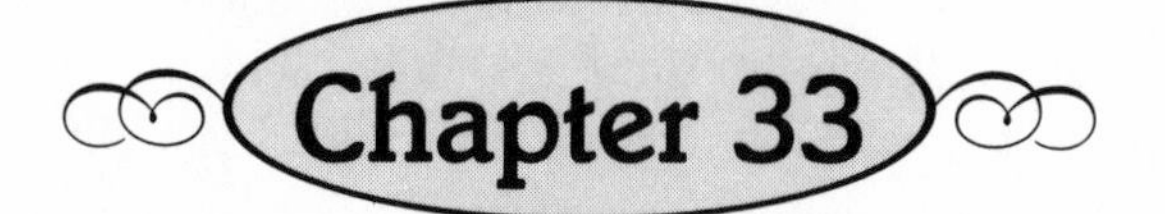

Chapter 33

Thank God. Fiona had gone out to Tookaringa to spend time with Steven. "I'll stay a week or ten days," she told Cassie, kissing her goodbye as she took off.

It was all Cassie could do to be pleasant to Fiona even though she knew it was not Fiona's fault. Fiona had no idea Cassie had fallen in love with Blake. She had no intimation that Cassie had become pregnant by him, that her heart was breaking because of him.

Cassie had to remind herself of these facts a dozen times a day.

She drove out to the radio station in the secondhand car the Flying Doctor Service had finally supplied for her. She didn't know how Betty and Horrie and the new baby lived in such a cramped space. The verandah Horrie had promised Betty before they were married had still failed to materialize, and they lived in two tiny rooms, like a blast furnace in summer. Yet Betty was never anything but cheerful. She spelled Horrie at the radio once in a while; she had a nice, reassuring manner with the Outback folks. She talked to them, as did Horrie, as though they were friends who had known each other for a long time.

There were no emergencies to attend to, but other phone calls brought about a change in the clinic planned for today at Medumcook, in the north. Stockton Wells and Mt. Everett had heard she'd be making the far north clinic run and called in to ask if they could be put on the route.

"I suppose we could stay out two nights," she told Warren on the phone. "Would Mary be interested in going? There'll be dozens of children to be inoculated and probably a lot of teeth to be pulled. I could use her help."

Mary's services were strictly voluntary, yet she never said no. Cassie wondered why she couldn't feel closer to Warren and his wife. They were certainly nice enough. Always cooperative. Perhaps it was because they were always the same. Nothing seemed to faze them. Nothing seemed to give them joy. They accepted everything with the same emotion—a sense of duty.

The three of them flew out shortly after ten-thirty. Mary brought the newspaper to read and then turned to knitting. She hardly ever talked on these trips. Cassie studied her for a while and then glanced out the window. She closed her eyes and imagined Fiona arriving at Tookaringa, saw Steven opening his arms to her, the first surge of life he might have felt since Jennifer's death. She heard Fiona saying, "Hello, Dad," visualized Fiona looking around Tookaringa and thinking, "Someday I will live here and be mistress of Tookaringa." Then Cassie thought—Fiona's children will inherit Tookaringa.

Maybe Fiona would move out there to keep Steven company. Move to where she now belonged. To a home that was now hers. Would it be good, Cassie wondered, to have Fiona out of sight and mind? Oh, God, when she'd so looked forward to her friend's return . . . when she'd waited for Fiona so they could take up their friendship, so she could share all that was in her heart.

She looked out the window at the increasingly green land below, at the tropical foliage . . . the banana trees, the palms, the sugar cane field, and envisioned Blake's hands touching Fiona, Blake leaning over to kiss Fiona, Blake saying to Fiona, "I love you," and she clenched her fists in her lap. Blake never again thinking of her, Cassie. Blake forgetting the passion they'd felt at Kakadu. Blake not even remembering what she looked like.

The only person who had sensed what might be within Cassie was, oddly, Chris. He'd appeared one morning shortly after Fiona's return, knocking—tapping was more like it—on the front door. Cassie had answered the door in her robe. Though she was sure he hadn't done so, she would have sworn he had bowed from the waist. His formal manner must be ingrained, she thought. He's like that even when he first wakes up.

"I've come at this early hour to invite you to breakfast," he said.

"To breakfast?" She brushed her hair out of her eyes.

He looked around, as though seeing if anyone were within hearing distance. "Yes," he said. "It dawned on me that you might need someone to talk to."

He'd known, of course, that Fiona had come home, married to the man Cassie loved.

Kind as it might have been, Chris was certainly not the one to whom she would unburden her soul. If she were going to do so, she needed sympathy, and Chris Adams was not a person to offer that. Nevertheless, Cassie felt a warmth toward him, as she had when he offered to send her to Townsville. She couldn't imagine ever crying in front of Chris and having him understand. He'd probably never even experienced heartbreak until Isabel died. He'd been married to the same woman for all those years. He'd never experienced rejection. He wouldn't know what unrequited love did to one's heart. He wouldn't know what betrayal meant. He wouldn't understand emotional pain, abysses as deep as the soul.

As she'd looked at him on the other side of the screen door at seven in the morning, she ran a hand again through her tangled hair. God, I must look a fright, she realized.

"Talk to someone?" she repeated. "What about?" No, she didn't want him to answer. "I don't know what you mean."

He stared at her for a minute, looking as though he didn't quite know what to do. "Well, in that case I'm out of line. I was afraid I might be." He turned, starting down the steps, when Cassie, ashamed of her curtness, said, "If you'll wait a minute, I'd love to have breakfast with you. That's the best invitation I've had in a long time."

"Well, I doubt that," Chris muttered.

"Come on in and sit down while I throw some clothes on. I won't be ten minutes."

Though he hadn't mentioned Blake and she hadn't admitted to the pain that wracked her spirit, they had managed to have a pleasant breakfast. They'd argued, and that took her mind off Blake. But then she and Chris almost always found something to debate. This time it was about aborigines. His claim that their brains were smaller, that they were just barely emerging from primitive existence, infuriated her. He did not consider them quite human. "Look at their jutting jaws. They look more like apes than humans," he had said. "Look at their practices, still of the Stone Age. Look at their inability to adopt white standards of sanitation, the work ethic, belief in one God."

Finally, Cassie shook her head and decided it wasn't worth fighting about. Chris's attitude said more about Chris than about the subject of conversation. But, irritating and incomprehensible as his attitude was, she did feel grateful for his reaching out. Two years ago she could never have imagined his doing so. But then, two years ago Sam and Fiona were her friends and Blake waited in the future. She could never have believed the depth of feeling Blake would engender in her, she could never have envisioned having an abortion. She could never have predicted any of the things that had happened to her.

In the plane, she sighed and Mary leaned across the aisle. "Anything wrong?"

Cassie looked at her blankly.

"You sighed as though the problems of the world were on your shoulders."

Cassie shook her head. "I didn't realize it."

Mary nodded and returned to her knitting.

The plane began to descend and Cassie looked out the window. They were coming in to Medumcook; Cassie had been there three times before. The plane had to land two miles out because the town was surrounded by palms and the Medumcook River slogged right through it. She had never been here in the Wet, when the river swept along like the Nile in flood, over a dozen miles wide and fathoms deep. Now, a few waterholes stretched between a trickle of water. Wooden whiskey cases were used as stepping stones from one side of the banks to the other.

The town consisted of one pub, on the bank of the river. The owner told her it had to be rebuilt every year after the floods. Warren handed mail to the postmaster-bartender. Eight people lived in Medumcook. A policeman, who covered more than six hundred square miles by himself. The postmaster-bartender. The owner of the pub also owned the local store, attached to the tin-roofed pub. A mile outside of town there was a cattle station, on its way to being one of the largest in the world, now turning out fifteen thousand head of top-grade Santa Gertrudis every year.

Fred, the bearded bartender, told them there would be a host of people coming in. They'd wait til nearly dark because "nothing stirs, not even snakes, in the blinding heat of the day at this time of year."

They had tea on the porch of the pub, whose tin roof rattled with the sounds of insects.

People began to stray in about five o'clock. A family came by truck, from seventy-five miles away. The woman was pregnant again, and the three small children had runny eyes, around which flies swarmed. One of the two little girls had a gash on her leg that was festering, a raw running sore.

Six men came riding in from the plains. Two had terrible toothaches, one had a boil. The others came along for a night of drinking under the stars.

Three men rode in from a camp twenty miles to the east, and one of them had a cough so bad that Cassie suggested he fly back with them and be X-rayed for tuberculosis. No, he'd have none of that. They stayed to drink and converse with men they'd never met or hadn't seen in years.

Four men rode in with their swags. They'd been mending fences and when one of them complained of a toothache, they'd all decided to come into town to spend an evening at the pub. By ten o'clock there must have been over a hundred men around the bar.

Fred said to Cassie, "I bet not a one of them has slept in a bed in nearly thirty years."

"Maybe you could do a good business," said Mary, "if you started a hotel."

Fred shook his head. "Nope. None of 'em wants to ever sleep in a bed again, I bet. They like the life they've chosen. Beds mean society, and that's what they're here to escape."

"What about you?" asked Cassie, pleased to discover she was able to enjoy herself.

"Me? I wouldn't know what to do back in town. I'd miss the Wet then, and that's what I like best. The floods—that's something I wouldn't want to miss. The rains from further north swell this little river, a little licking wave sneaks from waterhole to waterhole, trickling along, widening as it goes. From all directions creeks, surging with rainwater, create torrents and dash along, until it looks and sounds like the water's angry. It sweeps along animals, live and dead, and broken tree limbs catch anything they touch, rushing and raging. Why, one night between dark and dawn the river rose thirty-six feet! That was some night."

It was past midnight when the first men began to leave, a few riding off into the night, others throwing down their swags anyplace under the thick tropical foliage. Fred said, "I'll sleep out here. I made my bed up today and there's a sofa. You three can sleep in my place."

His place was a tin-roofed shack, hot as a griddle. Cassie tossed and turned all night. But in the morning, Fred fed them pancakes and the biggest lamb chops Cassie had ever seen and coffee that should have made their hair stand up straight.

"The abos'll be in now, in the morning. They'll come from all along the river."

Cassie looked out and saw four or five blacks already waiting.

It was early afternoon before they took off for Stockton Wells, a much larger town, one that already had a five-bed hospital. Cassie spent the afternoon discussing proposed monthly visits with the nurse, Sister Maureen, and then attended a man with fractured ribs, a baby with colic, a child with whooping cough, a pregnant woman with diabetes. She suggested the latter come into town the last three months of her pregnancy so that she'd be near the Augusta Springs Hospital, "just in case."

Aside from that, there were a dozen outpatients whom the nurse asked her to see.

By the time they'd finished it was twilight. Maureen insisted they stay in her home overnight; she could bunk in the hospital. They sat around drinking beer and talking until nearly midnight.

Cassie had barely fallen asleep when there was a pounding at the door that startled her so that she sat straight up. A voice called, "Doctor?" repeatedly.

Grabbing her robe, she opened the door. Standing before her was a tall, good-looking man with startled dark eyes.

"It's an emergency."

"Wait'll I get my clothes." Cassie could hardly see through eyes heavy with sleep.

Dressed and with medical bag in hand, she returned to the door where the man grabbed her other hand and began running toward the hotel, only three doors away. "She's out back," he said, not breaking his stride.

"I'm afraid she's going to bleed to death. She can't. She just can't." She wondered if the man were going to cry.

In the area behind the hotel was a barn and, lying on its side in one of the stables, was an immense horse, bleeding badly. There were two great gashes across its chest. Three men surrounded the animal, one of them patting her, talking soothingly, the other two making sure she stayed down, though she was making no effort to move. The pool of blood widened.

Cassie stood still. "I'm not a veterinarian."

The man who still held her hand looked at her pleadingly. "Doc, you've got to save Cleo. She's my only chance for The Cup."

All four men's eyes implored her. Cassie sighed and moved slowly towards the wounded mare.

"Heard shots about midnight. Not anyone trying to shoot her, I don't think, probably a roo shooter. But it must've scared her and she reared and stampeded into the barbed wire fence. Doc, you got to sew her up. You just got to."

Cassie knelt down next to the horse, whose eyes reflected the panic within.

"I'll need some lanterns."

In five minutes there were four lanterns swinging from the men's hands. "Put a couple of them up on that rafter," Cassie suggested, "and two of you kneel down here and be ready to hold the horse. I've given her a shot." She wondered if the amount of pain killer she had was enough for this big animal.

Within ten minutes Cleo began to grow drowsy; the medicine was working. Cassie clamped and tied off the bleeders and sewed the animal up. It took over an hour.

"Don't move her for a couple of days, and then only to take her home, in a truck if you can, and let her recuperate thoroughly. It will be a month at the very least, maybe longer, before you can ride her. And then break her in gently." She didn't know why she was saying all this. She didn't know a thing about horses. It sounded logical, though.

She was back in bed by two.

By mid-morning they were at Mt. Everett, a dusty little town just south of the green of the tropics, on the way back toward Augusta Springs. The air was rosy with dust. While they were there, attending to out-patients in the back room of the pub—one of three buildings in town—the pub owner announced that Templeton Station hoped the doctor could stop there to see an ill patient. It was only forty miles southwest.

They started a bit after two. The air was so thick with haze that Warren could hardly see. He called the radio station to check on the weather, then said, "A cold front's moving in from the northeast." Cassie didn't know what that implied.

She looked out the window, barely able to see the ground. They'd been in the air only thirty minutes and were so surrounded by dust that visibility was poor, though they were flying so low that Cassie could see trees and a herd of kangaroos through the dust.

"Want to turn around?" she called out to Warren.

He shook his head. "It should be straight ahead of us. Whatever's down there is so flat that it should be safe to land anyplace." With that the dust disappeared. They'd come through to the other side, and straight ahead of them, a bit to the left, was Templeton Station, purple bougainvillea shining bright in the afternoon sunshine.

Warren made a smooth landing despite gusty cross-winds.

Cassie ascertained that the woman they'd flown to see needed an appendectomy, so they loaded her onto a stretcher and into the plane.

"Why don't you sit up front?" Cassie said to Mary, motioning toward the seat behind Warren where she usually sat. "I'll sit in the back so I can be near the patient."

Mary nodded and strapped herself in.

Warren swung out, pointing down the landing field. Applying full power, he released the brakes and the right aileron. Slowly the tail rose as he headed down the homemade runway a couple of hundred yards. He eased the forward stick back, and the plane reeled sluggishly to the left. It was obvious he was not able to overpower the abrupt pitch to the left quickly enough to bring them back on track. He cut the power and brought the plane to an abrupt halt.

Turning the plane around, he returned to the take-off point. He leaned his head back into the cabin and motioned for Cassie to come forward. "That strong downdraft cocked us right before I could get up enough speed. The plane seems tail-heavy. Will you stand here in the cockpit doorway and can you roll the stretcher toward the front? Then when we get up, you can return to normal seating."

It was easy for Cassie to roll the stretcher frontward. She and Mary lashed it to the forward seat so it wouldn't roll and Warren nodded. "Fine."

He used full power and the plane began to roll again. Though the tail was still slow to come up, there was no swaying as the plane left the ground.

Cassie bent down to look forward and saw rows of trees straight ahead. The plane hadn't reached tree-top height and she looked quickly at the back of Warren's head. His neck was rigid. "The plane's not climbing properly," he said, as though to himself. "The sonofabitch isn't climbing."

Ahead of them, as they barely passed over the treetops, were miles of nothing except scrub bush.

Warren's voice was normal when he glanced up at Cassie and said,

"Think I'll make a full circuit to gain height before we set course." He began a Rate Two turn to port, veering slightly to the left.

Cassie asked, "Are you hoping to turn into the wind to gain air speed?"

He didn't answer. Cassie glanced at the altimeter. She'd flown long enough with Sam to know how to read a few instruments. They were flying at under three hundred feet.

With a shock she realized Warren's knuckles were white from the pressure he was exerting on the throttle knobs. My God, she thought, we're losing speed even with full power.

"Aren't we climbing?"

Warren shook his head. "We lost height with that turn." He turned to look Cassie straight in the eye.

"My God," she said aloud as the truth became all too clear.

We're in trouble.

"Now the nose is too heavy. Get back in the tail," he said, urgency in his voice.

Cassie wasted no time, squeezing herself between the stretcher and Mary's seat, rushing to throw herself against the back of the plane, sitting on the floor.

She could still see out the window and realized the nose of the plane was diving toward the ground.

The plane began to spin. She grabbed the legs of the back seat as they hit the ground before everything went black.

Chapter 34

A man's face stared down at her. "You all right?" he asked.

Cassie didn't know. I must have a concussion, she thought in confusion. The man stretched out a hand to pull her up from the floor of what was left of the plane. He put an arm around her shoulders and led her over to the edge of the plane, where the wall was missing. Someone else reached up to catch her.

Oh, God, what had happened? She looked up at the plane; the inside was intact. *Thank God. That meant Warren and Mary and their patient were okay. How in the world had the whole side of the plane been sucked away?* She was standing in its wreckage.

Beside the twisted mass of what had been the window, Mary was lying faceup, motionless. Cassie ran over to her. There wasn't a scratch on her, though her blouse was torn and her right breast lay exposed. Cassie leaned down and covered it with the ripped fabric. As she knelt to comfort Mary, she noticed the blankness of her eyes, staring straight up at the blinding sun.

Oh, my God.

Looking over at the plane, anxious to be of help to Warren when he discovered his wife, she saw two men dragging him from the cockpit, where he was wedged so tightly that she knew immediately he must have been crushed on impact.

Blood gushed from his nose, mouth, even his ears. His breathing was labored, torturous.

"Get him into the shade," Cassie ordered, reaching her hand to the back of her head, which suddenly ached terribly. The two men picked Warren up and placed him in the shade of the left wing. Cassie knelt down next to him. For a moment she couldn't see him, affected as she was by her own pain. She could tell by looking at him that he was nearly dead. There was nothing she could do.

She stood and looked around for their patient, horrified to see her body twisted around the stretcher, parts of which jutted through her.

Feeling useless and despairing, Cassie returned to Warren and sat, holding his hand, until he stopped breathing half an hour later.

She laid her head on his chest and wept.

Nearly a dozen people had gathered at the crash site.

A man she'd never seen before came over to her. "I've called your base radio station," he said, his hand on her shoulder. "They're sending someone out from Highcastle by ambulance. It's about a hundred miles so it'll be three or four hours before it gets here."

Cassie turned to look up at him, but all she could see were fuzzy outlines. The sound of the people gathering around her faded, and the dazzling rays of the sun were all she could see. I'm dying, too, she thought as the pain in the back of her head split it wide open.

It was too much of an effort to open her eyes, but she heard faint sounds—the swoosh of rubber-soled shoes on tiled floor, the faint, crisp sound of starched uniforms, and the inimitable smell of a hospital. She sank into unconsciousness again.

When she awoke next time, the first thing she felt was a hand around hers. She tried to open her eyes, but her eyelids only fluttered.

A familiar, flat voice said, "You have a concussion. Something hit you just above your hairline and fractured your skull. It's just an inch long but you'll probably be disoriented for several days."

She forced her eyes open. Chris Adams was sitting next to the bed, holding her hand.

"A sharp object nearly penetrated your left arm." Concern was etched on his face. "Right above the elbow. Luckily, it missed any nerves. It'll take you a few weeks to recover." He pressed his hand tightly around hers.

"Am I home?" Cassie asked.

"No, you're in the hospital in Highcastle. You've been here nearly twenty hours."

So what are you doing here? Cassie wanted to ask, but couldn't find the energy to speak.

When she awoke the next time, Chris was standing by the window, staring out into the twilight.

"What's happening to your patients?" she asked. Not *Hello,* not *How nice to see you,* not . . .

"I'm with one of them."

"Augusta Springs has no doctor?"

"Augusta Springs has no doctor right now." He didn't seem upset by the fact.

"Warren? Mary?" She had to hear him say it.

"They're both dead. Their bodies have already been taken back to Augusta Springs."

Cassie closed her eyes again. It was too much to think about. Three people dead, and she was alive. Why?

"Don't go doing that on me." Chris's voice filtered into her consciousness.

She opened her eyes again. "Doing what?"

"Feeling guilty. Don't go thinking it should have been you instead. That's sheer foolishness." He was leaning his arm against the wall, his legs crossed, staring at her from across the room.

"I wasn't thinking that."

"No, but you might. It's common enough. There's no rhyme or reason, Cassie, to why it's one person and not another."

Her sigh filled the room, and her eyes filled with tears.

"It's all over."

Chris walked over and sat in the straight back chair beside her.

She looked at him. "You must have felt that way when Isabel died."

"No, not for a moment," he said and his eyes looked like flint. "And your life is not over."

Oh, it was such an effort to talk. "I didn't mean my life. I meant the Flying Doctors. No plane, no pilot. Where to get either of them in wartime . . . "

There was a moment's silence. "You can always stay on in Augusta Springs. I need a partner, and heaven knows you're much better than Edwards was."

A fly buzzed beyond the window screen.

"Or, if you don't want me as a partner, go into practice on your own and we can assist each other in the hospital."

Cassie just wanted to go back to sleep, but she heard Chris's voice, as it grew fainter. "I'll stay until you're ready to be taken back home."

Two days later she was released in Chris's care. He laid her on the back seat of his car and spent a day and a half driving her back to Augusta Springs. He hardly spoke as he drove.

Cassie looked at the back of his head and wondered if she'd been wrong about him. He'd been so thoughtful and gentle with her. He was proving to be a friend indeed. He knew things about her that no one else in the world knew. Funny, she'd never have imagined that Chris Adams would have become her confidant, Chris instead of Fiona or Sam. She loved Fiona . . . did she still? Fiona's place in life was the one that Cassie had thought was hers. Did the envy, the jealousy that stabbed through her kill the love she'd felt for her friend? Knowing Fiona had shared Blake's bed, that he had made love to her . . . A knife twisted in her heart. She sobbed.

Chris turned his head to look at her. "You all right?"

Cassie nodded as a tear fell down her cheek. Never to know Blake's love again, never to feel his kisses, never to have him touch her, never . . . she began to cry, unable to stop.

When they arrived back in Augusta Springs it was nearly five. Chris helped her out of the car, but Cassie insisted on walking up the steps by herself. "You're going to be disoriented and weak for a few days," he said. "I'd better find someone to stay with you."

"No," she said. "I don't want a stranger around. I'll stay in bed, I really will. I'll just get up to get tea and toast or something."

When he'd made sure she had reached the bedroom safely, he said, "I'll run over to the store and buy bread, eggs, milk, that sort of thing."

He was back in half an hour, after she'd changed to her nightgown and slipped between the sheets.

He stood in the doorway to her bedroom, the bag of groceries in his arms. "I scramble eggs pretty well," he said. "How about that and some bacon and toast? And tea?"

His glasses were crooked, and a lock of hair fell over his forehead. He looked oddly boyish, and Cassie smiled at him. "Only if you'll stay and dine with me. You could sit here at my desk and we could eat together."

With one of his rare full-fledged smiles, he said, "Be right back."

When he returned, carrying a tray, there were daisies in a water glass along with the food. "They were the only flowers I could find," he said, grinning.

"It's lovely, Chris, it really is."

He brought his own plate and coffee in, placing them on the desk, sitting at it sideways so he could face her.

"I'll phone Horrie and tell him you're back."

"Maybe he'll have some idea of how we could go on. I'll have to get in touch with Reverend Flynn and maybe Don McLeod. They need the Flying Doctors in this area."

"You're beautiful," Chris said suddenly, as though pulling the words out of the air, surprising Cassie.

She stared at him.

"With the lamplight shining on your hair that way." He gulped his coffee, but his eyes never left hers.

I can never love him, she thought. He's bigoted and prejudiced and arrogant and cold.

As she sipped her tea, their eyes still locked, she felt stirrings deep within her. He was nice-looking—she had to give him that. Nice-looking in a regal, aristocratic, bloodless sort of way. Like Sam, he was too thin, bony. His chin was weak, but that wasn't his fault, that was genetic. She looked at his lips, aware of them for the first time. They were wide and sensuous. Made for kissing. She wondered what it would be like to have him kiss her.

His hands, around the cup, were strong. Long and slender fingers. A surgeon's hands. What might it feel like to have his hands touch her? What would it feel like to have his body cover hers, to have him naked next to her?

He stood up and came over to the bed, leaning down to lift the tray, then walked out of the room with it. She heard him washing the dishes in the kitchen and smiled, surprised at her own thoughts. He'd be shocked if he knew. But somehow she felt safe with him. She could never love him, but she needed someone to want her, even if only for tonight.

When he returned, standing in the doorway, his eyes were veiled as he said, "I'll be home all evening if you need me. You should be all right. But, just in case . . . "

"Don't go yet," she said. "Please."

He looked undecided.

"There's wine in the cupboard above the stove. Why don't you pour us each a glass?"

"Cassie . . . "

When he didn't move, she said, "Please."

He left and returned with two small jelly glasses filled with red wine. When he brought one over to her, she moved to the middle of the bed and patted the space beside her. "Sit here," she said. "I don't want to be alone."

He sat down, awkwardly, and Cassie noticed his face was flushed.

"I don't know how to thank you for all you've done, for taking care of me."

He drank the wine in one gulp and placed the glass on the bedside table.

She reached out and took his hand. His eyes did not leave hers. "What do you do for love now that Isabel's gone?"

He looked at her. Then his voice broke, "Oh, God, Cassie . . . "

She leaned forward, pulling him to her, her mouth meeting his.

He wrested himself away from her, standing up, an odd look in his eyes. "I'm going."

Yet even after he'd left, after the house was silent and dark and the only sound was the yelping of dogs in the distance, Cassie knew he wanted her.

When she awoke the next morning, Cassie started to leap from bed. The sun was shining in her window and she thought she must be late for the morning radio call. She pushed herself up on her elbow.

Then, everything came rushing back to her. The crash, Warren, Mary, her hospital stay, the drive back to Augusta Springs. Chris.

* * *

She spent most of the day in bed or sitting lazily on the verandah. In the early afternoon she did phone John Flynn, telling him there was no longer a pilot or a plane in Augusta Springs. They had ended the phone conversation with Flynn saying, "I'll see what can be done. Don't give up. But it will be some time before anything will happen. Getting a plane may be easier than finding a pilot with all the aviators gone to war. You just take it easy, and I'll see what I can do. I know QANTAS is hard put with most of its pilots having left the country. It may be up to us to try to find a pilot."

Both of them knew that wouldn't be easy. Everyone wanted to go fight the Nazis, and pilots were in great demand.

Horrie and Betty dropped by late in the afternoon. "Doc Adams called to say you have to take it easy," Betty said. She was pregnant again. "I brought you a casserole."

Cassie thanked her.

Horrie lit a cigarette. "I let Fiona know what's happened. She's coming right back. Wish I could rig up something so you could talk to patients from here instead of having to come out to the radio shack."

"I think I'll feel well enough to resume the radio calls in a few days. Now that I have a car, I can get out there easily without having to rely on anyone. In fact, let me try tomorrow morning."

"Doc says we shouldn't rush you."

"I'm a doctor, too." Cassie was touched that Chris was trying to take care of her. "Okay, make it the day after tomorrow. Even if we can't fly out, we can advise. Reverend Flynn says he's going to see what he can do, but it'll take time."

"What'll we do about emergencies?" Horrie scratched his head.

"Nothing. There's no way to get out to anyone. The only planes that can get petrol are the mail planes. Maybe if we have an emergency we can flag Mr. Brock. I don't know what else to say."

"With all this time on your hands," Betty said, looking at her husband with a twinkle in her eye, "maybe you can add a room to the house and put a verandah out back so's we can sit outside and get some air."

He raised an eyebrow. "I won't make any promises, but it doesn't sound unreasonable."

"I'm pretty good with a hammer," Cassie volunteered.

"Not woman's work," Horrie said, standing up. "Come on, hon. Let's not tire Cassie."

They'd barely left when Chris appeared, clutching a bag of groceries. He walked up the path, not looking directly at Cassie. "Thought a rare steak might be good for you. That and a baked potato."

Cassie was aware that she hadn't dressed all day, but had been sitting around in her robe. Suddenly she felt self-conscious. Her hair must be a mess, too. She ran a hand through it.

"I guess I feel up to getting dinner, at least one that simple," she said. "Am I eating alone?"

He looked at her and she couldn't read what was in his eyes. "I didn't know if you'd want my company." A blush crept up from his collar, across his cheeks, his forehead. He held the bag out to her. She stood up and took it from him. "Don't you think it might be nice if you kissed me hello?"

A startled look darted across his face, and then he leaned over and awkwardly kissed her cheek.

"Do you want to mix us drinks? I have wine that will go with the steaks, but let's have something first. A little Scotch and a lot of water for me. The liquor's in the cabinet above the stove," she said as she walked in front of him to the kitchen. "It'll take an hour for the baked potatoes, so we can make charming conversation."

Chris reached up into the liquor cabinet and found a bottle, looked around for glasses, and began to mix drinks. "Funeral for Mary and Warren is tomorrow night," he said. "I didn't know them well, of course, but if you like I'll accompany you."

Cassie scrubbed the potatoes, lit the oven, and accepted the drink that Chris handed her. She leaned against the counter, studying the amber liquid, and said, "That'd be nice, Chris. Thanks. But you know what? Something's wrong."

He cocked his head to the side and waited.

"I don't feel anything. I haven't mourned. I haven't grieved. I'm not depressed, except to worry how the Flying Doctors are going to continue. What kind of person am I?"

"Oh," he said, his voice relieved. "That's denial, Cassie. It's perfectly normal. Your mind hasn't accepted the crash, the deaths. When you do accept it emotionally, you'll probably crash yourself. It's just as well you can't work, you know, that there's no plane or pilot. You'll need time to get over this. Are you nervous about flying again?"

She shook her head. "Not in the least. I'm antsy about all these people needing my help and I'm not there to give it. I want to get in a plane and fly out."

"You don't understand what you're going through emotionally. When you can comprehend all this on anything other than a cerebral level, you'll be in an abyss, I imagine, knowing you."

She walked over to him and took his hand. "Do you know me, Chris?"

His hand wound around hers, tightening. "I don't know, Cassie. I don't know how well I've ever known anyone, myself included. I want to know you. I've wanted to know you for a long time."

They stared at each other.

She reached up to kiss his cheek. "Let me go change to something decent and comb my hair, okay? I wasn't prepared for a gentleman caller."

"You should have known." The edge of a smile trailed across his face.

"Maybe. But I wasn't prepared for this change in you."

"I haven't changed. The situation's changed."

"Perhaps so." She smiled at him. "But let me go try to look more alluring."

"You couldn't." He sat in the one big overstuffed chair. "But I'll be patient. After all, I've waited for what is it, two years? Comb your hair, if you must, though it looks rather attractive and wanton that way." She liked the way he smiled at her. It was the first time she'd detected any sense of fun in him.

She ran a comb through her hair, brushed her teeth, and threw on a pair of slacks and a beige silk blouse. But she didn't put on shoes. He'd have to accept her barefoot or not at all.

"There, isn't this better?" she asked. She was flirting and she knew it. She'd never played sexual games. It had always been so serious with her. Now, she was going to do what girls around her had been doing for years.

Chris's eyes met hers, and then he looked down again at his drink, finished it, and stood up. He walked out onto the verandah, and Cassie saw him staring into the gathering darkness.

When he came back in the room he stood in shadows. Then he moved into the light and took off his glasses, looking intensely at her. "You frighten me, Cassie."

How delicious. She frightened him. "Why, Chris?"

"I'm nearly forty-five years old and I've never known what it's like to be in love before."

Chapter 35

Well, this is the damnedest thing, thought Cassie. Of all people in Augusta Springs . . . in the world, come to think of it. Even after Fiona returned home, Chris came to dinner two or three nights a week, bringing a bottle of wine or a bouquet of flowers.

Both women were at loose ends. Fiona's job had long been filled by a young woman from Charters Towers. And John Flynn told Cassie, "I think we can get an old plane, but we'll have to outfit it for our needs. However, I can't find a pilot in the whole country who's not needed either in the war effort or by an airline."

Cassie continued the three radio calls a day but could do nothing to fly out on clinics or emergencies. She assisted Chris in operations, and saw extra patients when he was overloaded, but her days passed slowly. Fiona had nothing constructive to do all day, either. "Are you having a romance with the good doctor?" she asked.

Cassie shook her head. She could no longer divulge her deepest feelings to Fiona. "I wouldn't call it that. I think he's lonely without Isabel. We have medicine in common and I think he's come to understand that the Flying Doctors are no threat to him. He was very kind, taking emergencies for me when . . . when I wasn't here. And driving all the way to take care of me at the time of the crash. We talk medicine a lot."

"I think he's head over heels about you. He seems different, not quite so rigid. Not coiled up like a spring."

"If you mean he's not as abrasive, I agree. I notice it not only with us but with patients. Maybe age is mellowing him."

"He looks younger since Isabel died."

"I suspect he aged while watching the woman he loved die so slowly. And now, well now, he doesn't feel that terrible strain."

"It doesn't seem to me like you two talk to each other much at all when he comes to dinner. You're like mere acquaintances searching for something to talk about. I wonder if I weren't here if you'd even converse. The town is calling you an odd couple."

Cassie tossed her head. "We're not a couple."

"That may be, but if you are, you're a strange one." She read Cassie parts of the letters Blake wrote to her. There weren't many, but when there was one, Fiona was filled with happiness for days, rereading it until it scarcely held together.

"He's going out on bombing missions now," Fiona declared, her eyes blazing, her voice frightened. "Flying over the channel."

Cassie said nothing.

"Oh, God, how I wish I'd become pregnant. How I wish I were going to bear his child."

One evening Chris told them he had a patient who needed eye surgery and couldn't afford to fly or take the train to Adelaide. He'd suggested driving. The woman didn't know how to drive, however. They couldn't afford to take their three small children, and he wondered if Cassie and Fiona would consider going out to stay at their station for a week while the husband drove his wife to Adelaide. Fiona was used to small children, and together they might contemplate a vacation in the country, a change of pace. It might be good for them to feel useful since they'd been sitting around doing nothing for three weeks. He offered to take Cassie's radio calls three times a day.

"They live about forty-five miles southeast of here. You'd have to milk the cow but it's a small spread and wouldn't require anything else except taking care of the children."

Cassie and Fiona looked at each other. "Well, I need to feel needed," Fiona said. "Might be fun."

"I can drive you out on Sunday," Chris said, "and come get you the next Sunday. It's more like a dirt track than a road out there. There are no other homesteads nearby at all."

"Pioneer women," said Cassie, thinking it might give her insight into her patients and their lives. "Sure, I'm game."

"I thought you two might be. Thanks a lot." He got up to go. Cassie walked with him to the front gate.

He reached out to take her hands. "I can't sleep nights for thinking of you."

She put her arms around his waist and reached up to kiss him. There was no electricity, but it was pleasant.

Fiona came in from the barn, laughing, holding a basket of brown eggs. With her were the two eldest children, Laurie and Phil. "That smells wonderful," she told Cassie, who was frying bacon.

Cassie had just finished feeding the baby, and food was splattered all over the high chair. She didn't know if she'd want a steady diet of this, but for a week it was fun. The kids were dolls, especially the oldest one, Phil. He stood in the doorway, pointing out to the east.

"Look at the light out there," he said.

Fiona glanced back from where they'd just come. She walked over to the door. "Hey, Cass, come look."

In the center of the horizon, which was so bleak one could see forever, past the low scrub trees, was a glaring silver light. Flashing toward them, it was elongated, flat against the land.

"My God, it's fire," Cassie said. "It must be thirty miles wide."

The two women looked at each other.

"We can't possibly outrun it," Fiona said.

No, of course not. Not without any means of transportation." Cassie felt pressure in her chest. She looked around. "It's still far away. Let's eat breakfast."

"Eat breakfast?" Fiona's voice cracked.

"Of course. It's going to be a long day." Her heart thumping in her chest, Cassie turned over the sizzling bacon, reaching out a hand for the eggs Fiona still had in the basket she held. "Come on, act normal. Like we're going to have fun."

Fiona stared at her, then turned to the children. "Look at this breakfast! Let's eat." She plumped Laurie down in the chair next to her, patting the seat on the other side of her for Phil.

Cassie sat down, wondering what in the world they could do. She asked Phil, "How many sheep do you have?"

"Nine. Me dad just bought them. He's saved up for a long time. Their names are . . . "

"Nine," Cassie said thoughtfully.

"What are you thinking?" Fiona asked. She was forcing herself to eat the food in front of her.

"You know what? A fire won't burn over burnt ground. If we could send our own fire marching toward it, it would have to turn back on itself, extinguish itself. Or, at least it would skip the scorched earth we could create all around us. You know, fight fire with fire."

"How can we do that?" Fear caused Fiona's voice to tremble.

"I don't know. Let me think a minute. You wash up here, Phil and Laurie will help you. And I'll go reconnoiter, see if I get any ideas."

As she left the house, the dog, a blue, rushed up to her, licking her hand. She wished she'd brought it some bacon. It ran in circles around her. A knot formed in her belly. The sheep were in a paddock close to the house, grazing contentedly. She knew that sheep followed the leader, followed anything, would even jump off cliffs to their deaths if the leader did so. Could she control them? A notion began to jell.

She stopped to pump water into the pail, carrying it—with all her might—over to the paddock where the sheep were. They came running over as she poured the water into a trough, lapping it up in seconds. She stood watching them, trying to reject the ridiculous idea forming in her mind. Then she walked back to the pump. After three trips she said aloud, "Okay, you blokes, that's it. Now rest for a bit, because you're going to work all day."

The horizon glared. The fire seemed no closer but she knew it was licking up the miles. She had no way of gauging but she thought it would be hours before it was close enough to cause damage. She wondered how long, how painfully long, it took to burn to death.

Should they try to run? Sideways, even, out of the path of the fire? Could they run fifteen miles, perhaps more, today? Of course not. Not with three small children. The truck was gone and there wasn't even a tractor.

Returning to the house, she discovered Fiona standing in the doorway, holding the baby. "Have you got any brilliant ideas?"

"I don't know how brilliant, but unless you have a better one . . . "

"I don't have any at all. I want to run, but I know it would be futile. We can never outrun a fire, especially with children." So, Fiona had come to the same conclusion.

Cassie took a deep breath, hesitating. "What I've been thinking is that we'll get the sheep, all nine of them if we can, and with me on the outside we'll walk all around the house in an ever-widening circle. You and the kids can walk behind us, and hopefully our walking will tamp the grass down until it's so flat . . . "

"Tamping the grass down?" Fiona looked at Cassie as though her friend had lost her mind. "Do you see how thick this grass is?"

"I do." For a minute Cassie wanted to give up and start running, hoping they could outrun the fire. "So, we're going to have to walk round and round the house until we stamp it down. We can't go more than six miles because six miles a day is all sheep can travel at a stock rate."

"You sure have learned a lot."

Cassie brushed the hair out of her eyes with the back of her hand. "Little did I know it would ever be useful. Well, what do you think?"

"I think I'm scared stiff." Fiona turned into the house and put the baby in the crib. "But if we don't do anything, we don't stand any kind of chance. What if the sheep run away?"

"I don't know. Do you think it would do any good to tie them together?"

"And you hold onto them? If they start running do you think you can keep hold of nine sheep weighing well over a hundred pounds each?"

"Well . . . " Cassie laughed, despite the fear that shivered through her. "Let's see what we can do. You and the kids—you explain to them, you're more used to children than I am—help me round them up. Maybe the dog knows what to do. You keep the dog back with you, following me and the sheep, so he'll herd the sheep . . . "

It was easy to get the sheep corralled and once Cassie started walking on the outside, circling the little house, they walked along as though traveling on a stock route. Their hooves barely trampled the grass down. They walked around in the same circle for an hour, until Laurie began to cry. Cassie thought, I'll let her rest a bit, but she has to help. We need every pair of feet.

"I'll water the sheep," she told Fiona. "Find something for the kids to drink. For you and me, too." She could feel a blister forming on her heel.

Fiona tended to the baby and Laurie said, "I don't like it. I'm tired."

Cassie looked over at Fiona.

"We'll sing. I'll teach you some songs, some marching songs." Fiona smiled, though Cassie could tell she didn't feel like it. "Let's see if there's any string. We could tie some to a sheep and he can lead you. That'd be fun, wouldn't it?"

The second hour passed like the first except that Cassie's blister burst and it pained her with every step she took. She knew the children must be in worse shape, but Phil kept saying "I'm a man, and men don't complain." He gritted his teeth as he said it.

In the afternoon, after Fiona made sandwiches, she asked, "Can't the children take naps?"

"I want them so tired they'll have no choice but to sleep tonight." Cassie looked off to the horizon. The glaring pewter color had changed to a pale orange, growing in size as it drew nearer. "It's still miles away," she said, hoping Fiona would agree.

Fiona didn't say anything.

They walked all day, allowing the children to rest frequently. The dog, walking behind the sheep, never seemed to tire. Cassie made certain all the animals had water frequently. Finally the blisters hurt her so much that she took off the boots and walked barefoot through the furrows.

By six o'clock the sheep were done for. "Fix something to eat," Cassie told Fiona. "Anything. See if there's any coffee, will you? I could use some." She smelled the fire now, probably not more than fifteen miles away. Acrid smoke filled the air.

"Take the dog and the sheep inside," Cassie said to Phil.

"The sheep?" He giggled.

"Your father wants them as the foundation of his future stock, doesn't he? Put them in the kitchen."

Fiona said. "Smell it. Smell the fire." She put an arm around Laurie.

"Listen to it," said Phil, instructing the dog to lead the sheep into the house. "It crackles."

Laurie burst into tears. "We're going to burn up," she wailed.

"Hush," Cassie snapped. She knew if they were as tired as she, they'd fall asleep as soon as they had full tummies. She thanked the Lord for Fiona, for without her the children would be frightened to death.

Laurie fell asleep at the table.

"I'm so tired I feel I could die," Fiona said. "Do you think we're going to?" She picked Laurie up and carried her to the bedroom. The baby was already sound asleep. Phil sat on his bed, cuddling the dog, who had never been allowed in the house before. The poor creature's paws were bloody and he whimpered as he licked them. The sheep were shuttered in the kitchen, munching hay Cassie had brought in from the barn.

"Are you scared?" Cassie asked when the two women were alone.

"Aren't you?"

"Scared shitless."

"I think of Blake, and I regret that we never really got started. I've thought of him all day."

Blake.

Cassie stood and walked, barefoot, to the door. "Look at it," she whispered. "You couldn't describe it to anyone. Listen to that hissing, even though it's still miles away."

"How many miles?" Fiona came to stand beside Cassie, slipping an arm around her.

Cassie shrugged. "Not enough. I feel so useless, as though anything we do is futile."

"You've done all you can. I've just walked behind. I'm the one who feels useless."

"Maybe we both are. There's absolutely nothing we can do about that fire now."

"Yes, there is," said Fiona. "Light it. That's what we've been aiming for all day, isn't it?"

Cassie turned to look at her friend. "If we don't die from the fire I just may die of exhaustion." Fiona nodded in agreement. "What if it doesn't work?"

Fiona put her hand around Cassie's and leaned over to kiss her cheek. "Cassie, I have faith in you. But if it doesn't work, and if I have to die now, I guess I'd rather die with you than anyone else I can think of."

"I love you, too." Cassie put her arms around Fiona. "But I'm scared to pieces. I'm not ready to die. I don't want those three kids to die."

"You're a rock, Cassie. I couldn't have been this calm with anyone else. I keep thinking you're going to get us out of this. I know it. We're not going to die, we're just scared, and with good reason. You go light that fire and I'll pour us some coffee."

Cassie opened the door, where a chicken squatted. Picking it up, she tossed it inside and took the matches Fiona handed her and walked out toward the fire that was now rapidly approaching. She could hear the swishing sound of displaced air as the fire roared across the treetops, as it jumped from one tree to another. It hissed, and it was so bright she felt blinded.

As she walked through the trampled grass, Cassie wondered if the oncoming dragon would slay them. She could smell the fire on solitary gusts of wind. Though it was still well over a mile away she felt its burning, looking to make sure she wasn't ablaze.

Standing at the edge of the area of flat grass, which they had spent the entire day treading down, she knelt and lit a match. The gusts cycloned by the oncoming fire blew it out. She held her hands around the next match and nursed a spark of fire, blowing gently on it, thinking how ironic it was to be trying to set a blaze when one that filled the whole sky was rushing toward her. The spark caught, spreading quickly, and she ran to another spot, where she started another blaze. Whether it would rush toward the approaching holocaust that roared toward the house or whether it would rage back across the area where they had trod the break she wouldn't let herself contemplate.

Brief, furious bursts of scalding air and a crackling thunder took over. Her fire was heading outward, toward the oncoming inferno.

"I can do no more," she said aloud and, turning around, went back to the house, aware that her hands were trembling.

Fiona was watching from the doorway. "Coffee's on the stove," she said. "It's very hot."

"What isn't?" Cassie asked, her stomach tight with fear.

They sat down across the table from each other, each with a cup in her hands.

Fiona reached across to touch Cassie. "We're going to be an island in a scorched sea."

"I wish I had your faith."

Fiona reached across the table and put her hand on Cassie's arm. "You know what I've been thinking lately? Neither of us is doing anything useful because someone else has my job and you don't have a pilot. Remember Sam was teaching me to fly? Had me almost to the point of soloing when I had to go back to Ireland? What about if I go down to Adelaide and take lessons? How about me for your pilot? We could work together."

Cassie stared, her mouth half-open.

Fiona squeezed Cassie's arm. "I was afraid to mention it, afraid you'd hate the idea. I didn't want you to reject me. But really, Cass, I think I could be a pretty good pilot, and look at it this way. It's either me or no Flying Doctors out of Augusta Springs."

Cassie jumped up and came around the table, flinging her arms around Fiona. "Oh, I think it's just a wonderful idea. A beautiful idea. I can't think of anything that would be better."

Except being Mrs. Blake Thompson.

The crackling sounds of the fire became so loud that not even the baying of the dog could be heard.

Chapter 36

In the morning, when the pearl grey dawn first striped the eastern horizon from whence the fire had come, all that could be seen was scorched earth, felled trees. Smoke curled into the air from the smoldering, charred ground and all was deathly silent. No bird sang, no wind blew.

Cassie and Fiona had not slept all night. They opened the kitchen door to let the sheep out, but the animals huddled in the corner and would not go near the door. Cassie walked out, hoping they would follow, but the burnt ground was too hot and she jumped back into the house. Nothing within sight was alive.

She turned to look at Fiona, in the doorway, with a wan smile. "I think we survived."

It looked that way. She wondered why she didn't feel more elated. "I'll feed the baby. You take care of the older kids, okay?"

"You know what? I'm shaking," Fiona said, surprised. She held out her hands. "Look at me, now that it's all over. You'd have thought I'd have done that yesterday rather than now, when we're safe."

"Not at all," Cassie said, her voice matter-of-fact. "People often rise to emergencies and sail through them rather heroically, but after the trauma is all over, they cave in, sometimes quite unable to function."

"Well, I'm not that bad, just a little shaky." Fiona went into the children's room where the baby was standing in the crib, drooling and grinning with delight to see her. Phil was curled around the dog, who was licking his elbow. Laurie hiccuped in her sleep.

Cassie started coffee, wondering how they'd all walk over the still-burning earth to the outhouse. She'd have to rig up a substitute.

There'd be no chickens today to give them eggs. Without the storehouse would there even be enough food to feed them until the end of the week? Were there just four more days to go? No, three. Well, they could eke it out, she thought. But would the earth cool off enough so a car could drive over it by Sunday? Wherever she looked, mists of smoke rose into the air from the singed land.

Two days later, however, an old half-ton truck made it across the fifteen miles of burnt earth as Steven Thompson and Chris Adams drove over what had once been a barely designated road.

Steven threw his arms around Fiona, while Chris just looked at Cassie. "Jesus," he said, "once I heard about the fire I tried to get out here, but there was no way. Ever since yesterday we've been waiting for the earth to cool down enough so our tires wouldn't burn up. Steven and I kept telling each other you were all right, but . . . "

Steven interrupted, "I don't think either of us believed it. Do you know what it was like to see the house standing, to see someone moving in front of it? I told Chris that if any two women could live through this, you two could." He let go of Fiona and came over to Cassie, gathering her in a bear hug. "God almighty, I was never so glad to see any two people in my life." Tears welled in his eyes.

"How did you do it?" Chris asked. "How in the world did this bit of earth escape? It's like an island in the middle of hell."

He surprised Cassie by putting his arms around her shoulders, pulling her close. "Christ, I thought my life had ended," he said in a low voice. He held her to him, and his arms would not let her go.

* * *

Back in Augusta Springs, Cassie went directly to bed. She lay in her dark room, the shades drawn, shivering uncontrollably. Her teeth chattered. Fiona fed the children and put them to bed.

Steven said, "I'm going to sleep on the sofa. I'm not letting you two girls be alone."

Chris stayed, too, and stuck his head in Cassie's door every fifteen or twenty minutes. He'd come and sit on the side of the bed, stroking her forehead. But she pushed him away, saying, "Just leave me alone. I'll be all right."

When he left she burst into tears and could not stop sobbing. Fiona, Steven, and Chris all came to stand in the doorway. Cassie just wanted them out of there, wanted to be alone. She didn't even know why she was crying. Eventually she slept.

In the morning, she was awakened by the cries of the children, laughing and running around, waking Steven up. By the time Cassie arrived in the kitchen Steven already had coffee perking and was scrambling eggs.

"I didn't know you had these hidden talents," she said, trying to smile at him, yet wanting to do nothing more than go back to bed. But she couldn't leave Fiona with the three children. And besides, everything was safe now. Why did she feel so terrible, so cold, so dizzy?

As Steven poured coffee for her and handed her the cup, she fainted.

When she came to, Chris was bending over her. "We're going to get you out of here, away from noise and the kids. Their father will be coming through this afternoon, and Fiona will take care of them while I take you over to my house. You need peace and quiet."

Cassie was too weak to argue. He picked her up and carried her out to his car. "We can send for your clothes later," he said.

She sank into the seat gratefully.

He tucked her into his bed and drew the curtains. "I have to get to the hospital, but I'll be back at noon to fix you something to eat. Meanwhile, I'm going to give you something that will relax you and let you sleep."

She didn't awaken until nearly dark, when she smelled food cooking. She thought she ought to get up and go out to the living room and let Chris see he didn't have to bring dinner to her, but she couldn't force herself to move.

When Chris came in, he turned the light on and said, "Can you get up to go to the bathroom? You haven't all day."

Cassie nodded. Of course she could, but she tried to move and couldn't even toss the covers back. Chris leaned down and picked her up, carrying her to the bathroom. "I'll wait outside," he said, "but don't be shy, if you need me. We *are* doctors."

When he had her tucked back in bed, he said, "I have some chicken broth ready." He had plumped two pillows under her head.

"You get more than your share of taking care of sick women, don't you?"

His hand wound around her wrist and he held it tightly. "Don't ever talk that way. It's not the same. You're not Isabel." There was anger in his voice.

She began to shake, trembling so that her teeth chattered. Chris sat next to her, his arms around her, holding her close, running his hand through her hair, whispering, "There, there. It's all right. Everything's all right." The warmth of his body eventually quieted her, and she fell asleep next to him. He sat and held her all night, napping upright.

He gave her another shot when he left for work the next morning, but she was awake before he returned home. She lay in bed, rigid, thinking she couldn't bear any more. Why did Warren and Mary die and not me? Why am I alive? Why did Blake not want to marry me? Why did he choose my best friend? He's come between us, and I can't unburden myself to her anymore. Can't be as close as we were. Why did Jennifer die? That beautiful woman, in her prime. Burnt beyond recognition.

She wept, silent tears coursing down her cheeks.

When Chris arrived home he found Cassie curled in the fetal position, her face streaked with tears, staring wide-eyed into space. She wouldn't talk to him or even acknowledge his presence. When Steven came by later, Cassie stared at him blankly and both men knew she didn't see them.

"She's in shock," Chris told Steven. "I think it's all been more than she can assimilate. The war—her friends leaving, Jennifer's death, and then the plane crash. The fire was a catalyst. A comatose state is often induced when the person doesn't want to accept reality. It's a way of escaping."

Steven went over and brushed his hand over her forehead. "I thought she was going to be my daughter-in-law," he said, his voice low. "I had already begun to love her as such." Then he turned to Chris, "What can be done?"

Chris shook his head. "Time. Bed rest."

"Well, the children will be gone tomorrow," Steven said. "Fiona can take care of her then."

"No. I'm going to."

Steven looked at him. "Let me know if I can be of help in any way. I'm staying over at Fiona's."

Cassie heard it all as though through a tunnel, muted, a long way away. So Steven had thought she'd marry Blake, too. But no tears came. Nothing came.

Three days later when Cassie opened her eyes and was conscious of her surroundings, Chris was sitting in a chair by her bed, reading. He immediately closed the book and rose, moving to sit beside her.

"I have soup ready. Would you like some?"

"I'd like some orange juice," she said, sitting up. "That and a toothbrush. My mouth feels like a bird's nest. How long have I been here?"

"Five days." He stood up, starting for the door. "I'll be back directly."

Cassie arose and went down the hall to the bathroom, drawing water for a bath. When Chris returned he knocked on the bathroom door, and when he opened it he stood grinning, a new toothbrush in his hand.

Cassie smiled up at him. What a nice man he'd become. "I don't want soup. I want a soft-boiled egg and toast and tea."

When he brought it to her in bed, on a tray with a rose beside it, he said, "I'm sorry you're better."

She cocked an eyebrow at him.

"I mean, you'll be leaving now."

She reached out a hand to touch his arm. "Well, I hope you like me with more life than I've had. My whole body feels like I've slept in the same position for twenty years."

"You were pretty rigid. Want a massage?"

He'd never been so nice. "Wait til I finish this tea and I'll accept your offer."

He sat and watched her finish her supper. Then she turned on her stomach.

"I'm not an expert at this."

"That's okay." She pillowed her hands under her head.

"You have a beautiful body," he said.

"You've never even seen it." And then, "Harder, rub harder. It feels wonderful."

After a minute he asked, "Are you still in love with Blake Thompson?"

Her heart stopped. A ragged sigh escaped her. It was several minutes before she answered. She lay there while his hands massaged the tense knots in her shoulders. Despite his questions she felt herself relaxing.

"I don't know. Give me a definition of love."

His laugh was bitter, and his fingers dug into her upper arms. "I'm not an expert on such matters."

"Oh, come on," she said, turning her head sideways to see him better. "You and Isabel were married for twenty-some years."

He was quiet. His hands did not stop, though she felt them tense up. Suddenly he kissed her between the shoulder blades.

"You can't be interested in Isabel and me."

Cassie caught some indefinable quality in his voice, something she didn't understand. He stroked her legs and thighs, rubbing them so the tension flowed from her.

"Mm, that's nice," she murmured. He was relaxing her body and piquing her curiosity simultaneously.

"Turn over," he said.

She rolled over and saw a tenderness in his eyes she had not seen before.

He reached out to stroke her arms, to soothe the muscles. He released the knot that had gathered in her stomach five days ago. His hands wound down her legs, loosening the tightness in her thighs. She closed her eyes, relaxing completely under his touch.

He rubbed the inside of her thighs and she was filled with longing when he stopped. She opened her eyes to see him standing looking down at her and knew she wanted him to make love to her.

He looked at her for a long moment and then said, "Wait." When he returned he carried two glasses of wine.

Cassie sat up. When he reached out to give her the glass, she held his hand, turning it palm side up, kissing it.

She heard his gasp.

"Make love to me, Chris."

He stared at her and then knelt down beside the bed, his hand in hers. She moved his hand and put it on her breast, felt her nipples hardening. "Now. Here."

His eyes did not leave hers until he leaned over to kiss her, his lips hungry on hers, and she wound her arms around his neck, whispering, "Come to me, Chris."

He stood up, untying his tie, unbuttoning his shirt . . . until he stood naked before her. His body was hard and sinewy, the way she thought a man's body ought to look, and she threw back the covers, opening her arms.

Their love-making was frenzied and furious. He plumbed her depths and when she thought he was going to withdraw, she involuntarily cried, "No, don't," but he had no intention of doing so. He teased her until the only important thing in her world was his driving into her again and again. Her hips rose to meet him and together they moved in tandem with a wildness . . . a power beyond control.

The only sounds were her moans—sighs of ecstasy that welled up from the deepest part of her being. Her body shivered under him, rising again and again to meet his thrusts, wanting to pull all of him into her. Her muscles tightened around him and she heard him sob, heard him exclaim, "Jesus. Oh, Jesus Christ!"

Her breath came in short spurts as he left her, rolling onto his side, leaning on his elbow to look at her. Her breathing came hard. "I'd forgotten how good it can be."

He put his hands under his head and lay back on the pillow, staring up at the ceiling, though Cassie sensed that was not what he was seeing. Finally he said, "I've thought of this. Oh, God how I have fantasized about this since the first day I met you."

"Since the first day you met me?"

He nodded. "I've wanted to fuck your brains out for as long as I've known you."

She had never heard anyone talk like this. "I thought you couldn't stand me."

"I couldn't. But I wanted you. I did all sorts of things to try to get you and your body out of my mind. I thought this could never happen."

She reached over and ran a hand across his belly. "I never even thought about it."

"I know." Then he smiled. "Keep doing that, it feels good."

She leaned over and kissed his chest, running her tongue across his nipples. She felt him tremble as she bit him lightly, and he grabbed her, looking into her eyes, before he pulled her to him and began all over again.

"Tell me about you and Isabel," she said as they lay side by side.

"You don't want to know about Isabel and me."

"But I do," she whispered, curled against him.

He sighed. "Let me get some more wine," he said, arising and going to his kitchen. When he returned, Cassie said, "You have a beautiful body, too."

Chris looked down at himself and laughed. "No one's ever thought that about me."

He climbed into bed and plumped a pillow against the headboard. "You really want to hear?"

When Cassie nodded, he said, "I've never talked to anyone about Isabel and me."

"Isabel was the prettiest girl I'd ever seen. I met her my last year in med school. I'd never really had a sweetheart before. I met her at a church social and she was the shyest girl there, sitting on the sidelines while everyone else flirted and danced. That appealed to me. We began to date, doing the usual things, going to the cinema and skating and going to the beach. Her family invited me to Sunday afternoon tea. Her parents were more rigid even than I've become, and they seldom smiled, but her father liked the idea that I was going to be a doctor.

"Isabel told me she hated cities, they terrified her. She said she loved children, and certainly I wanted children. I was wild with desire for her. But we didn't do much touching. Well, I mean she did none, and seldom let me do any, but that was okay with me. I thought she was sweet and virginal and she wanted to save herself for marriage, that old chestnut. I had trouble falling asleep nights, wanting to make love to her.

"Like so many people of that age, or maybe any age, I got my emotions confused with my glands. I think that's why so many get married. So, that's what we did. We married the day after I graduated from med school, and I spent a year interning and then we took off for Augusta Springs, by which time I knew I'd made a gigantic mistake."

Cassie stared at him.

"Cassie, I never loved Isabel. Not ever. I married her because I wanted to go to bed with her and she hated every second of it. When I did attempt to kiss her, she drew back and said, 'I can't bear those awful wet kisses. It's disgusting.' When I did tentatively touch her, she brushed my hand away and said, 'Don't do that. I can't stand it.' She lay in bed rigid and unmoving. 'Get it over with, for heaven's sake,' she cried. Of course, I could do nothing with that attitude.

"Weeks, months would go by and we wouldn't touch, even in bed, sleeping as far apart as possible, until I'd be driven wild with desire, not especially for her, but for some woman, someone. And one night I took Isabel, hurting her and I didn't care. We'd been married nearly a year, for God's sake."

His voice shook so that Cassie thought he was going to cry. She reached out for his hand.

"She looked at me with what I can only describe as hatred and said, 'I never want to go through this again!' We never did make love again. We never came together ever again, not in twenty-two years."

Cassie was sitting up straight in bed, her mouth open. "Never again? Not ever again in all those years?"

He shook his head. "Never. Would you? Would you want someone who acted like that with you? Yet, you know what? She acted as though I was going to throw myself at every woman I ever met. She was a most jealous person. She would scream at me like a shrew several times a year, throw things at me, accusing me of affairs."

"Chris, are you telling me you haven't made love to anyone since you were what, twenty-two or three?"

"Make love? Have sex, you mean. Well, Cassie, I'm not totally neurotic. Sure, when I'd go to a city to a conference, I'd find someone. Prostitutes. Not too good for my ego, I must admit. Pay someone to sleep with me because my wife wouldn't."

"Why did you stay in such a situation for so long?"

He shrugged his shoulders. "Gutless. Because divorce is frowned on. Nice doctors aren't divorced. Because I thought something must be my fault. God, how I tried. I tried year after year until I thought I had no more to give, Cassie."

"Oh, Chris . . . "

"And when you . . . Jesus Christ, Cassie, you don't know what happened to me that day Fiona brought you to my office. I didn't approve of you or the Flying Doctors. I thought they had no right to send a woman doctor up here. But you know what happened to me? You and Fiona left my office and I started trembling. I had to sit down because I was shaking so badly. I took to walking nights to try to get you out of my system, but always found myself walking past your house, hoping you'd say 'Good evening,' fantasizing that you'd invite me in, that you might run your fingers over my hand, that you'd brush my arm."

"Really? I never imagined . . . "

"Of course not. But Isabel knew. I'd come home nights after you'd been reading to her, and she'd say, 'This is what you've dreamed about, isn't it? A beautiful young woman with the same interests as you and you wanting to get into her pants. But you know what, she won't let you, any more than I have. She's a lady, and ladies don't do it. She comes and reads to me and I can tell she won't want you, you and your disgusting male ways. You'll see. I'll die and you'll try to get her and she'll laugh at you. Ladies don't like it, you mark my word, and she's a lady. You won't get near her, even after I die."

"God, you've been a doctor long enough to know that isn't true. Why did you let it go on?"

Chris shrugged. "I've asked myself that question over and over again."

Cassie smiled at him. "You do know how to make love remarkably well. I want you to know that." She leaned back into her pillows and studied him. "Poor Chris. Isabel was wrong. I do want you to make love to me a lot. I like what we just did."

"Jesus, Cassie . . . "

She laughed and said, "No wonder you've been such a hard ass."

For a moment, he acted as though he didn't know what to make of the comment, and then he, too, broke out in a laugh.

"You make me laugh more than I've laughed in twenty-three years."

"That's not all you're going to do with me," she said, sliding over on top of him.

"I think I must've died and now I'm in heaven," he said, reaching up to cup her breasts in his hands.

"Nonsense," she murmured, looking down at him, "you're just beginning to live."

Chapter 37

The year and a half since Fiona returned had passed quickly. Fiona would never be the pilot that Sam was—she, like Warren, was far too cautious about taking risks—but she and Cassie worked well together. The only fly in the ointment was still Blake, despite Cassie's continued affair with Chris. Cassie could not bear it when Fiona read her parts of Blake's letters. They timed clinics at Tookaringa so they could stay the weekend and Cassie felt jealousy when Fiona and Steven openly enjoyed the affection of a father-in-law toward his beloved son's wife. Fiona would lean over and kiss the top of his head as she passed him, and he would reach out to catch her hand. They talked endlessly of Blake. Blake. Blake.

Cassie would get up and leave the table and walk across the lawn, down to the billabong. There, she stared at the swans and watched jabirus and spoonbills, bats hanging upside down in one of the trees. Look, she told herself, that part of your life is over. Blake's part of your past.

Then why couldn't Chris erase thoughts of Blake?

He never interfered about her patients anymore. They were hers, and she appreciated the change in him. She felt safe with Chris, even though they still argued often, not only about their old standby, aborigines, but about religion, politics, doctor-patient relationships, and about women's role in life. Cassie thought there should be no woman's role, that women should elect roles individually. Chris thought one of the problems of modern life was that women were not satisfied to be wives and mothers, and it upset the balance of society.

So what? asked Cassie. *So far it's all been tipped in favor of men.*

Within months of Fiona's obtaining her pilot's license, Cassie found her own house. She told Fiona that she and Chris needed privacy, which was true. There was no way he could slip into her bedroom as long as she lived with Fiona. The town knew they saw each other, were what they called "a steady couple," and wondered why they didn't marry, but there could be no public acknowledgment of their carnal relationship.

Though Chris supplied Cassie with far more than sex, and she knew it, she was in no danger of being in love with him. He had said to her, when she moved into her own house five blocks from Fiona's, "I know you can never be in love with me, but until Mr. Right comes along, let me be with you."

He loved to touch and, when they were alone, he held her close and hugged her often. He slept with his arm around her, and said to her,

"Isabel never touched me. I love it when you run your fingers down my arm. You don't even know you do it, do you? It's so natural with you. You aren't even aware when you lean over and put your hand on mine."

He was formal to her in the hospital, calling her "Doctor" and acting as rigid as he always had. But everyone in the hospital, everyone in town, knew they were seeing each other, so his formalities were laughable. Yet he had difficulty breaking down the barriers that he had built around himself over the years.

Because she and Fiona saw each other every day, Fiona did not mourn Cassie's move. Instead, she adopted two aboriginal girls from Mundoora and brought them to live in what had been Cassie's room. Their mother had died and the father had gone walkabout. She built another bedroom onto the back of the house and employed a housekeeper-nanny. She sent Anna, the older girl, to school and spent her free time preparing Marian for school and for white people's ways.

"I don't want them to discard their heritage," she told Cassie and Chris when they dined together, as they did several times a week. "But I want them to be able to fit into our culture, and not live on the fringes of society. They can return to their tribe and the old ways if they want to, but I want to give them a fighting chance."

She didn't realize there was no possibility of that. The children at school made fun of them and never included them in games or friendship of any sort. So Anna lost herself in books and managed to make better grades than most of the others. Fiona spent all her free time playing with them, teaching them, mothering them.

"Fiona, you're the ultimate mother. You could adopt every kid you see," Cassie said.

"Wouldn't you like to have children?" Fiona responded. "I think of having children all the time—Blake's children, of course." She turned to look at Cassie. "Why don't you and Chris get married and have children?"

"I'm not in love with him."

"Well, you spend more time together than most married couples. He's obviously insane about you."

Like Blake, though, Chris had never told her he loved her. "I don't want to marry him or anybody. I feel safe with Chris, and comfortable, and he's good in bed."

"What more can you ask?"

"Fiona, you don't even believe that. You were so in love with Blake, even though I didn't know it, that you couldn't open yourself to other men, despite your protestations. You know perfectly well it's not too smart to get married just for glandular reasons."

Fiona smiled. "I suspect that's why most people get married. And, besides, you're not in love with anyone else."

Cassie didn't say anything.

"Oh, my God," said Fiona, looking into her friend's eyes. "It's Sam, isn't it? You're in love with Sam."

Cassie shook her head and brushed her hand through her hair to keep it out of her eyes. "No, that's not it at all."

"Of course it is! You don't have to pretend with me. And he writes you those friendly but brotherly letters. You don't want him to know, is that it? Oh, Cassie, I had no idea." She got up and flung her arms around Cassie. "What will you do about Chris when Sam comes back?"

Oh, Fiona, you have it so wrong. "Maybe I won't have to do anything."

"You'll hurt him terribly."

"Chris knows I'm not in love with him."

"You're going to break his heart when Sam comes home."

"Sam has nothing to do with it." *Come on, Fiona, get off this tack. You're so off-base I want to laugh, except it hurts too much. You don't know I got pregnant by your husband. I'm the one who can't get over him. You're where I thought I'd be. You have the father-in-law I thought I would have.*

"Well, Chris has served a purpose, anyhow. You're much nicer to men in general. You've softened and it's nice to see."

Because I know he can't hurt me. I don't care enough. If he picked up today and left, what I'd miss is sex. And that's all.

But she knew it wasn't quite all. She enjoyed his companionship, sharing medical problems, seeing him relax and become gentler, more open. Not only with her, but with his patients.

* * *

On February 19, 1942, the Japanese Air Force all but destroyed Darwin. Hundreds fled in terror at the nearly-complete devastation, leaving burning cigarettes, half-finished jobs, meals cooking on stoves.

After Pearl Harbor, most children and women had left Darwin. The Japanese were too close. There were scarcely two thousand people left that fateful day when over two hundred and fifty died. Bombs sank ships and rendered planes immobile, homes were strafed; American and British as well as Australian ships—cruisers and destroyers in harbor—were decimated. British tankers exploded, American and Australian Air Force planes erupted in blazes of fire, tankers were wrecked, ammunition ships were detonated. Other planes were shot out of the air. Communication systems destroyed, panic took over.

People fled on bicycles, flat-top trucks, road graders, ice cream carts, anything that moved.

In half an hour, before ten-thirty in the morning, the physical damage was done and the Japanese planes turned back north toward their waiting aircraft carriers, leaving behind the wreckage of Australia's northernmost capital city, what had been a lazy tropical town of bougainvillea and lush tropical greenery, palm and banana trees, a community noted for its rebelliousness and drinking, its abhorrence of authority.

At noon, Japanese planes returned to fly over the R.A.A.F. base, bombing it to hell and gone, annihilating the airdrome and other buildings. Heavy thunder reverberated through the smoke-filled air; red and yellow flames filled the sky.

One month previously, the newest and best outfitted hospital in the nation had opened in Darwin. In a twelve-minute period six bombs fell and, while not directly hitting the hospital, caused considerable damage. Rocks crashed through the roof, glass shattered over beds and into operating rooms, wards were wrecked. All but one immobile patient ran from the isolated aborigine ward.

Communications were destroyed, and the rest of Australia did not hear of the devastation until hours later. For the next three and a half years Australia expected to be attacked by the Japanese again and the north coast *was* bombed sixty-three more times during 1942 and 1943. These bombings, however, were limited to the tropical edge of the continent. Never again was so much damage done nor so many lives lost as in the initial attack.

Nearly all of Australia's young men were in Europe and North Africa, and there they remained year after year.

On the morning call-in, three days after the bombing of Darwin, the Augusta Springs Flying Doctor Service received an emergency call from Heather Martin.

"Cully's been shot," she said.

"Is he dead?"

"No. It's his leg. He's bleedin' bad. Nothin' seems to stop it."

"What happened?"

There was silence at the other end of the line. Cassie waited and when there was no response she explained he should lie flat and elevate his leg to decrease blood loss. "Press on the femoral artery to stop the flow. The femoral artery? Okay, face the patient and halfway between the prominent part of the hipbone and the pubic bone—that's the crotch—on a line halfway between those two, feel for the femoral artery and press. We'll be there directly, leave here immediately."

"What in the world could have happened?" Fiona asked as they headed toward the plane.

Cassie shrugged. "Your guess is as good as mine. Do you think one of the girls shot him?"

Fiona pulled the stops away from the plane. "Do you think he attacked one of them?"

"Cully? Who knows? Doesn't seem likely, and you'd think any of those Martin girls could take care of herself."

They got in the plane and Fiona revved the motors. "I think the last we saw them was when we took Cully out."

"It took them long enough to talk him into going but there. Addie's hasn't been the same since. Cully might not be good-looking, but he sure could cook."

"Bertie always seemed to have a hankering for him, whether he could cook or not. I heard Estelle at one of those galah sessions, shortly after we took him out, say how delighted they all were and the girls managed to ride in from fence-mending or mustering just to eat. You know how unprepossessing he looked, thin and not even as tall as those big girls."

"I've been surprised they haven't sent for Don to come marry one of them. I was sure one would win him in the six months he's been out there."

Within an hour Fiona was circling over the Martin homestead, coming in for a landing on their always-perfectly-cleared claypan. "If only all the airfields were this well kept up," she commented.

No one came to meet them. Cassie grabbed her bag and began to run the quarter-mile to the house, along the picket fence and the stone path to the verandah.

All of the girls were standing on the porch. "Ma's inside with Cully," Bertie said. "The bleeding's done stopped."

Cassie nodded to the girls. None of them moved.

Billie said in a flat voice, "They're in Ma's room."

Fiona halted on the porch as Cassie slammed the screen door behind her and headed toward Estelle's bedroom, the downstairs one.

The drapes were drawn and Cully was lying on the bed, a sheet covering him, his leg obviously resting on pillows. A cool washcloth was on his forehead. Estelle was seated in a chair next to the bed. "Cassie, thank God." She stood up and held her arms out. Cassie hugged her and looked down at Cully. His eyes were closed.

"He's in a lot of pain, but the bullet went clear through," Estelle said, pointing to the blood-soaked bed linens.

"I need light," Cassie said.

Estelle raised the blinds and sunlight flooded the room.

"This is a clean wound," Cassie said with relief. She reached into her medical bag. "Cully, I'm going to give you something so you can sleep without pain. When you waken we'll have sewed you back together and you'll have to take it easy for a while. Now, I'm going to turn you over and . . . oh, he doesn't have any pants on."

She plunged the needle in his buttocks and turned to Estelle. "What in the world happened?"

"God, Cassie, I don't know whether to laugh or cry. All the girls have had a crush on him, from his first meal, from the minute he walked through our door. Even though he's not the most talkative person, we all fell in love with him. I think each of the girls was waiting to see who he'd respond to. They each found ways of courting him—little ways, you know.

"But, damnedest thing happened. Him and me. I'm a good seventeen years older'n him, but there it was. He's been sneaking into my bed every night for months.

"I didn't want the girls to know. Thought they'd be disillusioned with me, bedding a man close to their ages. Hell, he's just twenty-nine. And look at me . . . forty-six. And I thought they'd be angry with me, taking the only man they've ever known. They coulda stood it if he'd chosen one of them, but their mama!"

Cassie had taken sterile rubber gloves, antiseptic, thread, needle, sutures and was bending over her patient as Estelle talked.

"Well, Cully woke up early and leaned over to kiss me awake. He likes sex mornings best, so we were going at it when Bertie came bursting in, saw us messed up in the sheets with Cully's bare ass sticking out, and thought he was raping me. She ran and got one of the guns and aimed for his leg. She's a good enough shot she'd have hit just where she wanted. She didn't want to kill him, just wound him so's he could be sent to jail. Well, she was one surprised young lady when she found out how wrong she was. I guess they're all in shock to think Cully and I've been doing this under their very noses for a long time."

Cassie, her head bent over her patient, smiled to herself. Life certainly was unpredictable.

Estelle put a hand on Cassie's shoulder. "I don't want them resenting me. Find some men, will you, and send them out."

"There aren't any men in town. They're all away at war," Cassie said, observing her sutures, pleased with what she saw.

"Well, when you hear of any. When the war ends. Send them out one by one or a few together. Make sure they're nice, if you can. When the war ends lots will be coming home without jobs. We can put them all to work."

"And to bed," Cassie said without thinking. Then she looked up at Estelle, embarrassed.

Estelle smiled. "It's okay, Cassie. It's nature. I'd forgotten how important a part of life it was, being without a man for so long. But you know, after good sex I feel great all day long. Healthy." Then it was Estelle's turn to look apologetic. "Oh, I forgot. You don't know yet. Get married, Cassie. When the boys come home, find one and get married. Or marry Sam. That'd be a good life. The two of you working together."

Not likely, Cassie wanted to say. Not Sam. And she wasn't sure sex was worth all the pain it brought. At least it had brought misery with Ray and with Blake. Short, intense sexual forays led to lingering, abysmal heartache. She thought maybe she could do without sex from here on. Do without love.

It wasn't until she and Fiona were flying back to Augusta Springs that Cassie thought to wonder if sex and love were always inseparable.

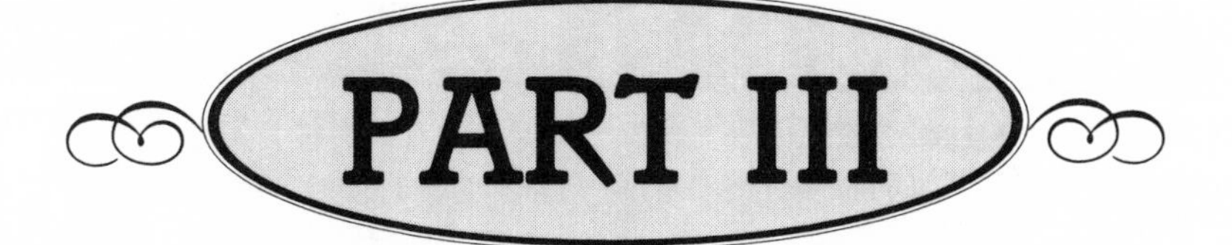

July 1944–January 1947

Chapter 38

"Marry me," Chris said for about the hundredth time in four years.

"Aren't you pleased with us?" Cassie asked, picking at her chicken sandwich. It was early Sunday evening and they were dining on Fiona's verandah. Fiona was spending the weekend at Tookaringa with her father-in-law, and Cassie had volunteered to stay with Marian and Anna. She had fed the children earlier and they were out back, playing on the swing Steven had hung from the tall silver gum tree.

"I'm pleased with us except that I always feel on edge, like I'm going to lose you. Our relationship doesn't give me peace."

"Do you think," Cassie asked as she reached across the table to run her fingers over his hand, "that a piece of paper is going to make that much difference?"

"Yes," he nodded. "I do."

"What do you want that you don't have now?"

"I don't want to have to sneak out of here before dawn. I want to be able to sleep next to you every night of the week. I want to come home to a house that's ours."

"You'd like to have children, wouldn't you?"

He shook his head. "I think I'm too old to be patient with children. I just want to have you. Though if you want children, Cassie," he said softly, leaning over the table, "I'd be happy about it."

Cassie stood up and looked at him. "More ice tea?"

"No."

"I do." She disappeared into the kitchen.

She wished she could love him. She wished she could tell him that he excited her, but he didn't. Well, now and then in bed, he did. She liked making love with him. He didn't thrill her the way Blake had, but he'd learned the things that aroused and delighted her. Still, something was missing—something she couldn't even find words to describe. She enjoyed him most of the time, but she didn't want to spend a lifetime with him. Some nights she was relieved when he left, enjoying time by herself. Sometimes even when she was with him a terrible feeling of loneliness came over her and she wondered what was wrong with her.

She returned to the verandah and stood in the doorway, looking at Chris. "You're a very nice person," she said.

"I don't know what brought that on," he said, his eyes smiling behind his glasses. "It's due mostly to you. I've been happier these last four years than I've ever been in all my life."

"Don't let it go to your head," she grinned. "You still have a few faults."

She looked through the screens to see a tall, thin, uniformed man walking up the street. He limped as he walked and his left shoulder was lower than the other. She hadn't seen him in town before.

"Who's that, do you know?" she asked Chris, nodding to the man slowly approaching.

Chris turned to look, squinting his eyes against the sunlight. He stood up, leaning forward. "Jesus Christ!"

"What?" She couldn't see the man's face but she was sure she'd never seen anyone who carried himself as the soldier did.

Chris turned to her. "It's Blake Thompson," he said, his voice cracking.

Cassie looked again as the soldier turned down the sidewalk that led to the house. It couldn't be. He was too thin. Too lopsided. Too . . . oh, God. She froze. It *was* Blake.

"Fiona?" Blake called, unable to see through the screening.

Cassie couldn't speak. She tried to, but no sound came.

Chris put a hand on her shoulder and then walked over and opened the screen door. "She's not here, but welcome home."

Blake looked at him, not recognizing him for a minute. "Dr. Adams, isn't it?" He reached out to shake hands.

"I'm here with Cassie," Chris said, nodding toward her.

Blake walked up the steps and stood framed in the doorway. Cassie hardly recognized him. He grinned at her, though his eyes did not smile, and he said, "No hug for the returning hero?"

She walked toward him and into the embrace his right arm offered as it slid around her shoulder. Her arms went around him and with horror she realized his left sleeve was partially empty. She pulled back, staring at the sleeve.

Blake pulled himself erect, and said, "Guess I have to get used to that reaction."

"Blake, you've lost . . . "

" . . . From the elbow down, yes. That can't be fixed but my leg's healing. They say I'll get over the limp."

The eyes of a stranger met hers.

"Come in, come in." Chris pulled Blake into the screened porch, gesturing toward a chair. "We're just having supper. Will you join us?"

Blake looked around. "Fiona. Where's Fiona?"

Cassie could hardly find words. "She's spending the weekend out at Tookaringa." Her heart was beating so fast she thought she might faint.

Blake sat down. "When will she be back?"

No *Hello, Cassie. Good to see you.* Nothing except *Where's Fiona.*

"Before dark, I'm sure. Shouldn't be more than an hour or so."

"How about a drink?" Chris asked.

Blake nodded. "Yes, thanks, that sounds just right."

"What would you like?"

Blake's eyes were empty. "I've missed Aussie beer. Got any?"

"Sure," Cassie said. "And a sandwich?"

Blake nodded. "Sounds good."

Cassie's hands were clammy. She had trouble swallowing. The only way she got to the kitchen was working hard to put one foot in front of the other.

As though in a trance she sliced the chicken, slapped mayonnaise and lettuce on the bread, and then she felt arms around her, heard Chris whisper in her ear, "Are you all right?"

No, she wasn't. She was anything but all right. But, instead of slumping against the counter she stiffened her back and turned to smile at Chris, kissing him on the cheek. "Of course. Anything between us ended a long time ago."

"I wish I could believe that," Chris whispered as though to himself.

"Get him a beer. You know where it is." Cassie's voice sounded impersonal and cool, even to her own ears. Oscars, she thought. Do they give out Oscars for performances like I'm giving? Like I'm going to go on giving when I see Fiona in his arms?

She waited for Chris to take the cap off the bottle, not wanting to be alone with Blake. Her legs began to shake and she fought to control them. She pleaded with the unseen gods not to let her cry. She blinked hard.

With Chris following her she returned to the verandah to find Blake sitting in the same position.

"Fiona wrote you have your own place now," Blake said.

Making conversation.

Cassie placed the sandwich in front of him and, taking the bottle of beer from Chris, placed it on the table, too. Looking at the empty left sleeve, she asked, "Is that why she hasn't heard from you in so long?"

"Yeah." He bit into his sandwich and then grabbed the bottle, swilling the beer and making a little moan. "I forgot how good beer can be."

"You're home for good, I gather," Chris said, stretching his legs out as he sat in the chair next to Cassie. His eyes were on her as he spoke to Blake.

"I'd say it's for bad," Blake said, his voice as bitter as his eyes were dull. He took another gulp. "Damn, that tastes good."

Cassie was fighting for breath. She consciously reached deep into her diaphragm for air.

Blake looked at her and said, "You're a sight for sore eyes, Cassie."

She was afraid her voice would break but she said, "How did it happen?"

Blake looked at his left sleeve. "Lose the arm, you mean? Plane was shot over Dusseldorf, but I made it back to the airfield. I caught a piece of shrapnel but the tailgunner and navigator didn't make it."

Cassie stared at him.

Chris said, "Fiona's going to be the happiest woman in the world."

Blake was silent a moment. "With an incomplete man? That's doubtful."

That's why he didn't write. He didn't even know if Fiona would want him. Oh, the idiot. What does an arm have to do with love? Cassie wanted to throw her arms around him, reassure him. "Fiona will love you no matter what."

Blake laughed. An odd, harsh sound. "So, she's become part of the Flying Doctors, huh? Imagine that."

"You'll be proud of her. She's been wonderful. We've had a grand time together."

Now, for the first time Blake looked straight into Cassie's eyes. Neither of them said anything.

"I can't picture her piloting a plane," he said.

Cassie blinked and stared out through the screen. "She's not only a pilot, but an anesthetist, she's pulled a couple of teeth, adopted two aborigine girls . . . "

At that moment Anna and Marian came flying around the corner of the house, Marian crying and holding up her hand. "Anna bit me," she cried, tears streaking her dusty face.

"I didn't mean to," Anna said, a guilty expression on her face. "We were just playing."

Marian ran to Cassie, but stopped short when she saw the stranger.

"Excuse me," Cassie said as she got up and took Marian by the hand. "I better wash this out and put something on it."

Marian's eyes grew round with fear. "Is it going to sting?"

Cassie picked her up and held her close. "A little bit, but just for a second. Come on, I'll kiss it. Anna, you come along, too."

She busied herself with the little girls as long as she could. When she finished putting a bandage on what was merely a scratch, she gave them milk and cookies and left them chattering in the kitchen. She went back to the bathroom and sat on the edge of the tub. Oh, poor Blake. Feeling like he wasn't whole because he'd lost an arm. Poor Blake . . . thin, wounded. The look in his eyes, barely alive. His buddies dead in the plane he flew back across the channel. And he looked at her as though they had never known each other in the way that they had. As though he knew her name and that was all. She could have been anyone. Pity was replaced with anger, with her own pain. Her own wounds.

She took three deep breaths and went out to the verandah again. "I'm not going to be much use to Dad without an arm," Blake was saying. "I don't know what I'm going to do."

Just then Fiona's little green roadster pulled around the corner. She'd been saying the first thing she was going to do when the war was over was buy a new car, one where there weren't dents and scratches, where the gears shifted smoothly, and you couldn't hear it coming halfway down the block.

Blake recognized the old car. He stood up and moved to the door. Cassie thought she and Chris ought to disappear and let this be Blake's and Fiona's moment, but she couldn't move and noticed that Chris made no move to do so either.

It was twilight; shadows hid the porch but Fiona's face was bright and clear. She walked up the path, her step jaunty, carrying her little suitcase. "Yoohoo," she called, her voice filled with anticipation, "where are my girls?"

And then she stopped. She dropped her bag and stood there a minute, staring at the doorway where her husband stood. Her face crumpled, her lips trembled, and her hand clutched at her throat. "Oh . . . " Tears coursed down her cheeks and she began to run, her arms open. She ran into the arm waiting for her, and burrowed her head into Blake's chest for an instant before pulling back and looking up at him, love and delight and joy filling her tear-streaked face.

She threw her arms around him and their lips met. Cassie had to turn away. As she did so, she realized Chris was not looking at the tableau before them, but at her.

"We shouldn't be here," he said, his voice low.

No, we shouldn't, she agreed silently.

"Oh, my God." Exultation was in Fiona's voice, her red hair swinging around. "This is the most wonderful—oh, darling, your arm . . . it doesn't matter. Oh, beloved . . . " In that moment she saw Chris and Cassie, as she clung to Blake. "Isn't this the most wonderful thing in the whole world?" She kissed him again, laughing and crying at the same time.

He hadn't said anything, but his right arm pulled her close, not letting go.

An icicle cut through Cassie's heart.

She grabbed hold of Chris's hand and said, "We're going."

Fiona and Blake never even heard them as they left.

They walked to Cassie's house through the darkening evening. When they arrived, Chris asked, "Do you want to be alone?"

Cassie felt her whole body shaking and wondered just what she did want. She thought of Blake holding Fiona close. She closed her eyes and remembered them kissing each other.

"No," she said. "And, Chris, this isn't affecting me like you think it is." *Liar.* "It's been nearly five years since I last saw him. Come on in. Let's have a drink."

He started toward the kitchen. "What do you want?"

"Scotch. A double."

"Cassie . . . "

"Don't you dare go, Chris Adams. Don't even think it. Stay here. Stay all night. I don't care if everyone in town sees you leave in the morning. For God's sake, don't leave me alone." She turned and her eyes blazed at him. "I don't care what you think. I don't even care what you feel tonight. Just don't leave me."

He reached out to her, touching a tendril of her hair. "Cassie, I never want to leave you."

She brushed his hand away.

While she waited for him to return with her Scotch she tapped her nails on the coffee table, her foot jerking back and forth.

She drank the Scotch in three swigs, and then turned to Chris. "Make love to me."

He sighed and looked at her. "Come here," he said, reaching his hand to touch her shoulder.

She turned on him as though with anger. "No. Come to bed." She stood up and walked to the bedroom.

He looked after her, shaking his head, murmuring, "My poor darling." But he followed her, already untying his tie and unbuttoning his shirt.

Her clothes in a heap on the floor, she was already waiting for him, standing silhouetted against the street light, her body lithe and wound tight as a drum. She stood there while he undressed, watching him in the semidarkness.

He lay down on the bed and looked at her, across the room. Then she ran and jumped on the bed, climbing on top of him, pressing herself against him, kissing him hard.

"Hurt me, Chris. Make love to me so furiously nothing else in the world will matter."

"Hurt you? Oh, God, Cassie . . . "

Her nails raked his shoulders as she pushed herself hard against him. She knelt above him, brushing her breasts across his mouth, saying, "Bite me, Chris!"

He did so, but gently, his hands reaching around her to caress her buttocks. She swayed above him, her body slapping against him, moving down his body, kissing his nipples, her tongue feathering across his belly, down . . . down . . . across the insides of his thighs. She crawled to the bottom of the bed and took each of his toes in her mouth, one by one. She kissed the arch of each foot, nibbled her way up each leg until she took him into her mouth and heard him moan.

"Christ, Cassie, be gentle."

She rolled off him, pulling him on top of her, their bodies undulating as she moved faster and faster, grinding against him until their rhythm was frenzied, their bodies twisting, gyrating in tandem.

"Now," she insisted and raised her body so he entered her easily, thrusting against her until nothing else existed. It was not love, even Chris knew that. He knew exactly what it was.

Cassie's legs wound around him, holding him in her, moving against him. She thrust herself upward in an arch, her nails strafing along his back, her breathing spasmodic and hard. She wanted him to erase Blake from her mind. From her mind and heart. She wanted Chris to consume her. Make her forget. Make her want no one but him. And she cried, "Chris!" as the wonderful, warm waves washed over her, again and again. "Don't stop! Please don't stop!"

He had no intention of stopping. He brought her to climaxes over and over again. When he could no longer perform, his tongue whipped her to ecstasy.

She didn't let him sleep all night. Near dawn he got up and put on his clothes. He couldn't be seen leaving her house at this hour. She didn't say goodbye.

After he left, she slept. Dreamlessly.

He didn't. He walked around his house, took a shower and brushed his teeth, and walked over to the hospital, where one of the nurses poured hot tea for him.

Not bad for a man of my age, he thought. Aloud, he said, "Damn. Damn. Damn."

Chapter 39

Cassie was awakened by the phone's ringing. It was Fiona.

"Cassie, is there any way we can cancel the clinic today?"

"I don't know how," she said, wondering if that were true.

"Have Horrie send them a message. Barring a life-threatening emergency, nothing in the world is going to make me leave Blake today."

Cassie hung up without even saying goodbye and lay there, staring at the curtain billowing in the breeze. Five years ago next month she and Blake were heading toward Kakadu. Five years and two and a half months ago she was in Townsville aborting his child. God, how glad she was she had done that. What might her life be like now if she hadn't? She didn't even want to think about that.

She got up and walked into the bathroom, turning the shower on for the water to get hot while she brushed her teeth. She stared at herself in the mirror. She didn't like what she saw. She guessed Blake didn't, either.

She shampooed and scrubbed herself in the shower and then turned off the hot water as she let icy cold water needle her. Five years, she thought, toweling herself dry. Wasn't it time to get over Blake and get on with her life? Five years where she'd stayed emotionally static. Wasn't it about time to do something about her personal life?

Standing naked, she phoned Horrie. "Call Winnamurra," she told him, "and cancel today's clinic. Blake arrived home last night and Fiona doesn't want to fly today. I'll be out for the morning call-in." Without waiting for a response she looked in her closet and pulled out a yellow shirtwaist dress. Then she found her high-heeled spectator shoes and drew on silk stockings. No one in town will recognize me dressed this way at this hour.

She phoned Chris, but there was no answer. He must already be at the hospital.

She glanced at her watch. Another half-hour before she had to take radio calls. She'd stop in and surprise him.

Ten minutes later she marched into the hospital and down to his office. He was sitting there, drinking his third cup of tea of the morning and his face lit up when she burst through his door. "This is a pleasant surprise." He stood, nearly knocking the tea over.

She walked over and reached up to kiss him. He raised his eyebrows.

"If I can find out where Don McLeod is, will you fly out to him with me and have him marry us?"

Chris was silent as he stared at her.

"What? Do you need time to think it over after all these years of proposing to me?" The tone of her voice was sharp.

He shook his head. "No, that's not it at all. Of course I'll marry you, any time, any place you say."

"I'll get Horrie to try to locate him." She turned and walked out of the office, back down the hall, across the hospital parking lot to her car. She drove out to the radio station, and she felt nothing. She was not happy or angry or sad or anything. She thought maybe she was dead.

She knew she was not being fair to Chris. Aloud she vowed, "I shall never let him be sorry I'm doing this to him. I swear I won't." Her knuckles were white around the steering wheel.

During the radio call-in she asked if anyone knew where Padre McLeod was. It happened he was at Yancanna. Brigid and Marianne had left long ago; their required two years had expired, and three pairs of sisters had been there since they'd left. But Marianne had married Chief and stayed, on call at the hospital for emergencies and raising her two sons.

Cassie didn't want everyone in the district to know her plans; she just said to tell the padre she'd be flying out within the next few days and not to leave without telling her.

"What's up?" Horrie asked.

"Cross your heart you won't tell?"

He grinned, "Not even Betty?"

"Well, swear her to secrecy, too. I'm getting married and I want Don to perform the ceremony."

"Cassie! So you're going to make an honest man of Doc Adams?"

She nodded and felt a tightness in her chest. Well, why not? He was good in bed, he loved her, he'd grown much kinder, he'd begged her to marry him for years. He was somebody to do things with, go to movies with and talk with—at least about medicine. They tended to argue when they talked of anything else that was important. Well, she didn't have to talk about important things with him. The gossip of the town was enough.

She stopped at the hospital again and waited for Chris to finish his rounds. "Don's in Yancanna. Want to fly out there?"

Instead of looking happy, Chris's eyes were pained. "Romla will never forgive me if I don't give her time to get here. I have to, Cassie. Aside from you, she's the only other person in the world I really love."

Nothing was ever simple, was it? "Phone her now."

Chris shook his head as though frustrated. "Okay." He sat down at his desk and called the operator. When Romla answered he explained immediately why he was calling. "How soon can you get here?" he asked.

They talked a few minutes and he looked at his watch. "Okay, tomorrow afternoon. I'll meet the bus."

He hung up and looked at Cassie, who said, "Except for the radio call-ins, I'll be home all day, barring an emergency. Come for dinner?"

She stopped by Fiona's, wanting to tell her she'd have to fly them all out to Yancanna tomorrow evening.

Fiona cried, "Married? Oh, Cassie, how wonderful! Isn't this sudden?"

"What in life isn't?" All day she'd noticed a hardness in her own voice, and hated it.

In the middle of the morning, Blake was still in his pajamas, sitting at the kitchen table. Cassie barely glanced at him.

"Let me get you tea," Fiona said.

"No, thanks."

"I think you'd better sit down. Would you prefer coffee? I have some news, too."

And Cassie wondered why she hadn't known it before. "You're leaving." Now her voice was dull. Of course. She should have known immediately.

"Blake wants me at Tookaringa."

"That's where she belongs," Blake said. "Not flying around the countryside."

Of course. Fiona would be mistress of the largest cattle station in this part of the world. As Blake's wife, that was her role.

Cassie sat down. "How will I find another pilot?"

"I know, I've thought of that. But, Cassie, dear, you do understand, don't you?"

"Of course." But her mind was reeling off, wondering if this were the end of the Flying Doctors until after the war. "I should have sensed it. No, I don't need coffee."

"When are you getting married?"

"Chris wants to wait for Romla to get here late tomorrow, and I want Don to marry us, so I hope you'll fly us out to Yancanna."

Fiona and Blake exchanged glances. "My father's arriving tomorrow," Blake said.

"We'll only be gone a couple of hours," Cassie said.

Fiona said, "Steven's so fond of you I'm sure he'd want to come to your wedding, too. But we can't all fit in the plane."

We all? Cassie hadn't envisioned Blake there.

"No. I hadn't planned for anyone to be there, really. Romla. Maybe you as my attendant. I don't want anyone there."

Fiona laughed and threw her arms around Cassie. "Do you really think the town will let you get away with that? So many people love you and Chris they'll be crushed not to come to your wedding. They'll really be insulted, Cassie."

"Oh, shit!" She really wouldn't even have bothered suggesting it if she'd known all this would happen. She just wanted to run away and get married. Run away. That's what she was doing, wasn't she?

Fiona's arm was still around her shoulders. "Come on, Blake and I can fly out and get Don and bring him here for the wedding. If you don't want a big church affair, we'll have it here, in the yard. A reception afterward. Romla can help when she gets here tomorrow night. Come on, Cassie. You can't just have a little wedding with no one there. The town would never forgive you."

Cassie began to cry.

Blake just stared at her the whole time.

"You won't have to do a thing," Fiona said. "I'll take care of it all."

"No, you should be spending this time with Blake."

"We will be together. He can fly to Yancanna with me to get Don. Cassie, you have to realize you're a public figure. So is Chris. You have to tell everyone on the galah session that you're getting married, in case they want to drive into town."

Why had she started all this? "I don't want any fuss. I just want to get married quietly. I want to do it quickly and get it over with and . . . "

Fiona laughed and shook her head. "This will be as big and important to everyone around here as Race Week. Well, maybe not quite, but . . . "

Dear Fiona. Cassie hated what she was doing, giving up this honeymoon period with Blake.

"And we'll expect you and Chris for dinner tonight. We'll make plans," Fiona went on.

"Chris doesn't care what we do. He just wants to get married."

"I think Chris will love a big do."

Cassie shook her head. "He's not a social being, you know that."

"Just wait. Chris will love the turnout. Between the two of you, you know everyone within two hundred and fifty thousand square miles."

Blake had still hardly spoken. He got up and walked out of the room.

Cassie looked up at Fiona. "I didn't mean to rob you of your happiness."

Fiona laughed. "Rob me of my happiness? My happiness is just beginning. I'm so happy I could burst. I didn't know anyone could be so happy. Oh, Cassie, it's wonderful you're getting married. I really thought you were waiting for Sam."

Cassie stood up. "You come over to my place for dinner. I'm a better cook. Besides, you don't want to spend the afternoon in the kitchen on Blake's first day home."

"Okay." Fiona leaned over to kiss Cassie's cheek. "I'm happy for you, darling. Just as I know you are for me."

As she drove home, Cassie thought *I am happy for her. I really am. I care about her happiness. I really do.*

She had been wrong about Chris. He was delighted with Fiona's plans. "Romla will love to help, if you can keep her from taking over entirely. This is right up her alley."

"I'd love to have her take over," Fiona said. "But if we're going to have a really big wingding, we better wait until Saturday night. Give people a chance to get into town. Everyone will volunteer to bake cakes and bring something. Why, this is going to be the wedding of the year."

Just what Cassie hadn't wanted.

Blake didn't say more than ten words the whole evening. He and Fiona left early.

When they had gone and Cassie stood washing the dishes while Chris dried, he said, "Where do you want to live? Your house or mine?"

"I don't want to think about all these things."

Chris kissed her on the neck. "They're just details. But I guess I don't want us to start our marriage in this house where I spent so many unhappy years with Isabel."

Cassie finished the last dish. "Why have you stayed there so long?"

He shrugged. "Guess I just never thought of moving."

"Well, I'm not nuts about this house, either."

"Want to buy Fiona's? You always liked that house, and she'll be leaving it."

"Chris, that's a lovely idea." She turned to smile at him, the first time she'd felt like smiling since Blake had walked down the path to Fiona's. "I've never been more comfortable in any house. Yes, let's ask her. Oh, I do like that idea."

As soon as the dishes were finished, Chris said, "I'm going home."

"You're going home? Why? No one will even be shocked now if you leave early in the morning."

He leaned over and kissed her lightly. "No, I want us to spend our nights apart until we're married. It's only five more nights, darling."

He had never called her that before.

"We've never spent five nights apart in all the time we've been together."

He smiled. "This will make Saturday night all the sweeter."

"Are you going to tell me last night wasn't the greatest we've ever had?"

"Saturday will be sweeter."

Romla did take over all the arrangements. She located enough records so that people could dance even though there was no orchestra available. She told Cassie she was thrilled they were going to be sisters and she was ecstatic for her brother. It's what she'd been wishing for ever since Cassie had come to Townsville so long ago. "I've loved you from the minute I met you," Romla declared.

The wedding was the event of the winter of 1944. People drove for ten and twelve hours to attend. All the hotel's shabby rooms, all of Addie's rooms, and nearly every guest room in town were occupied. There was no way to have either the wedding or reception at Fiona's. The ceremony was to be held in the Presbyterian Church, and the reception in the school gymnasium.

Steven had approached her the day before the wedding. "Cassie, you need someone to give you away. I'd be honored if you'd let me."

How ironic.

Don and Margaret stayed in her guest room, and Don claimed to be mighty pleased that she'd have Fiona fly all the way to Yancanna to get him. He told her Margaret was going to have a baby and he was accepting the pulpit at the Alice Springs church so he wouldn't have to leave her and the child. "I'm going to stop being a roaming padre and settle down to being just the reverend." He smiled.

"How will you like that?" Cassie asked. "So many people will miss you."

"And I'll miss them. But it has to be. I don't intend to lose touch, though." He put his hands on Cassie's shoulders. "Are you going to be happy, my dear?"

"What's happiness?" she asked.

"I think I know why you're doing this, but Chris Adams is a good man. He's even better since you and he have been going together. He had an unhappy marriage, has he told you? I knew all along. Don't make him unhappy again, Cassie."

Cassie was hurt. "What kind of woman do you think I am? I thought you liked me!"

"Like you? Cassie, I love you. Next to my Marg you're the woman I'd want most as my wife. You know that. I imagine you've always known it. That doesn't mean I have to think you're perfect."

"You know me better than that!"

He shook his head. "That's not what I'm referring to at all. I'm talking about purity of purpose. You may not be doing this for the right reasons, but then what *are* the right reasons for getting married? All I'm saying is, I hope you're the woman I think you are and you're not going to make Chris Adams unhappy just to try to prove to Blake Thompson that he doesn't matter."

Staring into Don's eyes, she whispered, "Is that what I'm doing?"

"I suspect so." Don put his arms around her. "But that doesn't mean you can't have a good marriage. You have to accept the fact that Blake belongs to Fiona and can never be yours. I think you've known that in your head, but now that you've seen it, you have to accept it as a fact and live your own life."

"Oh, Don, that's just what I told myself. I have a life to live."

"Well, Cassie, let's hope this is the way to do it."

The next day he said, "Have you ever had a penchant for flying?"

"What do you mean? I fly half the time."

"No, I mean being a pilot."

"Heavens, no."

"Well, I thought I might ask John Flynn how he felt about your learning to fly. There isn't another available pilot and you don't want this to be the end of the FDS, do you?"

Cassie cocked her head. "You know the rule. Doctors are not allowed to fly planes."

Don nodded. "Yes, but Cassie, that rule didn't take wartime into consideration. Either you learn to fly or the FDS is out of commission until the war ends."

"Let me think about it. I don't know that I could do it."

Don smiled. "Cassie, I can't think of anything you can't do if you put your mind to it."

She smiled at him. "Do you really think so, Don?"

"You love challenges. You thrive under pressure. I know you that well. I've seen you pass every test you've come up against. Maybe it's just what you need, my dear. I'd say that you need new mountains to scale."

Everyone in town and over a hundred people from the bush came to the wedding. Not even half of them could fit into the church, so the street outside was lined with people.

The party afterward lasted until nearly three in the morning, but Chris was called away at nine to attend a patient in labor. It was after midnight when Don and Margaret escorted the bride home.

Cassie sat up, waiting for her husband. Restless, she finally spent her wedding night writing a letter to Sam, telling him of the recent developments.

When Chris arrived at five-thirty, he was exhausted, having had to perform a cesarean.

He fell on the bed and was asleep in less than a minute.

Cassie climbed into bed next to him and listened to the roosters crowing, heard dogs barking, and wondered if Fiona and Blake were asleep. If they would soon wake up and Blake would reach for her and they would make love again. And again.

Chapter 40

"Nervous?" asked the instructor.

Cassie climbed into the pilot's seat, ready for her first flight at the controls. The instructor climbed into the seat to her right.

"There's no need to prime the engine," he said. Rob Wright was a tall, lean, chain-smoking man in his late forties. "It's a warm day. If the engine were cold you could give it a couple shots of prime and then turn the switch on and start up and let it idle a bit. But it's warm today."

Why wasn't this like the thousand other times she'd been in a plane?

"We're flying a tail glider so the tail wheel is low. That means the engine cowling is up front, blocking out what's right in front of you. We're going to taxi by using 'S' turns. You'll turn like an 'S' as you progress down the taxi strip. It's important for when you taxi off the ramp in case other planes are parked there. When you 'S' to the right, you can see to the left. Okay, let's taxi out to the end of the runway."

She'd studied hard and knew just what he was talking about. They'd been in the classroom for two weeks.

"Now," Rob said with a grin, "we'll use cigar."

Cassie turned to look at him. *Cigar?* She couldn't have heard him correctly.

"Yup," he chuckled. "CIGAR. 'C' is to check your controls. This Cessna has a wheel instead of a stick, so pull it back and forth to see if the elevators are working and use your feet on the rudder pedals. Wiggle the wheel to the right and left and look out to see that the ailerons are working."

He waited while she did that.

"Now for the 'I.' Instruments. This Cessna 140 doesn't have many instruments, but we have compass, oil temp and oil pressure gauge, and there's the rpm instrument, so we check to see that our altimeter gauge is set properly. This has to be set according to the atmospheric pressure. If you can't get this info from a weather station then you have to know what the elevation of the field is. Say it's twenty-five hundred feet above sea level. Set the altimeter accordingly. This is vitally important."

Cassie nodded, hoping she was going to remember this.

"Okay," Rob went on, "next is 'G' for gasoline. Remember when we were doing our check at the ramp I had you climb up that little ladder and take the fuel cap off and stick your finger in to see if you had ample fuel? Remember this has to be done on both sides as there's a tank on each wing." He continued talking, explaining that the "A" in cigar stood for air shrims.

"Last, 'R' equals revolutions per minute, or rpm. When you rev up the engine, look at the rpm indicator. Go to about fifteen hundred rpms. Now the plane has two sets of spark plugs, so if one-on-one cylinder goes bad you don't lose complete power. You also have two mag needles, which are similar to a car's distributor but they're much safer and more proficient." He went on explaining the intricacies they'd already studied.

"Okay," he said as he leaned over to clap her on the shoulder. "Ready for take-off? I'll do the take-off and then you get on controls with me. Now you hold the wheel on your side and put your feet lightly on the rudder pedals. This plane is tricky in the use of the brakes. If you use both the right and left ones simultaneously, the plane'll stop."

They looked carefully in all directions and pulled onto the runway. The throttle opened easily and quickly, a nice swift push, and they were rolling down the runway. "Push forward a wee bit on the wheel until we feel the tail raising in the air and hold it right there. Keep the plane in a straight line down the runway using the rudder pedals, and then as we gain speed of fifty-five to sixty, ease back lightly on the wheel—ah, that's it, good girl." He told her to put the tail in a slightly downward position and the nose came up. The plane started to climb. "We'll leave the throttle full open until we get up to about four hundred feet and have nice airspeed, maybe ninety mph, and then keep to that pattern. Here, watch what I do."

He made a right turn. "Now we'll climb up to an altitude where we'll do maneuvers. If we didn't have a beach like we do down there, we'd have to find some straight line, a railroad or a straight road. One of the first maneuvers is going to be a straight and level flight. I'm demonstrating to you the means for such, for it's not an easy maneuver with a gusty wind."

He flew to twenty-five hundred feet and then told Cassie, "Okay, now you're on the control with me and you can feel what's being done to the rudders and wheel. Look out and see the horizon, which has to be at a certain attitude regarding the cowling, like you'd look out over the hood of a car. There's a distance between cowling and climbing or descending or turning.

"Now that you've latched onto this we'll go into a shallow banking maneuver. Banks and turns. When you turn in a plane you go into a bank similar to a racetrack. The controls must be coordinated in order to get a certain altitude or keep the plane from stalling and losing speed."

Even after having flown as many thousands of miles as she had, the experience was new to Cassie. She'd never been so aware of her relationship to the earth, never been so conscious of a plane's turning, of what was below her. They practiced banks and turns.

"Now," said the pilot, "we're going to do stalls, whereby the plane stops flying and doesn't fall down unless you make the nose go straight down through some extraordinarily foolish thing. The plane will glide a ten to one ratio. In other words, if you're up one mile you could fly ten miles. Here, we'll go into a stall and throttle back a bit and slow the plane down. Pull the wheels back and keep pulling them until it won't go back any further. Then the plane's nose will drop."

Cassie's heart was in her mouth. She had never so appreciated Sam's and Fiona's abilities. "It'll fall like a leaf but it won't go right down. Hold the stick back and use rudders so it'll just dip and dip and dip and lose air speed." Which is just what it was doing. Cassie's throat closed and she didn't think she could breathe.

Rob looked at her and laughed. "We'll recover from this stall simply by pushing the wheel forward. Never make any abrupt actions but just smoothly ease the nose down. When you push the stick forward the nose drops and the plane picks up speed and is flying again."

Cassie looked over at him and inhaled deeply.

By the time she returned from a month in Brisbane and made a clinic run out to Tookaringa, Fiona was pregnant.

"Why don't you seem happier?" Cassie asked. "I thought it was just what you wanted."

"I'm thrilled. So is Steven."

There was a silence. "But Blake?"

Tears filled Fiona's eyes. "Nothing thrills him. He hardly even talks. He stays in our room and reads or stares out the window."

"This can often happen to men who have witnessed war, seen terrible things, seen their friends die. Maybe he wonders why he lived and they died."

Fiona nodded. "I'm sure that must be part of it, but he thinks he can't do anything, that his life is over."

Cassie finished the tea she'd been sipping. "You mean because of his arm?"

Fiona nodded. "Yes. He thinks he's not whole. He can't ride and wonders what use he is if he can't mount a horse out here. He can't brand. He can't muster. He can't do any of the things he's done all his life. He can't even get up on a horse."

Cassie had no answer to that. "But he can be a father and husband."

"He thought I wouldn't even want to share his bed now that he's lost his arm. He thought the sight of it would make me stop wanting him. Oh, Cassie." Tears fell down Fiona's cheeks. "I had to do everything I could think of to . . . to seduce him! I don't even know if he wanted it."

"My God, Fi, he's still a man."

"He doesn't seem to think so. Nothing Steven and I do seems to pull him out of this lethargy. He's not interested in anything. When we discovered I'm pregnant, for just a second some life flickered in his eyes, and he said, 'God willing, it'll be a girl.' I think he means that girls don't go off to war."

"Well, he can't spend the rest of his life feeling sorry for himself."

As she said that, Cassie realized she'd spent a goodly portion of the last five years feeling sorry for herself because Blake had left her. Maybe one couldn't control one's emotions. Maybe no one could get Blake out of his black mood. It would have to come with time. "The only wisdom age has taught me is that this, too, shall pass. Everything does."

Fiona managed a smile. "When I'm really happy I'm sure that's true, and that my happiness is going to end any minute. When I'm in an abyss I'm positive it's not true, that I'm going to be miserable forever."

"Well, keep in mind that it does pass."

Fiona reached out to put her arm around Cassie's shoulder. "You're right. I'll think of that each night. But, in the meantime, I wish there were something I could do to help him. I can't bear to see him like this. He was a giant, Cassie. And now . . . "

"Blake Thompson will be a giant again, you'll see. We'll come up with something. Partly it's this damn humidity. It's enough to take the life out of anyone. Now, before I go I have to check with Horrie for the call-in. I'll make it from your set, okay?"

Horrie connected her with Ian James's wife, who described what Cassie was sure was pneumonia.

"I'll fly right over," Cassie said. Since there were no other emergencies, she picked up her bag and told Fiona, "I'll see you in a couple of weeks. I'm off to the Jameses."

Fiona walked her to the plane. "It goes without saying that I expect you to deliver this baby."

"It goes without saying." Cassie kissed her friend goodbye.

She arrived at the Jameses forty minutes later. Ian James lay on his bed struggling to breathe in the heat and humidity. Cassie sat next to him, counting his gasps forty times a minute. He was sucking air in and obviously not feeling relieved; his lungs must be full of fluid and pus rather than open air channels.

"Has he been coughing much?"

Mrs. James nodded, her eyes filled with fear. "And bringing up yellow-green mucus with traces of blood in it."

Cassie felt for his pulse.

"Why is he so blue?" asked his wife.

"Because his blood oxygen isn't adequate."

"Is it pneumonia?"

Cassie nodded. She had to get him to an oxygen mask and to the hospital. He was sweating and his muscles were tight. She thought he looked almost like a prize fighter in his muscular exertions, struggling and gasping for breath.

"I'm going to have to take him to the hospital. I'll get word to you from Augusta Springs tonight. I have an oxygen mask in the plane, but if we don't get him to a hospital, well . . . "

She looked around. "I have a stretcher in the plane. Can you find one of your men to help me?"

"I'll help."

Together they lifted Ian James onto the stretcher and strapped it into the plane. Cassie bent over her patient, arranging the oxygen mask. His pulse rate had slowed down; his blood pressure was dropping. His gasping was less frequent and he was obviously losing strength, like a swimmer struggling in the water.

She revved up the motor and took off. It was the fifth time she'd flown alone. She had to concentrate on the flying, on the buffeting headwind that suddenly sprang up, but a large part of her consciousness was behind her, where she could not see. She struggled with the wind, wondering if that meant a tropical storm was heading her way. She prayed she would get to Augusta Springs before the weather broke loose.

As she flew south she lost the headwind and flew through tranquil skies. She wanted badly to be with her patient, seeing what could be done for him. Was the oxygen mask in place? Was he breathing? She twisted in her seat and looked back into the cabin, hearing a rattle and she knew the air was going past the fluid in the upper chest, making a bubbling sound.

She had a terrible premonition they were not going to make it in time. If she were back there with him, she might be able to do something. She understood why John Flynn had made it a rule that flying doctors could not pilot their own planes. She should be back there with her patient. She wasn't doing him any more good right now than if he were lying back on his bed at home. He'd probably rather die there than on the way to Augusta Springs.

And that's just where he did die. Fifteen minutes before Cassie landed, Ian James gave one deep gasp and a sustained sigh. There was no other sound.

When Cassie arrived home, Chris had a Scotch poured for her. She drank it in one gulp and explained what had happened, both with Ian and about Fiona's pregnancy.

"What's all this bullshit about our supposedly getting used to death?" Cassie asked.

"I suppose that's so it won't continue to pain us so much."

"Does it still get to you?"

"Not so much if I don't know the patient. But always when it's someone I've known a long time. Or a baby."

"Telling the family. That's the hard part. Telling her over the radio. It seemed so impersonal."

Chris didn't say anything.

"I'm going to shower," Cassie said, getting up and going to their room—the one she had when she first arrived in town.

When she came out of the shower, Chris said, "You're in no mood to get dinner. Want to go to Addie's?"

"Sure." She shook her head as she looked in the mirror. "Chris, how would you feel if I let my hair grow?"

He came over to her, looking at her reflection in the mirror. "I've always wanted to suggest that. I think I'd like it."

"Why *didn't* you ever suggest it, then?"

"Oh, Cassie, I haven't the temerity to suggest anything to you. If I'd said I'd like you to grow your hair, you'd never do it. You never accept suggestions. You seem to think they're orders and if there's anything you hate it's authority."

She looked at him in the mirror. "You make me sound obnoxious."

He smiled at her. "You do have those moments."

She did? It was a part of herself she'd never acknowledged.

Chapter 41

The day the United States unleashed the atom bomb that led to the end of the war, Cassie delivered Fiona of a nine pound, two-ounce daughter, whom they named Jenny. Fiona hadn't wanted to come in to the hospital but would rather have had the baby at home. Steven would hear none of that. He'd lost too many children by being so far from a hospital.

Cassie suggested Fiona come in to town three weeks before the baby was due and stay with them, in her old room. "It wouldn't hurt Blake to come, too. There's room."

When she told Chris she had invited them, he asked, "How do you feel about Blake being here, in our house?"

"I wish you'd get off that dead horse. I feel fine about it. Fiona's my closest friend and I want her to take every precaution. It's a twelve-hour drive, in case she starts labor. I prescribe coming to town several weeks early for all my would-be mothers."

"I know that," he said, "but after what you did with Blake's baby . . . "

Cassie's eyes blazed. "Can't you forget that? I have. Smartest thing I ever did. I don't feel anything for Blake anymore. Honestly. But I do care about Fiona. For heaven's sake, Blake's a failure. Ever since he got home he's just sat around like a dodo, doing nothing, hardly even talking. Depressing everyone out at Tookaringa. Do you really think I'd rather have him than you?"

"It's just that sometimes you seem so far away."

"That's what happens when you marry a woman who has a career. Not every minute is focused on you! My God, I have problems and worries and thoughts about my patients and my job, too, you know. I thought you knew that."

He nodded. "Sure. Sure. Sorry I mentioned it. As long as you can handle Blake's being here, I guess I can, too."

"You better. It's your bed I'm in."

"God, Cassie, there's more to relationships than that!"

"Is there?" She turned away from him, looking out the window. "I thought that's what made your marriage to Isabel so unbearable."

Chris sighed. "Sometimes I'm sure you and I will never understand each other."

She flared at him. "What now? It seems to me we understand each other very well. I put up with your narrow-minded bigotry, your rigid formality, your reactionary thinking. You tell me I'm flawed. How awful not to be. Keeps us humble, don't you think? You know about my scarlet past and I thought you had forgiven me. Apparently you haven't, because you keep throwing it at . . . "

Chris's hands flew up in the air. "Oh, Cassie, it's not that at all. I know you don't love me like you did Blake. I don't even ask that. I'm grateful for what we have together, even though I know you don't feel for me what I feel for you . . . "

Cassie's voice was loud and strident. "I care about you as much as I possibly can. I promised to love and cherish you and, by damn, that's just what I think I'm doing. At least I try to. I try as hard as I know how to make you happy."

"I know, my dear, I know." He walked over and put his hands on her shoulders. "My sadness is that you have to work so hard at it."

She looked up at him and reached up to wind her arms around his neck. She kissed him, her tongue running across his lips. Pulling his head down, she flicked her tongue in his ear. "Aren't you happy? Isn't this what you wanted?"

He pulled her close, his arms around her waist. "It's more than I ever thought I'd have."

"Then shut up about Blake and let us enjoy each other. At least you talk to me. He hardly talks to either Fiona or Steven."

One month later Jennifer Stephanie Thompson entered the world at exactly noon.

An hour later Cassie was summoned to an accident involving a jackaroo who had lassoed a cow. The animal had then run away with him, leaping through a barbed wire fence and pulling the poor man behind him, smashing him into the trunk of a tree and mutilating his arm.

By the time Cassie arrived, the remaining fragments of the arm were yellowish-grey and the man couldn't move it. His mates had soddened him with whiskey, but he was still in excruciating pain. Bones stuck out of his arm and the dead part jacknifed at a weird angle to his body. The man was pale from loss of blood, though his mates had tied a tourniquet above the elbow to stop the flow.

Cassie looked up at the foreman. "I'm going to have to amputate right here," she said. Amputation was something no doctor ever got used to. "Most of his arm is shattered, anyhow."

She dug into her medical kit and handed a knife to one of the roustabouts. "Sterilize this in a fire or boiling water. Quickly!"

When the knife was ready, Cassie cut through the remaining muscle and skin, tying off the big blood vessel and putting a clamp on the end of it, pulling it out a little bit and tying a loop of thread with four or five knots around the extremity. She pulled it tight so there would be no bleeding. Washing the stump of the arm with the boiled water in an attempt to keep bacteria out, she then smeared antibiotic ointment on it and dressed the wound.

"Carry him to the plane. I'll take him back to the hospital for further surgery."

As she flew back to Augusta Springs the clouds reflected purple on the cracked earth. My God, she thought, how long has it been since it rained?

The unconscious man behind her let out a low moan, and she thought of Blake, without his arm, and how it must feel to have a part of yourself gone forever.

"You're right," Chris said after Fiona, Blake, and the baby had returned to Tookaringa. "Blake hardly says a word. And when he does it's in monosyllables. Feels so damn sorry for himself."

Cassie spread raspberry jam on her toast. It was not a clinic day, so unless some emergency came along she was free except for the radio call-ins. An idea had been growing as she sat around and watched Blake refuse to communicate with anyone.

"It's not just the loss of his arm, I suspect. It's the loss of his way of life. If he could *do* things, if he could ride a horse, drive a car, all the things he used to take for granted."

"You have an idea. I can tell." Chris said, leaning back in his chair, and sipping the last of his coffee before leaving for the hospital.

"Did you read that article in the last medical journal about all the new things they're coming up with for wounded veterans? They've invented so many wonderful aids. Did you see the one about the electronic arm?"

Chris shook his head. "I haven't gotten around to that one yet. I was fascinated with the article on malaria. Did you know it was the outstanding medical problem of the war?"

Cassie hardly heard him. "I'm going to call Norm Castor and see what he can tell me, or who he can put me in touch with."

When she next flew out to Tookaringa, she arranged to stay overnight, so that she could dine with Blake, Fiona, and Steven. She waited until the middle of the main course and said, "Blake, I'd like you to fly to Melbourne and see a good friend of mine. Of my father's, really. Dr. Norman Castor. He has a doctor on his staff who's doing fantastic things with veterans who have lost an arm or leg."

A pin drop could be heard. No one had mentioned Blake's infirmity since he'd first arrived home. They pretended it wasn't there. Both Fiona and Steven were looking at Blake, waiting to take a cue from him.

"What good would that do? I don't want a piece of wood with a claw on the end."

Cassie plowed ahead. "It's not like that anymore. They make arms and hands that look real, with shapes like fingernails, ridges for tendons, even blue lines for veins. One would never know they're not real."

Silence again. "I would."

"Well, I wish you'd give it a go. It wouldn't harm anything. It would just take a couple of weeks out of your life. And it seems to me you've taken more than that out."

"What's that supposed to mean?"

Fiona reached across the table to touch him. "Oh, Cassie doesn't mean a thing . . . "

"Yes, I do."

Another silence. Though this time all three of them were looking at her.

"You go around feeling so full of self-pity you don't see or care what you're doing to your wife and father," Cassie said. "You're breaking their hearts every day of your life. You don't *do* a thing. You sit on the porch and stare out into a void. I bet you're not even thinking, unless it's of yourself and how you're not a man anymore because you lost an arm in the war. What about the people who gave their lives? You're not so bad off. Because you can't ride or go out mustering or shoot a gun you feel your whole life is over. What do you think all the millions of people who don't live in the Outback do? You could create a life for yourself. You just refuse to. You make your wife tiptoe around, you show next to no interest in your new baby, and your father does nothing except try to please you."

She stopped, breathing hard, wondering if she'd alienated all three of them.

"Of course, that's their fault," she went on when no one said anything. "They're letting you rule their lives, instead of going on with their own, instead of getting satisfaction out of all the wonderful things that life offers, they let you bottle them up, too."

Fiona's hand went to her chest. "Cassie!"

"It's true, Fiona, and somewhere inside you, you know it. If Blake had one shred of love for you and Steven, and if he'd only open himself to loving his child, he'd go to Melbourne and let himself be fitted for an arm. Dr. Castor tells me it restores equilibrium—he thinks you could even ride again. You can do anything you ever did before, except maybe tie a shoelace, and I've never seen you with shoes that require shoelaces!"

Steven asked, "Is this true, Cassie?"

"It takes time and will power. Self-discipline. But Dr. Castor says it's amazing. You're not the only one in the world who's lost an arm, Blake. Think of those who lost their sight, are paraplegic, lost both legs. Think of those who can never move again. Your manhood wasn't lost with your arm. You threw it away. Well, here's your chance to recover it and do something with your life, and be the person your father and Fiona loved." She stressed the past tense.

Fiona began to cry and left the table.

Cassie hoped she hadn't alienated her forever. She had felt she had to take extreme measures to get to Blake. She'd debated about trying to get him alone, but decided if she spoke to him in front of his family, her words might mean more.

In the nearly a year he'd been home, this was more than she'd said to him altogether. He'd acted as though she were invisible, but then he acted that way with his father and often with Fiona. And everyone else in his world.

Later, Fiona came to Cassie's room. "I don't want you to think I'm angry with you. I just, oh, Cassie, you were saying all the things I wanted to say. Sometimes I just can't stand it. I feel I'm living with an uninhabited body. So does Steven. All joy has gone completely out of our lives, and neither of us has had the guts to say this. Not that saying it will do any good. Cassie, I'm so miserable and I should be so happy to have my husband home—and a new baby."

Cassie put her arms around her friend. "If you lived in a city, I'd suggest going to a psychiatrist, one that's trained in terms of the repercussions of war. It still might not be a bad idea. But, Fi, really, these new arms and legs are wonders. I haven't seen one but I hear they're great."

"He'll never do it, you know. He won't accept help. He thinks he has to be able to do everything or he's second-rate. But thanks for trying. I just wanted you to know my crying didn't mean I was upset with you."

"Thank God. I was worried there for awhile, but it was something I felt I had to say."

In the morning Blake was waiting, alone, at the breakfast table. "Will you make the arrangements?" he asked. "I'll go to Melbourne to see this doctor of yours."

After leaving the plane at the airfield, she drove over to the radio station. She'd just make it for the four-forty call-in. As she usually did, she wondered when Horrie was ever going to build Betty a verandah. They had added two small rooms to the tin-roofed shack as the three children had come along. Cassie was always amazed that she had never seen Betty being anything but cheerful, though at least once a month for almost six years now Betty had nagged Horrie about a verandah. "Somewhere to be in the shade," she would say.

In front of the shack was a new utility, a shiny blue Holden. Hardly anyone ever came out here, and she couldn't help but wonder who was visiting Horrie and Betty.

She walked across the dust to the still-closed door and opened it, waving at Horrie, who was already stationed in front of the radio. As she closed the door, hands reached from behind her and covered her eyes.

Horrie's voice had a lilt to it. "Guess who?"

She stood still a moment and then, with lightning clarity, she knew. Before she could even say his name, tears scalded her eyes. "Sam? Is it you, Sam?"

The hands left her eyes and touched her shoulders, turning her around to face the grin on Sam's face. Throwing her arms around him, she said his name over and over again through a haze of tears. She didn't know that she'd ever been so glad to see anyone in her life. Yet she wasn't sure she'd have known him after so many years.

He was no longer thin; he was solid. He'd grown a bushy mustache, and there were crinkles around his eyes, crow's feet. He was pale under the bush hat that had replaced his baseball cap, but the old sense of fun was still sparkling in his eyes.

"Why didn't you let us know?" she asked.

"And ruin the surprise?"

"When did you arrive?"

"We got here about noon." Sam put his hands on her shoulders and backed away, looking at her. "You sure look good. I like your hair."

Self-consciously she brushed her hand through her shoulder-length waves. "It's so wonderful to see you."

"I came home on the assumption you need a pilot. Last you wrote you were doing it yourself. I just laughed and laughed. I figured there's nothing you can't do—but I'm still hoping you'll need a pilot."

"Oh, God, need one? I can't handle two jobs at once."

It was so good to see him again, to look into those laughing eyes, to remember what flying out with him had been like.

"Where are you living?"

"God knows. Addie's is full-up and the hotel's a fleabag. Been having breakfast with Horrie and Betty. Hey . . . " he walked to the door that separated the radio room from Betty's kitchen and opened it. "Hon, come meet the greatest doctor in the world."

In the doorway appeared a pale-blond, very pretty young woman, smiling. She was, Cassie guessed, about five or six months pregnant.

"Liv, this is the doc you've heard so much about. Cassie, my wife, Olivia."

His wife?

Before she realized she was saying it, she said, "Well, you can stay certainly with us until you find a place. I'm back in Fiona's—we bought it from her. And you can have her old room."

Sam took his hat off and held it. "I can't believe you're Mrs. Chris Adams. That letter sure shocked me."

Why was she so shocked to see Sam married to this blond girl? Olivia wasn't much more than that. Just the kind she'd have predicted though. Olivia probably giggled, she mused.

"Yeah, we're all growing up," Sam went on.

I guess it's about time, Cassie thought. We're grown up and with responsibilities that aren't always the ones we would have chosen.

Chapter 42

"I can't believe it," Cassie exclaimed to Chris. "She's so empty-headed I can't imagine why Sam was attracted to her!"

"You just forget," Chris said as he picked up his coffee. "Sam was always attracted to the prettiest girl in a group, and it didn't matter at all whether she had a brain cell clicking. In fact, I think he preferred it if she didn't."

Cassie shook her head. "Well, he seemed to be getting interested in Sister Claire when he left, and she was brainy."

"That was five years ago."

"I guess so. But Olivia seems—well, I'm just surprised Sam can be happy with someone like that."

"She's pretty enough that he can be proud of her but not so beautiful he has to worry about her. Did you see the way she looked up at him?"

Cassie shook her head as she folded her napkin. "A simpering, little-girl smile. As though anything Sam does and thinks is just perfect."

Chris laughed. "That has its charms, you know."

Cassie's eyes blazed. "I suppose you'd like a woman who agreed with everything you think and do? Who'd gaze at you with cow-like eyes . . ."

"It would be a refreshing change. But, no, my dear." He leaned over to take her hand in his. "That would bore me to extinction. I like my women feisty . . ."

"It's a damned good thing." Cassie relaxed and grinned at him.

"You're glad they found a house so quickly, aren't you?"

"God, ten days was almost more than I could stand, watching her giggle at everything Sam said, and he grinning and basking in all the adoration."

Chris stood up. "Forget Sam and Olivia. Forget Romla . . . "

"Forget Romla? I haven't thought of Romla in ages."

He shook his head. "I forgot. She called yesterday. She and the family are coming on Thursday. I'll tell you later why. It's a nutty idea. But forget her for now."

"No," Cassie said, pulling at his arm. "Tell me."

"Roger's bored with being a policeman in Townsville. And I think Romla, though she didn't admit to it, is bored with the life they're leading."

"She certainly was when I was there."

"Roger's willing to change directions and Romla wants a challenge. She answered an ad for manager of a hotel and guess where? The Royal Palms here."

"The Royal Palms? Sam says it's a fleabag, a nothing."

Chris nodded. "I know, I know. Nevertheless, she and Roger think they'd like to have a go at something new and when she heard the hotel was here she arranged for them to come look at it and see if she thinks it has possibilities. She was quite taken with you, you know."

"And I with her."

"Anyhow, they're all arriving Thursday."

"That should be fun. I'll enjoy seeing her again. You haven't seen her either except that time you went to Brisbane for a conference and stopped off. Of course, I thought Roger a crashing bore." She was beginning to wonder if they were running a boardinghouse.

"Crashing," Chris agreed.

The next day was the first time Sam had flown on a clinic run since his return from the war. As they flew out to Tookaringa, he commented, "Boy, it's parched and this is the rainy season."

Cassie had heard the men talking of a drought for the last year, but no one had run out of water yet and she hadn't heard of any animals dying of thirst.

"If it doesn't rain soon, things'll be in bad shape. Ever been through a drought?"

"Can't say I have," she said, realizing as she looked out the window how dusty the land below her looked. But then she was so used to that, to the great cracks jutting into the bowels of the earth, that this didn't seem much different.

"Droughts out here can ruin everything you work for. I remember about eighteen years ago when the floods came, it ended a five-year drought that ruined families, killed all the animals. People starved to death, left homesteads to go to the cities, gave up dreams."

Cassie looked over at him. "Sam, it is so good to have you back. You've no idea the relief I feel not having to do two jobs at once."

"I was afraid maybe you'd give up doctoring for flying."

Cassie shook her head. "I never really loved the actual flying. I don't have that sixth sense like you do about what does or doesn't work up in the air."

He never told her and she'd never have known—probably no one else in town would have, either—about his wartime exploits if Olivia hadn't shown her the article calling him "a flying ace, a legend in his own time, downing more German planes than any other Australian pilot." The article said he would fly lower and faster than other pilots, seeming to dare ground fire to strafe him.

A restlessness had taken him over. He found it difficult to sit still in social situations, and Cassie noticed that his eyes would glaze over and he would gaze off into space when people were talking to him. He wanted to waste no time readjusting to life, and was anxious to return to work.

Sam turned around to face her. "I'm real surprised you and Chris are together. I thought you and Blake . . . well, anyhow, you could have knocked me over with a feather."

Cassie stared out the window, looking down at the dry, dusty land dotted with hundreds of gum trees. A herd of roos leaped between the trees. "That was over a long time ago."

"Everything here seems like a long time ago. I wonder if anything will ever be the same again. I used to dream of coming back to all I knew and held dear. Now I'm back and nothing seems the same."

"Has so much changed?"

"Everything's changed," Sam said. "The whole world's different."

"Has anyone warned you? Blake's lost an arm."

Sam nodded. "Yeah, you wrote."

"He went down to Melbourne a couple of weeks ago and is back now. He got an electric arm. I'm anxious to see it. He was having psychological problems. But supposedly he can do anything with his new arm that he could before."

"Except feel," Sam said. He pointed. "Look, Tookaringa! I've still never seen any place to compare with it. Seems funny to think Fiona's out here. Boy, will I be glad to see her."

Fiona and Sam hugged each other and Fiona's eyes shone. "Cassie, it's a different world! Wait til you see him. How can I ever thank you?" She said to Sam, "This dear friend of ours may just have saved my sanity. And my husband's. Clinic doesn't start for another hour and I have food ready—coffee cake and fancy stuff. It's a celebration. Blake's even smiling."

"It's true," said his voice from behind them. "I *am* smiling. Sam, welcome home. Good to see you. Been a long time."

Sam shook his hand and looked at Blake's other arm as he raised it. "I'm still pretty clumsy," he said, but there was a buoyancy in his voice. He jutted his arm out to Cassie. "Feel it."

She reached out, uncertainly, and all she felt was dead plastic.

Blake was like a child with a new toy. "Inside there are electric circuits—levers, gears, and a switch just down by the thumb. I can switch the hand on and off. I can carry something, grab it in my hand, and turn the switch off. The damn hand will stay shut holding that thing forever. Isn't it amazing?"

What was amazing was the change in Blake.

"Look! They told me to pick up eggs and test myself that way. Well . . . "

"He's ruined just a couple of dozen eggs," Fiona said, bringing the coffee cake, coffee, and tea out to the verandah.

"See? It's run by a battery." He lifted his sleeve. "Big trouble is it works at its own pace, not quite as quickly as brain waves. However, you know, Cassie, next week I'm going to get back on a horse after—my God, can it be six years?"

He looked directly into Cassie's eyes for the first time in all those years, and his voice softened. "How can I ever thank you? You did me and my family a tremendous favor, Cassie. It was time for someone to get mad at me."

He and Sam sat on the verandah while Cassie conducted the clinic—she could heard snatches of their conversation, mainly Blake's enthusiastic voice. He was telling Sam something about "buying up land, a narrow swath of it all the way to the coast, over a thousand miles."

"You're going to own more than a thousand miles of land?" Sam asked incredulously.

Blake laughed. "Sounds like more than it will be. As this drought continues, if it does, more and more people will want to sell out and I can buy it up cheaply. Not that I want to take advantage of them, but it'll make land available that isn't for sale now. And I'll send my cattle ahead of the drought. It'll start here, near the center, first. I'll march them to the coast, keeping lands ungrazed and waiting for the cattle that'll have to go through it. I can send them that way every year, and keep them fat. But in drought times, I can get rid of them here before they starve to death or become too thin to be of any use. I'll get them to markets when the prices are high . . . "

Fiona smiled at Blake. "He's the only person I know whose dreams always come true."

"That's because," Cassie said, "he *makes* them come true."

"With more than a little help from the women in my life." Blake raised his plastic arm and saluted not only Fiona but Cassie. "If it weren't for her," Cassie heard him say to Sam, "I'd still be lying around feeling sorry for myself. She's a hard taskmaster." Then Blake added, "When are we going to meet this woman in your life?"

Fiona's eyes met Cassie's; did she still think Cassie was in love with Sam?

They didn't talk about the war. It was just as though those years had evaporated, as though life hadn't changed at all. And there seemed to be a new spirit of camaraderie between Blake and Sam.

On the way back in the plane that afternoon, Sam reached out to touch her arm. "I'm sorry, Doc. You had me fooled."

"Sorry about what?" Cassie asked, surprised.

"You're carrying the torch. Maybe he can't see it and maybe Fiona can't see it, but it's obvious to me."

Cassie sat up straight. "You're wrong, Sam. You're completely wrong."

"I'd like to be. Honest to God, I want to be wrong. And if you say so, I'll go along with it. But if you ever need a shoulder . . . "

"Go to hell, Sam."

He laughed. "Ah, that's like the old Cassie. I thought something was wrong, thought you were getting soft."

"Soft? Me? Forget it."

He reached out to take her hand in his and squeezed it. "It's good to be back working with you, Doc. I sure missed you."

She loved the feel of him squeezing her hand. Oh, how good to have him back. Somehow, in the time he'd been gone she felt they'd grown closer. Maybe it was all the letters they'd shared. She thought it was a good thing Sam was married. She just wished she could feel closer to the woman he loved.

The first emergency call since Sam's return was from Mattaburra.

A man's anguished voice cut through the static. "This is Gregory Carlton calling . . . " His voice broke. "My sister's shot!"

Horrie froze. "Shot?"

"Is she dead?" asked Cassie.

"Almost . . . get here . . . oh, God!"

Silence.

Cassie looked at Horrie. "Phone Sam and get him here. Cancel the clinic."

She took her sunglasses out of her bag and wiped them clean as Horrie rang the operator.

"Sam's on his way here anyhow."

Sam sauntered in five minutes later.

"Alison Carlton's been shot. Come on," said Cassie.

As they sped to the airfield, she told Sam, "The only help she's had out there while Greg's been at war is an old aborigine and his wife. Alison's run that place on her own. She stayed in my guest room the couple of times she's come to town. God, how terrible."

Had Greg just walked in, returning from Europe, and found Alison wounded? How long had she been lying there? Cassie couldn't imagine what might have happened.

They were in the air within ten minutes and at Mattaburra in an hour and a half. As they circled the homestead, Greg came running out of the house, waving. Sam coasted onto the field that was always held ready. As he cut off the motor and opened the door, a beat-up utility kicked up dust devils as it chugged around the homestead corner.

Cassie never would have recognized Greg. His eyes were unfocused and bloodshot, his hair awry, he looked—the only word she could think of was *crazy*. After over five years he did not even greet them. Except for the fact that he was driving the truck, Cassie would have thought he was in a comatose state. He turned the truck around and began driving to the house, muttering over and over again, "It's all my fault. Oh, God!"

"Is Alison alive?" Cassie asked.

For a minute she thought he didn't hear her, but he eventually nodded. "Barely."

Greg sat behind the wheel even after he stopped in front of the house. Cassie reached for her bag and jumped out of the truck. He did not follow as she ran up the three steps and across the verandah, swinging open the screen door to the kitchen.

Blood was spattered across the usually neat yellow walls. Clinging to the bright red ooze were slivers of flesh. Crumpled on the floor lay a woman's body, smaller and frailer than Alison's, her chest blown away. A pool of blood stained the wooden floor.

Greg had said Alison was shot. He hadn't mentioned another woman. Cassie headed towards Alison's bedroom as Sam entered the room. "Jesus!"

Alison lay on the bed, a hole where her left breast had been, blood staining her blouse. Cassie could see from the faintly heaving chest that she was still breathing. Clutched tightly in her hand was a pistol. Cassie heard footsteps behind her and before she could even turn, Greg burst into the room, throwing himself across his sister's body. Then he held her head between his hands, crying, "I should have known better. I thought it would solve everything. Oh, God, what have I done?"

Cassie moved to him, leaning down to touch his shoulder. "You didn't do it. The gun's in *her* hand."

His red-rimmed eyes turned to her. "I did it as though I pulled the trigger. Oh, Jesus God!" he sobbed.

"Let me examine her," Cassie said, though she knew the woman had but minutes left.

Greg slid away from his sister, weeping, his head in his hands.

"Who's the other woman?" Cassie asked.

Greg looked up at her, his eyes seeming to sink deeper into their sockets. "My wife," he said, his voice strangling on the word.

Oh, my God, Cassie thought as she examined Alison. "There's nothing I can do. Nothing anyone can do."

She put her arms around Greg's shoulders. It was obvious what had happened. Alison couldn't accept the fact that her brother had returned with a wife. It would have meant she no longer had a place here.

Sam stood in the doorway.

"Christ, we hadn't even been in the house an hour," Greg said, then began to weep again. "I should have written. I should have warned her."

Yes, Cassie thought, he should have. Her eyes met Sam's. "Police will have to come out and ask questions." She watched Alison breathe her last, and thought it far better than to have her live through an inquest, through a trial, through imprisonment. Meanwhile, Sam would have to get body bags from the plane and they'd clean up the mess. Certainly Greg was in no condition to help.

"Do you want to tell me how it happened?" She thought the police would appreciate the information.

He was silent for so long that Cassie walked into the kitchen, stepped across the body of Greg's dead wife, and put a kettle of water on to boil. She found rags in the pantry and began to scrub the wall. Fragments of skin clung to the damp cloth. She felt sick to her stomach. He'd had no way of knowing, Cassie told herself. It wasn't his fault. Alison must have known that someday . . . after all, Greg wasn't much more than in his early thirties, even now. Alison should have known that someday he'd want a wife, a family.

Cassie found a blanket in a hall closet and covered the wife's body.

The water on the stove boiled. She found tea, steeped it, and took a cup of it in to Greg, who was still sitting beside his sister's body, staring into her vacant eyes. He brushed his hand through the air, indicating he wanted no tea.

"I don't care whether you want it or not, drink it."

He looked up at Cassie and then took the cup from her as she sat down next to him to drink her own tea.

"I knew all along I was being unfair to Susan," he said, his voice shaking, his hands trembling. "But I thought it would solve our problems, end the lies we've been living all our lives."

She didn't want to hear this. Sam walked over to stand beside her, resting a hand on her shoulder as she sat erect in the straight chair, looking at Greg, hearing a bird chirp outside the window. A faint breeze rustled the organdy curtain. Cassie was afraid she knew what was coming.

Greg turned to look at her. "I thought if Susan came out here with me, if she and Alison could be friends, we could all . . . oh, Christ! I knew better. In my heart I knew better. I just wanted to break the pattern, the vicious cycle that Alison and I've lived in. I didn't love Susan. I've never loved any woman except Alison." He dropped his cup on the floor, bending over to put his head in his hands, crying ragged tears that tore through Cassie's heart.

At the same time she felt slightly ill.

"I thought," he wept, "that I could keep us from going to hell."

Cassie stood up and walked to the window, fingering the billowing curtain. In the distance she saw a black and white cow munching at a trough.

"Don't tell me," she whispered.

He didn't seem to hear her. "We came here after our parents died, hoping to escape society's strictures, hoping we might find a place that wasn't as uncompromisingly rigid in what it believed to be right and wrong."

In the hush, Cassie looked out the window, and she heard Sam say, "But you couldn't escape yourselves?"

She could hardly hear Greg's voice. "We tried, years ago, to stop ourselves. Alison toured Europe for nearly a year, and we hoped we'd each meet someone else. But we went mad with the separation. From the time we were thirteen and fourteen we found ways to escape our parents' supervision. We found an attic room where no one ever went, not even the servants, and we spent hours up there, under the eaves, doing things we knew were wrong, were evil, things that would send us to hell, but we couldn't stop. We loved each other so much that nothing else mattered."

Cassie wondered if she might be sick. At the same time, she felt enormous sympathy for Greg.

He got up and walked over to stand behind her, pointing to a tree near the fence. "We buried our child under that tree," he said. "I delivered the baby, and together we smothered him, so our sins would not be compounded. Even then we could not stop. I thought if I came home with a wife that Alison and I could not continue to live in this manner. I knew—Jesus Christ, I knew in my heart—that it was a vain hope. I knew it was unfair to Susan, that I was using her to exorcise the demons within me and within Alison. I knew I was not being fair, but I never meant for her to die."

Cassie could not turn to face him.

"I killed her as directly as I killed that son of ours. I might as well have killed Alison. I murdered all three of them," he said. Then with a bitter laugh he added, "And I had trouble killing a German soldier whose face I saw across the lines in North Africa!"

He's going to kill himself if we leave, Cassie told herself, knowing she would never tell the police what he had just told her. She would say Alison had killed the wife out of jealousy and that would be that.

She turned and put her arms around him, letting him cry on her shoulder, letting sobs wrack his body as he stood holding onto her. Sam's eyes were on her, and he shook his head slowly.

He disappeared and when he came back he brought two body bags.

To Greg she said, "Come on, fly back with us. You'll have to talk to the police. It'll be easier if we do it now."

"No." He shook his head, his body rigid.

Sam's hand touched her arm. "Don't," he said. "Leave him be."

She looked at him, and she knew he knew what Greg would do. He's telling me not to stop Greg. It's probably for the best. Again she thought she might vomit.

"I'll send police out tomorrow."

Greg nodded. "Yes."

In the plane, the only conversation Cassie and Sam had was when she asked him, "You know what he's going to do, don't you?"

"Of course," Sam replied, his voice dull.

And when the police did arrive, late the next morning, they found exactly what Cassie and Sam expected them to find.

Chapter 43

"I do think it's terribly exciting," Romla said, peering into the mirror, adjusting one of her earrings.

"It's awful," Cassie said, slipping a dress over her head. "I'd never even been in the hotel before. It's ghastly. Paper peeling from the walls. Rooms a shambles, mattresses sagging. The bar smells—it's all such a mess."

"Exactly," Romla agreed, smiling brightly. "Think of the challenge. Augusta Springs is growing, Cassie, and except for Addie's which—let's face it, is terribly plebeian—there's no place in town that's decent."

"Well, certainly the Royal Palms isn't a candidate. Zip me up, will you?"

"But that's just what it is," Romla insisted as she zippered Cassie's green moire dress. "You look absolutely gorgeous. I can really envision what that hotel could become."

"Romla, no one in this town will even bother to come to it, and there aren't that many passers-through."

"Name me a really good restaurant in town."

Cassie nodded, running a comb through her hair. "Addie's is the only decent place to eat."

"And it has such atmosphere, doesn't it? What about elegance? Romance? And mixed drinks, I mean like martinis and sloe gin fizzes and whiskey sours? They don't even know how to make them around here. What about dances?"

"Like tonight or at Addie's?"

"Sure, with not an ounce of atmosphere. Look at tonight. A dance at the gym! Don't you yearn for a little class?"

"I forget what class is like. As for dancing, this is the first time in all the years your brother and I've been together that he's even been willing to go to a dance. That's just because you're here and he wants to show you the town."

"Oh, Cassie, I could change the social life of this town!"

Cassie looked at Romla in her vibrant red dress, her green eyes sparkling. It was easy to forget Romla wasn't beautiful—her enthusiasm sparked life in Cassie. But Cassie knew no one person could change the social life of Augusta Springs. It was a dusty cow town, a rail head. True, more people had moved to it and there was a housing shortage, but she couldn't imagine Augusta Springs ever becoming a tourist center or a place where people would flock to live. But it *was* growing. Steven had just given a gift to add a new wing to the hospital and Chris was interviewing doctors to expand the staff. He'd run it almost single-handedly since before the war; now, he was overworked and tired all the time and agreed he needed a partner. He had said he wouldn't even feel jealous if a new doctor came to town. He needed another surgeon, and he could use a pediatrician.

"How about a psychiatrist?" Cassie asked.

"Not enough call for one out here," he'd answered.

But the Royal Palms providing a living for Romla and her family?

"Roger could run the bar and I'd run the restaurant and the rooms. The people who are considering buying it are willing to sink money into it to get it going. It can be bought for a song."

"How does Roger feel about moving here?"

"Oh, he says he's willing to go anyplace I want to go. He's ready for a change, too. He'd like it better if I'd go to Sydney or Brisbane, but he's willing to give this a go. Of course, Pamela's away at school anyhow, and Terry could only go to school here another two years, but that'd be true even in Townsville. He'll have to go away to boarding school. Right now he's enthusiastic about a move to the bush. Maybe we'll even have a school beyond eighth grade by then.

"Of course, Chris and Roger never get along, but you and Chris are the reasons I'm high on this idea. I haven't really spent time with my brother in far too many years. And marrying you is the best thing that could have happened to him." She hugged Cassie.

"Well, it certainly would be fun having you here."

"Okay, it's settled." Romla slashed lipstick across her mouth. "Let's go. I'm ready."

The school gymnasium was draped with robin's-egg-blue and white crepe paper; a strobe light, hung from the center of the ceiling, swirled around, casting shadowed patterns on the dancers. Since liquor was not permitted, a bar had been set up outside, though lemonade and soda pop were served from a long table in a corner. This was the first fundraiser the Flying Doctors had sponsored, aimed at purchasing new medical equipment. People had come into town from miles around, and no one had a free guest room. Addie's, and even the hotel, were filled up. Tomorrow morning there would be an outdoor breakfast down by the big gum trees along the river, which was now but a trickle.

"Roger will never get past the bar," Romla said. "I couldn't make him dance if his life depended on it."

The room, as was this whole part of the continent, was lop-sided with men. No woman was a wallflower. And Romla, despite her thirty-three years, was the center of attention wherever she turned.

Romla was right. Roger never even stuck his nose in the gym, preferring to stand outside, talking and drinking.

Though Blake and Fiona had not come into town, Steven had, and as soon as he saw Cassie he headed toward her. "Going to give an old man the first dance?"

"I don't see any old men," Cassie said, pretending to look around.

"Flattery will get you everywhere," he said, reaching out for her hand as the band began to play, "I'll Never Smile Again."

"And I thought I wouldn't," Steven said as he put his arms around her.

"Thought you wouldn't what?" Cassie had forgotten how delightful dancing could be.

"Smile again. I'll miss Jenny every day of my life, but I *am* getting pleasure out of some things again."

"Time does heal," Cassie murmured. Yes, a knife didn't cut through her heart every single time she saw Blake.

"Like dancing with you." He pulled her closer and they moved gracefully across the floor, which was becoming more crowded.

"You're a good dancer, Steven."

"And you're getting more and more beautiful. I like your hair long."

"Thanks," she said. "And you, I can tell, are enjoying being a grandfather."

Steven laughed. "I *love* being a grandfather. Fiona and little Jenny are the best things that have happened to us since . . . well, Jenny would have loved Fiona and her granddaughter. She always thought it'd be you and Blake. So did I. Maybe it was wishful thinking on our part. I certainly never suspected you and Chris would . . . "

Out of the corner of her eye, Cassie noticed Sam and Olivia in the doorway. Olivia looked as though she were about to give birth at any moment. She clung to Sam's arm and looked around the room. Cassie couldn't tell whether it was with fear or pleasure.

Sam caught her eye and waved.

Steven turned to follow Cassie's gaze. "Pretty thing, isn't she?"

Thing? Maybe that's what Olivia was. Cassie still couldn't warm to her. She and Chris had Sam and Livvie to dinner and her conversation centered around the pains and aches of pregnancy, how dry and brown Australia was after Suffolk, and how hot it was in Augusta Springs. Also, she hadn't expected Sam to be away on overnight clinics or pick up and rush out without warning so often.

Cassie danced with several of the men who'd come to town for the occasion, and then turned to Chris. "Do I have to ask you to dance?"

"My dear, I haven't danced in twenty-five years."

"You should have told me—I could have taught you. Come on, just shuffle your feet in a two-step. She took his hand and led him onto the dance floor. "What a Difference a Day Makes . . . " she began to hum along with the band. "Hey, you're not bad. You underestimate yourself," she murmured. His hand tightened around her.

She saw Sam walk over to the leader of the band and talk to him, then turn to search for her, waiting until the song ended before crossing the dance floor.

"My turn, Chris," he said, reaching for her. "They're gonna play our kind of music," he whispered. "Ready?"

"I haven't jitterbugged since the last time we danced together."

The bandleader began to sing, "Pardon me, boy, is this the Chattanooga Choo Choo . . . " as Sam swung her out, and a rhythm filled her that she had thought she'd lost. Sam caught her as she whirled out and back again, and their feet clicked in steps she hadn't practiced in six years. The light pressure of his hand on her back told her exactly what he wanted to do next, and she abandoned herself to the music and joy of the moment.

"Sam," she said, when they were close, "it is *so* good to have you home again."

"You've changed, Doc," he said, "but thank goodness your dancing hasn't."

"Changed? Is that good or bad?"

"I like it," he said with a grin, sending her twirling. "You're softer. Not as argumentative, but still a bit feisty. Hell, I'd hate to have you lose that. I'm glad to be back working with you, too, Doc. Glad to be dancin' with you again. Glad all's right with the world again."

But when the slow music began again, Sam smiled at her, bowed slightly, and headed back toward Olivia, who was sitting in a straight chair against the wall.

Cassie noted that Romla was standing by the punch bowl talking with Peter Teakle, and realized she'd seen them dancing together several times during the evening. Peter was someone she knew of but had not seen much. He spent most of his time traveling from one little bush town to another, overseeing his family interests.

Later, when Romla asked Cassie about him, Cassie said, "They own *the* store in all these little towns that have nothing more than a store and gas station. The whole Outback buys its supplies from Teakle and Robbins. They send to them for a bed or a new bassinet or a stove and for all their food supplies. Two or three times a year a caravan—used to be camels, but now it's trucks—stops at each of the homesteads, bringing supplies of all kinds. I think Peter's in charge of all that, so that's probably why I never see him. Of course, he was off in the war, and I think he just returned recently. I haven't seen him in years. Every eligible girl set her cap for Peter before the war, but he never fell for anyone, even though he led a pretty active social life, as I recall. But he's out of town more often than in. He gave you a rush tonight, didn't he?"

Romla nodded. "I know, and it was rather fun. I told him I'm married, and that didn't seem to bother him at all. He was just nice. I introduced him to Roger when we went outside, and when I told him we were moving here he said he thought we'd be a great addition to the town."

"Ah, so you've decided? The challenge is the thing that appeals to you, right?"

Romla put an arm around Cassie. "That and the opportunity to be near you and Chris. I need more in my life than just Roger. I need to accomplish something and be with people I love. I want to come, and I've spent the whole day thinking of what I can do for the Royal Palms and Augusta Springs. I'm going to shake it up, Cassie."

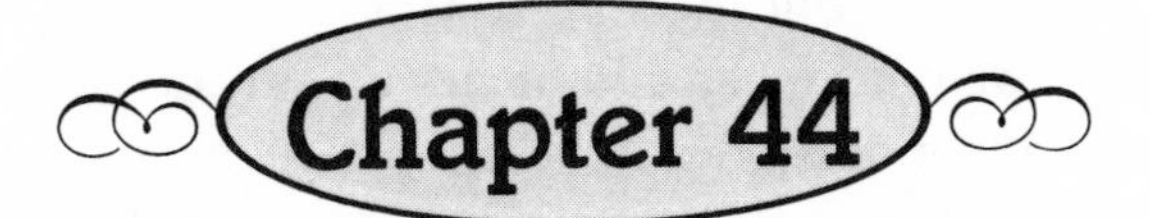

Chapter 44

"The only way I can even try to land is if you have some way of lighting up a field," Sam said as he grasped the mike. Horrie had called to tell them there was an emergency. Sam and Cassie had arrived at the radio shack simultaneously—Cassie was disheveled because Horrie had awakened her. Although it was just ten, she'd been asleep nearly an hour.

"You'll have to get cars and utilities lined up with their headlights on and set lanterns around the edge of the field. I can't land if I can't see what I'm landing on."

Not quite a hundred and fifty miles west there had been an accident, a car and a van filled with cattle. The driver of the van and the three inhabitants of the car were all seriously injured.

"We're afraid to move any of them," the caller had told Cassie. She'd looked at Sam and he'd taken the mike from her.

"I know the vicinity and I think I can get there in the dark, but being able to land will depend on how well lit the strip is."

He nodded as he listened to the caller and, before hanging up, said, "Look for us in about an hour and half." Then, turning to Cassie, he said, "You ready for a night flight?"

"We don't have a choice."

"Let me phone Liv," Sam said as he picked up the phone. Their baby was overdue. "Just my luck to have it born tonight."

"Chris is home."

Sam was back directly. "Okay, Liv doesn't think the baby'll arrive tonight and she has Chris's phone number memorized. Though, dammit, Cassie, I wish it were you delivering my baby."

Chris would have let her, she knew, but she had not mentioned it to him. There had been no question about who would deliver Fiona's baby, even though she had come into the hospital for the birth. Cassie had the idea that Olivia preferred Chris. She'd heard her say once, not realizing Cassie was within hearing distance, "Women shouldn't be doctors. I don't want a woman poking her fingers up me."

Silver from the moon's rays reflected off the plane. Stars studded the inkiness, but below them there was no light at all. Buckled into her seat, Cassie felt relieved that she didn't have to go on this journey alone. She closed her eyes and slept, awakening when Sam called back to her, "There it is. They lit the field up well. Good for them."

Leaning forward to look out the window, she saw a rectangle outlined about five hundred feet below. "I'm going to buzz over it a couple of times to get the lay of the land," he said, as though to himself. She looked at him and realized he wasn't wearing a hat. Actually, she liked his new bush hat so much better than his baseball cap. She also liked his mustache.

"Hold on," he called.

He bumped across the field, but—considering the conditions—Cassie thought it a near-perfect landing. Three men stood outside the plane, and one of them reached out to shake Sam's hand. "I'm Bob Mason—I'm the one who called. Afraid you'll have to get in my utility. It's close on to twenty miles away, but there's no flat land between here and there."

In half an hour they reached the scene of the crash. Cattle had escaped from the van and were roaming the countryside, blocking the road. The immense truck was on its side, and Cassie rushed there first. The driver was crumpled on the seat, dead.

She turned her attention to the car. The windshield and side windows were smashed and the front end was crushed in like an accordion. The woman from the passenger's seat had been thrown from the car and was lying inertly, blood coagulating on her head. She looked like a stick figure. Even before she leaned down to feel the woman's pulse, Cassie knew she was dead. Sandwiched in behind the steering wheel was the driver, his neck broken.

Whimpering on the ground lay a girl, perhaps twelve years old.

Cassie knelt beside the unconscious child and found the pulse rate slowed down to sixty. She was in a severe coma, her breathing rate increased from a normal twenty to thirty.

Cassie said, "I need a neurosurgeon. I can't handle this."

Sam's hand found her shoulder. "Of course you can. We just have to figure what to do."

"She needs hospitalization, but I dare not move her."

"What's an alternative?" Sam asked, kneeling down next to her, looking at her rather than at the child.

"Get advice from a neurosurgeon. I suspect it's a hematoma."

They were silent. How were they to do that in the middle of no where, over a thousand miles from a neurosurgeon?

"I've got a pedal wireless in my utility," said Bob.

"What good is that if no one's ready to answer on the opposite end?" asked Sam.

Bob scratched his head. "I could drive home and phone a hospital—tell them what frequency we're on and have a doctor wait for your call."

Sam raised an eyebrow at Cassie. "What about it?"

"Can't lose," she said.

Sam turned to Bob. "You got a wireless at the house, too?"

Bob nodded.

"Okay, the doc'll tell you who to call. You make radio contact after you reach him by phone, and we'll be on the frequency here. You listen in case you have to bring anything to us, okay?"

Bob nodded.

"Now," Sam said to Cassie, "what hospital do you want to contact for a doctor?"

The only neurosurgeon Cassie knew was Ray Graham. She told Bob his name and the name of the hospital that could contact him.

It was an hour before contact was made, an hour during which Cassie sat holding the young girl's hand, monitoring her pulse rate and breathing.

"What's a hematoma?" Sam asked.

"In simplest terms, it's a swelling containing blood."

"Okay, not in simplest?"

Cassie smiled in the dark. These terms meant nothing to Sam. She wondered why he even bothered to ask, but the fact that he did ask made her feel like she was sharing something with him.

"I suspect this is a subdural hematoma, associated with cerebral laceration. A fall, something slamming into the head. The treatment is to get rid of the blood clot."

Sam nodded. They talked of nothing in particular, until he said, "I thought about you and about Augusta Springs all the time I was in England. The worst part was not doing anything, waking up mornings with nothing to do unless we had a raid. Just sitting, all day long, playing cards, talking of home, or staring out into the fog, waiting for orders.

"Olivia was the first girl I met after I got your letter telling me you'd married Chris. She was a Red Cross volunteer and she gave me that letter. Such a shocker. It took me a couple days . . . Liv was pretty and she batted those long eyelashes at me. She handed me a pack of gum and smiled and said, 'Why, Captain, you look like you were just waiting for me.' It was all I could do not to reach out right then and there and grab her."

He was quiet for a while. In the distance a dingo howled. "She fed me for the next three weeks, and then we got married."

Cassie raised her eyebrows. "You only knew her three weeks?"

He nodded. "That was when I was in Dorset training other pilots, just like I'd done when I first went over. That was okay with me by then."

After further silence, he asked, "Do you love him, Doc?"

Just then they heard static on the pedal wireless Sam and Bob had hauled out of the truck. Sam twirled dials, glad Bob had left a flashlight with them. They could hear cows all around them but couldn't see them.

Then Bob came on the air. "I've got Dr. Graham. He's on the phone, and I'll hold it up to the transceiver here and hope you can hear."

"Dr. Graham, this is Dr. Cassandra Clarke out of Augusta Springs." She waited for her name to register. He must be surprised to hear from her after all these years she thought, and in the middle of the night.

"Yes, Doctor?" His voice sounded sleepy.

"I'm out here in the bush," she said, then described the accident and the condition of the young girl.

"Sounds like a subdural hematoma," Graham said.

"That's what I thought, but I'm not exactly sure what to do."

"You'll have to drill a hole in her head to relieve the pressure and let the fluid out."

"I don't have the right medical equipment here."

There was a moment's pause and then Graham's voice sprinted over the wires from Melbourne. "Someone up there must have a drill. Just get a drill from a garage, from a barn. Sterilize it in boiling water. Not too large a bit, of course."

"That'll take awhile."

There was a long silence, and then Bob's voice. "I'm bringing a drill right out, though it'll be half an hour til I get there. My wife will call Dr. Graham on the phone again and hook us up on the radio. I'll be right there."

Cassie turned to Sam. "A carpenter's drill?" A shiver passed through her. Drill a hole in the girl's head?

"Oh, Sam, I've never done such a thing." She looked at the girl, her face pale in the moonlight, her breathing coming more rapidly and shallowly. "She'll probably be dead by the time Bob gets back. Two hours will have passed since we got here."

He leaned over and said, "You can only do your best. You can't do any more than that."

They sat in silence until Bob arrived with two sterilized drills, each a different size.

They reconnected with Ray Graham over the wireless, which Bob pedaled while Cassie talked.

"Subdural hematomas are usually bilateral," said Graham.

"I know," Cassie responded, "but I don't know which side to try."

The almost-forgotten voice of Ray Graham crossed the miles. "It doesn't matter. She's going to die anyway if you don't do something. Try one side and if you don't get any blood, try the other."

Cassie looked up at Sam, who had wedged the flashlight in a firm place, leaving him free to help. "Hold her head firmly," Cassie said.

She took a deep breath and listened as Ray Graham led her through the operation.

"Make a small cut in the skin."

She did.

"Now, do you have any retractors?"

"Yes."

"Then pull away the skin until you can see the bone. It should be glistening white."

It was, even in the dark of night. The flashlight beamed directly onto it.

"Okay, now apply the drill and slowly advance it through almost half an inch of bone."

Sam made a sound deep in his throat.

Graham's voice continued through the static. "Instead of wood shavings at the end of your drill you'll get bony shavings and white watery stuff that looks like thick pudding."

"That's just what I'm getting," Cassie murmured. "Hold her head steady, Sam."

Sam was holding the girl's head tight but looking at Cassie's face.

Then Cassie shouted, "I hit a blood pocket and it's like striking oil!" Bloody water gushed out suddenly.

"You get the jackpot," Graham said. "The pressure will be relieved and within a few minutes some of the breathing signs and the pulse rate should reverse themselves. You can move her then, and fly her back to a hospital."

"Thank you, Doctor," said Cassie as the fluid continued to squirt from the head cavity.

"My pleasure," he said. "If you're ever in Melbourne, drop in. Good job, Doctor."

He hadn't recognized her. Her name meant nothing to him.

"You can sign off," Cassie said to Bob. "We can move her now and fly her home."

"What about these others, the bodies?" Bob asked.

"We'll take them along, too," Sam said, standing. "Any ID? Do we know who to notify?"

Bob held out a sheaf of papers. "We found these on the driver of the truck, and this is the wallet of the driver of the car. They're probably the girl's parents. Poor kid."

Sam took the papers and turned to Cassie. She nodded. He knelt down and gently picked up the young girl, stretching her out on blankets in the back of the truck. Cassie climbed in and placed the girl's head on her lap.

"I wonder if she has any relatives. Can you imagine how awful it's going to be for her to wake up and discover that her parents are dead? Look at the papers and find out where they're from."

Sam glanced at the driver's license. "Alice Springs," he said. "We'll have to phone the police over there. Have Constable Melby do it."

When Sam called Horrie on the plane's radio to request an ambulance, Horrie said, "Olivia's gone to the hospital. So has Doc Adams."

"Maybe I better take the controls," Cassie teased. "You're going to be a nervous wreck."

But Sam flew straight as an arrow and made a smooth landing on the brightly lit tarmac. Pale pink streaked the sky to the east.

"I'll follow the ambulance in my utility," Sam said, but in fact he beat it.

Cassie saw that her patient was settled before walking down to the waiting room where Sam was pacing. "Thought you might like company."

"Can you go see how she is? Find out what's happening?"

Cassie walked down the hall and through the doors, then down the hallway to the operating room. Peering in through the small windows, she saw a smiling Sister Frances holding a baby. She wrapped a blanket around it and placed it in Olivia's arms.

Cassie walked back to the waiting room. "It looks like Olivia's fine and you have a child—boy or girl, I don't know."

Sam let out a yell, picked Cassie up, and hugged her while turning around in circles. "I'm a father!" he shouted.

The young girl recuperated well physically, but not emotionally. When she heard of the death of her parents she stopped eating and, after four days, had to be fed intravenously. She didn't talk at all, but stared vacantly into space.

Her aunt and uncle lived in Tennant Creek and, when the girl was physically ready to be discharged, the uncle—a stringbean of a man—drove to Augusta Springs and looked at the silent child. "Got eight of my own," he said, a toothpick clenched between his teeth. "Don't know how I'll feed another." But he leaned over and kissed the child on her forehead. The girl smiled feebly and whispered, "Hello, Uncle Jack."

He gathered her up in his arms and carried her out to his utility, where Cassie bundled her in a blanket with a pillow under her head.

She watched them drive away, tears in her eyes.

Sam, who had torn himself away from his son, saw Cassie standing on the hospital steps, wiping away her tears. He went out to put an arm around her, but by the time he reached the front door, Cassie had disappeared.

A week later she received a letter at the Flying Doctor radio center.

When I awoke the morning after leading you through that middle-of-the-night hematoma, I found myself saying, "Cassandra Clarke. I know her." There can't be two doctors in Australia with a name like that. And memories floated back to me. It's been a long time, Doctor, but I hope you'll accept my apologies. I'm not proud of the way I treated you. I was afraid you'd make a scene and I never know how to handle such things.

My wife and I did divorce, after all, and I've married again. I have a two-year-old son, the joy of my middle age, the same age as my granddaughter.

I've wondered, over the years, whatever became of you.

Now I know, at least, what you're doing professionally. That was good work the other night, Doctor. Congratulations. You always had the makings of a really fine physician.

If you're ever in Melbourne, look me up. We'll have a drink together.

Raymond J. Graham, M.D.

Yes, have a drink together—for old times' sake.

Cassie shredded the letter and tossed the pieces in the air. Smiling, she realized she could finally put Ray Graham to rest.

Chapter 45

"I feel," said Fiona, "like I'm never going to achieve anything other than a woman's usual destiny."

"So what's wrong with that? You have three children . . . beautiful children, I may add."

"Cassie, my dear, you're just slightly prejudiced. And I adore them. I'm married to the only man I've ever loved and I'm inordinately happy. But is this it? Am I to live my whole life vicariously, through my husband and children?"

Cassie studied her friend as she sipped iced tea on Tookaringa's verandah. The clinic was over and she and Sam would be heading back in half an hour. They didn't stay overnight on clinic runs unless absolutely necessary, because Olivia wanted Sam home nights. Cassie suspected they'd had a big row about it, and Sam half apologized when he'd asked for as few overnights as possible.

"You must be busy all the time, with your children and Blake . . . "

" . . . and Steven, too, you know. Blake's off half the time, buying land and cattle, overseeing his other stations, fulfilling his dream. Ever since he bought that helicopter, I never see him. He's talking now of getting a Cessna, too. It's not that I'm lonely—I've more than enough to do. Don't get me wrong, Cassie. I love every single bit of it. I love my life. Yet, I feel I've lost a part of myself. I don't do anything just for *me.* It seems I've always pleasing others, doing things for them."

"I think," Cassie smiled, "that's called nurturing, and you've always been that kind of person, Fi, even when you were teaching."

"I wish I could do that again. It gave me such pleasure. Or flying, though it wasn't on a par with teaching. I mean, I got such intense pleasure from seeing a kid's eyes light up with a new thought or question. I yearn for that again.

"And I want so much to help the aborigines. I don't have the time and energy, but oh, how I want to start schools on these missions. I dream of it."

"Yet, look what happened to Marian and Anna," said Cassie. "You educated them, gave them the tools to be part of the white man's world, and what did they do when they graduated? Went back to their tribe. I see them a couple of times a year, sitting around, wearing torn clothes, looking and acting quite content."

Fiona sighed. "I know. Because, I suspect, they were made to feel like shit in a white man's world."

"Not just that," argued Cassie, pouring herself more tea from the pitcher on the table beside her. "But inbred ideas. They hate living in the houses we build for them. They trash them. They don't take owning anything seriously like we do, preferring to live under branch boughs, outdoors, part of the universe. They can't understand why we coop ourselves up in little enclosures . . . "

"And we can't understand why they don't want our comforts."

"Also, they're not allowed the freedoms we have. After all, it's illegal to sell liquor to them."

"Are you against that?" asked Fiona, running a hand through her newly bobbed hair.

"Actually, I'm not sure how I feel about liquor. But I do drink, and I believe in everyone's right to choose, even if it's their own destruction. We treat the aborigines like slightly retarded children, not responsible for themselves. Just because some of them seem to have a genetic propensity to drink themselves to oblivion doesn't mean we should forbid it. Lots of whites do that, too. I personally think it's physical rather than psychological. I'm not saying people don't drink when they're depressed, which only compounds the whole issue, and I'm against the harm liquor does. Yet I'm for a person's right to choose. I'd vote for their right to drink liquor if they want."

"The question remains, why would aborigines want to come to our towns and cities and be rejected, ridiculed, looked on with scorn?"

"So, why do you want to educate them?"

"To change the course of society. Someday, Cassie, some of them are going to show the doubters that they have brains, that they can accomplish the same things we can."

"But do they want to?"

"Much as we may resent it, and they, too, they have to evolve or perish. And I want to help in that evolution in some way."

Cassie stood up. "You're a born teacher, Fiona. You think the world can be saved by education."

Fiona smiled. "I wish I saw more of you. Twice a month isn't enough. I miss you in my life, and I envy your new friend, Romla. Not just that you two get to see each other all the time, but she's like you, doing something on her own that fulfills her."

"Well, her husband's helping. It's a joint venture, you know."

"Who are you kidding? I was in town and saw what she's done. That hotel is downright elegant. And dilled blanquette of veal! I mean, really! It's unlike anything we've seen around here."

"I can't imagine such a project succeeding in Augusta Springs."

"Well, count your blessings as long as they're here."

"She's hired a chef from San Francisco," Cassie said. "Can you imagine? And she's decorated each of the rooms differently. She and Roger have a room in one wing, and there are two bedrooms across the hall for the children. Romla loves it, and says she's never, ever cooking another meal. Of course, the bar is where they make the money."

"That's always so. But that's all her husband does, tend bar. And from the looks of it, he's going to drink up any profits."

"He better not. It's not their hotel. They're only the managers."

"Well, it's *her* project, and I envy her that. Not that I envy that husband. That son of hers is irresistible, though."

Cassie enjoyed her visits with Fiona more when Blake was away, when she didn't have to see him. Several times when he had about decided to give up mastering that plastic arm, Fiona had called her and she'd fly out and fight him. But that was all over. Nevertheless, the abrasiveness of those encounters lingered.

She and Fiona twined their arms around each other and started down the verandah steps, heading toward the plane out in the back field behind the outbuildings. Cassie was dressed in her usual bush clothes—tailored gabardine slacks, a cotton shirt with a kerchief tied around her neck to absorb perspiration, high-heeled boots, and her Stetson.

Fiona, likewise, was in slacks, but she wore a clinging silk blouse and sandals. Even in her expensively tailored pants she looked eminently feminine.

"There's not another bush wife who looks like you always do," Cassie told her.

"Blake likes me to look this way. I've gotten in the habit even when he's not here. Though I must admit, when he's away I don't always change to a dress for dinner."

Cassie thought there was another reason Fiona could always look this way: she had two nannies to look after the children. Fiona always recaptured her figure quickly, and Cassie could understand why Blake was proud of her.

Sam came pacing along the path from the opposite direction. "Just talked with Horrie," he called. "Emergency."

"I'm ready." Cassie leaned over to kiss Fiona's cheek.

"Ambrose Pulham's been killed."

Cassie remembered seeing Sylvia Pulham's black eye more than once when they'd stopped on brief between-clinic runs when Sylvia was pregnant. All five of those kids seemed petrified when their father was near. Last time they'd been called not because of Sylvia's pregnancy but because the littlest one had fallen from his high chair and suffered a broken nose and a concussion. They'd had to fly him to the hospital and the children had all screamed when their mother boarded the plane with the eight-month-old baby. Cassie never did believe he fell from a high chair.

When she talked it over with Chris, he said, as he had years earlier, "There's nothing we can do about it, Cassie. We can't interfere with families." But he added, "Christ, there's as much killing around here as in the war."

When Cassie had tried to talk to Sylvia, she reiterated again and again that the baby had fallen. No, her black eyes had been caused by her walking into a door—wasn't that silly?—and tripping and falling in the dark in the barn. How clumsy she was. No, the children weren't afraid of their father, it was just that they were so unused to strangers that they were shy when Cassie was around.

And now the oldest, Dan, had killed his father.

It was a purple and pink twilight when they landed at the Pulhams', bumping over the rocky ground. Pulham never had the landing field in good condition. No car drove out to greet them, and Sam carried Cassie's medical bag as they walked the half-mile to the house.

"Always looks and sounds the same," Cassie said, listening to the cattle lowing and the birds chattering in the branches as they settled in for the night.

"Did you expect everything to be dead?"

"I guess so." Cassie had to run to keep up with Sam's loping steps.

Sylvia was waiting for them, standing on the verandah, her arm embracing a post. She wore a clean apron over her dress and was holding a bloody raw steak to her eye. She opened the screen door and jerked her head toward the other side of the parlor. "He's in there." She did not follow them into the bedroom.

Ambrose Pulham had been shot straight through the head—one shotgun blast at close range left him headless. His body lay across the bed, his head spattered against the headboard.

His wife stood in the kitchen in front of the stove, her left cheek swollen and turning purple. She was frying bacon and potatoes. "The kids're out collecting eggs. They'll be in in a minute. Join us for supper?"

Sam sat in a chair, but Cassie stood in the doorway, unsettled by Sylvia's attitude.

Sylvia looked at Sam and reached for a cup, pouring tea into a mug. "Sugar?"

"No, thanks."

She plopped the cup on the table in front of him. "I'll set two more places."

"What happened?" Cassie forced herself to ask, feeling they must be in a dream.

"I'll tell you," said a boy's voice as Dan walked in from the back door. He carried a basket full of eggs and was followed by the younger children. No one seemed upset.

"I kilt him."

He handed the basket to his mother and turned to look at Sam.

"Wash your hands," said his mother. The children clambered around the sink.

"Wanna tell us about it?" Sam asked. "We'll have to tell the police over in Augusta Springs."

"Papa told me to clean the gun, the shotgun in the bedroom there, and then he told me to load it. It went off while I was . . . " His eyes went blank and Sylvia looked over at her son.

"While he was loading it. He didn't know about the trigger."

Sam shot a glance at Cassie. A fourteen-year-old boy in the Outback not knowing about a trigger?"

Sam leaned back in his chair, tilting the front legs in the air. "Let's try out self-defense."

The spoon Sylvia held clattered to the floor. "Let me feed the kids first and then we'll go into the parlor while they eat."

Dan said, "Me, too, Mama."

She nodded. Her swollen eye was beginning to purple.

When the four of them were seated in the parlor, Sylvia asked, "So you don't think the police will believe that?"

"Not for a minute," Sam said.

Cassie sat on the edge of the sofa, wanting to put her arms around both the mother and son. Sylvia turned to her. "You knew, didn't you? When we had to bring the baby to the hospital? You knew he hadn't fallen from his high chair?"

Cassie nodded. "I suspected. That and your black eyes when I've seen you over the years."

Sylvia said to Dan. "Take off your shirt, son. Show them your back."

His back was striped with raised white welts, some of the scars years old. One streak still oozed blood.

"Oh, my Lord," Cassie whispered. "Here, let me put antiseptic on that."

"He only did it when he drank," Sylvia said, her voice an apology.

"We'd hide his liquor and we'd throw it down the sink. He'd be furious but he wouldn't hit us. He only did it when he was drunk."

"How long has this been going on?" Cassie asked.

Sylvia shrugged. "Whenever he got drink into him."

"He beat Mama until she was bloody," Dan said, and his voice began to crack. "Then he'd rape her."

Sylvia shot a look at him. "How do you even know what that word means?"

"Mama, I'm not stupid. I knew what he was doing to you when you were crying and screaming. I saw blood on the sheets mornings. I heard you whimpering like a pup. I had to get out of the house those nights. I'd go sleep in the barn."

Sylvia got up from the sofa and walked over to her son, kneeling next to him, pulling his head against her. "Oh, son, I thought you didn't know."

He wrested his head away. "Mama, you never stopped him, not even when he beat me. Not even today when he started on Susie. You never, ever stopped him."

Sylvia began to cry.

Dan turned to Sam. "She began screaming right after lunch, and I thought, I'm not going to let him do it again. I'm just not. Last night, all night, I heard her crying, shouting, 'Don't, for God's sake, don't.' I went out to the barn but I couldn't sleep for shaking, and I vowed I'd never let it happen again. So, when I heard her shouting I took the gun down from the wall and opened the bedroom door and saw it wasn't Mama he was beating with a belt, but Susie."

Susie was just six.

"I don't care what they do to me, but I shot him and I'm glad."

Sylvia began to sob uncontrollably. "I'm glad, too." Then she said to Sam, "They won't send him to jail, will they? He's not yet sixteen. They won't send him to jail, will they?"

"Not if I can help it," Sam said. "But I think, boy, that we better review this story. Let's say your father was cleaning the gun. Get every one of the kids to swear to that and there's no way the police can prove otherwise. They won't even want to prove it. I'll tell them when we get back to town that he shot himself cleaning his gun. Happens all the time. I'll get a body bag and we'll take him back with us, and maybe no one will even come out to ask." He looked at Cassie. "You agree to that?"

"Of course." Sam, you're wonderful, she thought warmly.

"They can't put a young boy in jail, can they?" Sylvia asked again. "I need him here to help run the place. He's the only man I have now."

He wasn't a man, thought Cassie. A boy. He was a boy who would carry these scars with him forever, and not just the ones on his back.

Sam got the body bag and they zipped it around Ambrose Pulham.

"You want me to send someone out to stay with you a few days?" Cassie asked.

Sylvia shook her head. "No, we don't need no one."

Sam pulled Cassie aside. "Want to stay overnight or fly back? We got lights at the airfield now, remember."

"Let's let them be."

Sam lifted the remains into the plane. It was dark. Stars blinked in the velvet sky.

"Is it cold or is it me?"

"It's chilly," he answered. He started to get in the plane but looked at her standing, looking up into the heavens, and backed down.

Cassie was surprised to hear herself crying, soft little sobs. Sam's arms went around her and he held her tight against his chest. "What's going to become of them?" Sam smelled good.

"Maybe they're going to begin to live," he suggested, pulling a handkerchief from his pocket and handing it to her.

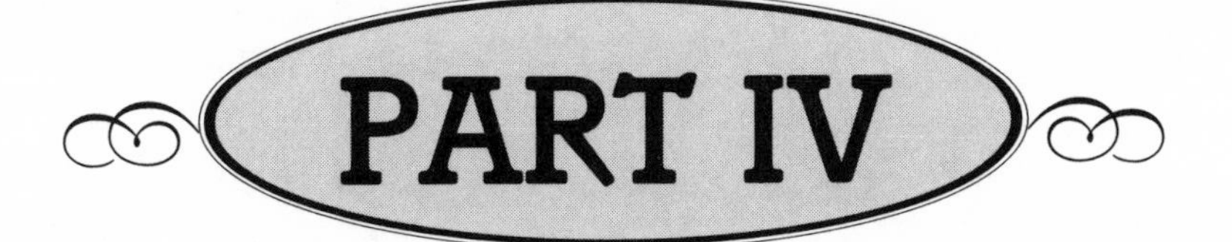

1948–1950

Chapter 46

In 1948 Cassie delivered sons to four of the Martin girls. Along with the two daughters she'd delivered the previous year, that made all the Martin girls mothers.

The drought was in its fourth year.

Numerous ranchers had lost all their stock and left their stations, moving into the cities and towns, taking on any kind of job that would feed and house their families until they could return to the land.

Chris delivered Olivia of her second child, a daughter. And Cassie brought into the world Fiona's fourth child, second daughter, in four years. She did not know that Sam had suggested naming their daughter after her, telling Olivia, "We can call her Sandy."

"Over my dead body," said Olivia.

"We can call her Sandra," Fiona suggested to Blake.

"Okay," he said.

So Sam's daughter was named Samantha and Fiona's was christened Cassandra.

Augusta Springs had become a town of over three thousand, adding a Methodist Church, another two teachers, and a social life of which Romla had become the doyenne, the arbiter of etiquette. She encouraged teas, ladylike affairs with cucumber sandwiches and a string quartet. Women met for lunch in the elegant dining room of the Royal

Palms. And while Addie's drew customers in as strongly as ever, it was for candlelit dinners of veal scallopine, chicken cordon bleu, lamb curries, and beef Stroganoff that Romla's dining room became famous. It was expensive and elegant. Her waitresses wore prim-looking pearl gray uniforms that nevertheless clung to their breasts, showing cleavage—which all had in abundance—and fitted tightly across their behinds.

"Every one of your waitresses looks like she could be in movies," Cassie told Romla. "Wherever do you find them?"

Romla just smiled.

She had imported a pastry chef who baked nothing but exquisite desserts. Augusta Springs had never heard of such a thing. Romla refused to allow anything to be fried. She was intelligent enough to keep steak on the menu, and her meals were aesthetic as well as gastronomic delights.

The dark-green-carpeted dining room was done in shades of pale and dark mauve, the light bulbs were pink, and the whole room was flattering to anyone who dined there. Even at breakfast, when there were no lights, people seemed to look better than out in the harsh glare of the Outback sun.

Romla gave parties. She threw the hotel lobby open to a ball during race week and catered parties by the score. She took on the task of raising money for the always-strapped Flying Doctors, organizing gymkhanas and costume balls, picnics and camel rides, riding into the hills for moonlight suppers. She brought a gaiety to Augusta Springs and a night life as well, inculcating social awareness into the ladies of the town.

But there was a thorn in her flesh.

Her husband.

He complained about the lack of entertainment available in Augusta Springs, so he invented his own. There was never an evening when there wasn't a serious poker game in the back of the Royal Palms bar, a table where the wealthiest men in town could be found three and four nights a week. The judge attended whenever he was in town; men like James Teakle's father and Old Man Stanley, whose ranch was one of the largest, managed to ride into town at least twice a week to attend the continuously running game. It was much too rich for most men's blood, and those who couldn't afford it played darts at Addie's. The men who came to the Royal Palms bar didn't drink and run—they were serious drinkers who could afford their vices. But seven nights a week the one constant player was Roger, the only one who couldn't afford the high stakes.

"The one place," Romla told Cassie, "that's making money is the bar. It'll take about two years to break even on the rest, they tell me. The bar's our security blanket. But, thank goodness, it *is* making money and our food is included in our wages, because we don't have a cent to spend on anything."

Cassie told Chris, "That doesn't make sense. The place is always full. The dining room is always busy."

"Maybe Roger's drinking up the profits," Chris said. "I know he never seems drunk, but that's heavy drinking going on there as well as gambling."

Cassie and Chris dined at the hotel a couple of times a week, not only because they thought the food divine but it gave them a chance to be with Romla and Terry. Most of the time Roger wouldn't leave the bar, so Cassie and Chris enjoyed their evenings with Romla. Monday evenings, when the restaurant was slow and when Romla turned the management over to the maitre d', she and Terry came to Cassie's and Chris's for dinner. And on Saturday afternoons, when Cassie wasn't on an emergency, she took Terry to the movies or played dominoes with him or took him hiking along the dry riverbed.

But more and more often Terry spent his Saturdays with Jim Teakle. Jim managed to be in town more than he had before, and he and Chris struck up a friendship, which surprised Cassie and delighted Chris, who took up skeet shooting again to spend Saturday mornings with Jim. They began to take Terry along, and taught him to shoot. Then Jim decided all boys should learn how to camp. He bought Terry his own swag and, on weekends out in the bush, taught him to make damper and strong coffee and to read tracks in the sand. Chris often accompanied them.

"He's a first-class fellow," Chris said. "I can't remember when I've had a real friend before. Not since school, that's for sure."

Jim Teakle was not only a first-class friend, but Romla thought him a gentleman. "Something I haven't seen in a long time," she allowed.

He began to attend the Monday night suppers, too, whether Roger came or not, and usually Roger decided he couldn't leave the bar. It was apparent that Romla had put pressure on him to come; when he did attend he ate and ran back to the hotel, not bothering to hide his impatience at the conversation and laughter that surrounded him at Cassie's.

Cassie could tell, as time went by, that Romla was putting less and less pressure on him, for he stopped coming altogether and she, Chris, Romla, and Jim Teakle became a regular Monday night get-together. Jim even took to preparing dinner in Cassie's kitchen when she was late on a clinic run or out on an emergency. Terry worshipped Jim, who talked to the boy as though he were an adult, asking questions and waiting for the answers as though they were important.

"It's nice for him to have a father figure," Romla said one Monday evening as she sat on a stool watching Cassie peel potatoes. Roger seems to have abdicated that job. He hardly talks to Pam when she's home on holiday. He quite totally ignores the children."

"Just them?" Cassie asked, adding salt to the potato water.

Romla was silent for a minute, then tears formed in the corners of her eyes. "No. Me, too. He doesn't even act as though I'm alive. We never have a meal together. He's been up too late the night before to share breakfast. Cassie, I think he's hung over every day. Yet he never seems drunk. All he lives and breathes for is that damn bar."

"You sorry you took over this job?"

Romla fought the tears, wiping them back before they fell. "No. Perhaps our marriage was over before we even came here and I'm just trying to blame it on the bar. On drinking. On anything other than the two of us. Do you know we have less money than we had in Townsville on a policeman's salary?" Romla burst into tears. "We each get a paycheck from the management—Roger for the bar, me for the hotel and restaurant. I've always endorsed mine and given it to Roger to deposit and Cassie, oh Cassie, I've just discovered we have *nothing*—not a cent—in the bank."

"My heavens, where's it gone?"

Romla wiped her tears away. "He's been drinking and gambling it away."

"Have you thought of separating?"

Romla jerked her head up and stared at Cassie, then burst into tears. "Oh, Cassie, I think of it all the time. Tonight I gave him an ultimatum: stop the gambling and drinking or goodbye."

Cassie began shelling peas, looking across the room at Romla, letting her cry. After a few minutes, she said, "You're scared, aren't you? Why?"

"No one in our family's ever gotten divorced," she wept, searching for and finding a Kleenex on top of the icebox. "He and I haven't even talked in years. It's been, oh, at least a year since we've gone to bed at the same time. Not that I want him to touch me, but it's symbolic, I think, of what our marriage has become. Is he getting it someplace else, do you think?"

"If he's drinking that would explain a lot. Whatever the reason, something's wrong with your marriage."

"Something," sniffled Romla, "has been wrong with our marriage from the beginning. But if I divorce, Chris will be ashamed of me, and what about the kids? Children shouldn't grow up in a broken home."

"Broken? What is it now? He doesn't pay any attention to them. All he cares about, whatever it is, is in that bar at the Royal Palms."

"Before we came here, he'd just come home from work, put his feet up on a stool, lean back on the couch, and close his eyes. We never did anything. It's been the most boring marriage I can imagine, but you don't divorce someone because of boredom."

"How long have you been married?" Cassie tossed the peas into a pot of boiling water and reached into the icebox for lettuce and tomatoes and green pepper.

"Eighteen years." Romla had stopped crying.

"Eighteen years of boredom? And now, all you've been working for is gone. You have nothing to show for it, no money at all?"

Romla shook her head. "Not a cent."

"I think this is what that writer, whatever his name was, meant when he said most people live lives of quiet desperation. How old are you?"

"Thirty-six." Romla paused and looked at Cassie. "I'm scared partly because I think I'm in love with Jim. He's the kind of father to my kids that Roger has never been. When Pam's home, Jim gives her more attention than her father does. Yet, he's never made overtures to me, never kissed me, never touched me except when we've danced . . . "

"You know perfectly well whenever there's a dance, Jim manages to be in town and doesn't dance with anyone but you. Well, a couple of courtesy dances, but . . . "

"I know." Romla half-smiled through her tears. "And I've wondered whether it's all in my mind or if it's real. He never says anything really personal and never holds me tightly . . . but he's so kind, Cassie! He's thoughtful, and Terry adores him."

"He's become close to Chris, too."

"I think about this every night. Every single night, and I think even if I got divorced he might not do anything."

"Don't get divorced for another man," advised Cassie, tossing the salad, adding onions and oil. "Get divorced for yourself. And the children. Then if something happens with Jim, so be it."

Romla got up from the stool and began to pace around the kitchen. Laughter could be heard from the living room. "I was brought up to believe you mated for life. If Chris would think me immoral if I divorced, I couldn't bear that."

Cassie went over to put her arm around Romla, who stood still for a minute. "No one really believes in divorce. But living in this kind of despair—that can't be what life's all about. Also, it shouldn't matter what Chris thinks. He won't stop loving you, won't disapprove. He'll be sorry, but he'll stand by you. Certainly there's never been any love lost between him and Roger."

"Funny, neither of us could stand the other's spouse."

"If Chris had had the courage to divorce Isabel, he wouldn't have spent so much of his life in misery. You better do some thinking. I hate seeing you as unhappy as Chris was with Isabel."

"Oh, I knew it! I always knew he was unhappy with her. And he never told me."

Cassie thrust silverware at Romla and said, "Go set the table and tell everyone to be ready in ten minutes."

* * *

Later that night as they undressed, Cassie asked Chris, "Would you be upset if Romla left Roger and divorced him?"

Chris gave her a sharp look. "Is that wishful thinking on your part?"

"She's dreadfully unhappy, has been for a long time. Now she's discovered he's gambled away all their money. Or drunk it up."

"The son of a bitch—though I imagined as much." He pulled on his pajamas.

"You haven't answered my question."

"I'd be delighted. If she needs my support, she has it."

"Tell her so," Cassie said as they moved toward the bed. Chris leaned over to put his hand on her breast. "And kiss me there, right where your hand is."

As he did so, Cassie murmured. "Oh, God, Chris, do that again. Don't ever stop." It felt so good. She arched her back.

Before they fell asleep, she whispered, "I'd like life to stay just like this. Remember to set the alarm."

Chris reached out to check the clock. "Nothing ever stays just like it is," he said.

In the morning, Romla told Cassie, "Roger's gone. Packed up and pulled out on the eight o'clock bus. I've a feeling he owes a lot of money to those men he plays poker with."

"What are you going to do?"

"First of all, I'm going to pay off his debts, every last cent, so I can hold my head up in town."

In the middle of the afternoon, as they flew back from a clinic down south, Sam asked, "Did the war change your life?"

She thought about his question. If the war hadn't broken out, Blake wouldn't have gone away. She'd have had no need to have an abortion. She'd be Mrs. Blake Thompson now. She never would have met Romla. She wouldn't be sharing her bed with Chris.

"Of course," she answered, watching a large flock of sheep on the red land below them.

"Nothing's turned out like I thought it would," he said. "I thought you were going to marry Blake. I mean, before I went away, you and he'd gone up north for a couple weeks."

"I thought you were going to marry Sister Claire."

"I might have," he said. "If you'd married Blake."

She wondered what one thing had to do with the other.

The silence stretched to minutes. In the distance a silver speck shone in the sun. Another plane.

"Are you ever lonely, Doc?"

She'd known all wasn't smooth between him and Olivia. She'd heard Liv object to the heat and the flies, the dry and the wet . . . over and over again. She liked the dances, when every available male wanted to dance with the fragile-looking blonde, the girl who looked like girls should look, dressed in pastels and ruffles, smiling at them with those big blue eyes and acting as though she was interested in everything they said. And she was, because they told her how pretty she was, and wasn't Sam lucky, and boy, could she dance.

"Don't Harry and Samantha help?"

"Sure. I'd lay my life down for them. My heart beats a little faster when they come sit on my lap or I pick them up or read stories to put them to sleep or answer their questions. I look at them and feel like my heart might burst. I feel immortal, and like maybe nothing else is important at all."

There was another silence and then Sam continued. "Maybe what I'm trying to do is figure out what happiness is. You don't seem unhappy. Do you have a secret?"

She thought a minute. "I'm not sure what happiness is either, but you're right, I'm not unhappy."

"But don't you ever get lonely?"

"Lonely? I don't have enough time to think about that. I used to be, but no, I don't think I'm lonely." Funny, she used to think she carried loneliness around within her.

"Loneliness has nothing to do with being surrounded by people—I've found that out."

She turned to face him and found him looking at her. "You know, before the war, everything was fun. But now . . . "

Cassie felt fear strike her chest. "You want to leave? Leave here? Leave the Flying Doctors?"

"No," he nearly barked. "It's not that. It's that . . . oh, forget it,

Doc. I'm sorry I brought it up. C'mon, let's talk about something else."

Cassie felt inadequate, wanting to say something comforting, but she wasn't sure what he was talking about. She felt like reaching out to touch his arm.

Sam said, "What about Blake's and Fiona's new house? Have you ever seen anything like it?"

"Never. Ten bedrooms and each with its own bath. Spread out like that, all on one floor. Fiona said as soon as all the furniture arrives they're going to have a party. She thinks maybe New Year's Eve." She'd met Blake at a Tookaringa New Year's Eve party. New Year's Eve, 1939. Nearly ten years ago.

"Steven will be lonely with that brood moving a couple of miles away. Wonder why Blake built it? Certainly the big house had room for all of them."

Cassie shrugged. "A new challenge. He thrives on them. He was born and brought up in that house and maybe he wants something new."

"But twenty rooms! Who needs that many?"

"It's not what he needed," Cassie said. "It's what he wanted, a showplace."

"Maybe Steven'll remarry now that he'll be alone."

"Jennifer's a hard act to follow."

"It's been nearly seven years since she died."

When they arrived back in Augusta Springs Horrie was at the airport waiting for them. He'd never done that before.

The minute Cassie stepped out of the plane, Horrie took her arm, his face pinched. "Cassie, there's been an accident. Get to the hospital right away."

"Can't Chris or Mel take care of it?" Mel Delano was Chris's new partner.

Horrie's face was white.

"It *is* Chris."

She looked at him, feeling Sam's hand under her elbow.

"What do you mean, it *is* Chris?"

"He's been hurt bad, Cassie. Romla called. Car accident. She wants you over there right away. My utility's waiting."

Chris? In a car accident? She shivered as she climbed into Horrie's truck.

Sam leaned in the window. "I'll follow directly."

Horrie talked as he sped along. "He was out at the old Curtin place. Hardly a car a week goes out there, and a big oil tanker came whooshing by and sideswiped him. His car turned over . . . "

"For God's sake, Horrie, why didn't you call the plane?"

"It just happened less'n two hours ago, Cassie. You were on your way back anyhow. You couldn't have gotten here any quicker. I thought it'd be better if you heard it from me than over the radio."

"Of course."

"Dr. Delano and an ambulance rushed out soon's they heard about it."

"I wonder how long he was there before someone found him?" Her mind didn't grasp the situation. It was another patient, not her husband.

"The driver of the tanker called in when he got to the nearest town. He returned to the scene of the accident and was waiting when the ambulance arrived."

"How bad, do you know?"

Horrie shook his head. "Romla just said 'bad.' "

Five minutes later they pulled into the hospital parking lot and Cassie ran up the stairs. Romla was standing in the hall.

"He's unconscious, Cassie, from the anesthetic. Dr. Delano . . . here he is now."

Dr. Delano, a short, thin, cherubic-looking Irishman, walked toward them. Cassie saw in an instant that Chris was dying. Delano shook his head and put an arm around Cassie. "You can go see him, but he hasn't much time left. I'm sorry, Cassie."

Romla burst into tears. "Oh, Chris."

"Come along," Cassie said. "Don't just stand here."

They entered the hospital room, which smelled strongly of disinfectant. Chris's eyes were closed but Cassie could see the faint movement of his breathing as his chest moved ever so slightly. Bandages covered his chest and a long gash, surrounded by dried blood, ran down his left ear and cheek. Cassie took hold of his icy hand.

His eyelids fluttered open. "Thank heaven," he murmured so faintly she had to lean closer to hear him. "I wanted you here. I waited until you got here."

She leaned over and kissed him.

"I've had the happiest years of my life with you," he said.

Cassie nodded and felt a hand clutching at her heart. "Me, too," she said.

"Never feel guilty," Chris went on, though she could feel the blood flowing out of him, thought she literally felt it sliding out of his hand. "I know why you married me. I know you never loved me . . . "

"That's not true!"

" . . . like I love you, but never feel guilty about it. You made me happier than I had ever been. To feel love like I've felt for you is worth all of life. It is much more important to love than be loved."

At the far side of the bed, Romla took his other hand and his eyes moved to see who it was. "Chris, darling, of course Cassie loves you as I do. You're the sweetest, most wonderful . . . Oh, darling, I've loved you more than anyone in the world except my children."

A weak smile flitted over Chris's face. "The two of you," he murmured, his voice a whisper, "have been responsible for all the happiness I've known." His eyes closed and he was gone. His body lay against the cold white sheets, and his left hand grasped the edge of the blanket, but there was no more breath, and no more Chris Adams.

Cassie looked at him and thought she would never see him clean his glasses on his tie again, never argue with him again, never . . . never do anything with him again. She heard Romla's sobs and turned to her sister-in-law, putting her arms around her, holding her close, looking over her shoulder to see Sam standing in the doorway, looking at her as, dry-eyed, she held the only woman who had ever really loved Chris.

Chapter 47

What made Cassie feel guilty in the months after Chris died was the fact that so little changed. Her work was the center of her life, as it always had been. She still dined several nights a week at the hotel with Romla, and Romla, Terry, and Jim came to the same informal Monday night suppers at her house. If anything, she and Romla grew closer. Romla filed for divorce, and it was as though a heavy burden had been lifted.

"You know," Romla said, "every single one of those men—the judge, Jim's father, and old man Stanley—all denied that Rog owed them anything. I know they were being nice to me, and I know they lied to me. I love every one of them. They'll never pay for another drink in that hotel, not while I'm there."

Terry came to Cassie's Saturday nights when Romla was busy at the hotel, and together they went to the movies after dinner at Addie's. After dining formally at the Royal Palms, Terry thought Addie's was exciting. He usually stayed overnight and after brunch on Sunday mornings Jim arrived to take him to church.

Cassie hardly ever ate alone. She didn't even have to walk into an empty house, because two weeks after Chris's funeral Sam presented her with a puppy, a black and white ball of fur who won Cassie's heart immediately.

She spent hours playing with the dog, and whenever she drove into the driveway, Bree's bark could be heard up the block, his tail wagging with ecstasy. By the end of the third week he was sleeping with her, and she trained herself to get up twice a night to let him out. He was house-trained by the time he was twelve weeks old. Nevertheless, she missed the warm human body she had grown used to.

One Sunday morning Sam appeared with a roll of wire, calling out as he walked in without knocking, "Where's a cup of coffee?"

Cassie and Terry had just finished breakfast.

"I've come to make Bree a fence," Sam said. "No dog should have to stay cooped up in a house all the long hours you're gone. So, I made a doghouse this last week, and now I'll surround it with a fence."

Just then Jim appeared, dressed in a dark suit with a bright red paisley tie. When he heard what Sam was going to do, he looked at Terry and said, "That wire looks unwieldy. I suppose we could skip church this one time and help Sam, couldn't we?" When Terry nodded eagerly, Jim added, "Wait until I go change my clothes,"

Sam grinned in appreciation. "Right nice of you both. I'll have Cassie amuse me while we're waiting."

"Can I take Bree for a walk?" Terry asked. He already knew the answer and had found the leash and collar on a nail on the back of the kitchen door.

Cassie was aware Sam was calling her by her name lately.

When she poured his coffee and he leaned back in a kitchen chair, she said, "You seem to have replaced Chris in Jim's affections."

"Nice guy," Sam said as he sipped the coffee. "Wonder when he and Romla will get hitched."

"I appreciate your kindness, Sam. All you're doing for me since Chris . . . "

"I'd do more for you if I could, Cassie. But everyone in town seems to be lookin' out for you. I bet you haven't eaten a meal alone since . . . well, since."

It was true. On the nights she didn't dine at the hotel, someone almost always invited her out. And if they flew in late from an emergency or an overlong clinic, Betty had something ready. There wasn't a weekend that a cake or a pie wasn't left on her doorstep.

Don McLeod had flown over from Alice Springs to officiate at the funeral, and he managed to write Cassie warm, supportive letters—one a week, with postscripts from Margaret, who was pregnant with their second child.

"You going to the Thompson bash?" Sam asked.

"I'm wondering if I should. You know, so soon after . . . "

"Blake asked if we'd come up Wednesday through Sunday. Suggested we could have the regular clinic Wednesday and there'll likely be accidents with so many races—and with so much partying, probably some fights. He thinks we can justify staying there a few days. Since Liv won't go anywhere without the kids, Fiona told us to bring them, and they can play with hers. Whole families are going to be up there."

"Well, put that way, if I'm needed as a doctor . . . "

"No rule says you can't dance and have fun, too."

"What will people think?"

"Hey, Doc, it's not so much what people will think as what *you* want to do. No sense two people in the same family dying."

Cassie reached out and put a hand over his. "Sam, you're a rock. Thanks for being such a good friend. Why don't you and Liv start coming over Monday nights with Romla and Jim? We have fun."

He shook his head. "Liv wouldn't enjoy it, Cassie. She thinks I spend too much time with you as it is. I waited til she left for church before coming over to build this fence."

Liv must be the kind of woman who found other women a threat, Cassie mused. Certainly Sam and she had nothing but a great partnership. He had never even kissed her, never even looked at her as though she was a woman. She'd never felt anything for him other than respect and admiration. Over the last few years, ever since he'd returned from the war, their friendship had grown so that now it was one of the sustaining things of her life.

"Huh? Funny, I hadn't realized that."

"Realized what?" Sam asked, getting up to pour himself another cup of coffee.

"Oh, nothing."

From the air it looked like a whole town had suddenly appeared overnight. Hundreds of tents had sprung up on the tableland six miles north of Blake's new home, in the center of Tookaringa's property—or at least the homestead property. Blake had a stretch of land that extended from Tookaringa down to Adelaide, if not directly, at least in a route over which cattle could pass without ever being on anyone else's land. Cassie had heard a rumor that he'd become one of Australia's largest land owners. During the drought he'd been able to buy cheap, just as he had predicted.

Blake had decided not only to hold a housewarming, but to inaugurate what he hoped would become an annual event: dances, picnics, and races that would attract horse owners from all over the country. The purse was big enough to make any trip worthwhile. Every station within at least six hundred miles had come and created its own little tent village.

"This is going to be some do," Sam said, pointing down at the burgeoning temporary town. "Look, creating that racetrack with those stands was no inexpensive proposition, you can bet."

It certainly wasn't.

"They paid all that money for something that's going to be used once a year?" Olivia wondered aloud from the rear.

"Well, sheepmen do it for shearing sheds," Sam replied, seeming to be apologizing for the extravagance. "That and bunks for the shearers. Shucks, they're not used more'n once a year."

But those were necessary for sheep-raising. This looked like it was created strictly for raising Cain.

"Sure hope there aren't any real emergencies to call us away from this," Sam said as he glided onto the field. "Looks like it'll be just what I need."

Fun, Cassie thought. That's what Sam needs.

"I hope I have the right clothes," Olivia's voice came from behind Cassie.

"You always look lovely," Cassie said. Olivia knew that.

"But I've never been to one of the Outback parties."

"No one's ever been to anything like this," Cassie said, picking up her medical bag and suitcase. She wondered if they'd be staying at the old house with Steven or if they'd be assigned bedrooms in the new mansion. Two such enormous homes on the same property and not even near each other!

There were four other planes already there, all single-engined Cessnas, and two helicopters. More and more Outback stations were buying planes. The world was getting smaller.

Cassie and Sam had watched the new house take shape for close to a year, but Fiona hadn't let them inside for the last two months. "Not until it's furnished. I want you to be overwhelmed," she said.

Overwhelmed was not quite the word.

On a low rise, with sweeping green lawns down to the narrow river that never dried up, the new homestead spread not up but out. Young, thin palm trees dotted the lawn, still strapped to stakes so they would not blow over. Geese and swans swam on the pond created by the dammed-up river, and two dogs ran across the grass, followed by a pony and cart carrying six children. A young woman walked beside the cart—the nanny, no doubt, or perhaps the new governess, now that the two oldest were ready for schooling.

Laughter floated through the air, and Cassie noted how Olivia's eyes lit up. "My goodness, I didn't know anyone really lived like this," she said, her voice filled with wonder.

"I don't know that anyone did before this," Sam said, picking up Samantha and hoisting her to his shoulders as they walked toward the house. "C'mon. I'll get the bags later."

Fiona, in navy linen slacks and a white silk blouse, ran down the verandah steps. "I've been waiting for you." She threw her arms around Cassie and held her tightly. "I can hardly wait to show you everything. We're going to have a marvelous weekend." She reached up to kiss Sam on the cheek, then turned to greet Olivia, putting one arm around her shoulders and smiling at the children.

"Livvy, I'm so glad you decided to come. We have lots of help to look after the children and you can just enjoy yourself. We won't have a worry in the world."

She led them to the house. "You're all in the west wing, on the opposite side of the house from ours." To Sam and Olivia, she said, "You and the children have adjoining rooms, but Linda can take care of the kids. She'll feed them supper and play with them and see they get to bed on time, baths and all."

"My goodness," Olivia marveled.

Sam grinned. "See? I told you."

"It's wonderful," Olivia said, her eyes bright. Cassie hoped things weren't as complicated there as she suspected. Olivia seemed happy right now.

Fiona walked over and put her arm through Cassie's. "Come take a tour of the house with me," she said.

"It's gorgeous," Cassie said, but thought it really was too modern for her taste.

The living room had to be forty feet square, perhaps larger. Persian rugs were scattered over it, and the overstuffed furniture was all white. It looked like an ad from an architectural magazine, Cassie thought. Everything was perfect, even the pillows that appeared to have been casually tossed. She couldn't imagine Fiona and the kids living in such a place. None of Fiona's warmth was reflected in her living room, which Cassie thought looked too sterile for the Thompsons. Of course, all the furniture in the other house had been chosen by Jennifer. Yet, Fiona's first house was still the most charming place Cassie had ever lived in, and she'd always bemoaned the fact that she didn't have Fiona's touch. But Cassie knew Blake had called in decorators from Sydney.

The astonishing kitchen was as modern and hotel-like as the living room, but there was a warmth to it. Shining copper pots hung from brass chains attached to wide, dark wooden beams that crossed the ceiling. There was enough counter space for half a dozen people to work, and the wooden table and chairs at the end of it overlooked an atrium not only filled with ficus and orange trees, but with birds singing from perches. Immense pink and yellow lotus floated on the fish-shaped pond. A screen to contain the birds covered the top of the atrium.

"Very impressive," Cassie murmured.

"Isn't it?" Fiona's arm tightened through hers. "Cassie, I never dreamed I'd live in anything like this."

"I'd miss the old house."

"I will, I know I will, but this is Blake's dream. I do worry about Steven, though. He's going from a house full of noisy us to solitude."

"It won't be solitude, will it? I mean, the bunkhouses are still over there, the office with the accountants . . . "

"You know what I mean. No warmth at nights. No one to talk with. I love that man. I couldn't stand to be married to him—he always has to be so masculine, so needful of power—but as a father-in-law and friend I love him. I see more of him than my husband."

"Maybe apartness is what keeps marriages fresh."

Fiona laughed. "Well, if that's what it is, I'll take it. Something works, though Blake never seems satisfied. He always needs new worlds to conquer. I think he was born with a restless soul."

She was leading Cassie down one of the corridors toward the bedrooms. "Each wing has five bedrooms. Of course, we take up all of our own wing. Here, this is our room."

It was as large as two of her bedrooms at home, done in dramatic shades of emerald and white. Fiona turned to Cassie. "I don't know whether Blake's upset with me. Last night I told him I don't want any more children. Three are enough. There are some other things I want to do with my life."

Cassie looked at her. What sort of response was she supposed to make?

"I want to see that these aboriginal children get some chance at education," Fiona went on. "And I want all these hundreds of Outback kids to get some contact with it, other than what their parents can teach them. Oh, sure, mine are okay; they have a teacher for a mother, a mother who has a million and one other things to do, too. I'm not thrilled to think of my children getting all their education from our governess, who is pretty good in some areas, but not all. And there's no common educational thread anywhere. It all depends on what the governess knows and how capable she is of teaching and . . . I've an idea in the back of my mind I'll talk to you about later. I've heard of some new and exciting things going on over in the Alice." She squeezed Cassie's hand. "Are you all right? You seem it, but I want to know—are you really all right?"

"I'm all right," Cassie said. "Better than I should be. I feel a bit guilty not to be more devastated. I was very fond of him, you know." Even to her own ears that didn't sound like much. *Very fond of one's husband.*

"You're so brave, dear, and so strong. Now, I'll send Henry out to the plane to get your bags. You can hold the clinic out back. I've got it all set up for you, under the plane tree. I suppose other times over at the old house on the verandah will be far more convenient, but this time?"

"Sure," Cassie said. "It doesn't matter to me."

"Wait til you see it all," Fiona went on. "Up where the race course has been built, Blake's had a dining hall constructed and three shifts of cooks for the week. He thinks there'll be some who don't sleep at all!

The bar's stocked with over six thousand bottles of beer, champagne, rum—you name it."

"Six thousand bottles? You're going to have a drunken orgy."

"Well, it's got to last four and a half days and there'll be well over a thousand people here. Some people began arriving Tuesday, erecting tents, organizing games, setting up the diesel plant, making sure there's enough wood and water. It's really quite exciting, all these people coming from so far away for a week-long party."

"You know Aussies'll go to any lengths for races. Well, come on, the sooner I get my work done the quicker I can relax and enjoy myself."

The clinic was routine except for a smashed hand. An aboriginal woman, obviously in pain but stoic, laid her hand on the table and looked at Cassie.

"What's this from?" Cassie asked, studying the finger.

The black woman said nothing.

"Fighting with shillelaghs?" Cassie asked. Nasty wounds were common in such fighting. She'd run across a dozen or so over the years.

The woman nodded her head.

The last two phalanges of the index finger were badly crushed. Cassie studied it carefully and then turned to the black woman. "I'm going to have to cut it off."

From the blank look in the woman's eyes, Cassie didn't think she understood. "Look, here at the second joint, it's smashed so badly it's of no use and will just cause pain. It will hang like that, getting in your way. It's better to cut it off."

The woman nodded again.

"Wait a minute," Cassie told her. She had to go get Sam to administer ether.

He was still in the house, having a drink with Olivia and Fiona.

"I knew I should have made a getaway," he grinned. "Should have gone over to the tent village. Hey, hon," he said, turning to Olivia. "Wanna come watch? You're always asking what we do."

"You, too?" she asked Fiona.

"I've seen this half a dozen times," Fiona said. "I don't need any more of it. Amputations don't excite me."

"Will I get sick?" Olivia asked Sam.

He shrugged. "I nearly did the first time."

"Then thanks but no, thanks. I'll stay here."

"He won't be gone long," Cassie assured her.

When she and Sam returned to the clinic set up on the back lawn, the woman was still sitting, her hand on the table.

"Let's move her to this cot, and then you can administer the ether, just lightly. This won't take long. I'd use novocaine but I think it's better for her to be unconscious."

He nodded.

Cassie cut the finger off at the second joint, leaving a flap of the strong inner skin. She brought that up over the stump and sutured it into place.

"Neatly done," Sam said.

"It is, isn't it?" She looked at the woman and realized she'd be conscious any minute. "You can go back to your wife," she said. "I'll be along before too long."

"I'll wait," Sam said. "Fiona says Blake and Steven will arrive for dinner. We won't even go up to the race track until tomorrow."

When they returned to the house, Blake and Steven were there. Blake threw an arm around Sam's shoulders, saying something Cassie couldn't hear. She went over and reached up to kiss Steven on the cheek as his arms went around her in a bear hug.

"Cassie, you get prettier all the time," Steven said, returning her kiss.

"She does, doesn't she?" Blake's voice came from beside her. He put an arm around her and said, in a low voice, "Are you all right? I mean, are you really okay?"

All too aware of his hand on her waist, she said, "I'm fine." She'd trained herself, over the years, to greet him as a friend. She no longer let her heart catch when she saw him or heard his voice. But she had to concentrate, make it an act of will. "After this week, you'll be one of the most famous men in the country, I imagine," she said, "what with this awe-inspiring house and the races. I hear people have brought horses from as far as a thousand miles."

He grinned, standing there towering over everyone in the room but his father. "That's what I hoped for. We're offering a purse that has proven to be irresistible. But come on, has Fiona given you a tour of the house?"

"That she has, and I'm bedazzled."

"Well, let's open the bar, then, and start having fun. We'll wait to go over where the crowds are tomorrow. Races start in the afternoon and in the evening there's a dance, so we'll stay for dinner, too. It'll be an all-day affair."

"What should I wear to that?" Olivia asked.

Fiona answered. "Just a nice frock tomorrow night. Saturday night everyone will wear their prettiest ball dresses and there will be two parties, one of them here."

The first race was held Thursday at one-thirty. Bookmakers gave odds under gaily colored umbrellas that protected them from the sun. A goodly number of women had come to the festivities and many of them wore slacks and jeans and Stetsons, just as the men did. The war had changed many things.

The stand was filled to overflowing, and the crowd was noisier than any Cassie had ever heard. First came the stockman's race, which was open to all. Ringers who thought they had good horses crowded into this one. The last race of the day was the aboriginal stockmen's race, and it was the most exciting of all. These stockmen seemed to disregard their own safety and made every run a close and dangerous one, filled with tumult.

Late in the afternoon the newly created Tookaringa Cup was run amidst wild cheering.

The dining room, an enormous thirty- by sixty-foot room with a kitchen at one end, was open around the clock. Fiona and Blake had set up a dressing tent for their guests, along with the other tents that were set in neat rows, tents that each of the stations had brought along with them. Cassie thought she danced with half the guests that night, but she didn't dance with Blake, and even Sam didn't rush over to her when they played some fast numbers, which they seemed to do less and less these days. Jitterbugging was on its way out. Just as well, she thought. I'm not as agile as I used to be.

Once during the dance Cassie was called out to minister to two ringers who had had too much to drink and had gotten into a fight. One of them required stitches. Another time she had to attend a man, also involved in a brawl, whose leg had been badly injured.

"He's got to go to the hospital," she said. "The nearest one is Yancanna. Get Sam."

"Well," Sam said as he revved the engine up for take-off. "At least you don't have to feel guilty about being here and having fun. See, I knew work would be involved."

They flew to Yancanna and were back before the dancing stopped, landing as a full moon rose exactly at the end of the brightly lit runway.

"You know," Sam said as they sat for a minute, looking at the moon. "We may be the luckiest people alive."

"I thought you were showing signs of discontent." Or even unhappiness, Cassie thought.

"Not at this moment," Sam said, his voice soft. "At this very moment I have all I could want."

He turned to look at her.

Chapter 48

The next day the stockyards teemed with horses and bullocks. First was campdrafting, followed by steer rides.

It was all a great deal of fun.

They'd just finished supper and changed clothes for the Friday night dance. The dining room ceiling was gaily decorated with crepe paper streamers. One end of the room had been transformed into a stage, where a band was tuning up.

Cassie said to Sam, "We know nearly everyone here."

Sam glanced around, nodding. "It means that we know nearly everyone within a five-hundred-mile radius."

She laughed. "That sounds pretty impressive, doesn't it?"

They were standing in front of the tent, waiting for Fiona and Olivia to finish dressing.

"Olivia seems to be enjoying herself," Cassie said.

"Thank goodness. Yeah, she's having a good time. I guess I haven't given her much of a life in Augusta Springs. She'd have preferred a city."

"Like Romla's husband, I suppose. Some people find the Outback boring. Is that Olivia's problem?"

"Cassie, I don't know what she likes. She misses green forests and meadows and her family and the stimulation of a city . . . or maybe it's just England. She'd like us to move back there." Seeing the look of dismay in Cassie's eyes, he went on. "We're not going, Doc. Not me. But that's what she'd like. Or a husband with a regular job, who'd be home weekends and for dinner each night."

Cassie reached out to touch his arm but their hands brushed each other. He held hers for a moment before Fiona emerged from the tent, Olivia trailing her. Sam's hand dropped to his side.

"Anyone seen Blake?" Fiona asked.

"I saw him and Steven a couple minutes ago, each going different ways," Sam answered.

Tonight there were no boots, Stetsons, or jeans. The men wore pressed pants and open-necked shirts, and the women were in skirts and high heels. Not formal—that would be for tomorrow night—but Sunday-go-to-meeting dresses with pearl or rhinestone earrings.

The sound of a fiddle wafted through the air as people slowly wound their way back to the dining hall.

"Just look at all those stars," Fiona said. "I never take them for granted."

"You never take anything for granted, Fiona," Sam said. "You still get as excited about everything as a kid."

"I'll take that as a compliment," she said, smiling over at him.

"Just how it was meant," he replied. Sam enjoyed being surrounded by three of the best-looking women around.

Blake was waiting at the entrance to the dance hall. He looked more handsome than ever, Cassie thought, in a blue shirt to match his eyes, his sandy curls cut close to his head, his strong, square face rugged and leathery from so much time in the sun. One would hardly notice his left hand, she thought.

He smiled down at Cassie. "The first dance is mine," he said. She hadn't danced with him in years. Not since the fall of 1939, when he would spend twelve hours driving into Augusta Springs to the Saturday Night Dances. She hadn't danced with him in a little over nine years.

The band began with an old smoothie, "Stardust." He reached out his right hand to take hers, drawing her to him. She felt the length of his body next to hers, felt him draw her close to him.

"I remember the first time we danced together," he murmured into her hair.

"New Year's Eve, 1938."

"So, you remember, too?" He pulled back so he could look down into her eyes.

"Of course. It seems like forever."

"It was. It was before the world changed, before we lost our innocence, before we knew how hard it all could be. I've never forgotten those weeks we spent together, Cassie. Do you ever think of them?"

"No," she said. "Never."

He pulled her closer. "You're lying. I was a coward, Cassie. You scared me shitless. No one had ever done to me what you did. I was afraid to send you letters, though I must have written a dozen. I always tore them up."

She looked up at him. "Why are you telling me this now?"

"Because I looked at you yesterday, as I have so many times over these years, and wanted you to know. I ran away from you, Cassie. I don't know what would have happened if the war hadn't come along."

Cassie stopped dancing. "Blake, this is no way to be talking to me. Stop it." She extricated herself from his arms and walked off the dance floor. Her heart beat erratically. What the hell was he trying to do?

Mac Hamilton grabbed her hand. "Come on, Cass. I didn't get a chance last night. I'm not going to let tonight pass by."

An hour later, Steven broke in. "I'd hoped you wouldn't disappear before I had a chance to dance with you."

She smiled at him. "You didn't even dance with me last night."

He grinned. "Why, Dr. Clarke, I'd swear you're flirting with me."

As they moved onto the dance floor, she asked, "How are you making it, living alone?"

"It's quiet. Awful quiet." He hummed to the music.

The next night, Saturday, while hundreds of others danced in formal attire to a twenty-piece orchestra in the dining room, sixty selected guests, the station owners and managers and other close friends, dined at the new mansion. A combo had been flown in from Sydney, and tables had been set up under Japanese lanterns strung among the palm trees. The immense living room had been turned into a dance floor for the evening. Every woman there had spent weeks shopping for a dress to wear to the most elaborate event ever held in this part of the world.

No one could come near to matching Fiona. She and Blake had flown to Sydney and Blake had explained to a designer there just what he wanted, with shoes dyed to match. She wore an elegantly simple scarlet satin gown cut so low that Cassie thought she'd be embarrassed. Diamonds flashed at her ears and a diamond necklace circled her throat. Certainly no one from any of the Outback stations had ever seen anything like it.

When Cassie had decided to come, she found an Indian sari tucked away in a closet, one she'd never worn, emerald green and gold-flecked gossamer silk. No one ever wore anything like that in Australia, she thought, smiling to herself about the impact it would make. And it did, but it wasn't comparable to Fiona's.

"You and Fiona are creating a sensation," Steven told her, sitting on her right at dinner. "You've changed, Cassie."

"How do you mean?"

"Oh, when you first came you were tough as nails. Abrupt, sensible, no nonsense."

"And now?" Her smile dazzled him.

"Well, maybe it's because you don't have to prove anything anymore. We all know what a good doctor you are. And marriage softened you. Your womanly side shows. You were good for Chris. He became a new man. You gave him a new lease on life, as I imagine you would any man."

"Steven, that's a lovely thing to hear. I like being a woman."

The trio had struck up, and the music could be heard across the lawn.

"Come on, let's go trip the light fantastic," he said, getting up and stretching out his hand. She grasped it and they walked up to the house.

They'd barely begun to dance when someone cut in. Cassie danced with a dozen people before Blake suddenly appeared beside her. "My turn. If I don't butt in I'll never get a chance. Or you'll go tearing off on another emergency."

He put his arm around her, and she felt again what she'd felt last night. As though she'd been deluding herself all these years—that making love with Chris couldn't do to her what being in Blake's arms did.

"You look beautiful," he murmured.

"I'm supposed to look exotic in this Indian getup," she said, wanting desperately for him to be impersonal yet yearning for his closeness.

They danced in silence for several minutes, and then he said, "Remember Kakadu?"

Her heart caught—she tried to breathe—and then it started beating again. But it was not hers. It was his that she felt pulsating against her right breast.

"That was so long ago. Forget it."

"Can *you?*"

She stopped dancing, looked at him, and walked away. She was scarcely three feet away when Sam grabbed her hand. "Hey, I think the only times I've ever danced with you was when we jitterbugged. Come on, Doc, let's try a real dance."

Anything, she thought, to get away from Blake.

He didn't hold her close, as Blake had. She fit easily into his arms, and they glided across the floor. "You're the easiest person in the world to dance with, Sam. Pure joy."

"It's reciprocal, Doc, completely mutual."

"Olivia's certainly having fun. Look at her!"

"You're a knockout in that outfit," he said, pulling her close.

She didn't even have to think when dancing with Sam. It was as though her body knew what his was going to do even before he did it.

Steven cut in before the song ended, announcing, "You've been too long gone from my life."

But when the next set began, Blake was beside her again. "My turn, Dad. You can't monopolize her."

As soon as she was in his arms, Blake said, "If you want to get away, Cassandra, you're going to have to work at it. So, you do remember Kakadu? I've wondered."

"Blake, what are you trying to do?"

"Just remembering," his voice whispered into her hair. "Remembering one of the peak experiences of my life. Remembering what it was like . . . to lie under the stars, to make love. Remember that aboriginal dancing? God, that had to be the most erotic night of my life." He pulled his head back and looked down at her. "It was for you, too, wasn't it?"

Everything faded. No one else was in the room. Only Blake's arms around her, his words. "Oh, Blake, I loved you so. I thought I'd die when you went away."

He pulled her closer, tight against him. "You didn't love Chris, did you? You couldn't have loved him after what we had, not that tight-ass."

Cassie jerked away. At one time she'd have agreed with him, but Chris became much more than that.

"You married before I did, remember? Let's forget all that. Leave it behind us."

"I can't forget."

"Don't be a fool!" she snapped. "How could anyone forget it? Leave it alone, won't you?"

He put his arms around her. "I think of you often," he said as they began to move to the rhythm of the music.

"Don't do whatever you're doing," she said, her body rigid. "Fiona's my closest friend."

"She's mine, too," he said, his voice low. "That has nothing to do with memories."

"Put them away in a box someplace and keep them there," she said. "You broke my heart once and I'm not about to go through that again."

He stopped, right in the middle of the dance floor, staring at her. "I did *what?*" Then, seeing others glance at them, he started to dance again.

"Cut it out, Blake. Just don't do this. Please, let's stop. I don't want to dance with you."

"Cassie, I . . . "

But she took off, forcing herself to smile at everyone as she cut across the dance floor, pushing through the screen door and walking out onto the lawn, where people still sat at tables under the swinging lanterns. She walked past them, across the wide expanse of trees, down toward the pond.

Leaning against one of the big gums that overhung the river, she consciously tried to slow her breathing.

"So, it's three of us now," said Sam's voice from the darkness.

As he walked out from under the tree all she could see was his silhouette. "*Three of you?*"

Sliding his hands into his pockets, Sam stood against the tall tree. His face was in shadow. "Yeah. Blake, the old man, and me." Then he turned and walked between the trees, disappearing into the darkness.

Cassie peered into the void but Sam was gone. He couldn't possibly have said what she thought she'd heard him say.

Blake, the old man, and . . . and me?

Chapter 49

The drought had lasted so long that people were calling the Outback "the dust bowl."

Sam complained daily about sandstorms.

He and Cassie were on a two-day clinic run down to Kypunda and beyond. They'd stayed overnight at Burnham Hill, then headed—right after breakfast—for Oliver's Lagoon station, about thirty-five miles further west.

"Visibility unlimited," Sam said with delight. "The dust must have settled—I don't even see a speck. Going to be as easy as pie today."

Cassie looked out the window. It had been months since they had seen the sky such an electric blue. The plane's silver wings sparkled blindingly in its glare. Crevasses cut great cracks in the dried-out earth beneath them. Everyone was hurting financially. Some of the stations were deserted. Others had no livestock. The landscape was littered with the carcasses and bleached bones of millions of sheep and thousands of cattle. Cattle weren't as badly affected as sheep since they were raised further north, in the tropics, and the drought was not as severe there as in the middle of the continent.

At Oliver's Lagoon, Cassie examined Mrs. Oliver, six months pregnant, and gave her two young children booster shots. She and Sam shared the Oliver smoke-o, luxuriating in the doughnuts the cook had just fried.

Then Sam asked, "Ready?"

The Olivers walked out to the Landrover; Fred drove Cassie and Sam the mile out to the landing field. As they rode, Cassie in the back seat and Sam in front with Fred, Sam stood up in his seat, gazing to the west. Cassie turned to see what he was looking at. A gigantic murky cloud loomed in the sky.

"Shit," Sam said, "it's a seething cloud of dust." He sat down and said to Fred, "I'll need an axe and ropes. We've got to belt that plane to the ground."

Fred looked over at him, swung the car around, and raced toward the shed. He and Sam dashed in and came back in a couple of minutes, throwing the rope and tools, rugs and old blankets into the seat next to Cassie, taking off toward the airstrip again.

"Doc, you'll be in the way. Just sit here."

She watched as Sam and Fred worked like madmen, strapping stakes into the ground and tying the plane to them until they'd used up all the rope. She heard Sam yell, "We've got to cover the air intakes or the dust'll block 'em forever."

She could tell from the expression on Fred's face that he had no idea where the air intakes were. Sam grabbed the mats, the blankets, everything, and jammed them into the shafts. Then he stood back and looked at the plane as the first savage blast hit. Sam ran to Cassie and said, "Get into the plane. You and Fred."

He jumped into the Land Rover and drove it in front of the plane's nose, pulled on the brake, and made a run for the plane, slamming the door behind him.

"That's to break the force of the wind," he explained, out of breath. "I don't know what else to do."

At eleven in the morning their world turned black, as dark as midnight. They could hear the wind funneling outside, heard and felt the strength of it. In the darkness Fred's anxious voice said, "Christ, I hope the kids are inside."

It was an hour and a half before twilight came, but the plane still rocked back and forth. Looking out the front window, Cassie was surprised to see the Land Rover had not turned on its side.

At last the storm subsided. Sam said, "God, look at all this sand."

The plane was mired in dunes of it.

Fred said, "I'll come back to help, but first I've got to go see if Laura and the kids are safe."

"Sure," Sam agreed as he reached out to put a hand on his arm. He opened the door and was about to jump to the ground, when he laughed. "Look, it's a sandslide. We can just roll down it," which he proceeded to do, laughing and whopping like a kid. "Fred, when you come back, bring a couple of shovels, willya?"

Fred reached up to help Cassie. "Come on, you may as well come up to the house and wait while Sam and I unearth the plane and Landrover."

Laura was fine, weeping with relief when she saw Fred and Cassie struggling across the sand. "Oh, thank God," she cried. "I wondered if you'd blown away."

Gritty sand covered everything—chairs, scatter rugs, stove, icebox, mantel, window ledges, picture frames, even the linen on the beds.

Two hours later, after they'd freed the plane and the Rover and made the airfield safe for take-off, Sam called Horrie. "Go back to Burnham Downs," Horrie instructed. "They had an accident due to the storm. We didn't even get it here."

It was nearly dark by the time they got to Burnham Downs, where the foreman's left leg and arm had been broken when the storm slammed him against a tree. He'd been carried up to the house, though Cassie imagined he must have screamed in agony. He lay on the floor in the middle of the parlor, his face ashen. The angles of his leg and arm were so unnatural it was nauseating.

Cassie knelt down and reached for his wrist, checking his pulse. "Can your fingers still feel?" she asked.

Homer, the foreman shook his head, his eyes pierced with suffering. Cassie nodded. "This is going to hurt but I've got to get this arm straight." With that, she pulled the arm down with such a jerk that it straightened. Homer let out a wail, then was quiet. "Sorry," she said softly. "Now, I've got to do the same with your leg, but that won't be as quick." She looked up at Sam. "I should have known better. Give me my bag, will you?"

She extracted a bottle of clear liquid and a hypodermic syringe. "Boil this for five minutes," she told Dan Elliot. She looked down at Homer. "Just a few minutes and you won't feel any pain," she promised. Her cool hand stroked his forehead.

Later, while Homer was still unconscious and after she'd straightened his leg, Dan found some boards which he and Sam sawed to the measurements Cassie requested. "They'll have to serve as splints until we get him to a hospital," she said. She placed them on either side of his arm and then wrapped it with tape. She did the same with his leg.

"He looks like a sandwich," Dan said, unable to suppress a smile.

Nancy came in to announce that she had supper ready and was expecting them to stay overnight. There wasn't much choice.

When Sam called Horrie in the morning, Horrie said, "It never rains but it doesn't pour."

"What do you have?" Sam asked.

"A plane's missing out of Oodnadatta. They want all the help they can get."

"My God, that's pretty far."

"We have no emergencies and they're asking for any planes within five hundred miles to come help search. Remember the Kookaburra? Planes came from all over the country to search for that."

"That was nearly twenty years ago, and they still haven't found it."

"I know. But you can't say it wasn't because no one looked."

"Okay. What frequency should we tune to?"

Horrie told him.

When Sam explained to Cassie what their day's mission was to be her first thought was for Homer, but Sam said, "You can keep him sedated. There's nothing the hospital can do for him but bed rest, is there? You have him fixed up fine."

"If he's fixed up fine, then why don't you leave him here and I'll take care of him while you fly down to Oodna?" Nancy said.

"I'd feel better if he's in the hospital and I can check on him for complications, that sort of thing."

"If you're going south, you could at least leave him here and stop for him on the way back. You'll need to fill up with gas someplace. It might as well be here."

Cassie's and Sam's eyes met, and she nodded.

"Okay," Sam said. "Thanks, Nance."

When they reached the search area out of Oodnadatta, the radio operator told Sam, "You've been assigned certain air space. You're to fly in thirty-mile legs, half a mile apart. Got someone with binoculars with you?"

Sam handed them to Cassie and then, irritation in his voice, said to her, "They're going on the assumption that a tiny Cessna over-shot its destination. Impossible in that headwind. If anything, it was pummeled sideways."

However, he followed their instructions for two hours, then radioed in. "Want permission to widen our coverage to one-mile legs so we can cover more ground more quickly."

The radio operator answered, "Let me check with the search master."

After a couple of minutes he came back on the radio, from six hundred miles away. "Permission denied."

"Shit," Sam growled. "This is a waste of time and fuel the way they're doing it."

They continued their legs, flying back and forth, Cassie staring into the bright glare of the sun. The land was nothing but brown, brown, brown, with cracks crisscrossing it. There was no sign of life and certainly no sign of a plane.

At five o'clock the radio operator announced the search was called off. The Cessna had been found two hundred miles east of where Sam and Cassie were searching. The pilot and passenger were both safe, though the plane was in pieces.

"We've got to refuel. Don't have enough to get back to Burnham Downs. I'll have to land and use our drums."

It looked flat enough to land anywhere with no difficulty. As he glided onto the hard-packed red earth, Sam said, "How about something to eat?"

Nancy Elliot had packed cold roast beef sandwiches. "Dear girl,"

Cassie said as she pulled them out of the paper sack. "We even have potato salad and pickles."

Sam refueled the plane from the forty-four gallon drums and stretched. It felt good to be outdoors. The sky was turning lavender in the west as fingers of gold surrounded the setting sun.

"We can't land at Burnham Downs in the dark," Cassie said.

Sam nodded, biting into the beef. "I'll let Horrie know. We can either fly all the way back to the lighted airfield at Augusta Springs and land and go out tomorrow morning to get our patient at Burnham Downs or we can stay here overnight and save gas and sleep under the stars."

They were silent for a minute, munching their sandwiches. Cassie saw the evening's first star on the eastern horizon. She felt at peace with the world.

"Well?" Sam asked, looking over at her.

"Whatever you want."

"Whatever *I* want?" He laughed.

"I don't care."

"Do we have enough coffee for breakfast?" he asked.

"If we just drink water tonight."

They finished eating in silence. After a while, Sam stood up. "I'll call Horrie. He's probably wondering where we are."

Cassie sat in the gathering darkness, the western sky purpling, growing blood-red into black. There wasn't a sound.

She and Sam hadn't said a personal word since the night of the party. Neither of them had ever referred to *Now there are three of us.*

She had been afraid even to think about what he'd been implying. For years, she'd felt safe with Sam. But he was married. And he was her friend, her partner. She didn't want her work—or her life—to be upset.

He was in the plane a long time. When he came out he had blankets under his arm and spread them out beside the plane. "Would you feel safer sleeping inside?"

She smiled, though it was too dark for him to see. "Safer, maybe, but not nearly as exciting. It's been years since I've slept out under the stars."

"Remember we did it our first run? That guy with a ruptured bladder? You operated on him out in the bush?"

"I thought I was in the middle of nowhere. It was the first night I heard them sing the cattle. It's still one of the most magical things to me, even though I've heard it half a dozen times."

He sat down next to her, his back against the plane's tire. "We didn't dream then, did we, that ten years later we'd still be working together."

She laughed. "I thought you resented me. I thought it was going to be a tough battle."

"So did I. You were tough as nails. More man than woman. You wore men's pants, you used four-letter words, you were matter-of-fact, and I thought you were a cold fish."

"I still wear pants."

"Yeah, and you still use four-letter words. But you're not tough as nails."

"No?"

"Nope."

The sharpness of the night air sent a chill through Cassie.

"I didn't even think of you as a woman in those days."

"Yes, you did," she disagreed. "You thought a woman had no right being a doctor. You disapproved."

"Maybe I did," he said, staring up into the inky night. The stars looked close enough to touch.

After a while he asked, "Do you miss Chris?"

Cassie hugged herself to keep warm. "Sometimes."

After a minute's silence, Sam asked, "I've often wondered, and it's none of my business. You don't have to answer. Did you love him, Doc?"

Cassie stared into the darkness. Stars seemed to sprinkle the sky right down to the horizon. "I didn't think so then, but maybe I did. I wasn't *in* love with him, ever. There wasn't any magic, any electricity. And there was a lot I never liked about him. But, yes, I think I grew to love him."

Sam didn't say anything.

"I took him for granted. Maybe too much so. The things about him

I didn't like—his rigidity and bigotry—irritated me. But he was a very good husband. I think he even became fond of the aboriginal girls Fiona took in. Maybe they taught him something. He realized Anna was intelligent. Do you know what? She contacted Fiona a couple of weeks ago about going on to school after all these years."

"Really?"

The bark of a dingo echoed in the distance as the light of the moon grew bright, etching the landscape in silver.

"I didn't know I loved Chris until after he died. That's the sad part."

After a while Sam said, "We learn so much too late. At least you made Chris happy. He was a different man from the one I knew before the war."

They were silent for a long time. Then Sam stood up and laid their swags out, about three feet from each other. He lay down on his. "You could've blown me over with a feather when I read your letter telling me you'd married him. I'd have thought if you were the only two people on a desert island, you wouldn't have gotten together. I was sure it'd be you and Blake."

Cassie said, "You wouldn't have won a bet from me. I'd have agreed." She crawled into her swag, relishing the warmth. Putting her hands under her head she looked above her. "It's magic, isn't it?"

Sam rolled over on an elbow and rested his chin on his hands, looking over at her. "What?"

"The sky. The night. The desert. Being here."

She fought the urge to reach out and take hold of his hand. She wanted to fall asleep out here so far from the rest of the world, feeling Sam's warmth and security. She drifted off into sleep and dreamed that he asked, "If you weren't in love, why did you marry him?"

And that she answered, "Who knows? Do you know why you got married?"

From afar, in a voice she could barely hear, he said, "Because you married Chris."

When she awoke before dawn and watched Sam, still asleep, she lay there wondering if that had really been a dream.

Chapter 50

"Ever since I flew around with you and saw all those little children who *needed* learning, I've been obsessed with it," Fiona said. "Now I'm determined to make time for it. I've spent years wondering what could possibly be done to educate these Outback kids, and now I think I've found the way, but the Flying Doctors have to cooperate. They're doing it in Alice."

"Doing what?" Cassie asked.

Fiona had flown into town in their Cessna—it was the first time she'd done it. "Educating via radio," Fiona said, her enthusiasm evident in her shining eyes. "I went to Alice and talked to the people over there. They're so excited it's thrilling. Oh, Cassie, it's unbelievable. They bring the world to these isolated Outback stations, to children who know nothing beyond their own fences. A teacher can tell stories, read books, teach arithmetic, stir their imaginations! A whole new world can open up for these children. Mine included, of course!"

Cassie smiled at her friend. She hadn't seen her like this for a long time.

"I thought correspondence classes were mandatory."

"Of course," Fiona agreed, brushing her hand in the air, "and I'm not knocking that method, but it leaves much to be desired, all by itself. A child works alone, unless Mummy helps and sometimes Mummy doesn't have the knowledge or the time. The child tries to learn to read and add and subtract and fills out forms and sends them to some impersonal being who corrects papers and sends them back. But this way, via radio—oh, Cassie, they'd be connected with a teacher and with other children. Their lives would be as bright and varied as their imaginations. They'd have contact with other children, hear other stories, other voices."

Cassie leaned forward, "I've always wondered when students have questions during correspondence classes, how in the world do they get answers that mean anything?"

Fiona clapped her hands. "That's it! I talked to Graham Pitt, the FDS director over in Alice, and he's a terrific radio technician. He tells me it can be done with sustained transmission. You'd need new equipment, but maybe Romla can have one of her fund raisers that she's so good at."

"When you're finished I'll tell you some news about her."

It was as though Fiona hadn't even heard her. "Of course, it means a whole new technique for some teachers," she continued.

"A real challenge, I'd say," Cassie said as she got up and went to the kitchen for more tea. She'd just found a new kind, blackberry, on the Teakle and Robbins' shelves. Fiona loved it.

"Do you want to try doing the teaching?" Cassie asked.

"Don't think I wouldn't love to, but I can't. Blake won't let me. I had to reassure him that my involvement with this won't interfere with our home life, with the children, with meals together. Don't get me wrong, he's very excited, too, about the idea that I might play even a small part in changing the level of education in this country. But, all I can hope to do is get this thing off the ground. Over in Alice they're calling it The School of the Air. Cassie, I think such radio schools can get going at every single Flying Doctor base. Do you know what a difference this will make to these children?"

"So, you want me to find out if the Augusta Springs section will sponsor this project?"

"Not really. I can do that. But I want to make sure I'm a speaker at the next council meeting, and you always attend them."

"I can call one, or we can get Steven to call one. He's back as head of the council now, after an eight-year hiatus."

Fiona nodded. "I'm glad he's letting himself get involved again. The kids brought life back to him, and now that he's alone again he's reaching out, thank goodness. What I wish for him is a good woman." Then Fiona laughed. "Well, if not good, at least exciting. Not just any woman will do. He's so full of energy himself and Jennifer could keep up with him, I think, though I only met her twice. He and Blake have their disagreements and Blake doesn't always win."

Cassie had let the tea steep and poured some into Fiona's cup. "How do you envision this working?"

Fiona stood up and paced, her hands gesturing in the air. "Well, I'd think we might choose a teacher and then fly over to Alice to talk to them there. A woman named Adelaide Miethke got the idea originally and has worked on it. I'd like to fly down to Adelaide—yes, isn't that funny, Adelaide from Adelaide? and talk with her or maybe she'd come up to Alice or even over here.

"You know, Cassie, I lie in bed at night long after Blake's asleep and think about this. It would have to be divided into different stages: children's stories and nursery rhymes, and then for those a bit older, numbers and language and spelling and then for older children . . . social studies, civics about our own country . . . then, later, about the world."

"Music. Can you have music?"

"Mr. Pitt says yes. The students can sing together, and hear music and talk to each other about it. It will be wonderful!"

Cassie thought it was already wonderful, watching what was happening to Fiona. Not that Fiona had ever seemed anything but happy since she'd married Blake, but now somehow Cassie thought she seemed like a desert flower in bloom. Her enthusiasm was contagious and carried Cassie along with it.

"Okay," laughed Fiona, "I guess I'll get off my soapbox, but I came to town to get your reaction to this."

"I think it's marvelous. We'll do all we can to help. I'm sure Horrie will, too."

"That's good, because we'll need him. We'll have to add a room onto the radio shack."

"Which will be good. We're getting too large for what we have. We need more sophisticated equipment and more people to work at the base. Horrie can't handle it all now that we can be reached twenty-four hours a day. We have the galah sessions and he has telegrams to send. It's become far too busy for one person, even though Betty spells him. But she's busy with the children. And you know what?" Cassie laughed. "She's finally taken it into her own hands, and by golly, she's building a verandah on that shack, all by herself! She says she's sick of sweltering in there in the summer and she doesn't have enough room, and she's building the whole verandah from scratch!"

Fiona giggled. "She's only waited, what? About nine years for him to keep that promise?"

"She's smart. Instead of getting mad at him for never getting around to it, she's decided his priorities and hers aren't the same and if she wants it, she'll have to take care of getting it."

"We might learn a lesson from that. Okay, what is it about Romla you were going to tell me?"

Cassie leaned forward. "Jim Teakle has finally proposed to her!"

"It's about time."

"Do you know what? Of course, don't tell this to anyone else. He'd never even kissed her until this year! After all these years of squiring her to dances, taking her and the kids on picnics, after all these Monday night suppers at our house . . . I'd taken for granted they'd at least gotten *that* far. He started a Boy Scout troop just so Terry could join. Of course, Terry's off at boarding school in Adelaide now, but whenever there's a holiday, Jim acts like Terry's his—takes him hunting and spends time with him like dads are supposed to."

"What about Roger? Does she ever hear from him?"

Cassie shook her head. "Not often. He sends the kids birthday and Christmas presents but he never bothers to see them. He's over in Brisbane and the kids are in school in Adelaide. Pam's at the university, studying engineering, of all things."

Fiona sat down. "When's the big day?"

Cassie shrugged. "Soon, I think. Romla says it's going to be *the* wedding of the year. Her first one was just a tiny thing, and she says this is going to be a blowout. She doesn't think a woman can get married without trousseau. She's upset she can't find any fancy lingerie."

"Sexy, you mean."

"Right. So, she's decided to open a lingerie shop in Augusta Springs, if you can imagine that!"

"If that were her only enterprise, she'd go broke. Women around here don't have money for such things. Besides, can you imagine any of the women out on those stations wearing something exotic to bed? Romla will go broke."

"I know," agreed Cassie. "But I guess she can afford to. She's made such a success of the Royal Palms that the owners have invited her to be a partner, with no financial investment at all. They're even going to build an addition."

"So the twentieth century is even coming to our part of the world. But, now that she's getting married, won't she stop working at the hotel?"

Cassie studied Fiona. "Why? She loves it."

Fiona threw her hands in the air in a helpless gesture. "Oh, it's just that working and being married . . . "

"But, Fi, her work excites her. Are you suggesting she give that up and be satisfied to clean house and cook?"

Fiona looked puzzled for a minute. "Well, we've always done that."

Cassie smiled. "Look at you with this new idea. I've never seen you this excited about keeping house and changing diapers."

"That's the kind of work you do for love, not pleasure."

"Where is it written that women shouldn't get pleasure from work?"

Fiona looked confused. "It's—oh, Cassie, if I insisted on doing this School of the Air teaching, Blake would have a fit. He wouldn't let me."

"Wouldn't *let* you?" Cassie's voice cracked. "Fiona, you're not his child!"

"I know, I know. But, after all, *my* job is to run our home."

"Which is fine," Cassie said, "if that's what you want. But Romla's at a different point in her life. Can't we each be different?"

"Easy for you to say. You're not married and responsible for a husband and children or a big house and servants. Oh, my dear, I'm sorry. I didn't mean . . . well, you know."

Cassie waved her hand. "I suppose sometimes you envy me and sometimes I envy you. But let's get back to this idea you want presented to the FDS. The Service has become so big now it has a total of eight bases around the country and employs twelve doctors. They're having a central meeting in Sydney next week, and I'm going. Steven's going, too, and I'll talk to him about your School of the Air, though I think you could plant some seeds, too."

"I already have. It's not Steven I have to convince, it's the other directors."

"I imagine it all hinges on money. I'll throw it in Romla's lap, though she may be too busy with wedding plans."

"Just mention it to her, and then wait until she's back from the honeymoon to pounce on her about fund raising. We have groundwork to do and it'll probably be a year before we can be ready."

"Fi, why don't you come into town more often? I love it when it's just the two of us."

"Since I have this project to work on, maybe I can fly over a couple of times a month. It's a luxury now that we have two planes, if you count the helicopter, too. Though I think the time for me to be away is when Blake is, too. He likes to have me around when he's home."

Fiona sat back in her chair and looked at Cassie. "Have you given any idea to getting married again? You've your whole life ahead of you. You're just thirty-seven. Still young."

"I don't feel so old, but marriage? I don't think so."

"I feel I'm in my prime. You are, too, Cassie. Share it with some wonderful man. Don't you want to have children?"

"If they could be as beautiful and well-behaved as yours." Cassie couldn't help wondering if hers and Blake's would have looked like Fiona's.

"You're not too old to have children, if that's what you want. I keep wanting to get past child-bearing age. I don't want more. Three's enough. Look around, Cassie. I bet you can have any man you want. Let's find a husband for you, a father to your yet-to-be-born babies."

"Don't do that to me, Fi." Cassie shook her head. "Besides, I know everyone in the territory. There's no one."

"No one?"

"Well, no one who's available."

Perhaps she should move, go someplace else. Set up a private practice. Meet new people. Start a new life. After all, she'd been in Augusta Springs a decade.

She'd look Sydney over next week.

Chapter 51

"I've been looking forward to this," Steven said as he took the seat next to Cassie. "I never get to see enough of you."

The thought pleased Cassie, too.

"How long," he asked, strapping the seatbelt on, "since you've been away from Augusta Springs?"

In the nearly-eleven years she'd been here she'd been out very few times. Kakadu with Blake. Townsville. A month in Adelaide learning to fly. Her father's funeral in Sydney three years ago.

"It's been three years."

"Longer than that for me. Blake flies all over the country, but I've no urge to see beyond Tookaringa. Or at least not much beyond Augusta Springs."

The stewardess asked if he wouldn't like her to store his Stetson. He grinned. "Already feel like I'm on vacation. Before I forget, Fiona said to be sure to tell you. Damnedest thing happened last week."

Cassie looked around. A large commercial plane was so different from what she was used to.

"The first time I came to Augusta Springs," she said, "it took me three and a half days. Now, it's going to be just a few hours."

Steven nodded, obviously ready to tell her his story. "Fiona and I were sitting on the verandah last Wednesday. Or was it Thursday? Doesn't matter. It was up at my place—we were having lemonade. It was about four o'clock and walking up the road we could see a woman in a long dress, carrying a carpetbag. We kept on talking but we were both looking at this figure getting closer and closer, wondering if it were a mirage. Heat waves shimmered up from the earth, you know how they do, and we had to wonder if she was real. No one *walks* up that road. Pretty soon we stopped talking and just stared at what seemed like an apparition. She was wearing Victorian clothes and shaded herself with an umbrella the same color as her dress, grey. She wore a ruffled, high-necked white blouse, with a great big hat like they must have worn in the 1890s. It was tied under her chin and I thought she might burst into song." He laughed. "Like maybe Betty Grable in one of her movies."

Now that they were airborne the stewardess approached, taking their orders for drinks.

"When we were sure she was heading for us, for the verandah, we looked at each other and both of us got up and went down the steps, walking toward her. She had blond hair pulled up under her hat and the bluest eyes I've ever seen, but she sure did look strange out there in clothes that must have been in style over fifty years ago."

Cassie wondered if he were making this up, but he was so enthusiastic and painted such a picture that she had to believe him. "How old was she?"

Steven raised his eyebrows. "I'd guess in her middle forties. She nodded her head at us and took a handkerchief from her wrist, from that long-sleeved jacket, and wiped perspiration from her brow. She asked Fiona if she were Mrs. Thompson. Fiona said yes and wouldn't she like some lemonade. She said that sounded wonderful and, after I took her bag, she followed us up onto the porch. We sat there like we were having tea in a Victorian novel. She had this soft, gentle voice you sort of had to strain to hear and introduced herself as Lucy Martin, recently arrived from England.

"Damnedest story, Cassie. She said she'd studied the maps and saw where there were aboriginal villages, and three of them are on the northern part of our property. They've always been there, about twenty miles apart, in sort of a triangle. She wanted our permission to set a tent up and live there. Her goal is to educate the aborigines. Can you imagine?"

"Fiona's been trying to do that for years," Cassie said.

Steven agreed. "She'd heard, who knows where, that Fiona was interested, which is one of the reasons she chose our land. She said she'd become fascinated with the aborigines when she was studying archeology in university. She had worked and saved money and taught, for all these years, to come live among what she calls the natives and study their ways. Can you believe that? She's been working toward this goal, she says, since she was nineteen years old, though she detoured into marriage. Her husband died two years ago."

"How did she get to your place?"

"Said she took the bus. You know, it passes now on the main road about seven or eight miles from the house. She walked from there."

The stewardess brought their drinks. "So? What did Fiona say?"

"You know Fi. She just stood right up and hugged the woman. I said Fiona ought to drive her up there in the Land Rover, but Fiona decided it'd be more sensible to take her there in the 'copter. Of course, I'm still not caught up in these modern marvels. And I had to ask her practical questions, like where would she get supplies? How was she going to eat? She said she'd eat when and how the 'natives' do and she'd left her tent behind a tree near the bus stop as it was too heavy and unwieldy to carry all the way to the house."

"What about her clothing? Did she explain that?"

He laughed. "Fi asked her. She said 'As long as I'm starting a new life I decided I should be able to dress any way I want and I've always felt an affinity for the Victorian era. So I had a dressmaker make me two outfits and I feel very comfortable, thank you, though it is a bit warm.' Fiona, of course, was sitting on the porch in shorts."

Cassie laughed. "What do you think the aborigines will make of her?"

Steven's mouth puckered and his eyes squinted. "Who knows? She didn't want our help—she wanted to start her new life as she'd dreamed of it. We did talk her into staying two days and Fiona gave her some books before flying her up to our northwest quadrant that's uninhabited except for the abos. About once every two or three years we graze cattle up there, but not often."

"Did you like her?"

"She's eccentric, but isn't that what makes our part of the world so interesting? How many nice, normal, well-adjusted people do you know up here?"

Cassie nodded. "It's true. Just about everyone is a little off-center; otherwise, they'd be in the cities or where it's easier to live, that's for sure. John Flynn once told me that he thought the Outback was filled with two kinds of people, those running from something and those searching for something."

"Perhaps." Steven leaned back in his seat. "I'm hoping you're going to let me wine and dine you during our one big adventure to the city. I've been counting on it. In the meantime, I'm going to catch forty winks." He closed his eyes and was asleep, just like that.

Cassie looked out the window and smiled at the story he'd just told. A woman appearing as though from a mirage, in the middle of this vast, nearly-empty continent, in clothes over fifty years out of date.

Aside from the loveliest benefit—that of renewing a kinship with John Flynn—Cassie was stimulated by the three-day meeting. One doctor and one councillor from each of the bases was present, and they shared ways to raise money and new techniques to promote efficiency. They also discussed a national policy which would still leave each section autonomous.

Cassie and the councillor from South Australia were the only two women there. However, unlike her experiences in med school and internship, Cassie was treated with respect by her peers. She had served the Flying Doctors longer than any of the other doctors except Allan Vickers, who was already a legend.

She was pleased to see Don McLeod there. He explained, "John has asked me to keep my finger in the pie. Even though I'm no longer a wandering padre, I manage to drop in on sections now and then and serve as a resource for the three padres out in the bush. The Alice is a central location, of course, even though it's a thousand miles from nowhere. It's the only one in the northern territory right now, too. Darwin has its own ambulance service. Of course, you fly into the territory now and then, I know, for emergencies. It doesn't seem like we'll ever have a large enough population to become a state."

"I can't believe it. Look how people are moving into the bush in South Australia and Queensland. I think the territory will fill up. Certainly in another twenty years it will be populated enough to be a state."

Don shook his head and held up his hand to stop her. "Lack of water will no doubt prohibit an expanding population. Also, the humidity up Darwin way, in Kakadu and Arnhem Land, can be excruciating for months of the year. It can render inhabitants close to comatose January through March, during the Wet."

"So I've heard. Well, I'm thrilled you're still a part of us. You hadn't mentioned that in your letters. How's your growing family?" He no longer wrote weekly but did manage to scratch off a note at least once a month, though never with details of his own life.

"Going to grow even more," he grinned. "Number four is on the way."

"My goodness, you make me feel old."

Don put an arm around her and kissed her cheek. "Want me to find you a husband?" he asked, only half-teasing.

"No, thank you. "I really am happy the way I am." But she was aware of a restlessness and reminded herself that she was going to look around Sydney and see if she liked it enough to leave Augusta Springs.

She did like it. In fact, she fell in love with Sydney all over again, remembering that wherever she was—San Francisco, London, Washington—she'd considered her grandparents' home in Sydney her home base. The old house overlooked the harbor upriver from Sydney, and she told Steven she wanted to go see it.

They not only saw the old homestead, freshly painted and looking as lovely as Cassie remembered, but knocked on the door. Cassie explained to the owners that she had spent much of her youth there, and asked if she could look at it again. The owners offered tea to her and Steven.

She and Steven and Don took the ferry across the harbor and spent an afternoon at the zoo. The day after the conference ended, she and Steven again took the ferry, this time across to Manly to spend an hour walking down the beach.

"Let's do something wicked," said Steven, so Cassie suggested visiting a nightclub at King's Cross, where she asked, "Do you really think they're prostitutes?" Two young women in short, tight skirts leaned against a light pole, smiling at the men who passed by.

"I think so," Steven said. "I didn't know nice young women knew about such things."

She looked at him. "I hope you're kidding. Do you think just because we're female we don't know about the seamy side of life?"

The nightclub wasn't wicked, but it was noisier and more colorful and filled with more people in more outrageous clothing than had ever been seen in Augusta Springs. Cassie and Steven danced to a band that blared so loudly they couldn't carry on a conversation, and they drank Scotch on the rocks and laughed a lot.

At her hotel room, Steven said, "Meet me for breakfast, before the plane takes off. Seven o'clock in the restaurant downstairs."

When she arrived the next morning, he said, "I don't remember when I've had more fun. I didn't sleep a wink last night, Cassie. Why don't you marry me? We could have a wonderful life together. I think I've been falling in love with you little by little for years. You make me feel so alive. Come live at Tookaringa with me."

Cassie was taken aback. "Steven, let's not ruin a perfectly lovely friendship. I love you. You're one of my dearest friends, someone I rely on, and someone I care a great deal about. But, I'm not in love with you. I want you in my life, though. I can't imagine my life without Steven Thompson."

"I was afraid of that. I know, I know, I'm twenty-five years older. I just thought . . . now that Chris, well, that you might . . . "

"I wouldn't be content to live at Tookaringa, either, Steven. I'd feel cooped up out there, and you couldn't stand a wife who still wanted to work, who wanted to fly out at a minute's notice, who had no interest at all in running a home . . . "

His smile was tinged with regret. "Okay, okay, you're right. I'd thought maybe by now you were ready to settle down."

"I don't know that I'll ever be ready for that." She remembered how Jennifer had stopped painting when there was a chance she'd become more famous than he.

When the plane descended into Augusta Springs, Cassie realized she'd forgotten to investigate whether or not she might like to move to Sydney.

She guessed that was an answer in itself.

Chapter 52

"The way he's shouted at me this last week! Acting like he didn't recognize me, tossing the soup I'd made across the room! I'm certainly not going to take that or let his shivering stop me from catching that plane," Olivia said.

"He's got malaria, Liv," Cassie said. "Malarial patients behave in bizarre ways."

"Well, I guess so! He acted drunk. He'd sing snatches of song and then break into tears. He swore—words I've never, ever heard him say."

Cassie nodded. "That's typical. People with malaria will be okay for several hours then break into sweats and shaking fevers. They're delirious, have hallucinations . . . "

"Yes, he kept seeing things that weren't there."

"They often fight their caregivers."

"Well, not me!"

Surrounded by suitcases, Olivia pulled on her white gloves and nodded at her two children. "I'm going back where people put these on when they go out someplace nice. I'm going to where there's lots of grass, and trees that lose their leaves in the winter, and where fog rolls across the heath . . . " Her voice was strident. "People don't die of malaria, do they?"

"Not ordinarily."

"I don't know why he'd want to get this right now. Just to make me stay? I wouldn't think he'd care. You're always off someplace in your damn plane. It was bad enough before, but ever since QANTAS left and Sam's employed directly by the FDS you'd think it was *his* plane."

"It is."

It was a beautiful Mark 1 tri-motor Drover that, compared to what they'd had, flew like a dream, despite its flaws. It came as close as possible to being a perfect Flying Doctor aircraft: it had a Lear 14d radio compass that picked up stations hundreds of miles away; it automatically gave a hearing in relation to where the aircraft was heading; and it had a wonderful amount of control below stalling speed. But it lacked stability and was likely to wander all about if you weren't careful. One couldn't read a newspaper or do much paperwork for fear the plane might turn around and go home. It was too heavy for the small engines, but at least the engines didn't guzzle fuel.

But aside from having to be watched all the time, it was a joy to Sam and Cassie, especially after putting up with the old plane.

"Well, it's so important to you because you don't have anything else. No husband, no kids, no one. But Sam does. I tell him to go back to QANTAS and get on some big overseas run, where we can live in a suburb of Sydney and go to concerts and movies and the kids can be exposed to something other than horses and sand and this godawful provinciality!"

Over the years Cassie had heard a few others—always women—talk like this. She thought it funny . . . she'd been brought up in three of the world's most sophisticated cities, yet to her, this was where the essence of life was. Everyone might know your business in a small town, but people cared. This was not only the heart of the continent, it was the heart of her life.

Olivia stopped pacing and looked at Cassie. "Tell me something about malaria." She glanced at her watch.

"It's caused by infinitesimal single-celled parasites which are transferred from one person to another by the anopheles mosquito."

Olivia looked impatient. "You want to put that in lay language?"

"Well, it was the single greatest medical scourge of the war. Men who'd built up no immunity came to tropical areas, and thousands became infected with malaria."

"So, how'd Sam get it?"

"I've no idea, but we do fly into tropical areas often. It's endemic with the aborigines. They go about their daily lives with no seeming difficulty, despite large numbers of parasites circulating through their blood. They don't have much energy but live whole lifetimes this way, unaware that they're infected. Sometimes what we take for laziness is just the effects of malaria. But because whites have no immunity, they can get seriously ill with very few parasites in their bloodstreams."

Olivia scrunched up her face. "Some little bitty things are running around in Sam's blood? Is it contagious?"

"No. You can only get it through a mosquito bite. And it doesn't have any symptoms at first. You know when Sam kept complaining about a headache? Well, a mosquito could've bitten him from a week to a month before that. What we're seeing now is the typical manic period that follows. Paroxysms, sudden chills followed by high fever and rapid breathing, then a sweating stage accompanied by a drop in temperature, hallucinations . . . "

"Then it's over?"

"Not necessarily. He can get the same symptoms again when more plasmodia are released into the bloodstream about every two to three days. I'm going to put him in the hospital so he has round-the-clock care. He'll sweat, so the nurses will have to change his sheets several times a day. We'll probably have to restrain him physically to keep him from hurting himself."

"Why Sam? Why now?"

Cassie stared unbelievingly at Sam's wife.

Liv lit a cigarette and blew smoke into Cassie's face. "Where's that taxi? Children—go stand on the porch and call when you see the taxi round the corner. Just like Sam, get sick so I have to take a cab."

Cassie had been prepared to tell her more about the illness consuming her husband, but Liv was obviously not interested.

"So, he's likely to have repeated attacks," Liv said. "You mean *all through his life?*"

"If you get a particularly dangerous type—and there are four types that infect humans—then all the organisms are released from your liver at once and there's only one bout with the disease, but it's extremely severe."

"So, how do you know which is which?"

Cassie had a feeling Liv wasn't even listening. "We don't know.

But if you don't treat it, attacks can recur for years and years. Of course, the patient slowly builds up defenses and attacks will occur less frequently, but they can last for up to forty years, two to three days at a time."

"Oh, that's great."

For you or for Sam? Cassie wanted to ask.

"Well, what can you do about it?"

Cassie shrugged. "Quinine, and I'm not even sure that's of much help. Maybe temporarily, but not in the long run. In children, high fever sometimes affects the brain, causing unconsciousness or convulsions. Researchers are working on more effective methods, but so far nothing's better than quinine or atabrine. We're lucky Sam's at the sweating stage. That means he's passed through both the cold and hot stages and is on his way to feeling better."

"Well, the last two days haven't been much fun, what with his moaning and me trying to pack."

The children screamed, "Ma, here's the taxi!"

In a flurry, Liv and the two children started lugging the suitcases out to the verandah. The cab driver opened the screen door and said, "Here, let me do that."

Olivia didn't even go back to the bedroom to say goodbye to Sam.

When Cassie went in to see him, he lay with his eyes closed, beads of sweat dotting his forehead. She sat down on the edge of the bed and he opened his eyes. "I'm going to get you to the hospital, Sam."

"Do I have to go?" She could scarcely hear him.

She nodded. "You need constant care for a few days."

For the next three weeks Sam alternated between sweats and chills for forty-eight hours and the weakness that followed for another forty-eight. The attacks came like clockwork, causing him to lose over thirty pounds. Cassie sat with him every evening.

When the seizures disappeared he was so weak he could hardly stand, but he asked, "When can I get out of this place?"

"I'd let you go now if Liv were home to take care of you."

He looked at her.

"Okay," Cassie said with a smile. "Do you think the town will gossip? I'll take you home with me, but when I'm out on flights you have to promise not to *do* anything or go anyplace."

His grin was weak. "That's probably the best offer I can get. I'd appreciate that mightily, Doc. I'm going bonkers here. Besides, you're a better cook than Liv's ever been."

"I'll have to work on fattening you up. You look as bony as when I first met you."

"Well, I didn't think *you* were any great shakes, either."

Cassie had missed Sam's company on clinics; luckily there hadn't been a single emergency that she couldn't handle alone. And she realized she was filled with contentment, looking forward all day to going home in the evening. For the first time since Chris's death she enjoyed planning menus, turning to cook books occasionally to prepare something special.

Sam was interested in every detail of her day. He wanted to know about all the ailments, wanted to hear how each station was doing, basked in their concern for him. He reminded her to make daily checkups on the plane, though they now had a maintenance man; all the pilot had to do was fly.

He lay on the chaise on Cassie's verandah and held court afternoons; it seemed that the entire population of Augusta Springs saw him at some time during the week. Sometimes Cassie didn't have to cook at all, and found herself disappointed when she found tureens of soup and the casseroles, pies, cakes, and bowls of flowers that had been dropped off for Sam.

"I feel like royalty," he said happily.

Gradually he regained his weight as well as his energy, but it was a slow process. Even when it seemed he had fully recovered, he realized he didn't have the energy to do half the things he had done before.

They both enjoyed the long evenings, sitting on the verandah. It wasn't until after nine, when the visitors had gone, that they began to talk of things they'd never talked of in all their years together.

"You know what surprised me most about the war?" Sam asked one evening.

Cassie, her head back against the cushion and her eyes closed, shook her head. "No, of course not."

"You."

She opened her eyes to look over at his silhouette in the dark. "What did I have to do with the war?"

"I found myself thinking of you, which I didn't expect to do. Hell, I didn't even think of you as a woman in those days, but I missed you."

"Oh," she said, feeling pleased, "you just missed our routine. We've always had such a good time together. I'd never thought of you as a man, either. I mean, not in *that* way, you know what I mean." Then why did she feel this way now, she wondered.

Sam was silent.

He stood up and walked outside. He sat on the steps, looking up at the stars. "Come on out. You should see these stars. The Southern Cross is as distinct as I've ever seen it."

Cassie didn't move. She had a premonition that something was about to change and she didn't want anything between her and Sam to change. "Sam, you're one of the few constants in my life."

He still gazed at the heavens. "So that means you can't come look at the stars?"

"You're just lonely, with Liv gone."

He sighed. "Cassie, I've been lonelier living with Liv than I ever was living alone."

"Why did you marry her?"

"Such a stupid reason. I told you once. She was the first girl I saw after I got your letter telling me you'd married Chris."

"You thought I was going to marry Blake when you went away."

"True." He was quiet for awhile. "And at the time that didn't bother me. It didn't begin to disturb me until I got to England, but I accepted it. I'd been an idiot not to realize how I felt about you, but your damn competence and feistiness and no-nonsense manner put me off. It wasn't until I left for the war that I began to see beyond all that. I kicked myself but then I figured I couldn't ever have competed with someone like Blake Thompson anyway. I hadn't been ready for someone like you. I was young and thought that what was important about a girl was how pretty she looked and how soft she felt. You were good-looking, but you sure weren't soft. But when I got your letter that you hadn't married Blake but Chris! You know what I did?" He laughed. "I never told you, did I? I smashed my hand right through a window. Broke the glass and nearly broke my hand. Bloody mess."

Cassie stared over at the dark shadow that was Sam. "No," she said, her voice barely a whisper. "No, you never told me."

"It's okay. It's in the past. I wasn't ready then anyhow. I still thought women should stay home and cook and have babies and agree with everything I thought."

"Well, hasn't Liv done all of that?"

"She has indeed. Except for saying yes to this land I love. And I find myself bored out of my skull. Of course, she isn't a bit interested in all the people we see out in the bush. She doesn't care about what we do every day. She's not concerned about the emergencies, the things you and I consider exciting and rewarding. No, Cassie, I'm not lonely because Liv isn't here. That's not what's wrong with me."

Cassie stood up and walked from the screened-in porch to sit beside Sam. She reached over and took his hand. "I'm sorry, Sam. I know you're depressed, too, because of what you've just gone through physically. You know there's no one whose happiness I care more about. You've become my best friend."

He squeezed her hand. "Funny, isn't it? The paths our lives take. If you had your life to live over, what would be different?"

Cassie sighed. She thought a moment. "I wouldn't have gone off to Kakadu with Blake all those years ago."

"Ah, so you suffered a broken heart. I've spent all these years wondering who said goodbye to whom."

"No one said goodbye at all."

"So he and Fiona came as a shock, huh?"

She nodded. "Fiona's never known she married the man I loved."

"Is that the past tense?"

"Don't you think love has to be shared or it becomes masochistic? Blake and I haven't shared anything in so many years sometimes I wonder how I even talk with him."

Suddenly Sam turned to her and she could see the whites of his eyes in the darkness. "So that's it?" He slapped his forehead. "And all this time I thought . . . Cassie, you married Chris when you found Fiona had married Blake. That's right, isn't it?"

"It seemed like the thing to do."

"Oh, Cassie, dear Cassie, and I didn't even know you were suffering." He reached out and put an arm around her shoulders and drew her close. "So, you've never known real love either."

"God, we sound like tragic characters, don't we? But I'm not unhappy, Sam."

"I wish I could say the same. I feel trapped. I know what I want and I can't reach out for it. Do you believe in those chestnuts? Duty. Honor."

"I don't know what I believe. I don't think you should hurt someone if you can help it, yet it isn't right to sacrifice yourself for someone else's happiness, either. You're thinking of Liv, aren't you? And the children."

"Of course."

They sat staring into the darkness, Sam's arm around her shoulders. She finally said, "Right this minute, I'm happy, Sam."

"I am, too. But I'll tell you what. I think I'm gonna go home."

She sat upright. "At this hour? Sam, it's nearly midnight. Wait til tomorrow, at least."

He stood up. "Nope. I'm going now, this minute. I'm going to walk—I don't even want a ride. Give me three days on my own and then I hope I can fly out again. I'm getting itchy."

"This is silly," she said.

"Never let it be said I haven't done a bunch of stupid things in my life. Dinner was good, Cassie. I could get used to your cooking. And I appreciate your hospitality, but it's time to get goin'."

As she watched him walk down the path and blend into the night, she realized he hadn't called her Doc once tonight. She stood on the steps, hugging herself as the night suddenly seemed chilly. She stared into the darkness long after Sam disappeared. For the first time in a long time, loneliness engulfed her. She was surprised to find a tear trickling down her cheek.

Chapter 53

She couldn't sleep. Well, not quite true. She fell asleep with little trouble, but she awoke at two and lay tossing until after four. Sam.

Cassie had taken Sam for granted all the years she'd known him. What was it now, ten years? No, eleven. He'd been away for six, but he'd been back for four and she'd seen him just about every day of her life since then.

They worked together like clockwork. They had but to glance at each other and knew what the other would do next, what was needed. Now that she'd flown planes herself, Cassie could look at the weather, at the terrain below, or at the clouds on the horizon and know what Sam would do. Not that she'd have done exactly the same thing, but she knew what Sam would do.

Sam made her laugh. Sam gave her comfort. Sam kept her in touch with the community. While she bandaged wounds or gave exams, he was with a group of people, finding out what was happening. He was the one who told her what a success the School of the Air was, and he was the one who picked up the mail and brought lessons to the Outback, sometimes discussing them with the children. He often gathered a group around him and Cassie could hear him telling them, with animated gestures, of the latest movie he'd seen. A year ago he'd bought an old guitar and taught himself to play. He kept it in the plane and when there were a bunch of kids around, he'd get out the guitar and sing songs to them, teaching them the words. After a few months, the children sang along with him, and were waiting for him when the plane arrived at clinics. "Liv can't stand my singing," he told Cassie. "So, I have to rely on captive audiences." While he'd never make it in a nightclub, Cassie thought he had a fine voice, and she enjoyed listening as he sang. Even when he'd just strum the guitar and hum along, she found herself relaxing.

He'd asked Cassie to teach him how to give inoculations, and he relieved her of that duty while she attended to cases no one else could handle. He was always on the lookout for help that stations told him they needed: governesses, jackeroos, cooks, accountants and, lately, pilots, though most of the station managers and owners learned to fly their single-engine planes or helicopters themselves. Blake had started that revolution in this part of the country.

Sam was as much a part of Cassie's daily life as breathing. But at two in the morning she realized she'd never really looked at him. She'd never been to a movie with him. She'd never had dinner with him and his wife. Though she'd had many meals with Sam before the war, she couldn't remember ever having dined with him and Liv, if you didn't count the big housewarming out at Tookaringa.

He'd said, "I married her because you married Chris." But there'd never even been the possibility of something between them, certainly not back in 1939. And now, of course . . . of course what? Well, for beginners, he was married. Then there was also the fact that being with him was so comfortable, he was so much a part of the fabric of her life, that there wouldn't be any electricity. But—there'd been little electricity with Chris and that had worked. If not beautifully, at least adequately.

What was she even thinking about? Suddenly Sam was alone, and he'd spent nearly a month in her other bedroom. They'd spent so many evenings together, talking, sharing. But they'd spent every day together for years and that hadn't made a difference.

Or had it? Wasn't that partly what made her life and work so wonderful? Had she ever been as happy flying with Warren, or even Fiona? Certainly not by herself. No, it was Sam. Sam was the difference.

She dragged herself out of bed at six-thirty. She'd just finished showering when the phone rang. It was Sam. "Look, I want to fly out today. If I get too tired you can take over. I've been grounded too long."

As she sat in the cockpit next to him, she decided she'd never noticed the pulse beating in his temple. Never studied his long, slender, capable-looking hands on the wheel.

"What're you looking at?" he asked, smiling.

"You."

He laughed. "You've been doing that every day for years."

She shook her head. "I don't think so."

"Sure you have."

"Well, you look different."

"How so?"

Cassie closed her eyes, wondering if mustaches tickled.

They were both wearing shorts, and she thought what nice legs he had. How come she'd never been aware of them before? She heard him humming and turned to him.

"You're glad to be back in the air."

"*Am* I! I feel I could fly without this plane. I haven't felt this good in a long time. Years maybe." Then he broke into "Some Enchanted Evening." Cassie couldn't help laughing.

The challenge for the day was an immense black man with a toothache. Cassie leaned him back against a tree and pulled at the infected tooth. But, whenever she pulled, the man's head came forward along with the tooth. Nothing she could do would give her leverage.

Sam got three other men and together the quartet sat on the enormous fellow while Cassie pulled the tooth. Later, it was something to laugh about.

They received word that they now had a dental hygienist at the little northern town of Armbruster, which had only recently become a clinic run. It was a tiny hamlet, and they had visited it only twice. There was a school that went through the sixth grade, even though there were only seventeen students. If they could bring dental tools, the hygienist would service the students and anyone else who needed dental care. So they made a run two hundred miles out of their way.

Armbruster lay along the banks of a sluggish river overhung by tall trees. Cassie thought it the most idyllic-looking hamlet she'd seen in this part of the world. The rocks along the river were striated and colorful; children splashed in the water, and women washed their clothes on rocks. There was only one dirt road in town, but there were two dozen houses. Every one of them looked alike except that they all had different flowers growing in their gardens. Banana trees, papayas, mangos, grapefruit dotted the backyards, and cotton grew in the fields behind the houses. There was a general store, run by a toothless man. Though it wasn't a Teakle and Robbins store, he said he bought most of his goods from Jim Teakle. A different man owned the gas station, which consisted of a lone pump in the yard next to the store. Across from that was the ubiquitous pub, without which no Aussie hamlet existed.

"She'll be in at noon," the pub owner, Terrence Quirk, said in reference to the hygienist. "She's got to ride in and it's close on to a dozen miles outta town."

He invited them to come over to the pub for "a spot of tea" while they waited. They'd no sooner been served than Cassie looked up to see the most beautiful woman she'd ever seen standing in the doorway. Diminutive, with long black hair, she wore jeans, a large man's shirt, a Stetson, and high-heeled boots that probably brought her height up to five-two. Her olive skin accentuated the almond shape of her eyes.

"That's her," Quirk said.

The Oriental beauty walked toward Sam and Cassie and stuck out her hand. "I'm Tina O'Keefe." She smiled, and the whiteness of her teeth against her golden skin was dazzling.

She sat down and ordered coffee. "This is kind of you to come so far out of your way just to deliver these." She picked up the box of dental instruments and peered into it. Her English was impeccable. Cassie didn't know what she'd expected.

"You new around here?" Sam asked.

"Somewhat," she said. "I was brought up in Darwin." When she saw surprise on Cassie's face, she laughed and said, "I know. You forget there's a Chinese population here, don't you? My great-grandfather came here in the gold rush in the mid-eighties, so I'm a fourth-generation Australian."

"Tina? That's not an Oriental name, is it?"

"No," she said as she sipped her coffee. "But my husband had trouble pronouncing my Chinese name. So we compromised on Tina."

"O'Keefe," said Sam. "You're married to Irish O'Keefe?"

"Have been for close to a year," Tina said. "You know him?"

"I flew with him during the war. My name's Sam Vernon."

Tina's face lit up. "I know you. Between the two of you, you won the war!"

"That's us," Sam grinned. "Never met another man as daring."

"He says the same of you. Too bad he's not home or I'd take you back to dinner."

"Where is he?"

"Well, we're just eking out a living," Tina said. "He's mustering, but he's over in the Kimberleys now. He takes jobs as they come. He's been there close to a month, and probably won't be home for another three or four weeks."

"Leaving you all alone?" asked Cassie.

"It's either that or give up the spread we're trying to start, though the bottom's going out of the cattle business, it seems. He's got a real operation going. He has his own helicopter and also hires two other pilots and their 'copters, three bull-catchers . . . "

"What's a bull-catcher?" Cassie interrupted.

Tina looked at her. "You two don't know anything about mustering with planes?"

Sam said, "I've heard tell."

"I'll tell you how it's done," Tina said, enthusiasm in her voice, her dark eyes shining. "Irish is the best in the business."

"He sure was the best pilot I ever flew with," Sam agreed.

"Any big station has many rogue cattle . . . "

"That's cattle that are runnin' around, unbranded, wild," Sam explained to Cassie.

Tina went on. "In order for a big station to get properly restocked you've got to muster all these rogues out of the canyons and hollows, and keep them from roaming around. These cattle don't want to get near any man, so Irish moves his men . . . he has two pilots and three bull-catchers and their gear, a handful of stockmen and a cook, and a mechanic in case something breaks down which it almost always does."

"That's a lot of men and machines."

She nodded. "You're telling me. The bull-catchers drive trucks with rollbars—big bumpers that can deflect a bull and go anywhere after a bull. Bulls can't escape them. Anyhow, you do aerial reconnaissance and see where there are large hordes of cattle and you figure out how they're moving, like toward water, and then Irish sends his stockmen and trucks into the area and the pilots run the cattle in. Takes a bit over a day to set up a portable mustering yard. It's pretty big, looks like regular stockyards, and has paddocks and races for loading cattle onto trucks. The men set up two big walls of hessian about eight hundred meters by six hundred, and the cattle are herded in. The hessian isn't very strong and it sways in the wind; if they pressed hard against it, the cattle could break through real easy. But somehow they never even try.

"Anyhow, it's an art getting those cattle from wherever they are into this funnel. It has to be done easy so it won't scare them. Sometimes a stockman has to jump from a 'copter and roll a bull over by the tail, strapping his hind legs together."

Even though Cassie had lived in the Outback over a decade, she had never heard mustering described this way. "Sounds dangerous."

Tina grinned. "Men love it. At least the men who are attracted to this kind of life. They wouldn't want any other job. The hours are long and hard, but the pay's good. It can all be done in about a sixth of the time that mustering without planes and 'copters used to take. Uses fewer men, too."

"What will all the aborigines do without mustering jobs?"

"When you get machines to do the jobs men did, it costs less money but men lose out," Sam said. "So-called progress doesn't always bring a better standard of living for everyone."

"So you stay home while he's out working?" Cassie asked.

"Just lately," said Tina, smiling. "I was the Chinese cook Irish hired. He didn't know I was going to be a woman. I worked out with the mustering unit for two years. We got married, though, six weeks after we met, so then it was 'our' unit, and I mustered as well as cooked. But our aim has been to have our own spread, raise our own cattle. We saved enough to buy a place, but Irish still has to work to pay for the cattle we want—and the upkeep. I'm staying home and breeding cattle and building up our spread. He's only gone half the year."

"You live alone half the year?"

"That's why I had you bring these tools," Tina said. "Actually, I trained up in Darwin to be a dental hygienist and did that for nearly a year—it was so boring I knew I needed a more exciting life than that. But here, I thought, while I'm waiting for Irish, I need some people around, so I thought I might take care of their dental problems. I'll do the school children for free—I figure that's my contribution to the community. But if anyone else needs a tooth pulled or a cavity filled, I can pick up a little extra change, put my education to some use, and maybe get to meet everyone around here."

"A friend of ours does mustering from his helicopter," Cassie said. "I wonder if he knows about your methods."

"Who?" Tina asked.

"Blake Thompson."

Sam's eyes narrowed as he looked at Cassie.

"Oh, we have the contract for Tookaringa," Tina said. "Well, the two north quadrants, anyhow. Blake does the other two himself—Irish taught him how. We always love going over there. I go out sometimes, spending three to four weeks in each quadrant. Fiona comes out at least once and we have a big barbecue. I love that woman."

"Who doesn't?" Sam agreed.

They talked with Tina until the middle of the afternoon. When they left, Cassie said, "She's someone I'd like to get to know better."

As Sam revved up the engine, he said, "You should meet her husband. Irish is one in a million."

Cassie closed her eyes. She usually napped when they flew back late-afternoons. But Sam's voice asked, "Want to take in a movie tonight?"

She opened her eyes and looked over at him. He was grinning. "What do you have against a nice platonic time at the movies with a married man?"

"Actually, you make it sound just a little dangerous."

His hands stayed on the wheel, but his eyes met hers. "Doc, it got to the dangerous stage a while ago, and you know it as well as I do."

Chapter 54

The last time Cassie could remember being so happy was when she and Blake had spent that time at Kakadu, over ten years ago. It was as though her emotions had been on a tight rein all these years, and she realized that's where she'd purposely kept them. She had vowed never again to open herself up to the pain that invariably seemed to follow joy.

But this was different. She had few illusions about life now. Sam was married. Their relationship couldn't go anywhere. Yet each day she awoke with a sense of joy. Each day she could hardly wait to get to the radio shack, which now had five rooms, all for business, while Betty and the kids had a home of their own next door complete with verandah. The town was growing, and at the once-secluded radio station, Betty had neighbors within walking distance.

The heightened awareness of each day was because of the subtle change in her relationship with Sam. Neither of them acknowledged it verbally, but when their eyes met they lingered. As they flew, they would look at each other and grin in silence.

On the Monday evenings when Romla and Jim came to dinner, Sam began to appear, uninvited but welcome. They would play cards afterward or go to the movies. When Cassie and Sam sat next to each other in the dark, their arms would touch. One night Sam reached over and took her hand in his, holding it for the rest of the film. Cassie never remembered what that movie was about, but she felt the warmth of Sam's touch for days afterward.

For the first time in over a decade she put Blake Thompson completely behind her. Not that there was a future with Sam, but there was the present, and for that she was grateful. She doubted he would ever have the ability to excite her the way Blake had when they were young, but she treasured every moment.

Even the colors of the days changed. The sky was bluer, the flowers more vibrant, the earth redder.

Romla said, "At last you're over Chris's death. I've felt guilty being as happy as I am when I knew what you were carrying around inside."

Then she told Cassie what *she* was carrying—a baby. Her eyes shone with delight when she cried, "At my age!"

She was two years older than Cassie.

"So, you're going to settle into domesticity again."

Romla laughed. "You know me better than that. Why would I give up the things I love? We can still live in our apartment in the hotel. All those old fuddy-duddies who laughed at my lingerie shop are eating crow. I could live on my income from that alone, and very nicely. Do you know I bet ninety percent of my customers are men? Well, maybe not quite. They come in, so shy and awkward. But now the Outback is dotted with more expensive and revealing lingerie than you'd ever believe. I often wonder if their wives wear any of it. All I know is I'm making a bundle. And now that his father's retired, Jim runs Teakle and Robbins. Why, Cassie, Jim and I have built an empire, and we're still making plans. I have no intention of giving up any of it. I can do it all—and have a baby, too."

One day in September Sam and Cassie flew out to Kypunda to bring a governess in for a gallbladder operation. It was after ten before Cassie could leave the hospital and when she walked out into the spring night, Sam was waiting.

"I knew you didn't have your car with you and I don't like the idea of your walking home alone at night."

She laughed. "I've done it for years."

"I know," he said. "You've done many things alone for years."

"I like your doing this," she said, slipping her hand through his arm as they walked along.

"I didn't bring my car because I wanted to walk," he admitted. "Shall we stop in at Addie's for a nightcap?"

"A beer sounds good."

"Yeah, I think so, too."

Addie's was always crowded late in the evening, the back of the front room filled with teams of men playing darts. Sam and Cassie chose a small table in the corner, where it was dark.

When the waitress brought their beers, Cassie said, "My back always aches after performing an operation. Must be tension. You'd think I'd get used to it."

"You'd think I'd get used to you, too, yet every day you're new to me," he said, not looking at her, staring over the top of her head at the dart players.

Not for the first time Cassie wondered if a mustache would tickle.

Sam's eyes met Cassie's. "I don't want Liv to come home."

Cassie sighed. "I don't either, but we're just playing games. What about Harry and Samantha? You couldn't live without them."

Sam didn't answer but downed his beer. "Come on. This wasn't such a good idea. Let's get out of here."

When they had turned off the main street and were walking toward Cassie's, Sam took her hand in his. They didn't say anything until they reached her house.

"You know, if we start something we can't finish, we won't be able to work together, don't you?"

Cassie leaned against the screen door and looked up at him. "All I know is I've been happier lately than I can ever remember."

Sam moved his body against hers. His arms pulled her to him, and mouth captured hers. She wound her arms around him, tasting him, feeling his hunger, knowing it had been a long time since she'd felt so alive, since she'd been kissed and felt it in every nerve of her body.

"What are you laughing at?" he murmured into her neck.

"The fact that mustaches don't tickle." She hoped he wouldn't stop kissing her.

But he pulled away, his arms still around her waist, pressing their bodies together. "I have some bridges to burn before I do what I want to do, Cassie."

He whistled as he walked back down her path, and she stood staring into the darkness long after he had disappeared. She wondered if she had ever felt happier.

* * *

Two days later, on their clinic run to Stockton Wells, he grinned and said, "I have something to tell you."

She looked over at him expectantly.

"Nope," he shook his head. "Tonight. How about the hotel for dinner?"

"Must be important," she said. "Not even Addie's?"

"It is important. And I don't want you to take it casually. I want you to get dressed up for an important occasion."

She laughed. "Will I know how to act? Should I be on my best behavior?"

"I hope not."

Just then Horrie cut in on the radio. "Got an emergency out at Tookaringa," he said. "Divert your clinic run and get there as fast as possible. Fiona's been thrown from a horse."

It was just after ten.

Sam reached over and took hold of Cassie's hand.

For the next two hours Cassie's heart was in her mouth.

Once they arrived at Tookaringa and Sam opened the aircraft's door, Cassie ran toward the house. Blake was sitting next to a pale Fiona, who lay on their enormous bed.

"Christ, Cassie," he said, standing as she rushed into the room. "There's not a mark on her, but she's in and out of consciousness. The cinch slipped and, as the saddle started to slide, the horse reared. Fiona fell off and the animal came down right on top of her."

Cassie sat down next to Fiona, whose eyes fluttered open. Internal bleeding, she was sure of that. Fiona's voice was barely audible. "Cassie, dear Cassie."

Cassie kissed her forehead. After a five-minute examination, she had the sense that Fiona had but a short time to live.

"Tell me you can do something," Blake's voice ordered.

She looked at him, feeling helpless. "I don't know, Blake. I don't have an X-ray machine . . . " And even if she had, there probably was nothing to be done.

Cassie sat back down beside Fiona, who opened her eyes again and whispered so low Cassie had to lean down to hear. She reached for Cassie's hand. "Cassie, my dear. My beloved friend. Do you know what worries me the most? Leaving the children. Who will take care of them? Who will give them the love every child needs." Cassie pictured the three of them, ages six, five, and three. "Will you take care of them? Be a mother to them?" A pleading intensity filled her eyes. "Blake, too. He doesn't know it but he needs someone to take care of him. He never even knows where his socks are. Please, Cassie. I can die in peace only if you promise . . . "

"Shh, Fi, you're not going to die," Cassie lied. She hoped she wouldn't start to cry.

"If I do, promise. Please, Cassie, promise you'll take care . . . "

"Of course, Fi. Of course, I will."

"You're not going to die, Fiona." Blake's voice was insistent. "You know I can't live without you."

Fiona struggled to move her head to the left so she could see Blake. "Remember to kiss the children every night," she said. "And don't let a governess bring them up. You do it. You and Cassie. Bring Cassie into your life. She'll bring up our children as she would have her own, if she'd had . . . " The end of the sentence hung there, never to be finished. Fiona sighed, then with a short burst of air, breathed no more.

Cassie turned a bewildered face toward Blake, who fell to his knees and burst into tears, his arms stretched over his dead wife. Cassie got up and walked around the bed. Kneeling down next to him, she put her arms around him, dampening the back of his shirt with her tears.

Standing in the doorway, Sam observed it all.

She and Sam tried to lend comfort to Blake and the children for the rest of the day. Blake decided on cremation, and Sam agreed to take the body back to the funeral parlor in Augusta Springs, where a memorial service would be held in a week. That would give everyone in the vicinity a chance to make plans to come to town. Steven made the plans, as Blake was too immersed in grief to think clearly.

"I'll stay over here," Steven told Cassie. "I won't let him be alone." Tears were near the surface of his eyes, too. "I loved her like a daughter," he said, over and over again.

Cassie felt a part of her had been ripped away, but it wasn't until nearly twilight, when she and Sam, with Fiona's body, were flying back to town that she allowed herself to cry. Great, gasping sobs. Never to be with Fiona again. Never to hear her laughter, never to feel her hugs, never to . . . ever. Never, ever.

The hearse was waiting at the airport and Fiona's body was whisked away before they'd even descended from the plane.

Sam put an arm around Cassie. Both cars were at the airport, but he said, "Come on, I'll drive you home."

"No," she shrugged his hand off her shoulder. "I want to be alone."

As she got in her car she remembered Sam had invited her out to dinner. "You had something you wanted to tell me?"

"It can wait." He leaned over and closed the door.

At home, after two drinks of straight Scotch, she went to bed and as she fell asleep, she heard Fiona's whisper, *Be a mother to my children, Cassie.*

Chapter 55

The next morning, during the radio call-in, Cassie told Blake that if he'd like to fly to Augusta Springs to get her, she'd come out and stay at Tookaringa for the weekend, take care of the children, and just be there for him and Steven.

Blake accepted her offer.

Sam hardly spoke all day. There was no clinic scheduled and Cassie solved the emergencies over the phone. She went around like a zombie, hardly hearing anything said to her. Romla tried to comfort her by inviting her to dinner. But all Cassie could do was weep. *Fiona, gone.*

Fiona's and Jennifer's lives had each been snuffed out so quickly in freak accidents. It was hard for those left behind to accept the sudden shock and the finality of it all.

"What will those children do?" Cassie asked.

Romla shook her head. "I don't know, dear. What do any children do who lose a parent? Blake has all the money in the world to hire good nannies and governesses. Certainly they'll be taken care of better than most people's children at such times."

"Men don't know what to do with a skinned knee or a sore throat . . . "

"Blake will get married again, I imagine. What is he, just forty?"

"Thirty-nine."

Romla put her arm around Cassie and smiled. "Maybe you. You're both . . . "

Cassie raised her head, eyes blazing. "How can you talk like that at a time like this?"

"Pretty gauche, huh?" Romla said contritely. "I'm sorry. The thought just popped into my mind."

And Cassie realized she had awakened with the same thought. *Be a mother to my children, Cassie.*

If not a mother, at least a beloved aunt. The two younger children had not yet absorbed the fact that they would never see their mother again, but all three of them were cranky and a handful.

Blake relinquished responsibility for them and rode out alone on his horse, leaving at dawn Saturday and not returning until dinnertime. Steven stayed at Blake's house. "I remember how I felt when Jenny went. I thought I couldn't go on living. And it has never been the same. But telling him time lessens the pain isn't any help now."

"No," agreed Cassie. "Let him grieve. But what are you going to do when I have to go back Sunday night?"

"We'll manage," Steven said.

On Sunday, Blake sat on the porch and stared into space—into that wide-open view that every place in this part of the continent offered. But at four, when Cassie said she really had to go, he stood up and walked out to his Cessna, and they talked of Fiona all the way back to Augusta Springs.

"You've been a brick, Cassandra," he said. "I can't tell you how much I appreciate your being there . . . here. She loved you more than a sister, you know."

"Yes. I do know."

Blake got out of the plane in Augusta Springs only to refuel. It would be dark when he returned to Tookaringa, but they had lights around the perimeter of their airfield now.

"Will you call me if I can do anything?"

He nodded. They'd all be in town in three days for the funeral.

"Plan to stay with me, all of you."

"You don't have room for all of us."

"Maybe Steven can stay with Sam. Steven and little Jenny. Sam has three bedrooms. I'll ask him."

When she did ask him, Sam said, "Sure," but the look in his eyes was strange. As if somehow everything in the world had changed.

After the memorial service Cassie wanted nothing more than to fly back to Tookaringa and take care of the two men and the children. But there was no way she could be spared. The ceremony was barely over when she and Sam were summoned to the far southwestern part of their territory, a part to which they'd never gone as there were no stations there.

One of the drivers on a camel train had been crushed. His son had ridden fifty miles to the nearest town, barely a dot on the map, to reach a radio. He would wait for them in the town; there was no way he could describe how to find the camel train from the air.

The land over which they flew was flat. There was nothing as far as the eye could see. Just flat red earth, not a tree in sight. Not even cracks in the earth, just flat sand.

The sun beat down on the only street in the town, which was over two hundred and fifty miles from any other habitation. Not a soul was in sight as the plane descended, but when Sam opened the door, an Afghan in long pantaloons appeared and a blast of hot air hit them with force.

Then Cassie saw several Afghans sunning themselves outside their huts while another led a herd of goats around the village's perimeter. On a sand dune, several small children played. But back across the town, where there were half a dozen houses, nothing moved. A car was parked outside what passed for a hotel, but one wondered how the vehicle got there and where it could go. There were no roads, or else they were covered with sand. A small stockyard groaned with penned-up cattle. The lone windmill that generated power from the Overland hung in silence.

"My father is ill," said the young bearded man, his headdress and pantaloons unlike anything Cassie had seen. She'd barely heard of these people who had been imported from Asia so many years before. She had thought the camel caravans were all further south. The young man before her was probably a third-generation camel driver. She could understand why they were needed in this deserted area where there were no visible roads and no railroad. He explained that his father had been taken sick and was unable to go on. They had placed him in a grove of trees, and the son had ridden back to town, where the constable had called the Flying Doctors.

Coming from behind one of the huts was a boy leading three camels. Sam and Cassie looked at each other. Sam grinned. "Ever ridden a camel?"

"I've never even seen one."

The camels approached, the tassels from their elaborate saddles jouncing cheerfully. Their hind legs looking too slender to balance their heavy bodies, they padded on the balls of their feet, light and rhythmic, trotting with an easy grace, as though they were dancing, rolling from side to side.

Cassie looked to the horizon and saw nothing. "Wouldn't it be easier to fly?"

"Come on," Sam said, "let's have an adventure."

Cassie cocked her head. "Let me get my medical bag."

They traveled over mile upon mile of shimmering gibber plains. For the first two hours, from horizon to horizon there was not a distinguishing mark on the landscape. How the young man who led them knew where they were going, she had no idea. The sun slanted to the west and was the only indication of direction. There was no grass, only dry riverbeds that even when full must have only been trickles.

"It looks sterile and dead," Cassie muttered after an hour.

Sam called over to her. "Look at it! Doesn't it make you feel dwarfed? We must look like ants from the air."

"Why does that seem to elate you?"

"God, look at these colors. Red, yellows—look how the sun lightens them up. And look at that green-grey saltbush over there." They rounded a low hill. "How can you say *dead?* See that olive green mulga spreading everywhere?"

The country played tricks. Distant objects, of which there were very few, were highlighted in bold relief. Blue-water mirages danced on the horizon. In the northern distance were sandstone hills, ruby and bronze in the clearness of the bright sunlight. A sandhill looked like a distant mountain as the glare of the stone gibbers fused reality with hallucination. Was it a mile or ten miles away? The world became two-dimensional; nothing broke the line of vision, nothing reinforced it. Only the flat, interminable, immeasurable desert.

The silence that engulfed them was beyond any stillness Cassie had ever known. Anything she thought to say became irrelevant before she could say it.

They traveled for three hours; Cassie constantly feared she would fall off the jiggling camel. A trio of men and a camel train appeared in the distance, along with another mirage of palm trees. The young leader pointed, and Cassie could not tell whether the group was five or fifteen miles away. They hardly seemed to come closer, until suddenly they were there. It was no mirage. There really was a grove of date palms.

"I feel like I'm in Morocco," she said.

Sam smiled at her. "Were you ever in Morocco?"

She had to laugh.

Waiting for them was the nearly unconscious patient, surrounded by three friends, all in the same costume as the young man who had guided them across the desert.

None of them would permit a woman to examine the patient. The patient whispered to one of the men who, looking at Cassie, relayed the message. "He would rather die than have a woman touch his body."

Cassie and Sam looked at each other.

"From the symptoms," Cassie said, "I've a feeling it's a kidney stone. I guess you'll have to be my fingers." She told Sam how to feel and what to look for.

The Afghans would not even let her watch while Sam knelt down beside the patient. Cassie turned her back to the men and talked to Sam. "He's got a crampy, colicky pain that comes in waves. It probably is felt in the flank area underneath the ribs and slightly in back and radiating around the belly and down the groin and even into the testicle. See if that's right."

"Feel his balls?" asked Sam.

Cassie had to smile, though none of the men saw it. She nodded. "Well, just communicate this in some way. They probably won't even let me say the word to them."

They all understood English, so the men knew what Cassie was saying. The patient moaned.

"If it's what I think it is, it's really an awfully acute pain, similar to very severe labor pains, and would be associated with blood in the urine, too. See if you can discover if that's true."

It was.

Cassie sighed. "The only thing that will alleviate the pain is a shot of morphine, probably given rather frequently. Will they let me give him a shot?"

Sam and the men murmured to each other. "No."

"Well, you've given them before. The pain will stop only if the kidney stone falls out of the urethra into the bladder."

"What's that?" Sam came over to stand beside her.

"The urethra leads from the kidney to the bladder. If the stone falls out of the urethra the pain, which is a muscle-cramping pain, will suddenly be over. Then later he'll urinate a little stone that should look like a tiny rough rock."

"And what if that doesn't happen?"

"He stays in excruciating pain, and surgery is required. The only thing we can do now is relieve his pain." While talking, Cassie knelt down and took a vial of morphine and a syringe from her medical bag. She nodded to Sam. "Find a cotton swab and the alcohol. Rub it on the spot where you'll give the injection." She didn't have to tell him how; he'd given hundreds of shots over the years.

The sun was beginning to sink over the horizon, its vermilion rays shooting straight up into the center of the sky.

"Now what?" Sam asked.

"I guess we stay here overnight. We certainly can't get back to the plane. You and the young boy can leave at dawn to get the plane. You can figure out how to fly back here, can't you?"

Sam grinned, sliding his hand into his pants pocket and drawing out a compass. "Can I? What a question to ask me!"

Cassie looked around. "Certainly anyplace here is flat enough to land, isn't it?"

"You thinking of taking him back to the hospital?"

"If he doesn't pass a kidney stone tonight."

"They won't let you give him morphine while I'm gone. They won't let you near him."

"We'll see. By tomorrow, if he's still in this bad pain he'll know the relief the morphine can provide and he'll beg for it."

"Willing to take your chances with their food?"

Cassie made a face. "Why not?"

They weren't sorry. Fava beans, couscous, tabbouleh, yoghurt made from goat's milk. The dishes were exotic and very tasty.

"It'll take you three hours to ride back to the plane," Cassie said, "and how long do you think to fly back?"

"Bit over half an hour."

As soon as the sun had disappeared the temperature dropped and Cassie felt cold. One of the cameliers brought a quilt. "There is only one. I'm sorry," he said.

"Makes for coziness," Sam said.

They sat close together, wrapped in the camel-scented quilt, staring at the stars that blanketed the sky.

"Is Fiona one of them, do you suppose?"

Sam didn't answer.

"What were you going to tell me last week, the day Fiona died?"

"It doesn't matter right now."

"What was it, anyway? It seemed important at the time."

"Liv and I have agreed to a divorce."

It hung there between them. It was as big as the sky.

"Oh, Sam." And then, "What about the children? How can you live without them?"

"We still have details to work out, but she's staying in England. I guess I'll have them during school holidays. It's better than having them grow up with so much tension in the household."

"How do you feel about it?" She couldn't see his eyes.

"I suggested it."

"And how did she react?"

"She'd wanted to suggest it. How do you feel about it?" he asked.

"Why did you say it doesn't matter now?"

He hesitated. "Things seem different than they did a week ago."

She knew what he meant. *Be a mother to my children, Cassie.*

Again he asked, "Well, how *do* you feel about it?"

"I don't know," she said. "It's such a surprise."

"Is it, Cassie? Is it, really?"

She crawled under the quilt and closed her eyes.

Was it really?

Something changed.

By the time Cassie became aware of it, she couldn't immediately pinpoint when it had changed or why.

The contentment she had felt for the few months before Fiona's death vanished. But she was too wrapped up in taking care of the people at Tookaringa to be aware that happiness had flown the coop.

When she did realize it, at first she took for granted it was because Fiona was dead.

And then she realized that there was no more of the bantering that had always existed between her and Sam. He was silent as they flew their missions. He was as helpful as ever; his relationships with the various station hands was the same, filled with laughter. He assisted her medically and sensed when she needed help—she never had to ask. He was at her elbow, ready when she needed him. Yet when he might have been in the way, he was not there. He read her like a book. But his *joie de vivre* was gone. And the intimacy that had begun between them had disappeared.

She flew out to Tookaringa via Blake's helicopter late every Friday afternoon and checked in with Horrie Saturday mornings. The radio at Tookaringa stayed on, tuned for any emergencies. She played games with the children, made idle conversation with Steven and Blake and went out riding with them, and tried to find things that would make them all laugh. There weren't many. None of them found much to laugh about in life without Fiona.

Blake flew her back to town Sunday afternoons. It was Steven who always said, "I don't know what we'd do without you, Cassie."

After working a full week and emotionally exhausting herself weekends, Cassie was in no mood to prepare dinner for the usual Monday evening get-togethers. Romla said she understood and invited Cassie to dine at the hotel, but Cassie wanted only to have a snack and go to bed early. One Monday the gathering was cancelled, near the end of the clinic run. Sam said, "Want me to pick up a couple of hamburgers?"

Cassie shook her head. "I just want to go to bed." She was asleep before nine.

As Cassie spent her weekends up north, her relationship with Sam became more formal than it had been even eleven years ago. When she had the time, she wondered why. One Friday noon, coming back from an overnight emergency run to the Birdsville AIM hospital, Sam said, "You goin' up to the Thompsons' tonight?"

"Uh-huh." It seemed to Cassie she'd never been more tired than she'd been the last two months since Fiona's death.

Sam nodded and set his lips in a thin, tight line.

"Why?"

"Oh, nothing. You haven't spent a weekend in town since Fiona's death."

"Those children need me."

"Yeah. Sure."

"What's that tone of voice supposed to mean?"

"Nothing."

Because she wanted to believe him, she did. "It would be nice once in a while to have a little time to myself. I'm so busy I don't have an extra minute. Tuesdays I have to shampoo, Wednesdays do my laundry, Thursdays . . . "

He held up his hand as though brushing away her complaints. "You're only doing what you want to be doing."

"I told Fiona . . . "

"Don't defend yourself to me."

"Is that what I'm doing?" she asked. And she turned from the clouds ahead of them to face him. "You think I'm going out there to be with Blake?"

Looking straight ahead, he nodded and raised an eyebrow. "Bull's-eye."

She didn't respond, deciding not to get involved in a conversation like this on a Friday afternoon when Blake would be picking her up in two hours to go to Tookaringa.

Blake. She had been telling herself all this time that she was doing what Fiona had begged her to do, being a mother to her best friend's children—who were also Blake's children. She had not loosened her heart strings when she was up at Tookaringa or even when she thought of going there weekends. It was too soon after his loss. There wasn't yet room in his heart for another woman.

Is that what she hoped for? Maybe it was time to take a good look at her motives.

"The cook is so impressed with you," Blake said as they neared Tookaringa, "that he said to tell you he's preparing something special for you."

Cassie laughed. "I bet I know what it is. He was telling me that when he worked as a chef in that Perth restaurant, his specialty was duck à l'orange."

"My God," said Blake, and he smiled for the first time in a long time.

"It's nice to see you smile."

"Well, I think I'm going to make it. I feel I'm part of life again."

It *was* duck à l'orange. And it was perfect.

By the time they had finished dining, it was nine.

Cassie put the children to bed, kissing each of them, promising to have a picnic the next day.

"You know what I'm going to do?" Steven said. "I'm going home. Not, Cassie, that the high point of my week isn't enjoying your company, but I haven't been home for a long time. I'll come back tomorrow, for dinner, and for a rousing game of cribbage in the evening. But I think I'll go sleep in my own bed."

Cassie and Blake were left in the soft night air. In the distance a dingo bayed. They sat silently for a while and then Blake said, "I was just thinking of our time together at Kakadu."

"That was a long time ago." Yet she remembered every minute of it.

"Nobody had ever knocked me for such a loop. I couldn't think of anything but you."

Then what happened? Cassie wanted to ask. But she knew what had happened. War had happened.

Blake stood up and walked over to the rattan loveseat where Cassie was sitting. He took her hand. "You scared me."

"Scared you?"

"I wasn't in control of myself. I think I was glad the war came along, that I could get away from my feelings. That I could distance myself from you."

"You seem to have done that very well."

"I've never done it. It's been a sheer act of will to keep away from you. Whenever you've entered a room, whenever . . . "

"Don't! Don't do that to Fiona's memory!"

Blake looked bewildered. "It has nothing to do with Fiona's memory. I had a happy marriage. Fiona was a wonderful wife. But that didn't stop me from wanting you all these years. To have you marry someone like that priggish Chris . . . it broke my heart, Cassie."

"*That* broke *your* heart!" She stood up and walked to the end of the porch, staring out into the night.

"Cassie, I've never stopped wanting you." She heard his footsteps, felt him stand behind her, so close that their bodies touched.

For eleven years she'd wanted to hear those words. His hand touched her shoulder and turned her around. "Tell me you've felt the same. Tell me that all these years you've never forgotten those weeks we shared, that . . . " His mouth pressed against hers as his arms encircled her, pulling her close.

His mouth was as she remembered it, and his embrace brought memories rushing back. He feathered kisses on her eyelids, on her cheeks, down her throat.

She pushed him back. "I'm not prepared for this," she said, breathing hard.

"Not prepared? It's been eleven years! Not ready? Do we spend our lives waiting until we're ready? Cassie, my children are ready for you. Steven's ready for you. I'm ready for you."

What did that mean? "I have to have time. I can't go this quickly from family friend . . . "

"To wife and mother? That's what I'm asking. For God's sake, did you think . . . "

"No," she said as she brushed his hands away. "I didn't think anything. I'm just not ready for this!" She was in shock.

Blake reached for her hand, holding it tightly. "Okay," he said, smiling at her. "Then start preparing. I suppose it is too soon after Fiona's . . . but we need you, Cassie. The kids need you. Steven needs you. I need you. We exist from Sunday night to Friday evening, until you come back into our lives. You help us feel whole again."

She'd sensed that. Why else had she given up her time to come up here every weekend? She was needed, she knew that.

She'd carried the torch for Blake Thompson for over a decade—she knew that, too. Why wasn't she happier? Why didn't a thrill run through her? Why . . .

"Give me some time," she said, turning away.

Blake reached out and put a hand on her arm, pulling her to him. He leaned down and kissed her again, a slow, lingering kiss. "Christ," he whispered, "I haven't had a woman in over two months!"

She pulled away from him.

"I'll see you in the morning," she said as she walked briskly away across the verandah, through the immense living room, and turned down the west hall toward her bedroom.

She didn't know why she felt as she did. She didn't know how she felt.

Had she come here every weekend since Fiona's death hoping for this? Why had Blake's actions shocked rather than pleased her?

She tossed and turned. He'd just asked her to be the second Mrs. Blake Thompson, hadn't he? To be a mother to his children. To be mistress of Tookaringa.

Not a word about love. But then, it was too soon after Fiona's death for *that.* He wanted her. He said he'd always wanted her. What that meant, she was sure, was he wanted her body. *I haven't had a woman in over two months!* Well, too bad. She hadn't had a man in years.

It would mean a whole different life. Maybe she was ready for that. She'd been a Flying Doctor for over a decade. Perhaps a change would be good. She'd thought, for a while, of moving to Sydney. But it hadn't been because she didn't like her job, didn't love the patients who had become part of the fabric of her life. She'd brought every baby born in her territory into the world for the last eleven years. She knew so many patients. She was welcome in every home in an area larger than most European countries—she even felt loved in the majority of those households. That wouldn't be easy to give up. Yet she knew Blake would insist on it. He wanted a mistress of Tookaringa, someone to mother his children. He wanted the household to run smoothly. He wanted someone to be there to talk with Steven and keep him company when he, Blake, was on one of his buying trips or out mustering. He wanted someone to make love whenever he wanted. He hadn't made love to anyone since Fiona died and he wanted a female body.

And here she was. Ten years ago they'd spent two weeks making mad, passionate love and he thought they could recapture that. He probably thought she'd gotten a career out of her system and would be willing to settle into a traditional role. Well, she had to admit that lately she'd been thinking it might be nice—wonderful, even—to have a family. If Romla was having a baby at age forty, why couldn't she have a child or two? Romla was not only continuing on at the hotel, but she and Jim were buying out the partners. Romla's lingerie shop alone could have supported them. Together Jim and Romla were carving out a mercantile empire and Romla was not about to give that up. Cassie wasn't sure she wanted to give up her medical practice for good. What might be nice—now that the territory had become so busy—was maybe getting another Flying Doctor and they could take turns flying out. One could handle emergencies when the other was on a clinic run. They could take turns being in the air and away from home. She could spend time at home with her family. A family? She'd never wanted children with Chris. Why?

Chris hadn't been enough to keep her happy—she had always known that, and so had he. She needed her work in order to feel fulfilled. No, she could never have been satisfied with Chris. Could she be satisfied with Blake? She loved his children. She loved his father. And she'd thought she loved him for all these years.

Then why hadn't she felt more when he drew her into his arms and kissed her tonight? Why didn't the blood rush through her veins, why hadn't her heart pounded? Maybe no man could do that anymore. That kind of thrill might only be for the young.

Unable to sleep, she arose and went to sit by the window, her arms on the sill, staring out into the bright moonlight.

What had happened between her and Sam, she wondered. Why had he been so withdrawn lately? Since when—since Fiona died, wasn't it? She tried to pinpoint it. Why didn't they share themselves with each other anymore? Was it because of something between him and Olivia? Was Liv coming back, after all? Or was it because she'd spent every weekend at Tookaringa?

Why did Sam float in front of her when Blake had just proposed? Why wasn't she happier? Why was she thinking of Sam instead? Why was she even hesitating about Blake's offer?

Funny, she thought, we think we know ourselves so well, but often we don't know ourselves at all.

* * *

She awoke just before dawn. Looking out the window, she observed a thin band of pale pink on the horizon, but the sky above was still dark.

"I know why," she said aloud. "Blake and I have grown apart and Sam and I have grown closer."

For a few weeks there, right before Fiona died, she'd thought she and Sam were falling in love. Then he'd turned away and she'd involved herself with Tookaringa. Or had it been the other way around?

His aloofness, she was suddenly certain, was because he thought that she and Blake . . .

Blake wanted her to give up her life and start a new one with him, with his children, with his father. And though they were all dear to her, she realized she did not want to give up her own life, the one that gave her such satisfaction.

But she would like to share it, and spend not just her days with Sam, but all of her life.

How did he feel? Did she dare ask him?

Chapter 57

There was a loud knock. Blake opened the door and peered in. "Call for you. Emergency."

Cassie didn't even pull her robe on, but rushed to the radio in Blake's den. Horrie's voice said, "Sam's already taken off. He'll be there to get you before too long. Baby's coming at Witham Hill."

"She's not due for another month."

"Tell that to the baby," Horrie said.

"I'll be ready."

"Not even Sunday sacred?" Blake asked.

"No time is sacred," Cassie said. "Or, maybe it's that all time is sacred."

Blake grinned. "You look irresistible. Do you wake up like this every morning?" He was already dressed and ready for the day.

"I'll just have time to get dressed and get something to eat."

"Breakfast is ready." He leaned down to kiss her lightly. "Start living for yourself and not for all your patients. It's time."

Was it?

When they heard the plane's engines, Cassie grabbed both her medical bag and overnight bag and turned to Blake.

"Same time next Friday?" he asked.

They started off at a brisk trot toward the landing field.

"We can wait a decent interval, six months if you like, for the formalities. That will give the Flying Doctors plenty of time to find a replacement. But you can keep coming out weekends."

Was she a "replacement" for Fiona? Someone to step in and take her place? Have it all work smoothly? No interruption? Anyone competent, any doctor at all, could replace her? She couldn't tell whether it was Blake's words or her own feelings that were irritating her. He seemed to think her answer was a foregone conclusion. Anyway, he wasn't waiting for an answer.

What she mainly wanted was to talk with Sam, and try to find out what was in his heart. She thought she knew him so well, yet she could not tell at all what he had been thinking for the last month.

Sam had not cut the engines, but stood in the doorway, the steps in place. He walked down and reached out a hand. Blake shook it.

"Cassie tells me," Blake shouted over the engines' roar, "that you and Olivia have split. Sorry to hear that."

"Yeah. Well." Sam followed Cassie up the steps and closed the door.

"Good time?" he asked as he slid into the cockpit seat next to her.

She nodded and smiled, a smile he didn't see as he concentrated on take-off.

"George said Henny's having a bad time. Of course, that was several hours ago, and she may have had the baby by now," he said.

"Let's call and find out," Cassie suggested.

But Henny hadn't had the baby. In fact, her husband was on the verge of hysteria. "God, Doc," George's voice cracked, "this is the third one and I thought it got easier. Nothing seems to be happening, and she's in awful pain."

Cassie told Sam, "I bet you anything it's a breech—the baby hasn't turned head-down yet. You should have called me. Blake could have flown me down there, or at least to Augusta Springs to meet you."

"Wanna pour me some coffee? Haven't had my quota yet and it's nearly ten."

After handing the cup to Sam, Cassie poured one for herself. "I always feel such pleasure at the thought of delivering a baby." Then she was sorry she'd said it. It would no doubt remind Sam about his own children, being raised half a world away.

"Haven't you ever wanted children of your own?" he asked.

"Lately I've begun to think it would be nice."

"You and Chris . . . you never wanted children then?"

Cassie shook her head. "I guess I wasn't ready. Or Chris wasn't the one I wanted to have children with. It's a helluva responsibility." Then she asked, looking over at him, "How are you going to bear it, not seeing Harry and Samantha? Not being with them as they grow up?"

Sam was silent, drinking his coffee, writing something in the log strapped on his leg. She heard him sigh. "Do you think I haven't spent sleepless nights about this over the years? Doc, I don't have an answer. I love my kids more than life itself. Should I stay in a lousy marriage to be with them and lose my temper all the time because I'm so damned unhappy? How about their growing up with so much tension and anger? I have to give up something. I finally figured I can't go on being this unhappy, can't spend whatever time I have being so miserable."

Cassie peered out the window. There wasn't a cloud anywhere. She had never heard Sam so emotional. "I imagine most parents who get divorced have to face that, don't they?"

Sam shrugged.

Cassie leaned over and put a hand on his arm. Raising an eyebrow, he glanced at her. "What brought that on?"

"I spent part of the weekend thinking about you. We haven't talked much lately."

"Not my fault," Sam said.

"Partly it is. But partly it's because I haven't even asked about what's going on with you and Olivia. You've been so quiet. I should have tried to break through that."

He reached up to put his left hand over hers, which still rested on his arm. "I spent much of the weekend thinking about you, too. My divorce will be final in three months. It's time we talked, Cassie."

"I think so, too."

"But let's wait til after this baby's born, so we won't be interrupted."

After a minute, she said, "Blake asked me to marry him."

They sat in silence. Sam didn't turn to look at her. He didn't say anything but kept his eyes straight ahead. Finally he asked, "You going to give up the FDS? Move out to Tookaringa?"

"You're taking a few things for granted."

He still didn't look at her. "Like what?"

"Like I accepted."

Then he turned to face her, his eyes intense. "You didn't?"

"I don't want to give up my job. I'm important to all these people and they're important to me. I want everything. I want my job. I want a family . . . "

"You do?"

"I want everything life can offer. You know, the only time I ever thought I really had love—love that made me think nothing else in the world existed—was for three weeks over ten years ago. Not much out of thirty-eight years, is it? Well, suddenly I realize I want that, too. I don't want to be a substitute for someone else. I want what I have now and everything else, too."

"So, you're saying no because . . . "

"I didn't say no."

The light went out of Sam's eyes.

"But I didn't say yes."

"What the hell you doin', Doc?"

"I woke up this morning knowing I had to talk with you, Sam. But not while we're flying out. I want us to be someplace where we don't have to concentrate on anything but . . . "

"Doc, you got it!" He reached out and put his hand over hers. "Funny thing, I went to sleep last night knowing that we had to talk. I decided I wasn't going to stand by another minute . . . "

He held her hand all the way to Witham Downs. Except when she poured him another cup of coffee.

The problem was exactly what Cassie had predicted—Henny Poulson's baby was upside down, feet first and unable to move. The poor woman had been in labor over eight hours and was in terrible pain.

"Don't let her die, Doc," her husband pleaded.

"She's not going to die," Cassie said after examining the woman. "Let me wash up and all of you get out of here."

"Will you need me?" Sam asked.

"Yes. Amuse George. Drink coffee and keep his mind busy. The baby will be here before we know it. Thank goodness we arrived no later than we did."

She turned to George. "Do you have blankets and clean sheets? This is going to be messy and it would be nice to protect the mattress as much as we can."

After she washed up she returned to the bedroom and she and George lifted the agonized Henny, spreading blankets and sheets under her. "Okay. Get out of here," Cassie ordered.

George did so willingly.

"This is going to hurt," Cassie warned her patient. "I've got to turn the baby so it will come out. It's upside down, and can't budge. Its legs and arms have to be put in alignment so they don't flail around and keep the baby from coming out or tearing you. I have to get up there and move it around. I've given you something to relax you but I need your help."

"I can stand the pain if I know it's going to be over soon and if I know the baby's all right."

"The baby's in good shape," Cassie said. "Strong heartbeat, but it's not any happier about being where it is than you are."

She did not say aloud that there was always the chance of mental retardation in a breech birth. She shoved her rubber-gloved right arm up into Henny. If she were in the hospital she'd have done a cesarean. It could be performed under anesthesia; it would be less painful and less dangerous for the baby. This way, if she sedated Henny too much the baby could be anesthetized also.

One of the baby's feet poked through the vagina. Cassie had to straighten the legs so they would come through together. She reached in, pulling the elbows close to the body so the hands would not impede progress. As she gently pulled, the hand and forearm settled alongside the baby's body. Okay, now, here came the feet.

As the feet plunged into the world, Cassie pulled them upward at an angle, gently easing the torso out and pulling the legs straight up toward the ceiling. She could see the nose and mouth still in the vaginal orifice.

With her free hand she reached for the forceps lying beside Henny and clamped them around the baby's head. Holding its feet in one hand, she eased the head out under the pubic bone.

Before the arrival of the placenta, Cassie laid down the forceps and suctioned out the baby's mouth. The sweaty baby let out a mewling cry.

The placenta slid out, accompanied by a rush of blood. Cassie sighed with relief. It was all over. She cut the umbilical cord and placed the baby inside the curve of Henny's arm. Too exhausted to speak, Henny looked at the baby.

"It's a girl," Cassie said, as she cleaned up. "A perfect little girl."

Sam stuck his head in the door. "Was that signs of life we heard?"

Cassie grinned. "It was. A lovely daughter. I need some towels and water. Let's get some clean sheets, too."

"Can George come in?"

"Why don't you have him wait til it's neater. Tell him everything's fine and give me five minutes."

It was twilight before Cassie felt comfortable about leaving Witham Downs. They'd stayed for supper and she'd cleaned up the kitchen. She had hoped Sam would want to return to Augusta Springs and not stay overnight. The weather looked perfect, cloudless. Now that the airfield could be lit, there was no danger about returning home at night. Maybe Sam would come over and they could talk. Have a glass of wine and . . .

She looked over at him. All day, since she'd left Tookaringa, she'd been aware of him. She'd flown with him all these years and had taken him for granted. Now, eleven years after first meeting him, five weeks after he'd kissed her, she was aware of him wherever he was. When he entered a room, or when he'd stuck his head in the kitchen and asked, "Need any help?" or when they'd sat around having a beer before dinner. Everything about him stood out: the way his fingers wound around the can of beer; the crinkles around his eyes when he smiled; the sound of his laughter. She liked his mustache, and the way his Adam's apple moved when he swallowed. The way he always tilted his chair back.

She liked the way he looked relaxed yet was always ready for any emergency, always attuned to other people's needs. She wanted him to kiss her again.

Last night, Blake's kisses had not kindled the feelings she'd remembered. She had not reacted like she had when his lips touched hers so many years ago.

Maybe Sam wouldn't send a charge through her, either, but if Sam wanted her . . . she could settle for something less incendiary if she had to. All these years when Sam had been by her side . . . well, maybe it was a good thing. Neither of them would have done anything dishonorable. If he'd really been going to stay in his marriage their hands would have been tied.

She felt his hand on her shoulder, his voice in her ear. "Ready?"

"For what?" she turned, smiling at him.

Their eyes locked. A smile played across his face. "For whatever."

"Yes, I think so."

"It's about time."

"It is that."

There'd be another hour before total darkness. Sam hummed as they took off.

They flew, without talking. As fingers of vermilion and rose streaked the darkening western sky, Sam said, "We can be back home in another hour. But I have a better idea."

"Whatever it is, as long as we're alone and can talk and . . . "

"And?"

"Tomorrow's Sunday. We don't have to be anyplace in particular."

She could feel the plane beginning to slow down, and she knew he was getting ready to descend, that they would land in the middle of what the world thought of as no man's land. He picked up the radio and called Horrie, telling him they'd be back in the morning.

Sam landed the plane with the last rays of light to guide them. "Come on," he said, grabbing her hand. As they walked back through the plane, he picked up a blanket. "Let's do our talking out under the stars."

But when Cassie descended the steps, he reached out and put his arms around her. "Before you say anything," Sam said, "I want you to know I love you. I not only love you, but I'm in love with you. I couldn't be happy with Olivia not only because we are so different but because she's not you. There, I've tried not to say any of that for the last five years." His mouth moved down onto hers and she knew that this was what her whole life had been heading toward.

He looked down at her, and she could see his face even though only a sliver of a moon was rising. "You can't marry Blake. Maybe you loved him before the war, but you're in love with me. I know it even if you don't."

"But I do know it," she said, leaning against him. "I thought I was falling in love with you before Fiona's death, when you were recuperating at my house. Those days were so happy. But then this last month you've seemed so far away . . . "

"I know. And it *is* partly my fault, because I thought you and Blake were back together. But last night, I thought, I'm not leaving without a fight."

"Were you going to fight for me?" She reached up to kiss him again.

"With every ounce of my being." He took her hand and led her to a grove he'd remembered. "Come here, woman."

She did, sitting beside him. He pulled her close.

"It took me a long time to realize," she said. "I thought we were too comfortable with each other. Certainly before the war we weren't . . . "

"I was. I just didn't realize it. By the time I realized it, half a world away, it was too late. There wasn't a single night, Doc, that I didn't think about you just before I fell asleep. I thought about you every one of those days I was gone. Soon I'll be free, Cassie. Free to ask you to . . . "

She laughed. "In some ways you're a prude, aren't you? You're going to wait until your divorce is final to ask me to marry you?"

"Me? A prude? That's just because . . . " He reached out and drew her to him, his hand fondling her breast.

"Because?" She laughed as her mouth covered his. Then she whispered, "Don't stop. That feels good."

When he could talk he said, "Because I didn't want to compromise you." His hand slid down her back, pulling her closer.

"How d'ya feel about making love with a married man?"

"Why don't we find out?" she murmured as his tongue ran along her lips.

He hesitated a minute. "I don't have anything with me. What if you become pregnant?"

"It wouldn't be the first six-month baby. Wait a minute." She slid out of her blouse as his hands ran over her. "Oh, God, that feels good. I don't think anything ever felt so good."

"I want you," he said, ripping his shirt off.

She moved away from him, standing to slide off her shorts.

"Don't move," he said, as the moonlight struck her body. "Christ," he whispered, "I've dreamed of this. I've wanted you for so long, so many years."

He stood and walked toward her, reaching to pull her to him, his mouth meeting hers as he picked her up and laid her on the blanket, their naked bodies touching.

In the middle of what many call the Great Australian Loneliness, the only sound was Cassie's crying out in the night.

In the distance, heat lightning flashed across the horizon. A single clap of thunder followed.

"What the hell are you laughing about at a time like this?"

"I thought there might not be any electricity between us."

He laughed, too.

Afterword

In the summer of 1988, while researching my first book about Australia, *The Moon Below*, I fell in love with a continent—both its scenery and its people. While there, I had two particular strokes of good fortune which, I did not realize at the time, would influence my life and add great excitement to it.

In Alice Springs—where I stayed just thirty hours on that first visit (two years later I would visit for ten days)—I wandered into the Royal Flying Doctor Service base. A part of it is devoted to an historical museum, which fascinated me. I viewed a video recounting the history of the Service and explaining the present role of this unique, dramatic, and heroic group of people. I'm a sucker for noble deeds and, as I traversed north through Darwin and Kakadu National Park and then took a bus halfway across the continent through the Outback, the idea of the Flying Doctors stayed very much with me.

The second stroke of pure luck that would have far-reaching consequences: near Cairns, on the gorgeous northeast coast, my two daughters, Debra and Lisa, and I took a tourist train to Kuranda. Sitting opposite us was a charming couple on holiday. Informal and relaxed, in jeans and a baseball cap, the man joined my daughter as they both leaned out of the train window, taking photographs. We ended up spending a good portion of that day together. When we parted he gave me his card and I discovered they were Chief of the Royal Australian Air Force Marshal Ray Funnell and his wife, Suzanne.

They sent to the U.S. for a copy of my first book, *East of the Sun*, which had just been published and then wrote a flattering letter to me. Thus began a correspondence which led to a flourishing friendship.

When, a year later, I still couldn't shake the idea of the Flying Doctors even though I knew it would be another two years before I could begin a book about it, I wrote to Marshal Funnell asking if he knew whether it would be possible to obtain permission to fly out with the RFDS should I return to Australia. He opened doors I never even knew were there. When I did visit again, in the summer of 1990 (their winter), I was offered hospitality I had imagined was reserved only for royalty. The Funnells welcomed me with warmth and friendship, and Tony Charlton of Melbourne made the arrangements for my unforgettable visit.

The time I spent there was the trip of a lifetime. I flew thousands of miles and many hours over and into the Back of the Beyond on clinic visits and emergencies. I flew in pressurized and non-pressurized planes of various sizes and in a helicopter. I rode a camel and traveled overnight on the famous Ghan railroad to Alice Springs, the heart of the continent. I was a guest of the warm and hospitable Lois and Lisle Litchfield at their famed Mundowdna, a 640,000-acre sheep station near Maree in South Australia, where they let me participate in mustering sheep in preparation for shearing. I spent a night in Oodnadatta, now an aboriginal town. I not only received unbelievable hospitality but partook of life as it is lived in the Outback.

In the process I met many interesting and wonderful people, and got to know one of the most remarkable men I've ever met. In 1935 the Reverend Fred McKay began to traverse thousands of miles of the Outback, at the urging of the Reverend John Flynn who founded the Flying Doctor Service. Both of these men changed the face of the country. In 1951, when Flynn was dying, he urged that Fred McKay succeed him. Fred gave his total working life to the cause of the Flying Doctors, at the same time fulfilling a term as Moderator of all Presbyterians in Australia and helping to form the Uniting Church.

I had the great fortune to meet Fred McKay and spend a good deal of time recording his stories. He generously offered to open the Royal Flying Doctor Service archives in Canberra to me. He and his wife, Meg, were hospitable beyond description and a friendship that I value deeply has ensued. I am privileged to have had his support and enthusiasm while writing this book. He has encouraged me at every turn. I could not have done much of this without his stories, his openness, his cooperation, his friendship. I had fallen in love first with a continent—and then with a man. I am only one of a great many who love Fred McKay, a man of solid achievement who commands great respect in his country. In many ways he has had a unique life which has bred in him a simple greatness. He is one of Australia's national treasures.

There are others I must single out to thank for their cooperation and help:

Chris Roff, Chief of the Victorian section of the RFDS;
Peter Dossett, Chief of the South Australian section of the RFDS;
Tony Wade, in charge of the Port Augusta RFDS station;
Dr. Ashleigh Thomas, of the Port Augusta RFDS;
Steve Byrnes, in charge of the Alice Springs RFDS station.

I want to thank Brigid Delano, Mary Ann Miller, and Dorothy Butler for reading much of what I wrote as I went along.

And not least, my editor, Ann LaFarge, who encourages, supports, criticizes constructively, and adds joy to my life and writing.

The history of the Royal Flying Doctor Service and QANTAS are inexorably bound together. QANTAS is the oldest, most continuous air service in the world. They were able to get off the ground financially by supplying the fledgling FDS with its first plane and pilot. The money earned from that contract supplied QANTAS with the backing necessary to become the giant it is today. And the QANTAS plane and knowledgeable pilots (for many years QANTAS supplied both plane and pilot) enabled the FDS to begin its operations.

All of the medical incidents are based on actual cases handled by the RFDS over the years. The incident about the pilot and his wife dying in a plane accident is based on a similar accident where the pilot and Timothy O'Leary's wife were killed.

The Royal Flying Doctor Service is still largely supported by individual contributions. No one in Australia is too far or too poor to be taken care of. No one on the island continent is more than four hours (at the very most) by plane from expert medical care, unless—of course—a person lives in a city and has to find his way to an emergency ward and then wait in line.

I read dozens of books about Australia and the Royal Flying Doctor Service. Those that I found particularly valuable were Ernestine Hill's *The Great Australian Loneliness* and *Flying Doctor Calling;* Arthur Affleck's *The Wandering Years;* Michael Page's *The Flying Doctor Story, 1928–79;* Jane F. Karley's *A Mantle of Safety: The Flying Doctor Service;* Margaret Ford's *End of a Beginning;* Elizabeth Burchill's *Innamincka;* Ruby Langford's *Don't Take Your Love to Town;* Keith Willey's *The Drovers;* Douglas Lockwood and Ainslee Roberts's *I, the Aboriginal;* Harry Moss's *10,000 Hours;* W. Scott McPheats's *Flynn of the Inland;* Timothy O'Leary's *North and Aloft* and *Western Wings of Care;* Robin Miller's *Sugarbird Lady;* Douglas Lockwood's *Australia's Pearl Harbor;* M. Duncan-Kemp's *Where Strange Paths Go Down;* Mazie McKenzie's *Fred McKay;* Jim Anderson's *Billarooby;* Patsy Adam Smith's *Outback Heroes* and *Hear the Train Blow;* Ion Idriess's *Cattle King;* and Mary Durack's *Kings in Grass Castles* and *Sons in the Saddle.*

Ajijic, Mexico
March 1993